THE DOORS OF DAMNING DESIRE
WERE SWINGING OPEN

Amity could not believe her ears—or her fate.

She had come to Venice as the happiest of women, bride of handsome and gallant Mario da Riva, a man who was heir to all the power and position the fabled city could offer.

But now Amity was learning the truth about Venice, her husband, and herself.

Her husband's cynical, sensual brother was holding her in an iron embrace, his aroused lust clear to her as he pressed her backward.

"Don't you know our customs?" he said. "In our city, wives have the duty and the pleasure of serving their entire new family—and now it is your turn to become a true woman of our city . . ."

Amity was beginning to learn
why Venice was called the most wicked
and wanton place on earth—yet even
now she still had fearfully far to go. . . .

ECSTASY'S EMPIRE

Big Bestsellers from SIGNET

ECSTASY'S EMPIRE
GIMONE HALL

A SIGNET BOOK

NEW AMERICAN LIBRARY

TIMES MIRROR

Publisher's Note

This novel is a work of fiction. Names, characters, places, and incidents are either the product of the author's imagination or are used fictitiously, and any resemblance to actual persons, living or dead, events, or locales is entirely coincidental.

Copyright © 1980 by Gimone Hall

SIGNET TRADEMARK REG. U.S. PAT. OFF. AND FOREIGN COUNTRIES
REGISTERED TRADEMARK—MARCA REGISTRADA
HECHO EN CHICAGO, U.S.A.

SIGNET, SIGNET CLASSICS, MENTOR, PLUME, MERIDIAN AND NAL
BOOKS are published by The New American Library, Inc.,
1633 Broadway, New York, New York 10019

First Printing, August, 1980

1 2 3 4 5 6 7 8 9

PRINTED IN THE UNITED STATES OF AMERICA

Pennsylvania
1776
The Fight for Freedom

1

Winter wind whined about the quiet Quaker meeting-house as Amity Andrews smoothed her green muslin apron over the fawn silk of her Sunday gown and tried for the hundredth time to catch the eye of Silas Springer. Why was Silas so solemn when often before he'd been a scandal in meeting with his smiles and his ardent glances that indicated his mind was on other things than prayer? Was he having second thoughts about marrying her?

Or was he, like the others, thinking about the British, the thousands of rough regular soldiers and brutal Hessians bearing down on Pennsylvania through the New Jersey country-side, wreaking devastation as George Washington's army retreated before them? General Howe had sworn to be in Philadelphia by Christmas, and in the December wind it seemed to the Quakers that they could already hear the shout of harsh commands and the sound of heavy boots in the snow.

At the bloody battle of Long Island, the Hessian jaegers had skewered Americans to trees with fixed bayonets while they pleaded to surrender, and soon only the icy Delaware would separate the Hessians from Pennsylvania, the Holy Experiment of godliness and peace.

For days fugitives had been fleeing up the road past the Andrews' Bucks County farm, pausing to warm themselves by the fire and drink hot cider or liberty tea made of ribwort root, before heading on toward the Lehigh Valley with their wagonloads of furniture and household goods. The small whitewashed rooms of the Fountain House Inn and the Cross Keys Hotel were filled every night. In the dining rooms people talked of nothing but war as they supped on roast mutton and drank Lisbon wine. In Philadelphia Tories were being rounded up and sent south so they couldn't join the British. Trenches were being dug around the city. The Continental Congress itself was ready for flight.

No wonder the Congress was ready to desert Philadelphia! Although it would be another year until the signers of the Declaration of Independence made their names public, the Loyalists knew their identities even now, and as the British Army progressed, the soldiers hunted down these traitors with special wrath.

Only the Quakers were staying in the city, outwardly calm, holding their meetings just as they were doing here in the Bucks County countryside, bent on defending their beloved land, not with long Pennsylvania rifles, but with the strength of their faith.

A terrible tension filled the usually tranquil air of the meetinghouse, but Amity thought only of Silas Springer. This very day it would be announced that he and she had completed the long Quaker process of betrothal, and having "passed meeting," had permission to wed. Small wonder that Amity wasn't thinking of the British when the mere sight of Silas was enough to make her breathless.

Silas was a fine figure in his square-cut coat, long flap waistcoat, and yellow buckskin knee britches. His head of copper-colored hair was almost too bright and striking for a Quaker, worn without powder or wig in the unpretentious way of the faith. Time had honed the color of his hair to this arresting shade; as a child he had been a carrot-top. But it was not only his hair that made Silas stand out among the youth of the meeting. His handsome boyish face with its lean cheekbones and sensual curve of lip already showed tracing of character. It was a parchment on which manliness would someday write with pride. Then he would be sturdy as an ironwood tree, and his clear gray eyes, shaded by his broad-brimmed beaver hat, would not show confusion as they did today.

What a different expression he had worn the day last summer that he had come upon her picking wineberries for jelly, her bonnet adrift in thistle and Queen Anne's lace! She had planned cleverly for him to find her, singing at the top of her lovely soprano voice, knowing all the while that he was working in a field nearby. But when she had turned around and seen him watching, the passion of his gaze had unnerved her, and she had sprung for her discarded apparel.

His hand had been quicker than hers, and he had thrust the bonnet into his pocket. "Thee should not have sung like a mockingbird if thee didn't wish me to find thy nest, Am," he said. "Thee are sixteen now and in need of a husband to see that thy bonnet stays put. Thee well knows to remove thy bonnet only when the Holy Spirit moves a Friend to speak in meeting."

"Thee shouldn't talk, Silas Springer," she taunted. "Thee are an old bachelor of eighteen thyself and always late for meeting because thee have no wife to hurry thee along. I will take a husband when I'm ready, and then thee will have to be careful, creeping up on me!"

The look in his eyes made her step backward, and her strawberry-blond hair caught among the berry brambles, twisting among the thorns like a golden spiderweb. He laughed at the sight of her trapped by the bushes, her face growing pink with effort.

"The Devil take thee, Silas!" she cried out, vexed. "Thee might help."

As he lifted her silky tresses, the threads winding over his fingers, he lost control, and his lips sought hers, gently at first, then more urgently. A girl of Amity's upbringing should have run away, but the fresh currents of her yet-untried womanhood pressed her to remain. She responded to his kiss tentatively at first, then with a vigor that surprised him. Tendrils of her hair were yanked painfully from her head, left behind on the fuzzy wineberry stalks as she moved into his embrace, ravenous with appetite she could not explain, far past teasing and enticing, herself the victim of the sweet snare she had set for him.

Together they sank into the soft grass, abloom with dandelion and Queen Anne's lace, his eager hands tracing the swell of her breasts as they tightened beneath her loose calico slamkin. She struggled, her body arching, scarcely knowing whether she fought for release or for a greater imprisonment. She moaned as he drew away; then in a fog of bliss she heard the words he spoke with awe and determination.

"I shall be thy husband, Amity! No one but me!"

Twice they had declared their intent in the monthly meeting of elders, and a committee had been appointed—two men to check into the "clearness" of the groom and two to do the same for the bride.

The two women had come to call on her. "Do thee understand what is required of a wife, Amity?" they asked.

"Yes," she said promptly. "Each is to love, nourish, and support the other."

"But the physical side, Amity? Did thy mother tell thee before she died? Are thee prepared to accept this part of God's plan?"

She was puzzled and did want to make a good impression. "I have kept house for Father these five years," she said. "I can cook a fine hasty pudding, card tow, spin linen, make candles, and scrub the pewter to a shine."

"We meant something else, Amity," they said.

She grew pale as they explained to her the duty of a wife that she must take on.

"It's necessary for the getting of children, Amity," they said gently. "If thee are lucky, thee may enjoy it in time."

Amity thought it the oddest thing she had ever heard that men and women should behave like the beasts in her father's fields, but not wanting to show doubt, she had swallowed her fear and pledged to accept her duty. She longed to mention the matter to Silas in hopes that he would reassure her, but embarrassment had overcome her. Had the men spoken of it to Silas, too? Did he fear it as she did? Perhaps that was what he thought of so solemnly! Not connecting the strange duty with the emotions that had rushed over her when he had kissed her, she felt a swell of solicitude for Silas.

Her father's powerful voice interrupted her thoughts. Silas, like the other men, removed his hat and placed it on his knees in reverence for the spirit that moved Friend Andrews to speak.

"Let us be grateful, for the Lord has sent us a time of testing," said Thomas Andrews. He was a large, imposing man, big of heart and soul as well as body, and well respected. Every eye turned toward him; every ear harked to hear his wisdom. Even Amity set aside her distress to listen.

"It is our law that since God dwells in every man and every life is sacred, our ministry shall be one of love. It is our faith that we shall never bear arms against our fellowman. We must not forget how our forefathers suffered for these beliefs, cruelly imprisoned, paraded through the streets. Others suffered the hardships of a new world to create Penn's Holy Experiment. Now that great dream has passed from our hands into the hands of violent men, and we must have the courage of those who went before us. I say to you, hold strong! Be joyous! We are chosen to live our faith! For Whig shall call us Tory, and Tory shall call us Whig, and we shall have enemies on every hand. But Friends, it is written that we shall reach the Peaceable Kingdom and the lion shall lie down with the lamb!"

A great sigh of assent ran around the room as Thomas Andrews took his seat again on the deacon's bench.

Silas Springer had given close attention to Friend Andrews' words, his jaw set hard, cupped in hands well suited to planting and plowing, hands soon to find a happy task in caressing beautiful Amity as his wife. In a week he would sit with her on the marriage bench, she in her black wedding hood. Before the gathered Friends they would speak vows, one to another, and they would sign the marriage certificate. She would write there for the first time "Amity Springer." There would be a party, and then when the night had grown late, he would carry her away to his under-the-eaves-style bed in the house where now he lived alone. Oh, how he loved her, and he must wed her, lest his overwhelming desire for her drive him to the sin of bedding some tavern wench.

But though it was settled, he knew guiltily that it was unfair of him to wed her and subject her to the crisis that he dared to entertain with his faith. "These are the times that try men's souls," Tom Paine would write this winter of 1776, words that could apply to no man more than to Silas Springer. For while Silas lay awake at night restless with desire for Amity, he struggled with another desire, a desire that his creed made more sinful than any sin of lust. Silas Springer longed to be with the Continentals, as brave as they were ragged; he desired to overthrow tyranny and make men free. But for love of Amity, he was certain he would be there now.

Listening to her father's words, Amity sat stunned as she began to realize what war would mean to her people. She had heard all her life that it took more courage to stay out of a fight than to get into it. For the first time her faith would be more than words from a book. Chosen by God to live her faith! She trembled with fear and with the excitement of challenge. She must be equal to whatever came!

Then she was aware that Silas had risen. He looked, if anything, more troubled than before, his fingers whitening on the rail of the bench in front of him. "Friends, I have read the words of John Locke, Voltaire, and Thomas Paine, and I have yearned for justice. But I did not know how much I yearned until now, when the enemy is at our very door. The Holy Experiment was but the beginning. Seed of a nation— that was William Penn's vision, and the Revolution will make that a reality! I cannot sit by while the British overrun mankind's finest hope! Help me seek the will of God, for I have lost my conviction; and I feel born for no other reason than to hear the music of freedom and to help banish tyranny from this land!"

"Thee mean fight, Friend Springer?" This question came darkly from the deacon's bench.

Silas drew in his breath, and Amity saw the pewter buttons quiver on his velvet coat. "I hope with all my heart that God may yet show me a way that I may not lift my hand in violence. And yet . . . yet . . . I will fight if I must!"

Murmurs of horror arose as he spoke these words bravely. Amity was ill with disbelief.

"Thee know what it will mean if thee join the Continental Army, Silas Springer?"

"Yes. It means that I will be read out from the Society of Friends. It means I will be as dead to everyone that I love; and if I die in truth, I cannot be buried in the hallowed ground. That is the penalty for any man who fights."

The meetinghouse fell silent again. There was only the rattle of windowpanes buffeted by the wind. How could it be so quiet when Amity's world was exploding in a sudden and unexpected end? Silas fight! Read out from the Society of Friends! Her father would never allow him to marry her! She'd be read out as well!

The room swam, the wide, random-width floors tilting up to join a fuzzy maze of prayerful Quakers. Out of the confusion came Silas' face. He was looking at her, his gaze direct and frank, his gray eyes alight with a fire she had never seen before. She jumped up with a cry and ran from the place.

2

She had dinner on the table when her father returned from meeting. Chicken and potatoes, hot biscuits, and rich churned butter. Outwardly she had regained her composure, hung away her good clothes for her slamkin and blue checkered apron.

Amity's father looked at her sharply as she busied herself

about the table. Surely it was a blessing to come home to a meal already prepared, but it did not distract him from the problem at hand.

"Daughter, thee cannot marry Silas if he joins the Continentals. Thee cannot wed out of meeting."

"Thy sister, my Aunt Zenobia, did," she said, setting down a dish and almost breaking it.

It was the wrong thing to say. Thomas' expression went thunderous. The subject of his sister Zenobia was a delicate one. "I shall not have thee end like Zenobia, child!"

Amity thought of her vivacious aunt who had wed a sea captain and now lived in a fine house in Philadelphia's Society Hill. The house was filled with elegant furniture and fascinating knickknacks. It was hard to see that Aunt Zenobia had ended badly, but among the Friends her name was spoken only in whispers.

"I would sooner see thee in thy grave beside thy brothers and sisters!" cried Thomas, beside himself.

The thin band of Amity's courage broke and she gave way to tears. "But I love Silas, Father. I can wed no one else! What am I to do?"

Thomas Andrews softened and patted her hair gently. He hated to see her wisteria-blue eyes filled with weeping, for she reminded him so of her mother, who had died with the last of the babies. She was the only child God had left him; all the more reason life must go well for her. At least his sons lay where they might not be tempted like Silas Springer.

"It's the disease of young men to think that the sword can change the world, Am," he said.

"Are there many like Silas, Father?"

"Too many. I have heard that Quakers from Philadelphia have joined the fight. The Free Quakers they call themselves. There are Quakers fighting from Boston. And General Greene of Washington's staff is a Quaker. Oh, it is not that I do not want to separate from England, but with time, it might have been done in a peaceful manner."

"It could not, Father! The British are brutes!" Amity was aghast at her outburst. She had been unaware that her mind had harbored such uncharitable thoughts. But thankfully her father only laughed.

"It's a good thing thee are a girl, Am, or I'd fear thee'd be ready to fight like Friend Springer. Think, Amity. Silas did not say he would fight, but that he was tempted. Maybe thee can find a way to prevent his joining General Washington."

"I? But how? I'm only a woman, Father!"

"It's because thee are a woman, Amity. And God has given thee powers thee do not yet dream of. It's a shame thy mother is not here to advise thee, but if thee love Silas thee will find a way. Now, go out to the barn for me. That old banty hen's cackling as if she's laid a new egg, and I shall be wanting a custard for supper."

Amity dried her eyes, and putting on clogs and a woolen cloak, went out into the cold afternoon. Heavy bluish clouds hung over the long house of russet stone that seemed already settled into the earth, looking worn with centuries, though Papa had built it himself less than thirty years before. Light from the setting sun reflected from the windows and made the slate roof glow vermilion.

She supposed it was no wonder that the house seemed so much one with the hillside. Like many other settlers, Amity's family had lived first in the dirt-floored basement while their home was being constructed over their heads, and the arched, whitewashed bake ovens were still there in testimony to those first years. Farther down the hill was the diminutive spring-house, where Amity had retreated on many a childhood afternoon to fashion her own private world with her corn-husk dolls and to listen to the gurgle of water running on to the grassy pond.

Beyond stretched fields of corn stubble, and here and there oaks left standing among the rows seemed to float against the rosy sky like angels with gray arms outstretched in benediction. To the west, shadows spilled over the wooded slopes of Buckingham Mountain, where the notorious Tory-loving Doan gang was supposed to have a hideout called Wolf's Rock. Moses Doan was as handsome as he was evil, they said, but Amity thanked her stars that she had never seen him.

Dear God, if ever any land had been created for peace, it was this Bucks County, which William Penn had named for his own home in England. A land of peace, but it should be a land of freedom, too.

Now, for a long time, it had been neither. Could Silas be right that there was no way short of war to save it? And what had her father meant when he had spoken of the powers God gave to women?

The huge bank barn was gloomy and warm, the cows all stirring in their stalls. One wall was built into the earth, stalls and stables on the first floor, the second for threshing grain.

The barn was a great improvement on early structures of unchinked logs and roofs of rye straw. It was her father's pride.

Carefully Amity put her hand beneath the little red banty hen. It had a foul disposition and would peck her if it could. She frowned, for the nest seemed empty.

"That banty's laid no egg, Amity," said a voice. She turned, and the hen flew up noisily between her and Silas, still dressed in his meeting clothes, bits of straw clinging to his coat and his linen shirt. "I begged thy father to let me see thee. Oh, Amity!"

He had his arms around her, kissing her as he had in the berry patch. She struggled against him angrily, and he stepped back, still holding her, as though afraid she would run away. "Do thee hate me for my words in meeting?"

"Hate thee? No, Silas. But neither do I understand. We are people of peace. Thee might have told me thy plans before I sewed my marriage hood!"

He released her, acknowledging that he could no longer claim her. She felt a chill where the warmth of his hand had encircled her tiny waist.

"Amity, help me find the strength to keep from joining the Continentals, for nothing holds sway over me but desire to own thee as thy husband and desire to fight the Revolution," he pleaded.

His glance held her; she felt lost in his love, as she asked with a shuddering breath, "How, Silas?"

Already she knew, as she remembered her father's words. She knew even before he had taken her chin in his hand, loosened her bonnet strings, and tangled reckless fingers in her curls as he pulled her lips against his. The straw wafted a scent of sweet invitation. She did not know whether it was God's will for her or her own, but the force of it was all but irresistible. She did not know exactly what would happen if she crumpled to the floor and opened herself to his embrace, but she intuited it must not happen before they had pledged their vows. Sensing the enormity of her power over him, she pulled her lips from his with a moan. Her sturdy clogs dragged her back with their weight as she walked toward the door.

"Thee may kiss me whenever thee like, Silas," she said determinedly, "but not until thee has renounced war and sat on the marriage bench."

Young Silas gazed after her, anguished with desire, but

nonetheless admiring her proud flight. She had set the alternatives of his life before him succinctly. For the bliss of her love he must cleanse himself of his list for revolution. Body and soul shouted that he must have her, but Amity or revolution, he could not have both, and the other called to him so strongly that he did not know which passion would win.

He followed her out of the barn and saw her slender form poised tensely at the foot of the grassy ramp. Beyond lay a scene that had completely claimed her attention. In the yard her father was in conversation with a British soldier, his splendid red coat with its blue cuffs and turned-up coattails contrasting sharply with the simple tow cloth and buckskin of the Quaker. The soldier leaned on his Brown Bess musket, his wigged head snowy beneath the black cocked hat with its silver officer's cockade.

The Britisher, his face florid from the stinging cold, was warming himself with swigs of rum from his canteen. Voices carried. The soldier's, strident; the Quaker's, steadfast. They were having an argument.

"I am a Quaker, sir, and cannot provide you with supplies," Thomas Andrews was saying.

"Blast!" cried the officer. "I know what you are! But even scum like you, too cowardly to chose your side, cannot stand by and see a fellowman go hungry. See here, I am offering you the king's gold—a fine profit on your flour and potatoes."

"I am sorry, friend," replied Thomas calmly. "I am pledged against violence and cannot give aid to any man for the purposes of war."

"Then I will take it by force, if I must, and keep the money for my trouble."

"Do as thee must," said Thomas stoutly.

The officer cursed. "Give me the key to the root cellar, then."

"No. That would be an act against God."

The officer grasped Thomas Andrews by the collar. Amity marveled as she saw her father will his muscles to remain lax, offering no resistance. "By 's blood, I'll break the door down if you don't give me the key!"

"Do as thee must," said Thomas again, less loudly this time, but only because his breath was almost choked off. The officer shoved Thomas away in disgust, sending him sprawling in the snow.

"The key, Friend!" bellowed the officer scornfully.

But Thomas Andrews lay unmoving where he had fallen.

Infuriated, the Britisher struck Friend Andrews with his musket butt. "Get your worthless carcass up from there!" he screamed.

"Stop it! Stop it!" Silas rushed forward, inserting himself between the soldier and Friend Andrews.

"Get out of the way, man, or I'll deal with you, too!" cried the drunken officer.

Silas ignored him and lifted Thomas' head onto his lap. Blood ran onto the snow. "You've hurt him. He's unconscious!"

The Britisher was taken aback. He had not really intended to injure the Quaker, but he was more than a little drunk, and to show concern or to apologize would be to lose face. He represented the king! The sooner these colonists learned that King George wasn't to be trifled with, the better. His face went livid with wrath as he thought of his empty stomach. Oh, he'd had some dried beef and cold biscuits in his satchel, but he'd hoped for much more. He'd intended to add an apple pie to his store or at least a jar or so of jam, some flour, sugar, and potatoes. He and his company were separated from Howe's command, scouting for the main army off in New Jersey; and they must fend for themselves, while their fellows had fine rations. It hadn't been so difficult in New Jersey, where people put red ribbons on their doors to show loyalty; but since they had crossed the Delaware into Pennsylvania, it seemed that everyone sided with the Continentals. Twice on this quiet Sunday afternoon he'd exchanged shots with farmers in his quest. A Quaker farm had seemed the obvious solution, but even the Quaker had thwarted him. He'd endured enough for one day. By heaven, he represented the king!

Quickly he wrapped his riding quirt about the waist of the pretty Quaker girl. "You'll get the key, little Friend!" he said.

Amity was very pale, her eyes large and purple, like violets in her white face. She looked down at her father's still form and remembered his words in meeting. *Be joyous, for God has sent us a time of testing!*

"I cannot get thee the key," she said in a whisper, determined to stand up to her faith.

The Britisher laughed unpleasantly. "You'll get it, all right. I'll wager it's in the barn."

He yanked her against him, the softness of her buttocks against the lower section of his uniform reminding him of another sort of sustenance that he had been without. This girl

• 13 •

was a morsel that would more than make up for the frustrations he'd suffered this day. Very young she was. Probably a virgin, although, since Quakers didn't give rings, her lack of one didn't necessarily mean she was unmarried. He studied the face of the lad who stood a few feet away, clenching and unclenching his hands, as though in spite of all he could do, they would be fists. Was this boy her husband?

No, he decided astutely. The pair of them had come from the barn. The lad had straw on his clothes, and her hair was rumpled. He'd interrupted the boy in some activity related to what he had in mind himself. He laughed again, a sort of derisive hoot. The circumstance whetted his appetite even more, and made him all the more determined to have her. No doubt the lad had made her all hot and ready with his clumsy pawing. She'd get more than she'd bargained for!

What about her beau? Was he likely to make trouble? He was still a stripling, not so big and heavy as the officer, but he looked dangerous, the muscles of his neck throbbing as he fought to control his anger. Ah, but the boy had no weapon, and the officer had his trusty Brown Bess.

Amity sought Silas' eyes as the soldier dragged her toward the barn, far more aware of the thunder of his expression than of the grip of the Redcoat's arms around her.

"Silas! Thee mustn't! Remember thy faith!" She saw his awful conflict, for if he lost faith, he might lose her, too; and she was dearer to him even than faith. Suddenly she thought of a way she might remove him from temptation, as her glance fell again on her unconscious father. "Silas, help Father!" Go for the doctor!"

Amity did not have a chance to see whether he went, as the soldier yanked her into the dim barn. She would have the last laugh on the Britisher, she thought. The key was not in the barn, but in the house, hanging carelessly by the money drawer beneath the window through which, in harvest season, Thomas Andrews paid his field hands. A wonder that the cellar door was locked at all! Locks were contrary to the Quaker faith, since a Quaker depended on God's protection. Once, before Amity had been born, there'd been a rumor of unfriendly Indians in the neighborhood, and Father had drawn the latchstring. But the matter had troubled him, and he'd risen to unfasten it. In the night the Indians had come and tried the door. It's being unlocked had so unnerved the savages that they'd gone away without murdering the family. Since then the Andrews house had never been locked.

The value of the philosophy was borne out in the present situation. If Thomas had not locked the cellar door to discourage a goat whose habit it was to nose it open, the soldier would have already taken his provisions and departed. Thomas would not be lying unconscious.

The soldier was delighted that Amity had sent her beau away. Maybe after all she wasn't as pure as she seemed. Maybe she knew what it was she felt pressing against her slamkin from inside his blue trousers. He was well aware that a fine uniform had its attraction for the fair sex, and perhaps a Quaker girl was no exception. Perhaps the uniform excited her. Surely none of her menfolk were ever likely to wear one!

With a drunken grunt he spun her around to face him, crushing her soft breasts against the buttons of his coat. His mouth was on hers, his rummy tongue shoving between her little teeth. She gagged and almost fainted, for quite aside from never having been so kissed, she had never tasted spirits.

She pushed his foul-smelling lips from hers with both hands. Annoyed that she did not want him after all, the soldier flung her to the straw as easily as though he were shifting a sack of flour.

In an instant he was atop her, crushing her breath away. She blocked her face with her arms to protect herself. If he were trying to kill her, he was going about it in a peculiar way, she thought in terror, but perhaps this was some special torture only soldiers knew. She hoped Silas had gone, because she did not know how much longer she could resist the temptation to call out to him to save her. Fighting the urge to scream for help, she struggled valiantly against the soldier, certain she would sooner die than cause Silas to break faith and have the sin upon his soul.

The man continued his filthy overtures, his eyes oozing lust, gasps of anticipation issuing from his throat. If he were not trying to kill her, then things could be no worse. She had only to endure, and soon he would be done.

But suddenly his finger probed unthinkably where she had not dreamed that fingers could go, stroking and exploring the intimate depths of her body. Her stomach convulsed, and she began to shudder uncontrollably. The soldier mistook her revulsion for aroused passion. He took special pleasure in thinking that he had made her desire him against her will. He struggled with fastenings and put his hand into his open britches, pressing his shoulders heavily against her breasts so that she couldn't change her mind and escape.

Amity felt a wave of relief as he ceased his activity beneath her petticoats; then new horror washed over her as she saw what he had drawn forth. As he yanked her skirts higher, over her waist, Amity thought of what she had been told by the women's committee. Why, that was what he intended to do to her! Profane her with the act that God intended for the sacred union of man and wife! Surely faith did not require her to stand it! She began to scream, hysterical with outrage and loathing.

The disgusting weight lifted from her body, and cold air rushed against the sweat he had left behind on her bare skin. As the rafters spun in focus, Silas stood with the soldier in his furious grip. The Quaker's face was black with fury as he shook the redcoat by the neck, making the soldier's heels trace little paths in the dirt floor as he rocked to and fro. Silas' grip tightened, and the soldier's breath rattled.

Amity was about to see a man die!

"Silas! Enough! Thee are a Quaker!" She cried. But perhaps the force of evil in the barn had become strong enough to stop her voice. Perhaps it was only her heart that shrieked so, because Silas did not seem to hear her. Silas spoke to the soldier, his voice coming between gritted teeth.

"I am pledged not to lift my hand against another human soul! But thee are not human. Thee were hatched from the Devil, not born of a mother's womb! I do not believe that God made thee!"

Amity scrambled to her feet, trying to put herself between them. "Silas, don't kill him!" she sobbed. "I love thee! Oh, Silas, if thee love me, don't kill him!"

Slowly Silas turned and looked at her. She saw him struggle with himself, and remembering what both of them had to lose. With a great trembling, Silas loosened his grip. The soldier tumbled forward, gulping painfully, impeded by his fallen trousers.

Amity looked at Silas, his face transformed with joy. "Oh, Am! It was God's test! I've been tried and not found wanting! I've kept the faith and can wed thee clear! Oh, I do love thee!"

She ran to embrace him, but as she did so, the malevolent redcoat struggled to his knees and reached for his Brown Bess. Happiness turned to dismay as she saw him lift it to his shoulder. He was not six feet from Silas when he pulled the trigger, and the flash of the powder pan lighted the barn for an instant stark as death. Blackness and a roar followed. Circles of red and blue blinded her and gunsmoke burned her lungs as she screamed again.

A body lay on the barn floor.

"Oh, dear heaven, I've killed him, Amity!" Silas' voice was high-pitched with strain. "I meant only to spoil his aim!"

Her vision cleared and she saw Silas standing with the pitchfork with which he had tried to jar the soldier's rifle. Blood ran from its prongs, and wind rushed in through a hole that the musket had blown in the wall of the barn.

She ran to him, and they wept in each other's arms.

"I've killed! I've killed," he moaned. "I can never marry thee now, Amity," he said, choking on the words.

"But, Si! Thee didn't *mean* to! Thee had no choice."

He shook his head. "I said I didn't mean to. I thought I didn't. But, Amity, it was no true accident! I saw him with thee, and I wanted him to die!"

"We'll hide his body, Silas, and no one will find out," she said desperately.

"No. It's no good. I would live a lie, and there would be no end to it. I have not told thee the worst."

"The worst, Silas!" She could not imagine what could be worse.

"It pleasured me to see him die. I can never sit with thee on the marriage bench, Amity. I cannot live my life as a Quaker now!"

She knew that he was right, that the life they had planned could never be. The wedding linens in the big curly maple chest Father had made her would go unused, the wedding hood unworn, the children unborn. But they clung together, savoring the warmth of their love for a few moments that must last them a lifetime.

Then he helped her move her father into the house and cover him with blankets by the fire. She saddled her mare and rode for the doctor while he dragged the soldier down to the pond, and having weighted his clothes with rocks, broke the ice and shoved him beneath. Having done with the soldier, he gave the dead man's horse a smack and sent it galloping down the road. Then he worked until past dark to repair the damage to the barn. The Britisher would have comrades, and for the sake of Amity and her father there must be no trace of his having been here.

Amity was waiting for him in the house, sitting with her needlework, her face wan in candlelight.

"Is thy father better?" he inquired.

"Yes. Weak with a fever, but the doctor has applied a poultice of pokeweed to the wound to keep away infection," she said.

"I'll be going, Am," he said.

"Home, Silas?" she asked, but her voice was hopeless.

"To join the Continentals," he answered.

She had known already, for he carried the Britisher's Brown Bess musket and had slung the powder horn over his shoulder.

"Oh, Amity, as long as I live, I'll love none but thee!" he said softly.

"Nor I any but thee!" she returned.

He kissed her so that she felt that the world had stopped and forever become the moment. Then with enormous effort he released her, and without looking back, went out and closed the door behind him.

She built up the fire and sat for hours, watching her father and weeping by his bedside, until exhausted she drifted into a nightmare of slumber. Far into the night she wakened as the door burst open with a furious wallop. She leaped up, certain it was the comrades of the drunken soldier bent on retribution. She seized a poker from the fireplace, but it was only the wind that had done the deed, howling into the room and sending showers of sparks up the chimney. She shut the door, trembling, aware of the poker in her hand. She had thought they were coming to do to her what the dead officer had narrowly failed to, and she knew that she would have defended herself to prevent it, no matter what violence had been required. She was filled with a great emptiness of heart and soul as she felt her father's forehead and found the fever had broken. Thomas Andrews slept peacefully, for he had no battle of spirit to fight, and she marveled at the great strength of his faith. Someday she might find it, but not here, not now. The world had intruded on her quiet Quaker existence and shaken it to the core. She was, after all, like her Aunt Zenobia and must go seeking for her life beyond the gentle meeting.

3

A line of pink lighted a cold pussy-willow sky as she donned her heavy duffel cloak and rode away from her father's house. At the foot of the hill she stopped and looked back, remembering all the sweet scenes of her childhood. She could never return, for Father would have to disown her, however it pained him. Overcome with sadness, she almost turned the horse to return before she had started. But then with a flip of her riding stick to the animal's flank she sent it galloping, her face buried in its mane, her cloak flying out behind.

By the time the sun was up, Amity was trotting along the eastern slope of Buckingham Mountain. Shaggy hemlocks on either side of the trail sheltered her from the wind as the morning sun rose, filtering through the branches. By a rocky streamlet she dismounted and took bread from her saddle pouch for her breakfast.

"Out early, miss, eh? Up with the birds, so they say, though any bird with sense has gone south by now," said a man's voice.

She whirled, not being able to locate the speaker.

The man laughed. "Down here, miss."

She saw a little fire in a nook among the rocks. The man beside it was lean and dark, with black hair and heavy brows slanting toward a steep nose. She could have easily thought of him as fierce, but he seemed more bemused than dangerous, like an inquisitive brown bear, blending into the surroundings in his fringed buckskins. No wonder she hadn't seen him.

"Won't you join me, miss?"

She hesitated, unable to dismiss a sense of threat, more frightened of him than she would have been before the British soldier. He grinned and patted the rocks beside him, set a small iron skillet over the flame, and began to slice sausage into it. Amity remained where she was, and he seemed to forget all about her.

The rocks looked warm, bathed in the heat of the fire, and her stomach clenched as the meat began to sizzle. She remembered that she had gone without her supper last night, and hunger overcoming her innate dislike of the man, she scrambled down to join him.

He acknowledged her arrival with a smug gaze, his sharp eyes belying the laconic movements of his body. He'd known she couldn't resist, and he hadn't wasted energy coaxing her. Now he didn't bother welcoming her to his fireside, as if he were always so sure of women. She hated the intimate way he looked at her, as though he knew things about her she didn't know about herself.

But why should she distrust him when he'd done nothing wrong, only generously asked her to share his fire and his breakfast? He hadn't the look of a farmer, she thought, nor somehow of a soldier, though General Washington approved of buckskin gear for the Continentals. Frontier clothing, suggesting all sorts of cunning and competence, inspired terror in the British regulars like no other uniform, Washington said. Was it clothes that made this man seem so cunning and competent?

"It's dangerous for a girl traveling alone these days," he remarked. "Perhaps we'll ride together a way. I'll escort you, if we're heading in the same direction. You're a Quaker, by the look of you. Perhaps you're going to Virginia. The Continentals are sending Quakers there out of Philadelphia, lest they help the British. And the Congress is in Baltimore already. Perhaps you're off to join some kin. South is the way sparrows are flying, girl!"

"Are *you* going south?"

"No. Only a bit. South and east to the river. I've business to tend."

"Are you a trapper, sir?" she asked quizzically.

"Trapper?" He thought it over, seeming amused, though Amity saw nothing amusing about her question. "Aye, I should say that's exactly what I am."

"You are too far east for good beaver, then," she said, puzzled.

"Oh, there's game about. Perhaps I've been after fox." He laughed, and Amity found it unpleasant, though she supposed she should be glad he was enjoying their conversation. She, on the other hand, was not interested in talk at all. Her mind was only on the food and on the journey ahead of her.

"I'm headed for General Washington's camp," she said.

"Well, Washington's camp is in my direction, so you can ride along. There's redcoats lurking in these woods."

"I know," said Amity with a shudder. "I'd be glad for a man's protection. We can't be far from Wolf's Rock, somewhere up the mountain, where outlaws hide."

"The Doan gang," he said with a nod.

"Yes. Those scroundrels! They rob and loot and line their pockets with gold in the name of the king!"

"I hope you're not carrying gold, miss. However, there's worse they might rob of a lovely woman. Ah, I've seen them, and they are devils, every one. But you stick with me. I've a good Pennsylvania rifle, and I'm afraid of nothing on two legs or four."

He took a pair of tin cups from his leather pouch, and having wiped them on a none-too-clean sleeve, filled them with a bitter tea from his boiling pot. He handed her one. Then, whittling a point onto a stick, he gave her that, too, indicating that she should spear the sausage with it as he was doing. The meat was delicious, the spicy kind made by the German Mennonite settlers; but she flinched as the hot tea ran into her stomach.

"Wretched stuff, eh?" commented her host sympathetically. "We'll have better soon, when the war is over."

"When the war is over. But that cannot be soon," she replied, thinking how far the embattled Continentals had to go to defeat the well-equiped British.

"Ten days, miss. General Washington has sent a dispatch warning Congress that the army cannot last more than that. They'll starve or freeze if nothing else. If General Howe only sits and waits, they'll surrender."

Amity choked on her food, suddenly realizing that her host was a Tory. She put down the stick. "I've heard of no such dispatch," she said.

"There's many a thing I've heard of that you haven't," he said. He towered over her as he went to mount his horse. He was well above six feet, she thought, and handsomer than a Tory had a right to be.

She didn't want to ride with a Tory, but she had no choice. She kept her silence as the sun rose higher, shimmering on a crust of snow. They went south, out of the woods and over fields of frozen corn stubble to the twisting River Road. Ice churned in the rapids of the Delaware, cold and bright through the leaning trees of its clifflike banks.

The Tory studied his companion admiringly, watching the

jounce of her breasts and buttocks. "Why would a Quaker be going to the Continentals?" he asked finally, breaking the long silence.

She had a mind not to answer him, but she knew it must be said, if only so that she knew she had courage to say it. "Why, I am not a Quaker any longer. My . . . husband . . . is with Washington already, and I am going to join him." She had not realized before she spoke that it would be necessary to own Silas as her husband. But they would be wed, of course, perhaps this very day.

Certainly he'd be glad to see her, she told herself. He'd understand that she could have a crisis of faith as well as he. In times such as these, women no less than men must make devastating decisions. He'd know how much she loved him, having run away to follow him.

While she was occupied with her thoughts, they reached Coryell's Ferry. He reined in his big black horse and bid her farewell. "This is as far as I go, girl. You'll find the Continentals in the woods about Bowman's Hill."

"Will thee catch thy fox near the river?" she asked.

The Tory laughed his unpleasant laugh. "Aye, I hope to. It would be a feather in my cap, for he's a clever old fox that has slipped many a snare. You'll be needing the password to get by the sentries. They change it every day, but this morning it will be 'boiled stone,' which is the best dish they have to eat. Tell the sentry 'boiled stone,' and you'll have no trouble."

"How would a Tory like thee know the password?" she cried furiously.

"Ah, I did say I'd heard many a thing you hadn't," he reminded her, his voice ringing on the cold air. "Give George Washington a message for me, little Quaker. Tell that old fox that Moses Doan will catch him yet!" And digging his heels into his horse's flanks, he galloped away.

Amity sat gaping after him for a time. She had breakfasted with one of the notorious Doan gang! What sport he had had of her, pretending to protect her! She recalled the indecent way he'd looked at her, and thought he'd been laughing at her all the time, perhaps toying with her, debating whether to rob her and steal her horse or whether to perform upon her the indignities for which the soldier had died in the barn. She thanked her stars it had suited him to do neither!

Her horse was lathered and panting when a voice from a bramble thicket called to her to hold up. She obeyed, nearly tumbling over the mare's neck as she reined in.

"Give the password," came the command.

" 'Boiled stone,' " she answered promptly.

The bushes parted, and a girl no older than herself stepped into the road, brandishing a musket. She wore a short calico gown that showed her ankles in woolen stockings and old, worn brogans on her feet. Over the gown was a shorter striped-linsey skirt, and on her head was a broad white cap with ruffles.

"I thought thee were one of the Continentals," said Amity in confusion.

"So I am," replied the girl, pushing wisps of tangled hair from her face.

"But—"

"I know. I'm a woman. Though it's hard to remember it sometimes, living as I do. I'm not the only female who carries a musket for George Washington. Some have even lied about their sex to do it. I'm glad you knew the password, so I didn't have to shoot you."

"There are some who know it who *should* be shot!" cried Amity. "You must take me to General Washington right away! I've brought him a message."

"Have you? What message?" came the curious female rejoinder.

"Well, I suppose it's all right to tell *you*. The outlaw Moses Doan is scheming against the Continentals. He said to tell Washington he was going to trap him, and he knows the password. It was he who told it to me."

The female sentry leaned on her musket and looked uninterested. "Oh, Moses Doan. General Washington is aware that the Doans spy on him. But he's slick, Moses Doan. He can't be caught. And if ever anyone could get the password, it would be him."

"But how would he learn it? Would one of the men tell him? Surely no one would!"

"There are ways it might be learned. Not from a man, most likely."

"From whom, then?"

"A woman. There's hundreds here, and many man-hungry widows among us, wasting to feel feminine again. Perhaps he offered a bottle of French perfume he'd stolen from a lady in a coach. More than likely, he offered himself. There's not a woman wouldn't lie still for him, so they say."

"Well, I wouldn't!" said Amity, only vaguely following her companion's drift. "He's arrogant and ill-mannered."

"Did he try to make love to you?" The girl looked at Amity with new speculation.

"Love? No. Certainly not!"

"Then you don't know what you'd have done, do you?"

"I . . . am betrothed and have no interest in any but my fiancé," said Amity.

The other grinned. "Well, now, if you say so. But there's a war on, and we shouldn't stand here gossiping all day in the road. My name's Grace Turner, by the way."

"Amity Andrews. Are you certain we shouldn't tell General Washington about Moses Doan?"

"Pshaw, it's nothing. The general won't send men on a wild-goose chase after the Doans. Is your fiancé in camp? I'll help you find him."

She gave a whistled signal to call another sentry to watch the road and then led the way into camp, where men in all sorts of uniforms huddled about fires. Some wore the blue coat of the Continental Army, but many more were in buckskin or brown homespun. Raccoon caps mixed with black felt tricornes. Some of the men carried little tomahawks engraved with the word "liberty" thrust into their belts. But no matter what the uniform, all were ragged. Stockings were tattered and seemed glued on with dirt. Feet were wrapped in burlap that left traces of blood in the snow.

Grace stopped to inquire after the Quaker named Silas Springer and returned shaking her head. "They say he's been sent on a mission upriver, where the British had a mind to cross a patrol. You can share a tent with me until he comes back."

In another section of the camp were little lean-to tents occupied by women. Grace stopped beside one where a girl in a dirty woolen cloak was trying to start a fire, fanning it with her apron. "The wood's run low," she said in an irritated tone. She was obviously pregnant, and so thin that she seemed all baby. The great balloon of her belly made her list as she tried to balance herself.

"Is there anything to eat?" asked Grace.

"A fish. It's not big, and I spent all morning catching it. I didn't have time to gather wood."

"A fish!" Grace was delighted. "A wonder some soldier didn't take it for his rations, Isabel!"

"Not where I hid it," said Isabel, grinning now. She lifted the hem of her dress, and they saw the catch tied to the ruffles of her petticoat.

"But that's too small to make a meal of," said Amity thoughtlessly.

Isabel's pleasure faded and her expression grew morose as she took notice of Amity for the first time. "I suppose *you* expect to eat too. But we can't feed you. We haven't anything but the fish and one frozen potato."

"Oh, but I've food enough for all of us," declared Amity, happy to be able to make a gesture of friendship. She opened her saddlebag and produced several loaves of crusty bread, a jar of strawberry preserves, and two mince pies. Isabel and Grace gasped and hugged each other, until Isabel broke into a fit of coughing.

"Why, you're ill, Isabel!" Amity cried.

Isabel regained her breath and smiled. "No, I'm all right. Grace takes good care of me, and a meal like this will make me strong."

Before long they had the fire going, the fish frying, and a pot of liberty tea brewing. The little campsite took on the atmosphere of a party. Giggling at each other's ravenous appetites, the young women devoured the jam and bread like children, smearing their faces and then sticking out dainty tongues to lick away every delicious drop. Even Isabel's hollow face turned pink and satisfied.

"I wish you could have brought more," sighed Isabel when the rest of the bread and one of the pies had been tucked away for saving, by Grace's order. "Oh, dear, I didn't mean to seem ungrateful, Amity."

"Oh, but I should have brought more," said Amity, angry with herself. "Only, I was too bent on catching up with Silas to think of it."

"Never mind, Amity," said Isabel. "It only proves you're a woman. We all make fools of ourselves over men."

"Not me!" said Grace. "Not anymore. I'm done with men!"

"Perhaps she really is," said Isabel shyly. "There's a dozen that have tried to woo her since her Clem deserted."

"Thy husband deserted and left thee here?" asked Amity, startled.

"Yes. He's probably with the Tories now, cozy and warm in Trenton. I would have none of it when he wanted to change sides." Grace was a pretty girl, with heavy chestnut curls worn loose about her neck for warmth. Many a man would want to stroke those curls, but beneath Grace's easy manner was a sternness that argued for caution.

"At least I didn't end with a big belly like Isabel," Grace snapped, unable to stand Amity's pity.

Isabel's face fell, and her eyes clouded with injured feelings. Compassionately Amity tried to set matters right. "There, now, Isabel, a baby's a blessing and a part of God's plan. Thee should be happy. But can't thy husband find some lodging for thee?"

She had said exactly the wrong thing, she saw, as Isabel began to sob.

"Isabel's husband was killed on Long Island," Grace said with a sigh. "They'd been married less than a year and were mightily in love. The British burned everything, so she's nowhere to go. No home and no money. She might have got a position as a tavern wench, but who would hire her as she is?"

"I don't mind being as I am!" said Isabel with surprising strength. "And I'd much sooner be with the Continentals than ogled in a tavern. Thank heaven General Washington tolerates the likes of me. I know I'm a drain on the army, though, eating what's meant for the men and slowing down the march."

"Oh, how you talk," said Grace. "There's many that cause more trouble than you, with less reason. Why, you wouldn't even ride the baggage wagons, Isabel!"

"I try not to be too much bother."

"There, now. Of course you do. We all do."

Amity lay awake that night, too cold and miserable to sleep in the lean-to. The frigid little tent was a far cry from the warm bed she had always known, and she wondered if she had the courage to starve and suffer for liberty and love. Could she possibly be as strong of spirit as Grace and Isabel?

In the morning Amity began to try to do her part, too, carting water from the river in a pair of buckets yoked over her shoulders. Grace was again on sentry duty, and the password had been changed. Amity wondered if Moses Doan knew this one, too. Once, on her way up the steep bank, icy water sloshing over her skirt, she thought she caught a glimpse of a tall, dark form sliding stealthily among the trees. She studied the vegetation, seeing only shadows blowing.

Should she have told George Washington about Moses Doan after all?

No, she reassured herself. If anyone of her sex knew the business of the Continentals, it was Grace, who moved competently and good-naturedly among the men, privy to all sorts of camp gossip. If Grace didn't think it necessary to speak to the general, then it wasn't.

Beside Grace, and even Isabel, Amity felt hopelessly inept. She would never have the stamina to stand cold and lack of food as a matter of course, as they did. They were as devoted to the Continentals as Amity should have been to her faith.

"Perhaps you should go home, Amity, now that you see what it's like," suggested Isabel, as Amity paused by the fire.

The weather had turned unseasonably warm, and Isabel seemed lighthearted, seated in the lee of the wind in the bright December sun. She was carefully mending the lace of a ruffled white lingerie stock, feeling important in her task. Grace had brought the basket of mending and had pointed out that this garment belonged to Washington himself.

I could go home, she thought. Father would deal severely with me. But he would love me still. It's not too late. I haven't married Silas or done anything yet to be read out of meeting.

She could take Isabel with her. Grace had told her that she did not expect Isabel's baby to live. The mortality rate was high among infants born to the women of the Continental Army. Even if the child were born healthy—and that was unlikely, with its mother so undernourished—it would soon die from the weather or starve because its mother was unable to provide enough milk.

Isabel did not share this gloomy view and chatted gaily about the approaching birth. "If it's a boy, I'll name him for his father, of course. And if it's a girl, her name will be Gracie, because Grace has helped me so," she told Amity.

At first Amity had thought her attitude marked her for a simpleton, but she was beginning to realize that Isabel was stronger even than Grace. Beneath her chatter was a will that would not be denied, and Amity felt her own resolve harden to wait for Silas. Her eye constantly sought the perimeter of the camp, watching for his patrol to return.

"There's a farmhouse near the river," she told Isabel. "I'll go and ask if they'll take thee in."

"No." Isabel shook her head. "That's General Greene's headquarters."

"General Greene. Why, he is a Quaker. I'm sure he'll offer sanctuary.

"I will not cause more trouble than necessary to the Continentals, Amity. There are a dozen women at least with child. The general cannot take them all in."

Isabel stayed in the lean-to as day followed day. Amity watched signals flashing from the sharp peak of Bowman's Hill to the Continental supply point in Newtown and wondered what they meant. Men worked at building breastworks to keep warm, and steam heat rose from their damp, burlap-covered feet when they pushed them close to the fires. She worried about Silas. Had something happened? Shouldn't he be returning?

The soldiers were quick to admit her to their campfires, loving to tell her stories of their exploits of the Battle of Long Island and since. They joked about the formidable Hessians in Trenton, who dyed their big mustaches with shoe polish and plastered their hair with tallow and flour. One soldier had a grisly trophy, a Hessian's waist-length pigtail, cut from beneath the enemy's tall metal-fronted hat. It made the girls' spines creep to see it, and Grace would not allow Isabel to look, for fear it would "mark the baby."

"It's savage," said Grace. "Like an Indian taking scalps."

On the far side of the river it was said that hundreds every day were taking advantage of the British offer of clemency, pledging the oath of loyalty to the crown. Perhaps many on the Pennsylvania side would have taken it, except that they were not allowed to cross the river.

It was nearly Christmas. The soldiers rejoiced that Howe would not celebrate the holiday in Philadelphia after all, unless he wanted to swim his entire army across. Washington had held the British at bay by commandeering all the boats that the enemy might have acquired to make the treacherous crossing. Now and then the situation was accented by the rattle of American artillery or the popping of muskets. Amity soon ceased to notice the sound of guns. She was becoming inured to camp life. She had learned to cook tasty stews for the men from the toughest piece of meat, sometimes she helped to forage for the horses, and she was proud of her accomplishments. She thought she had nothing more to learn.

But one morning they heard a group of women crying hysterically for help from the New Jersey shore. The Continentals answered the summons, rowing across beneath British fire. The daring rescue accomplished, the women were brought ashore weeping, their hair askew, their faces wild with horror, their clothing torn. One was only a little girl.

"Dear heaven, what happened to them?" asked Amity.

"Raped by the Hessians," said Grace, her mouth set.

Amity thought immediately of the English officer Silas had

killed in the barn. The thing had been done to each of them, even the child. So this was war!

The Jersey men will be flocking to our side now," said Grace matter-of-factly. "Those poor women will be needing the comfort of their own sex. Let's go see what's to be done."

Practical Grace! She was seasoned and level-headed. Nothing unnerved her. Amity knew she should follow, but she was unequal to it. Ashamed to find herself so fainthearted, she nonetheless fled down the road to avoid facing those sisters with their ravaged bodies and spirits. Worse, she knew that her motives for flight were ignoble. It wasn't so much that she couldn't stand the sight of their suffering as that she couldn't stand the terror of knowing how close she had come to being violated herself.

Overcome with mindless panic, she dashed deep into the woods, until, feeling herself too far away from camp for anyone to hear, she began to scream, covering her face with her hands.

Bushes nearby crashed urgently, and Amity froze, afraid to uncover her eyes and see whether she had perhaps aroused a British scouting patrol. The dark image of Moses Doan rose in her thoughts. It could be he, since he spied on Washington's camp. Would he expect to have his way with her this time, now that she knew who he was? He was used to feminine favor, Grace had said.

She cringed as hands seized her shoulders familiarly. Then a voice said, "Why, Am, whatever are thee doing here?"

"Silas!" she cried joyfully, and turned to embrace him.

All the dreadful hardships of the camp seemed to melt as he held her, the grueling uncertainties vanished now that he had found her. She rose on waves of ecstasy as he kissed her, her lips and cheeks and hair and eyes.

"Oh, Silas, I was frightened thee might not come back! But now everything's all right. We'll be wed, Si! I could not keep the faith either, for I had not the faith to live without thee!"

"Wed!" he said in a dazed tone.

"Yes," she replied with a laugh, drawing back to see his relief that he did not have to live his life without her.

Instead she saw troubled eyes that frightened her. "Silas, do thee still love me?" she asked in alarm.

"Oh, Amity, of course I love thee. Didn't I say I would love no other? And I won't ever. But it's not so simple. I've broken faith and killed, and I can't wed thee. Go home to thy father, Amity. Can thee imagine I would wed thee here, even if I could? Can thee think I could see thee live like the camp women, cold and hungry? In battle I would always be a coward, thinking that I might die and leave thee with a baby."

"Thee are foolish, Si," she said boldly. "Thee might convince me if I were still on my father's farm. But I am not, Si! Oh, at first I thought I could not stand one night in the camp. But now! Now I am as much a part of the army as thee, in a woman's way. I can build a fire, and wash and mend, and tend the sick. I'm not afraid of being cold and hungry so long as I'm with thee. And as for a baby, why, my friend Isabel is to give birth any moment, and she is happy. I would sooner bear thy child in a lean-to than not bear it at all!"

"No, Am!" He was shouting, angry at himself and at her. "Thee are still a Quaker girl."

"Thee killed to save me. I am partly to blame," she pleaded.

"I killed the officer to save thee, but I joined the Continentals to save liberty. War is not the same. I have killed another already."

The anguish in his words shocked Amity to silence. How could she deal with a soul in such torment?

"I didn't have to kill him like the soldier in the barn," Silas went on. "He was only trying to steal a boat. I was hiding in the bushes and had the only clear shot of my patrol. So I fired, when I might have held still and let him take the boat. But I was a soldier and had to shoot him, though he hadn't lifted a hand against me. That is war, Amity. It's different from what I imagined!"

"But thee will stay and fight anyway," she said softly, reading his expression.

"Yes. May God forgive me. I can't abandon the cause of liberty!"

"And I will stay and be thy wife," she cried strongly, "since I cannot abandon thee!"

"Thee will go home, Amity! This very day, thee will go home. Do thee know what today is?"

She shook her head, having lost track of the time. "It can't matter what day it is, Si," she said wonderingly.

"It's Christmas Eve. I will not have thee in a camp of war on the birthday of the Prince of Peace."

He stalked away, certain she would obey, and after a little while she followed him, heading back toward camp with no intention of doing as he had commanded.

4

Amity wondered what had come over her. Although Quaker in theory acknowledged their women as equals, she had always obeyed a man. Her father had been her master, and she had expected her husband to be her master as well. He was not her husband, of course. Was that what made the difference? Or had the weeks in the camp honed in her a desire to control her own destiny and to live her life on her own terms—like Isabel, who refused to ride in the baggage wagon, or Grace, who carried a stout Pennsylvania rifle, even though her husband was with the enemy across the river.

Amity walked back to the lean-to in a temper, choking on angry tears. Isabel was tending the fire as Amity threw herself onto tattered blankets and began to weep.

"Why Amity, has something happened?" cried Isabel.

"Silas is back," Amity managed to say.

"Silas is back? And you are crying? Those aren't tears of joy."

"Silas told me to go home. He doesn't want me here."

"Poor Am." Isabel rose from the fire to put her arms about her friend and drew in her breath sharply.

"What's wrong, Isabel?" said Amity fearfully, forgetting her own troubles.

Fright was written on Isabel's thin features, but her little mouth set bravely. "I've felt strange all day. I think it's near my time. Don't let's tell Grace yet. No need, and it's Christmas Eve."

"But there's nothing special about this Christmas Eve, Isabel," she protested, wanting very much to tell Grace, who would know what to do.

"Christmas Eve is always special," returned Isabel. "Haven't you heard? There's to be a bonfire, with a bit of rum for all the men and fiddlers for carols and dancing. It's rumored that the general has a special Christmas present for the troops, and everyone is hoping it's food, of course."

"Very well. Then we'll not tell Grace about Silas either," said Amity.

In a little while Grace returned in high good humor, the incident of the Jersey women put behind her. "What shall we have for dinner, Isabel?" Grace asked.

"Oh, there's potatoes, though they're moldy," said Isabel with a sigh.

"Then we ought to have pheasant, since it's Christmas Eve," Grace said, drawing forth a bird. The Continentals could spare little ammunition for procuring such small game, but Grace had charmed a soldier into showing her how to set a snare. The real trick had been to hide the device so that no one would find the prize before her. She had been checking the trap for a week.

The aroma lifted Amity's spirits in spite of herself, as darkness descended, pressing the landscape into a flat monochrome of black. Usually Amity dreaded the fading of the light, but this evening the night seemed to hide the harsh reality of the camp, cloaking it in an unaccustomed mellowness.

Amity exchanged her calico slamkin for the fawn silk meeting dress, which she had brought with her, carefully folded to be her wedding gown. The white fichu, which she crossed over her bosom and knotted behind, would not be so clean tomorrow or probably ever again, after it suffered the smudges of the campfire, but what matter? When she had left home, she had committed herself to Silas as surely as if she had already spoken her vows in meeting. She had come too far to go home. Silas would simply have to change his mind. Her womanly powers had not been enough to prevent his joining the Continentals, but could they at least suffice to make him wed her?

A ranger wearing a japanned leather helmet with feathers and a beaded band rapped his fist on the tent canvas. "The general wants to see you, miss."

"The general? What general?" Amity had not made the acquaintance of any officer of that rank.

"Why, General Washington, of course," came the reply.

"General Washington! I shouldn't have thought him aware of my existence," she said in amazement.

"Well, he must be. You're to come to General Greene's headquarters, where Washington is having dinner tonight. I've been sent to bring you."

What in the world could the commander of the Continental Army want to see *her* about? Heart pounding, Amity followed the ranger's moccasined feet through the bitter night. Sparks jumped from campfires, and the air was filled with the aroma of woodsmoke. A distant fiddle struck up a Christmas carol. They came over a little rise, and she caught sight of the farmhouse where Greene had his headquarters. In spite of shortages caused by the war, a single candle shone in each window, the peaceful glow a simple but eloquent proclamation of Christmas.

"I'm glad they didn't save the candles," she said.

"Truth, there's no better use they could have been put to," he agreed, motioning her inside. "Hurry, now, the general's waiting."

The warm house seemed strange after her weeks in the field, the main room cozy with its low beamed ceiling and pine floors spread with Oriental rugs. The only illumination came from the blaze in the fireplace, its rough-hewn mantel set with Bucks County redware. A tall figure turned from the fire as she entered. In his blue coat with yellow epaulets and his buff waistcoat, George Washington looked every inch a general. She had seen him before, riding his big white horse about the camp, and she had thought him impressive, even then. But up close, he was even more compelling. Lightly powdered hair swept smoothly into a queue, bound with a black silk ribbon. The large straight nose seemed to measure the dimensions of the man, suggest the force of his character. The mouth was stern; but most telling were the deepset eyes half-hooded by their lids, as though he wished to hide the worry and compassion that showed within.

"Miss Andrews?"

"Yes, sir," she murmured.

"It has come to my attention that although you are residing with the women of the army, you are not the wife or widow of one of my men."

She blushed uneasily. "Yes, it's true," she said.

Anger leaped to Washington's face. "Then why in blazes are you with the troops?" The heat of his wrath made her tremble as he paced, hands clasped behind his back.

"I came in good faith, sir," she said in a small voice, "to marry Silas Springer."

"He asked you here and then refused you? I shall have him reprimanded!"

"Oh, no. He didn't ask me." Amity was quick to defend Silas.

"You came uninvited. Dear heaven, isn't it enough that I

must put up with desertions and militias that turn Tory when called to fight? That I must ask my men to withstand so much, men who would follow me to the end of the earth? Must I be dogged by feminine romantics as well?" He seemed to be talking to himself, lost in reflection. He paused, and she wondered what she should say, but then he began again, this time without a doubt addressing her. "Can't you understand what a drain unnecessary women are on the army, Miss Andrews? The wives I must keep, and the widows I would never desert, but you, Miss Andrews, must leave. I am expelling you from the camp."

Expelled! It seemed so much crueler and more final than when Silas had told her to go home. She had defied Silas, but this man she would never be able to defy. Devastated, she gathered her courage to plead her cause. "My friends and I take very little from the rations, sir! We fish and trap, and when we catch nothing, we go without. We wash, mend, cook, carry wood and water, and nurse the wounded. In battle women have loaded the rifles and swabbed hot cannon. The Continentals would be hard pressed to do without us!"

Washington's fury was unabated. "Confound it, young lady! This very minute I am wasting precious time dealing with you, at a moment when I have matters vastly more important to consider. I am not unaware of the female contribution to the war, but—"

"General, I think this is not so simple as it seems," said a deep voice. She had not seen a man seated in the shadows in a mahogany armchair covered with French brocaded taffeta. Heavy eyebrows accented his firm features, and his uniform was much like Washington's, though without any frill of lace on the cravat. "This man Silas Springer has already distinguished himself in the acquisition of the Durham boats and has been promoted, though he's but lately joined the army. He's a Quaker.

"I'm General Greene," the speaker continued to Amity, his voice gentle. "Thee are a Quaker, too, child? Was thy Silas disowned from meeting and lost to thee? Thee followed him, but he will not have thee disowned, too, for marrying him?"

Amity nodded, weeping at being addressed in the familiar Quaker manner in this strange place. She remembered that her father had told her that General Greene was a Quaker himself.

General Washington's anger seemed to cool a little. "Well, Miss Andrews, there are few of my soldiers that I value as much as the Free Quakers, who risk not only their lives but their immortal souls for liberty. If you were a man I would enlist you at once for your spirit, but I cannot take responsibility for women, especially an innocent young one like you. The British troops have behaved abominably in Trenton; even their commander, Colonel Rall, has a reputation for sporting with the ladies. But perhaps you did not see the effects of Hessian misbehavior. There were women brought over this morning."

"I did see them, General," she answered, eyes down.

"Then perhaps you will understand why I wish to save you from such a fate. I'll send a soldier to escort you home at dawn."

The immediacy of her departure took her breath away. "But couldn't I have a few days, sir?" she burst out audaciously. In a few days Silas might weaken, she thought, with a clearer idea of what feminine wiles might accomplish than she had once had.

"I'm sorry, Miss Andrews. It must be tomorrow morning. Take my word, it's the best thing you can do for your Silas and the Continentals."

The cold air seemed to have increased its bite as she left the house, stunned with the finality of her fate. A good thing she'd become used to the cold, she thought. Her father's welcome was likely to be as cold as the Continental camp. Amity wandered toward a huge bonfire in the center of a field, thinking not of the gaiety around it, but only of warmth. There had been an air of expectancy in the farmhouse, a sense of urgency in Washington's face and in his busy pacing. He had had dangerous matters on his mind, but what matters exactly? The sense of urgency seemed to be outside, too, in the very stillness of the trees and the lap of the ice-filled river. Something was about to happen. Something more than the arrival of Christmas.

Grace was dancing with a soldier, who clutched her waist as he spun her enthusiastically about. Her laugh rang out and her face glowed in the firelight. She saw Amity and called out, "Why don't you dance, too?"

Amity made herself smile, not in the mood at all for festivities. "Where's Isabel?"

"She said she was too tired to come."

"Then I'll get a cup of cider to take to her," Amity said. She pushed her way through to the fire, where a great iron pot hung over the flames. After jostling for position, she received her cup and headed into the darkness again. Strange that Isabel hadn't come. She had been looking forward to it so much.

The lean-to seemed very quiet, and the fire had died almost to embers. "Isabel?" she called.

A moan came in answer. She pulled back the flap and saw her friend lying there, her legs drawn up against her stomach, her eyes big and dark as the night itself in her white face.

"Oh, Isabel! Is it time? Is the baby coming?"

"Yes. I'm so glad you're here, Amity. I didn't realize when Grace left—" Her voice was choked off in a wave of pain that convulsed her. "I didn't dream it could hurt this much," she said when she could speak again. "It's as though it doesn't *want* to come out, and I can't say that I blame it, either."

Isabel was shivering uncontrollably, but at the same time she was drenched in perspiration, her clothing clinging to her, beads of moisture standing out on her forehead.

"Grace was right, wasn't she, Amity?" she demanded hysterically. "My sweet baby is going to die!"

"There, Isabel, try to be calm. Worry does no good. Thee must think of God and have faith." Amity spoke the words she knew a Quaker woman should speak, but even as she did, she wondered what good faith had done her mother, who lay buried in the same grave with the last little brother.

"Oh, Amity! I mustn't lose it. It's all I have in the world! Even if it's born alive, it will starve," sobbed Isabel, uncomforted.

"Grace and I would never let it starve! We will find a way to feed it somehow!"

"Do you promise, Amity?" Isabel clutched at her words.

"Yes. Yes, of course," Amity's pledge had been rash, she knew. But now she had no choice but to affirm it and to take it to her heart as a sacred vow. Grace would help, of course, and be more capable than she.

"I believe you, then," said Isabel, more willing to trust Amity than an unseen God. "*You* would never fail a promise." She was panting as violently as though she had run a foot race, and she was still shaking, though Amity had built up the fire and thrown her own cloak over her.

"I'm going to get Grace," she said, heading off to the bonfire at a dead run.

Midway she stumbled against Grace in the darkness, on

her way to check on the mother-to-be. Amity gasped, too out of breath to say more than "Isabel . . ." but Grace understood at once.

"Go and see if you can find some blankets," Grace commanded. "See if you can find an officer who will give up his hut for the night."

Amity nodded, glad that Grace intended to deal with matters at the lean-to. Yes, she thought, she must find shelter for Isabel. Why, even her father's cows had the comfort of the barn when they dropped their calves. She thought of General Greene's headquarters. The house had seemed empty. A family had lived there, she'd been told, but they must have gone away for Christmas. Why not ask General Greene to take Isabel in? There would be a bedroom with fresh sheets and feather pillows.

The guard lowered his rifle to challenge her as she approached the door. "It's all right," she said, smiling at him. "I was here earlier to see General Washington. He told me to come back, or he'll be angry!"

The soldier hesitated but stepped aside. Opening the door and closing it quickly behind her before he could think better of it, she peeked into the room where she had left Washington and Greene. No one was there. She glanced curiously at maps spread on the table, aware of the prominence of the Delaware River. Where had they all gone?

Frustrated, she paced before the fire, much as Washington had paced earlier. Then it occurred to her to look upstairs. She could at least find a suitable room for Isabel, and she'd be occupied during her wait. Running up the wedge-shaped stairs, she quickly chose a small bedroom, and having plumped pillows on the low-framed maple bed, began nervously to build a fire.

Below her came footsteps. Voices wafted up through the fireplace. Washington, Greene, James Monroe, and others were discussing the maps.

"The boats are behind Hog Island, where no one can see them," said Washington.

"The Durham boats?"

"Yes. The largest, stoutest vessels around, used for hauling iron ore to Durham Furnace, north of here, where our bullets are made. But they will serve another purpose tomorrow!"

"When do we attack?"

"Tomorrow night. Colonel Rall won't be expecting us. It's Christmas, and he'll be carousing. He had no instinct for the jugular. If he had, he'd have beaten us by now. This is our last chance, gentlemen. The enlistments of most of our best soldiers expire at the end of the month, and we cannot expect them to reenlist to sit idly starving here. We must have victory! Victory must be our Christmas present to our brave soldiers!"

Washington's Christmas present to his men. Not rations, but victory, wrapped in gunpowder and blood instead of paper and ribbons. Now she knew why Washington had said she must leave at dawn. A battle was imminent. Amity trembled, without courage to go downstairs and reveal herself. Obviously her request for Isabel would meet rejection. The generals couldn't admit a passel of women to their headquarters on such a night. She knew now why the family was absent from their house. They hadn't gone; rather they'd been sent away. She doused the fire and hid behind the bed, hearing every detail of the plan in spite of herself. Would they think she'd hidden in the house on purpose? Would they think her a spy if they found her? She was, after all, a Quaker, and a Quaker's allegiance was always in doubt.

The conference went on for hours. At last Washington distributed copies of an essay written by Thomas Paine, to be read to the men as they crossed the Delaware in the Durham boats.

" 'The summer soldier and the sunshine patriot will, in this crisis, shrink from the service of his country,' " she heard Washington read, " 'but he who stands it now deserves the love and thanks of man and woman!' "

After a long while the house was quiet. They had gone out, she thought, to begin preparations for the attack, or perhaps to warm themselves with a last glass of ale before beginning to give orders.

Amity slipped downstairs and let herself out, murmuring good night to the sleepy sentry, who thankfully must not have mentioned her presence to his commander. Good night! It was almost morning. The stars were pale, and the Jersey palisades appeared in silhouette against the sky as she ran through the snow, carrying blankets she had taken from the house. Fear clutched her as she approached the lean-to, gasping for breath, the cold air hurting her lungs. And then she heard the cry of a baby.

Joy transcended the cold as she stepped into the lean-to and saw Isabel's blissful face. "It's a girl, Amity," Isabel whispered, and Amity was shocked at the thinness of her voice. "Healthy, too, isn't she, Grace?" the voice pleaded.

"Yes, it seems so, Isabel. She's a fine baby. She's beautiful." Grace's words ended in a sob, and Amity turned on her with sudden alarm. All was not well after all!

Frantically she began tucking the fresh blankets about Isabel and the infant, but Isabel seized her hand and reminded her, "You promised you wouldn't let her starve or freeze, Amity—you and Grace. Oh, it's so hard to leave her here when I've only just held her." Amity started to cry a protest, but Grace's quiet voice stopped her, making the promise again. "We'll take care of her, Isabel."

Isabel's grip relaxed, and she gave a long sigh as if sinking into a deep feather bed. Her eyes closed gently.

"She's asleep, poor thing," Amity whispered.

"Yes. Forever. It's a blessing, Am. She's with her Reuben, and soon they'll have their Grace, most likely."

"The baby! But thee promised that it wouldn't starve! And so did I!"

Grace turned on her fiercely. "I said it to be kind, you idiot! We'll do what we can, of course, but it's bound to die."

"Thee are terrible, Grace," said Amity, her chest heaving with angry grief.

"I'm realistic. Next I would be loving the baby the way I loved Isabel. It will die, Amity. And who are you to be so righteous? Where were you all night?"

"I cannot tell thee, Grace!" she said with a sudden new burst of trepidation. There were clever spies in the camp, she knew. She must not breathe a word of what she had heard. She must take no chance on being the cause of ruining the Continental surprise in Trenton tonight.

"Never mind, I can guess," said Grace. "You were with your Silas, trying to persuade him to marry you, with your kisses and that pretty dress. You had better get from my sight for a while. There was a cow wandering in the woods yesterday. I heard her bell. Go and see if you can find her. We'll need milk for the baby."

Tears streamed from Amity's eyes as she went on her errand, and crystals of ice formed in her lashes. She had not a friend in the world, she thought. The Quakers would shun her when she returned home. Isabel was dead, and Grace was justified in her anger. As for Silas, he had been strong enough to keep away from her. He hadn't come to the lean-to to look for her during the night, or Grace would not have thought she was with him already.

A rustle in the bushes attracted her attention, and she

turned to follow it, making a noose in the rope she had brought to slip over the cow's head. The sound came again, but now, strangely, it was behind her. She went after it, puzzled, wondering how the animal could have got there without her seeing it.

Increasing light laid the black skelton shadows of bare trees across the snow, but still Amity could not see her quarry. A mist blew from the sculptured snowbanks along the river, stinging her already freezing cheeks. Suddenly she glimpsed a dark form, and then she was flung to the ground.

Above her loomed the evil, mocking face of Moses Doan.

5

"Don't scream, little Quaker, I've a knife at your throat!"

She glared up at him furiously, half a mind to disobey, but the gleam of sharp metal, no more dangerous-looking than the gleam in his eye, dissuaded her. "What do you want of me?" she said.

"Don't play games, Miss Amity. You know very well what I want." His face was rugged and virile beneath his snow-dusted coonskin cap, and his chin of black beard glistened with wax that he had rubbed into it to make it shed snow and sleet better. The beard was crusty with ice anyway, but beneath it his mouth seemed like hot coals. Something in its sensual twist told her how it would heat her body if he kissed her.

She was not exactly afraid of the outlaw. After all, she had breakfasted with him once, and he had not proved dangerous then. But then she had had the feeling that he could be dangerous, perhaps in more ways than one. She had that feeling now as his expression seemed to dare her to try to run away.

"I don't know at all what thee want, sir. I was looking for a cow to milk for a newborn child. If thee have any decency, thee'll help me look."

The outlaw grinned, showing rows of white teeth. Everything about him was as perfect and natural as the earth itself.

He was a beautiful predator, like a hawk, able to take one's breath away with the grace of its deadly flight.

"Decency, Miss Amity. Why, you know I haven't a shred of it, now that you've been talking to the camp women. And most likely you won't have a shred of it yourself when I've done with you." He laughed in the suggestive way he had, filling her with a thrill of dread. Instinctively she thought of the soldier in the barn and tucked her skirts about her ankles.

He noted her motion, and to her embarrassment, guffawed. "Now, that's not necessary. I may have no decency, but I have pride. When I lift a woman's skirts, she's always willing. But that's for later. I told you I was out to catch a clever old fox."

"George Washington," she blurted.

"Aye, you've a good memory. Have you as good a memory of what you heard in General Greene's headquarters last night? Tell me or I may kill you."

"They were celebrating Christmas, that's all," she said, aware of his businesslike knife. He might have pride about not raping women, but doubtless killing them was in another category. "I was only looking for a place to bring a friend in childbirth," she added, glad there was a kernel of truth to her story. She was an unskilled liar.

He glared at her, not believing her for a moment. "More went on last night than babies being whelped."

"How would thee know?" she demanded.

He chuckled. "I took a mug of cider at the bonfire last night. Nobody noticed a stranger on Christmas Eve. I know almost everything that goes on in this camp. And something *is* going on. That old fox is up to something, and you know what it is!" His tone turned soothing, and Amity felt more alarmed than ever as he bent over her, pressing his lips to hers. The sensation was jolting, all the more so because it was like a draft of forgetfulness. For a moment sweet warmth filled her, her will was as lost as though she had whiffed opium, like sailors' wives in Philadelphia.

"Tell me about the Continentals, Amity," he murmured. "They are getting ready to march. I know, because they are all mending their shoes, those that have them."

His words brought the world back into focus. She was aware again of the cold and the snow, but more than anything else, of the danger Moses Doan posed to the Continentals. General Washington had said that the entire future of the colonies depended upon surprising the British at Trenton. Moses Doan must not be allowed to decide the course of the war!

"I won't tell thee," she said. "Kill me if thee like."

Bemusedly, his eyes shrewd, he lowered the knife. She drew a breath of relief.

"Let me go back, then, if you're not going to help me find the cow. I must find food for the baby."

"Let you go! Of course I can't. Why, you'd run right back and tell them I was here. If you won't tell me what the Continentals are up to, I'll have to spy to find out. Washington's brave, I give him that. But he can't succeed on a march in weather like this. You'll come with me, Amity. Give me your hands."

Wonderingly she held them out and he bound them loosely with the rope she had brought for the cow. Then he tied the other end to his belt, so that he had her on a lead. Taking a handkerchief from his pocket, he bound her mouth tightly.

"There, now, you'll not be giving the alarm, done up so, little Quaker, though you can't be kissed, either, and I know you liked it."

She fought to speak and tell him how she had hated his kiss as she stumbled after him, helpless as livestock, down the muddy riverbank.

Before noon he had found the Durham boats in a wooded cove between Hog Island the shore of the Delaware. Silas, who had helped acquire the boats, was among the heavy guard. If only she could cry out to him! But even if she alerted the Continentals, Moses Doan might get away. He was too slick to be caught, Grace had said.

Doan chuckled at the sight of the boats. "They'll be frozen and their powder wet before they even get across. But I'll report this to Colonel Rall, anyway, and take my reward. The only question now is when. Today, is it, Miss Amity?" Her glare made him laugh again.

He withdrew and built a little fire in a cave in the riverbank and cooked himself a meal, dousing his hot tea liberally with rum. "I'd feed you, Amity, but you might scream and rouse someone," he apologized. "Would you promise to behave?"

Amity shook her head and went hungry, but at least she was warm. Exhausted, too, she realized, since she had not slept the night before. She dozed; then a muffled sound roused her. Drums! Moses Doan was grinning, pulling her to her feet and over the riverbank, then down into the snow to hide with his arm flung over her.

The line of Continentals came into view, their faces set

with the determination of liberty or death, their ill-shod feet wrapped in burlap, leaving bloody traces in the snow. Up and down the line Washington paced on his white horse, as though he knew it would give his men heart to see him; and his own magnificent courage was mirrored in their eyes. Amity was transfixed by the sight, but the outlaw thought it funny, and tossing her onto his saddle, he climbed up behind. "Now, Miss Amity, we'll ride upstream and swim the river." Insolently he put an arm around her waist and pulled her against him. The push of his nether regions against her buttocks disturbed her strangely, and she did not feel more complacent when he set the horse to galloping. Then the frigid river numbed her legs and took her breath away. The horse snorted and gasped. Its powerful shoulders churned amid the curds of ice. If they did not freeze to death before they got across, he'd ride to warn the British—unless she could stop him. It might cost her own life, but what did she have to live for without Silas? And what better way to die? She could not die to give life to another, as Isabel had, but she could die for liberty!

The summer soldier and the sunshine patriot will shrink in this crisis, but he who stands it now deserves the thanks of men and women.

She would have to take Moses Doan's life along with her own. Two lives, and she a Quaker! But Silas had said war was different, and like Grace, she had become as much a member of the Continental Army as though she had enlisted.

The outlaw was bound as much to her as she was to him. What affected one affected both. Without allowing herself to think more about it, she flung herself from the saddle.

Moses Doan gave a shout of surprise as her movement jerked them both into the river. She could not possibly swim, tied as she was. "Dear God, forgive me," she prayed beneath the icy water. She would drown and pull him down with her in the black depths.

To her surprise, she bobbed up again, struggling to breathe, the instinct for life strong even though she had chosen death. To her horror she saw the outlaw floating beside her, the knife in his hand. He was going to kill her, she thought, with a greater terror of being murdered than of drowning. But then she realized his intentions. He had slashed the rope between them and cut himself free. Now he would get across. She would drown without weighting him down like a rock. No doubt he was a strong swimmer himself.

Then his arm went about her neck, pulling her with him through the Delaware's treacherous currents. She could not imagine why he had bothered to save her.

The outlaw did not know either. "You tried to kill me, damn you!" he bellowed, icicles already hanging in his dark hair, as he found footing on the far bank. "I should have let you drown!"

He seemed to expect her to answer him. A one-sided yelling match did not satisfy him, and remembering she was gagged, he tore the bandana from her mouth. "There. Scream all you want now. There's no one to hear you. Scream till you're frozen solid. It won't be long. I'm going in that barn there. You'll come, too, if you've any sense."

"Go with you? Never!" she cried, and began to shout, hoping to arouse someone on the opposite shore. But before long she realized her efforts were futile. Even if someone heard her, the message could never be understood across that distance. The hem of her skirt had frozen stiff, and she knew he was right. She must seek shelter or die.

The house that had been near the barn was a burned ruin—a chimney fire, perhaps, or maybe someone had lived here who had loved liberty too well. No other structure but the barn was anywhere in sight, and she had no alternative but to go inside. Pushing open the door, she felt warmer, and then suddenly she drew in her breath. In the center of the barn stood Moses Doan—stark naked.

She stood gaping at his muscled shoulders as he toweled himself with a horse blanket. Then he raised the blanket higher, and she stared at the lean, powerful legs and the manliness between.

"Get your clothes off, too," he said, acknowledging her presence with his command.

She hesitated, then, knowing it had to be done, hid herself in a stall and began to strip. "Is there another blanket?" she asked.

"Maybe," he said curtly. "Look for yourself."

"I . . . thought perhaps you'd hand it to me," she wavered.

"I might, and then I mightn't. Can't think why I should. I'd be dead now, just another cake of ice in the river, if you'd had your way."

She gave up, and having removed all her clothing, hung her gown over the stall. A pile of hay suggested warmth, and crawling in, she buried herself deep in its sweetness.

The outlaw's shadow fell across the opening of the stall. In his hand he held another blanket. "Are you warm, Miss Amity?" he asked mockingly.

"Warm enough," she said, teeth chattering.

He caught sight of her in the hay and grinned. "It appears to me you'd get warmer with company in there," he said.

"No, thank you!"

"Well, now, I know I'd be warmer."

"Stay away!" she warned.

"I'm coming in," he said matter-of-factly. He put a foot into the haystack, and instinctively Amity began to scramble out. Her bare breast swung into view, all covered with bits of shining straw. The outlaw's expression made her remember her nudity, and she sank back.

The outlaw grinned.

"Can't you build a fire?" she asked desperately.

"Nothing to build it with. But putting a man and woman together is like striking flint. Especially a spirited woman like you. A spirited woman warms a man better than spirits from a whiskey bottle."

His bare skin was touching hers, the thick hair of his chest tickling, and to her amazement, she realized he was right. A peculiar heat was growing inside her. Why, she might have been lying close to a stove! The sensation was so welcome that she did not protest when he put his arms around her to draw her closer. His fingers began to work on her bare back, caressing her, and the heat grew to a flaming fury. Now he was kissing her roughly, as he had when he'd caught her outside the camp, and again his lips drugged her. But this time he did not interrupt his kisses with requests for Continental secrets. Secrets of another sort were his will, and she surrendered them helplessly in the face of the conquering army of his lust. A demon of desire possessed her as his hands and lips moved everywhere.

Deep inside her, something screamed that this could not be happening. He was a Tory! He was the enemy! She had just tried to kill him, and now she hated him more than ever for doing this to her.

Powerless, she felt his hands in the intimate regions that the British soldier had violated, and she exerted herself to seize his hand to pull it away. Somehow she pushed it deeper instead, and gave a moan of agonized ecstasy. The outlaw sighed and rolled himself atop her. Now she felt a different thrust against her body.

"No!" she said, the word coming out not as a word at all,

but as a tortured sigh of assent. There was a quick moment of pain and then a rhythmic motion, so gentle it might have been a mother rocking the cradle. The sweet sensation lulled her, and her body relaxed and opened to him. But her insistent demon overcame her with demands, and she began to push her body against his. Arms locked about his neck, she began to cry, growing tense to bursting, unable to breathe, until finally the gentleness deepened to savage urgency in both him and her. The motion was faster as his body beat harder and harder into hers. Then she felt herself exploding, falling like a shooting star from a summer sky, and she held more tightly to the outlaw to save herself.

Finally she was aware only of silence, the darkness of the barn, and a sense of warmth. The spy stroked her hair. She remembered that she hated him, but that did not seem to matter. What mattered was that he had mastered her. She had not known that she possessed this weakness, and the discovery disgusted her. He had degraded her in more than body, for he had done it with her consent, and degraded her soul. He was worse than the British soldier that Silas had killed.

Moses Doan had been as good as his word. He had taken her without forcing her, and he had left her, like himself, without a shred of decency. She began to cry, and he said, not unkindly, "No use in that, Miss Amity. The milk's spilled now."

He was right, she supposed, though she couldn't help weeping. He turned his back on her carelessly, and in a moment he was asleep. She knew she should remain awake to mourn her virtue, but the warmth and the delicious aftermath of passion were too great, and soon she slumbered beside him.

6

She awoke to the sound of snoring, and looking down at him, shivered at the memory of what had happened. Had it happened? It seemed like some dream she might have had beneath the icy surface of the river. Only the ache between her legs told her that it must be true as she slipped out of the straw into the chill of reality.

He was at her mercy now, as he slept, just as she had been at his earlier. She had only to use his own knife on him. But Amity knew she couldn't kill him in cold blood, not as he lay sleeping. He had, after all, saved her, if only for his lustful purpose.

Her gown was dry, though her cloak was still heavy with moisture. She took the horse blankets instead, and saddling Doan's horse, led it quietly outside. It was dark, and hail had begun to fall, rattling and hissing in the trees. She was tempted to go back, but no fate could be worse than that she degrade herself with him again.

He would not sleep much longer. Now was her only chance to find the Continentals. They must have crossed the river, too, by now, if the boats had not upset in the current. She had only to ride toward Trenton and find the line of march, and they would send men back to capture Doan and defeat his goal.

Amity galloped south through the night, eager to put distance between herself and the sleeping spy. The hail was punishing, and the wind whipped the inefficient blankets she had pinned around her. Perhaps the army had not managed the crossing after all. She saw no sign of it or of the troops that had been supposed to join it on the Jersey side. She had ridden far and was nearly frozen again; and although she had stuffed straw into her shoes in the barn, she was afraid her feet were frostbitten. Then in the distance she saw lights, and began to ride toward them. There must be a village where she could ask someone to share a fireside. Perhaps there might even be men there sympathetic to the Continental cause. They would relieve her of her errand and go to capture Doan themselves. Leaving the river road, she turned toward the lights.

"Halt!" cried a voice, and Amity was weak with relief. Soldiers. She had found the Continentals. But as the sentries gathered around her, she saw that their coats were not Continental blue. They were red!

She had found the British. Or they had found her. They were staggering with drink and resentful of having to stand duty on Christmas night, had been of a mind to desert their posts and join their comrades, who were partying in the town.

"What are you doing behind our lines, miss?" they asked.

"Seeking sanctuary," she answered quickly. "I wish to declare my loyalty to the king."

"On Christmas night, miss?"

"Is there a special time to be loyal to King George? I don't want his majesty's men to burn my home when they cross the river."

"You come from Pennsylvania?"

"Yes."

"How fare George Washington's troops? As poorly as we hear?"

"They are starving, the miserable wretches."

The soldiers chuckled. "Let's take her to the colonel," one said.

"Aye, She'll be a lovely Christmas present for him, and he'll give us an extra ration of rum."

Heart heavy, Amity let them lead her away, and soon they were in the cobbled streets of Trenton. Here and there oil streetlamps flickered through sleet, and sounds of gaiety echoed as drunken soldiers stumbled from one door to another.

"Here we are, miss. Lucky we found you, and not the Hessians!"

They bid her dismount and led her inside, where a number of officers sat feasting around a table with a lace cloth and a candelabrum. The aromas of roast beef, potatoes, carrots, and corn pudding made Amity feel faint.

"I'm Colonel Rall, child. So you've come to declare your loyalty! What's your name?"

"Amity, sir," she answered, trying vainly to keep her eyes off the food.

He followed her gaze. "Won't you join us for dinner? Afterward we're going to play cards."

He filled a plate for her and sat her next to the fire. Amity ate ravenously, pulling off her shoes to warm her feet. There were other women in the room. Amity was aghast that some of them sat shamelessly on the officers' laps and poked tidbits into their mouths. They wore satin or silk open-robed gowns that displayed elaborate petticoats beneath and were adorned with lace, feathers, colored foils, and tassels. Coiffures were built to great heights over hair pads, with rows of jeweled, powdered curls.

Amity endured their scornful glances with some embarrassment for her own disheveled appearance. Her beautiful meeting dress was torn and crumpled, and bits of straw hung in her hair. Nonetheless the colonel insisted that she sit beside him as he played his cards, and now and then his hand dropped familiarly to her knee. She shuddered under his touch. He was the beast who had ordered the massacre of the hapless Americans on Long Island, and after her experience with the outlaw, she knew what such attentions meant. Hail slapped against the windowpanes as she watched the flicker of the colonel's ringed fingers in the candlelight and tried to think of a plan.

Colonel Rall was winning. He drank heartily and insisted that she have a glass of Lisbon wine. "You bring me luck, child," he said. "I'll see that you're rewarded."

A soldier entered and bent over to whisper in the colonel's ear. "Not now," said Rall. "Can't you see I'm ahead, you fool? I don't want to see anyone now."

"But it's the spy, sir. Doan," Amity heard him say. Her heart pounded. He was here!

"Blast!" said Rall. "Give him dinner and a bed, and I'll see him tomorrow."

Amity was wild with glee. After all that had happened, the British commander was going to refuse to see the outlaw. The morning would be too late. The outlaw would not receive his pay for his effort. She laughed to herself as she imagined the spy standing outside in the sleet, while she basked in the Britisher's approval. How angry Doan would be! How furious if he could know that she was inside! He had had sport of her, but the victory would be hers and the Continental Army's!

The soldier who had brought the message of the spy's arrival disappeared and returned again. She blanched as she saw the folded piece of paper in his hand. "Doan asks only that you read this note, sir," he said.

"Oh, very well."

Amity tottered to her feet. She must destroy the paper! Seize it and throw it into the fire! But it would do no good. If she destroyed it, they would know that it had been important. The room spun, the candles flowing into giddy circles of light. Just as she fainted, she was aware that Colonel Rall had caught her in his arms.

Dimly she knew that he carried her up the stairs and laid her gently on a bed. She felt that she wanted to keep sinking into the feather mattress forever, until she reached some perfect oblivion. Visions of the Continentals flashed in her fogged mind; she saw the blood of their footsteps, the determination and love of liberty on their faces. It would be a massacre if Rall read that note! And Silas was with that march!

In her swoon she seemed to see General Washington standing by the fireside again in the Pennsylvania farmhouse. "Go home, Miss Andrews," he was saying. "It's the best thing you can do for Silas and the Continentals." Once more her soul surged with longing to prove herself as valuable as if she were a man.

Her vision cleared, and the officer was not George Washington, but Colonel Rall, gazing on her anxiously. The corner of the outlaw's note showed in the pocket of his waistcoat. He had not read it!

She stirred, and when he saw she was conscious again, the Colonel's expression changed. He had a reputation with women, she remembered as she read in his ardent gaze how desirable she was to him, lying there with her fire-and-honey curls spread over the pillows.

Her stomach convulsed as she realized he was thinking of using her as the outlaw had, but this man had none of the outlaw's evil attraction. He pretended to straighten the covers around her, and his hand grazed the curve of her bosom.

"Are you feeling better, Amity?"

"Yes," she said, suddenly understanding what she had to do, understanding that he was far more interested in her than in the note in his pocket. Tonight she would be more valuable to the Continentals than any man in Washington's army. She would sacrifice for her country the thing that no man could. She'd use what the outlaw had taught her and she'd use it to thwart him!

"I would feel easier if my bodice were loosened," she sighed with a smile.

The colonel complied eagerly with her request, his hands moving hastily on her fastenings. The touch of his hot fingers made her flesh creep.

"It's warm in here, sir. Do remove thy coat and be comfortable," she suggested. He obeyed with alacrity. She breathed a sigh of triumph when the waistcoat with the message still in its pocket fell carelessly to the floor after his red jacket.

After that, she forced her mind away from the proceedings. He sank his teeth painfully into her nipples, shaking his head back and forth like a dog savoring a meaty bone. Sweat ran from him, and his hands left sticky ooze on the skin on her stomach as he worked his way to his goal between her thighs. Amity's legs trembled with dread. She had not guessed it could be this bad. It would be worse when he pushed her legs apart and inserted himself. She wondered if she could stand it. She must! She stuffed bedclothes into her mouth to keep from screaming. He would exhaust himself on her, and when she had subdued him with his own fatal lust, she would burn the message.

A knock came on the door, and a voice called to the colonel.

"I'm coming," he said, and with a grunt sat up and began to button his trousers.

"Oh, don't leave so soon!" she begged in panic, as he donned the waistcoat.

Colonel Rall laughed wickedly. "My dear, you are a lovely morsel, but I was winning at cards. I'll be back later, and to-morrow we'll buy you a new gown with the winnings." He slapped her rump familiarly as he went out.

Amity wept. She was saved, but liberty was lost. Then through her grief she heard the sound of shots. Below, chairs scraped and overturned in confusion as the card game broke up. She had held him long enough! The Continentals had arrived!

Running to the window, she saw that the sun was up. Cheering Continentals were charging through the streets, breaking through doors and into houses. Artillery batteries, massed at the ends of Trenton's main street, cut down groggy Hessians as they rushed into formation. Colonel Rall was galloping to join his regiment, which was marching down King Street into deadly American fire. The bugles and drums kept playing even as the British broke and ran; then even that semblance of order was lost. Through the wind-driven snow the cry of "Liberty" rang everywhere as the tattered Continentals turned months of defeat into resounding victory.

Footsteps sounded on the stairs. The Americans were checking the upper stories for snipers. Whoever came would think her a Tory, finding her here in Colonel Rall's headquarters—why, in his very bedroom, dressed in only her chemise and petticoat!

She grabbed at her gown, but it was too late. The door opened, and she would sooner that any other Continental had opened it than the one who stood there.

"Silas," she whispered.

The triumph of the victory vanished from his face as he

saw her. All her life she would be haunted by the betrayed look on his features, of utter bewilderment and pained surprise, as though a Hessian had been hiding there and had run him through with a bayonet.

How she loved him! How she wanted to run to his arms and ease her own hurt against his stalwart chest. Something told her she could not. Innocence had ended for Silas when he had killed; she understood that better, now that innocence was ended for her, too. How long it had been since summer, when he had found her amid the berries and thistle, her bonnet in the grass. How long it had been since he had pledged, "I shall be thy husband, Amity, no one but me!"

Thunderstruck, he waited, as if hope were too natural a part of his nature to die easily, as if he had loved her too well to believe what he saw. If only she could utter words that would dispel appearances!

She longed to tell him all that had happened. How the outlaw had dragged her along the riverbank to find the Durham boats, and how he had swum the river with her. She wanted to confess how she had escaped and beg forgiveness for the desperate way she had kept the British commander from learning of the approach of the Continentals.

But she knew it was better this way. There was much Silas might forgive, much she might ask him to forgive. But her moments in the haystack with the outlaw must be part of any honest tale she told him, and she could never ask forgiveness for the worst of her degradation, her delirious enjoyment of the Tory spy.

She was no longer the girl he had pledged to sit with on the marriage bench, just as he was no longer the same man, since he had killed the soldier in her father's barn. She knew that life had separated them, and the time had passed forever when they might have married.

Going back in the Durham boats, the soldiers were so cold they had to stamp their feet in rhythm to break up new ice that was impeding navigation. The Hessians, to the tune of their own drums and fifes, were marching south, in their arched metal-fronted hats and their shining boots. And all along the way Americans laughed and cheered at the sight of them under their ill-dressed, ragtag guard.

Colonel Rall was dead, a spy's note found unread on his body: *Washington is coming on you down the river. He will be here afore long!*

Philadelphia
1778

7

"**I**'m off to Mrs. Bingham's tea party, Amity. Won't you change your mind and come?" Amity's Aunt Zenobia studied her niece bemusedly as she pulled on her York tan gloves and tied the horsehair strings above her elbows.

It had been almost a year and a half since the girl had appeared on her doorstep, only a few days after the glorious victory of the Continental Army at Trenton. She had had a harrowing story to tell of how her young intended bridegroom had joined the Continentals on the eve of their wedding and been disowned from the Society of Friends.

Love had prevailed over faith, and Amity had run away to join him. There it should have ended well, Zenobia thought, but it hadn't. Amity, unable to face the humiliation of returning home, had come to Philadelphia instead.

Zenobia couldn't condemn Amity for running off to Silas. She herself had been disowned from meeting when she had fallen in love with a dashing young seaman in the China trade. Zenobia smiled as she thought of John Willet. Never had she regretted the rash love that had separated her from home and family. That had happened almost twenty years ago, when she'd been scarcely older than Amity, and there had followed a blissful decade before the jealous sea had claimed him from her. Luckily, he'd left her wealthy, with a three-story home in Society Hill. Unluckily, he had left her no children. But Zenobia wasn't dissatisfied. She had had John.

Amity had run away for love. In that much the pair were alike. But Zenobia would have never let love slip through her fingers. She would never have allowed herself to be sent home like an errant puppy. Zenobia suspected Amity wouldn't have, either. She suspected there was more to the story.

Why else would Amity toss so in her sleep at night? Why so often did Zenobia find her standing by the flicker of her small oil lamp, trembling, her eyes, normally reminiscent of lilac blossoms and summer skies, a stormy purple. Among the pillows Zenobia would always find Amity's nightcap, testimony that she had thrashed and tossed until it had come off, and her beautiful curls would be tangled in shimmering cascades about her quivering shoulders.

She made such a sensual picture standing there that Zenobia never doubted that the dream or the nightmare was about a man. But that was the question Amity's aunt had not been able to ask. Oh, she had tried. But Amity always sensed it coming and changed the subject. Dream or nightmare, that was the crux of it. That was what Zenobia longed to know. Had the man been Silas? One of the brutal Hessians? Perhaps the very line between dream and nightmare was thin. Perhaps Amity herself would not want to admit which it was.

Even as a child Amity had had a way of reaching for life that did not befit a Quaker. Zenobia well remembered a day little Amity had been left in her care while Thomas Andrews had been selling his produce at the High Street Market. Attracted by azaleas in her aunt's garden, the child had pinned a row of the flowers in the brim of her bonnet. Amity had intended to remove them before her father returned, but the blossoms had left a stain. The stain of vanity, Thomas had called it when he'd punished her. Now Amity had reached for the forbidden bloom of love. And that, too, had left its stain.

Zenobia pinned on her chip hat with its double row of puffs of lilac ribbon and adjusted the layers of her open-robed gown of pomona green silk, the lace-trimmed flounces of its sleeves and the edges of its low, squared bodice. Zenobia had given up Quaker simplicity when she had married John, along with "thee" and "thy," about which John had teased her so. Zenobia couldn't help smiling as she checked her appearance in the arched Queen Anne mirror in the parlor. She was still beautiful; John would have approved. He used to joke that he had chosen her for features that would last—a nose that was straight instead of upturned, a mouth frankly soft and wide, not girlishly saucy or rosebud sweet.

"The officers will all by vying to pour tea for you," said Amity, coming up behind her. Like Zenobia, she did not consider herself really a Quaker now, and she, too, had given up "thee" and "thy" after her months in the sophisticated company of her aunt.

"British officers!" said Zenobia with a snort. "It's not for such pleasure that I'm going."

Amity laughed. "But have a good time anyway. It's a lovely, warm day, and you are more adept at enjoying yourself than I."

"I suspect that you are remaining at home exactly because of the weather," replied her aunt. "You would rather sit in the garden than waste away the hours flattering Tories in hopes of collecting some scrap of information for the Continentals."

"Why, Aunt, that's not the case at all. It's simply that Grace is busy and can't tend Gracie. Go and spy for us both—and eat enough tea cakes for two."

Amity drew a breath of satisfaction as Zenobia left the house. Her aunt had been right. Amity was giving herself a day of vacation. She had not even asked Grace to take baby Gracie.

Amity had been spying for the Continentals ever since the British had come to occupy the city in September. It had been a winter of such display and gaiety as Amity could never have imagined. The British had put on amateur theatricals, revived horse racing, given lavish dinners and balls, in spite of food scarcities caused by the Continental river defenses—the ingenious *chevaux de frises* sunk beneath the water to pierce the hulls of ships that passed over.

In November Grace had come from Valley Forge with Isabel's baby. The child could not endure another winter in the cold, Grace had said, reluctantly taking a job in a tavern. The work had been exhausting, the indignities worse. When two handsome young officers had offered her a position as their housekeeper over their tankards of Cyder Royall, Grace had sensibly taken them up. The soldiers had not been enthusiastic about an infant, so Gracie had fallen to Amity. Grace came to visit almost every day. Between them the two girls had spoiled the baby horribly, Zenobia said.

The house was quiet now, the only sound the ticking of the grandfather clock, carved with flame-and-urn finials at the top. Behind its door was painted a green, twisting serpent, and Amity, like other harassed adults of the era, had told Gracie that a snake was inside, to keep her from playing with the pendulum.

But this afternoon the toddler was not into mischief. Instead she was snoozing angelically upstairs in her crib of curly maple. The servants had been given the day off, too, and were away from the house. Amity had had a hard time getting used to being waited upon by a cook and maid. Their presence made her nervous. Alone, Amity indulged herself in setting the house to rights herself, dusting the latticework of the Chinese Chippendale chairs and the porcelain Longton Hall peacocks on the pedimented walnut mantel. Amity loved her aunt's house, where bits of scrimshaw and pieces of jade set in velvet-lined rows of shelves breathed the excitement of far-off places, along with Uncle John's models of ships. John Willet had furnished the house with the finest Tabriz rugs brought from the Middle East, with scrolled silver sauce tureens from England, with wallpaper that had traveled from France in the hold of his vessel. Double doors led from the dining room into the garden, walled from the dirty cobblestone street. There bluejays called among plantings of bushy rhododendron, yellow roses, sweet william, and blazing red geraniums. Warm sunlight fell onto the grass, and breezes stirred the tulip trees.

Zenobia had been right. It was to sit in the garden that Amity had forsaken her duty at Mrs. Bingham's tea. Oh, she'd be asked after. She'd been quite the belle of the season. Strange she should have been, when her heart had never stopped breaking over Silas. When she had never been able to forget the instant that he had opened the door of Colonel Rall's bedroom, and she had realized the hopelessness of their love.

Was it the loss of Silas' love she mourned, really? Or that dark passion that had so profoundly interfered with their young love? The frightening desire she had found with the outlaw?

Silas commanded a regiment now, having distinguished himself not only at Trenton and Princeton but also in defense of the river forts, where a brilliant trap had been sprung on the British. At Brandywine he had shown himself an asset even in defeat. These things Amity had learned from Grace. She had never seen Silas again.

Now and again, news of him came from the British officers, too, as they quaffed their ale and spoke of the daring and intelligence of Silas Springer. He had begun a boyish idealist and become a warrior of skill and fury. Amity thought that his belief that she was a turncoat had aided the transformation.

Amity had done what she could for the Continentals. She had helped collect the supplies that Philadelphia women managed to drive straight through British lines to Valley Forge. And more than one raid on a grist mill or furnace in the countryside had been thwarted because Amity, Grace, Zenobia, or others like them caught wind of it as they danced the minuet in Philadelphia.

Amity strolled into the garden to cut flowers. All alone, she closed her eyes, imagining herself in Bucks County again, as she rested in a white wrought-iron chair. How she missed her home, especially in the summer. The wonders of the city could never replace it! She would have traded Zenobia's fine house and well-planned gardens in a moment for the simple farmhouse and a tangle of may apple and jewelweed, field daisies, and cornflowers.

She could never go home now. Even Father was gone. He'd been shipped off to Virginia for his refusal to take the oath of allegiance to the United States. The wagon train had been stoned, and he had been killed. She mourned him along with all else that the war had cost her.

She tried to think back to that time when she and Silas had courted, but other thoughts kept intruding—the same sort of thoughts that interrupted her sleep at night. She thought of Colonel Rall, for whom she'd been merely an interlude in a game of cards—an interlude that had cost him a battle and his life. More often she thought of Moses Doan, who had spared her life but not her virtue.

Unbidden, the dark outlaw came to her mind, standing over her stark naked as she lay equally unclothed in the haystack. The power of his broad shoulders seemed to intensify as it dropped down to his furry chest and narrow hips. The part of him meant for passion was like a shaft of flame, turning the chill of her body to fire before he had even touched her.

This was the dream she had more often than the dreams about Rall or the soldier in the barn. She supposed she would never experience such a moment again, that miracle of degradation and passion that had fired her soul to bursting. She would forever be cold in heart and body.

Oh, not that she had not had many chances for a turn between sheets since the British had come to Philadelphia. But the masculine gropings she had endured behind Society Hill jardinieres and beneath dinner tables had inspired only quick slaps of her ivory fan or well-placed kicks of her little silver-buckled evening slippers.

What would become of her? she wondered. Half of her

was still ingrained with the rich idealism of a Quaker, and that part longed to merge with a gentle strength like Silas! But the other half! The other half had gone wild at the outlaw's touch! If only she could be sure she would never repeat her wanton behavior!

But Amity could not be certain. Moses Doan and his gang still roamed the Bucks County hills, evading capture, and their every exploit, reported faithfully by the Philadelphia newspapers, was devoured by young ladies who had never seen Moses Doan, but who felt faint with excitement at the very thought of him. He was the worst sort of brigand on the high road, though his bent for relieving the rich and pompous of their possessions had given him a sort of Robin Hood reputation. How many girls had enjoyed his thieving ways since that Christmas night at Trenton? How many had he robbed of the possession that could never be retrieved?

If they met again, she would show him, she vowed, beating at the shadowed memory. She picked a rose, pricked her finger on a thorn, and frowned as she tucked the blossoms into her basket and started into the house.

In the doorway she paused, puzzled, as a whiff of tobacco smoke assailed her. Strange, since Aunt Zenobia had never taken up pipe smoking like so many Philadelphia women. Cautiously she followed the aroma to the door of the parlor and stopped in amazement. In the middle of the floor sat a whole collection of luggage—a camel's hump trunk, several portmanteaus, a gentleman's black leather hatbox, across which lay a cane switch-style walking stick. Peeking around a door, she caught a profile view of a man ensconced like a prince in her aunt's best brocade wing chair, his perfectly turned calves, clad in stockings of cobweb silk, stretched languorously across the cushion of the matching footstool.

She knew what it meant, and in a flash of rage she dashed across to the luggage, seized the long, limber walking stick, and shutting her eyes tightly, began to lash at him.

"Get out! Get out of this house! There'll be no British quartered here! General Howe has promised! He'll have you court-martialed if he finds you here!"

The cane thunked against his frock coat, whistling as it whipped through the air. The sound made Amity ill, but she was too angry to care. She had been imposed upon once by the British officer at Trenton, and she did not intend to spend a night under the same roof with another one. Oh, it was one thing to dance and flirt with Britishers to milk them of imformation, but sharing accommodations was quite another! She well knew what the conquerors wanted of the women of the fallen city! She and Aunt Zenobia had been fortunate so far, since General Howe had taken their excuse of being defenseless females alone as reason enough that they should not quarter men in the house.

Defenseless! She was not that! Quaker principles aside, no man would take advantage of her ever again! Not an outlaw, not a British officer, not this man or any! She pulled back the stick to hit him again, but it refused to come. Opening her eyes, she saw that he had grabbed the other end of it. She yanked at it in a frenzy. He yanked back harder, and too stubborn to give way, she toppled into his lap without letting go.

She landed bottomside up, with her soft round buttocks over his knees, and temptation seemed to overcome him. She screamed as she felt her dimity skirts lifted above her waist. Next came her hooped petticoats, and then nothing was left but her lacy drawers. Curls tumbled from Amity's cap and blood rushed to her head as she hung with her nose a mere inch from the carpet. Her breasts strained to tumble from her low bodice as she kicked mightily, trying to injure him with a buckled slipper. But a delicious thrill ran through her at the touch of his hand on her bare skin, and an expectant ache started between her thighs, which were pressed against his hard, muscled ones.

Horrified by her own reaction, she fought harder. Why, she had not even seen his face! No, that was not exactly true. It had been a very handsome face, smooth-shaven, with a patrician nose and a sensual mouth that had reminded her uncomfortably of the outlaw. Her breath stopped in her chest as she waited for him to lower her undergarments and fling her helplessly to the floor.

Instead she felt a stinging smack on her neither region. She was still reeling with surprise as the second and third blows followed the first, ringing resoundingly as her ripe flesh bounced against his hand. Disbelieving, she steadied herself against the chair and twisted around to look. He was actually spanking her, his features brimming with satisfaction.

He let go of her, and she skidded off onto the rug, her skirts sighing as they descended around her. She leaped up, bursting with indignation and fury, but aware nonetheless that she had been bested.

"By heaven!" he cried, a little breathless himself. "Are all American women as quick-tempered as you?"

"Are all the British as loutish as you?" she shot back. "You might have knocked, at least, before you trespassed into a private home!"

"I did knock. But no one answered. The door was open, and the foolish carriage driver had gone off already, leaving all my lugguage on the sidewalk. I'd have taken more care if I'd known what I know now! Truth to tell, I thought this a peaceful Quaker household, my dear. It seems I've much to learn, and so have you, if you cross swords with me again." His eyes twinkled now, gleaming with rich amber light. "I'll be glad to teach you, if you dare, but for now please bring me some refreshment. Ale if you have it, but if not, a cool glass of that abominable liberty tea. There's a good girl, and I'll not report your conduct to your mistress. I'm not British. Mrs. Willet will be glad to have me here, you'll see."

"Oh!" cried Amity in helpless rage. He had a slight accent of a kind she had never heard before, and taking a moment to study him, she realized that he had told the truth about not being British. Whatever his nationality, he was an aristocrat, and to judge by his clothes, very wealthy. His frock coat of exquisite flowered damask boasted buttons of French silver plate. A short-skirted waistcoat parted over tan cashmere britches, and his macaroni cravat was silk and lace, tied in a bow under his proud, unyielding chin. His hair swept back from his high forehead in waves. Oddly, it was his own hair, lightly powdered. She would have expected any gentleman of his obvious social stature to wear a wig. But more than anything else, she noticed those eyes.

She had never seen any like them, and they were difficult to assess, since she was afraid to hold them with her own. It was as though their compelling depths might draw her hopelessly into his thrall. He had taken her for the servant. Well, she would disillusion him about that! Then perhaps she would bring him his ale and spill it down his fine waistcoat. It would serve him right. But she stood hesitantly, remembering that he had vowed to teach her another lesson, should she "cross swords" with him again.

She trembled, hating him, not caring who or what he was, only that he should not take up residence in this house. Who *could* he be to dare walk in and install himself bag and baggage? Who could he be to be so certain that her aunt would want him? Amity was certain that Zenobia would not.

While she tried to decide how to give him his due, the baby began to wail upstairs. Grateful for the interruption, she raced upstairs to tend the child. She took her time, brushing out Gracie's dark curls, which were like Isabel's.

"Mama!" said the cherub, tugging at Amity's disheveled curls.

"Oh, dear," Amity sighed. Gracie had called Grace "mama" when she had first come to Philadelphia. Grace would not be pleased by this transference. "I'm not your mama, sweet. I suppose Grace is, and *she* has no choice but to keep house for those British scroundrels. Heaven only knows who *we* have in *our* house now. What's to become of us, with the world so topsy-turvy?"

She hugged the child in still-quivering arms, and sensing Amity's discomposure, the baby began to cry again, ending in a fit of coughing. The little girl had had the cough ever since she had been brought from Valley Forge, and Amity frowned, wondering if she should administer a dose of mithridate.

She had exaggerated Grace's position, perhaps. Grace was treated more like a fine lady than a housekeeper, to hear Grace tell it. The officers were forever vying for her company, and once had made a shambles of the parlor during fisticuffs over who might escort her to the horse races. Amity could only hope that Grace used nothing but the customary pan of hot coals to warm their beds on chilly nights.

But no matter how pleasant a situation it might be for Grace, it would never do for Amity! *She* would never inhabit the same house as any of King George's lustful troops! And as for that arrogant person—she could not call him gentleman—downstairs, she would as soon tolerate his presence as have a passel of the big Philadelphia rats that Aunt Zenobia's calico cat kept the house clear of.

But he was not a Britisher, she reminded herself. No matter, she hated him anyway. She hated him because he had behaved so abominably, she told herself, not admitting that her own conduct had been less than perfect, not admitting that she really hated him, not for the indignities he had dealt her when he had had her over his knee, but for causing her the same unrest the outlaw had. He had set currents of desire running within her again, like a recurrence of a dread disease which she had hoped was conquered.

She played with the baby awhile before she grew calmer and curiosity overcame her. What had happened downstairs?

Was he still sitting there? A wonder he had not followed her upstairs to choose his bed! A quiver to trepidation at that prospect was followed by the unsettling notion that he might have left the house and gone from her life forever.

A little later, carrying the baby as a sort of shield, she crept downstairs. At the turn of the steps a hearty masculine laugh told her he had remained. Her aunt's laughter joined in, genuine and melodic, not the controlled little titter she used to reward Tories for their compliments and jokes. Zenobia had not even taken off her hat, Amity saw as she descended.

The intruder was drinking ale, while Zenobia sipped or pretended to sip liberty tea. She seemed to have forgotten her teacup, her gaze rapt on the elegant stranger. Did he have such an effect on all women? Even on Zenobia, who had never thought any man worth notice since Uncle John?

He looked up and saw her, and a slow smile started over his handsome face. Amity wished that she had not taken such pains to brush her hair up high and fasten it into a perfect chignon. She had changed her dress, too, discarding the dimity for something she had hoped would give her more confidence before him, a yellow silk with puckered draperies behind and a flounce to the skirt. It was fancier than anything she might have worn in the days when she had been in good standing in the Society of Friends, and she wore it self-consciously, with a black velvet ribbon high about her slender throat, a concession to vanity, though she had never yet worn jewels.

He leaped to his feet as she entered, his heels coming together as he made a deep bow and lifted her hand to his lips. But he kept her fingers in his an instant too long, and his eyes caught hers with a flicker of a twinkle.

"Amity, my dear, I should like you to meet Don Mario da Riva," said Zenobia. "Don da Riva, my niece, Amity Andrews."

Amity smiled a trifle smugly. Now he would see what a dreadful mistake he had made! She was no servant girl. And she would tell her aunt he must be ordered out summarily. It would be a sweet revenge!

But Don da Riva did not bobble. "Ah, we have met," he said easily. Why, he had not taken her for the servant girl at all! He had merely pretended to, to avoid having to apologize to her! He would smirk no longer when she had told her aunt of his scandalous behavior!

He surprised her by reaching for Gracie. Apparently no female was too young for his charms, because the child went to him, accepting the gold watch he took from his fob pocket to amuse her. "A beautiful child, madam," he said, "though she must take after your husband, with that dark hair."

"No," she said in confusion, "I'm not married." She flushed furiously at his lifted eyebrows. "Gracie is a friend's child."

"Oh, I do beg your pardon," he said, but he did not look at all repentant. He had meant to ascertain her martial status, and it bothered him not at all that he had managed to embarrass her. She, on the other hand, still knew nothing about him.

"Amity, Don da Riva has just come from Russia," said Zenobia.

Russia! Perhaps he was a wild cossack. That might explain his behavior. But no, he hadn't a Russian name.

"I'm Venetian, Miss Andrews," he explained. "My family's palazzo is on the Grand Canal. We're a seagoing republic, and supervising the building of ships at the arsenal has been my specialty. But Venice is too confining for many young men, and I have lived in London and Paris and other capitals. Most lately I am from St. Peterburg, where I have been advising her majesty Catherine the Great on the building of a new Black Sea fleet, with which she hopes to conquer the Crimea."

She sat down slowly and stared at him. "Are you acquainted with the empress herself, sir?"

"Indeed. She's a most remarkable woman, who thinks more of her country's destiny than of herself. She is the most powerful woman in the world, but she has written herself a list of rules to live by to keep from losing touch with her people. She showed it to me herself over chocolate in her apartments one morning. I had a chance to know her well, since I was quartered in the Winter Palace."

The Winter Palace! And now he wished to quarter here? Surely the most lavish home in the city would be a comedown. Why was he in Philadelphia, anyway? She looked sidewise at her aunt, and saw her studying him with the same speculation.

He put his hand into his pocket and drew out an envelope. "The letter of introduction, Mrs. Willet. I mentioned that I had brought one. It's from a friend of yours in Russia."

Whoever could Aunt Zenobia know in Russia? Amity wondered as her aunt took the letter eagerly, turning it in her hand.

"There is only one person with whom I am acquainted in St. Petersburg, and surely he would not . . . But, why, it is. It's from Caleb Beale!"

"Pray tell, who is Caleb Beale?" Amity burst out impatiently.

"A Quaker, a member of the same meeting as I when I was a girl. But he decided that God had called him to be a public Quaker, and he went away. He has been traveling ever since, and has been well-respected everywhere. He has been close to many a seat of power."

Amity had heard of such people, quiet and unheralded, but persistent in their attempts to turn violence to peace and influence the leaders of the world to the principles of enlightenment. Wherever a king or emperor sought to learn the will of God, there would likely be a public Quaker, who might be brought quietly to the private chambers when generals and ministers had been dismissed.

"What does he say, Aunt?" Amity demanded, wildly impatient as Zenobia studied the letter with exasperating deliberation.

Zenobia seemed to pull herself back from some disturbing long-ago memory. "Why, he asks that I extend every courtesy to Don da Riva, and hopes that I can find room for him in my home. I suppose he doesn't know that I am widowed. It's not quite proper, but what matter, sir? We shall be delighted to have you. This is wartime, and nothing is quite normal."

"It will never do!" cried Amity. "I must speak to you privately, Aunt!"

"It *will* do, Amity." Zenobia's tone brooked no argument. "Caleb Beale would not send us a guest we cannot trust." Zenobia had lost her Quaker standing when she had married, but faith had mutated to fiber. Most unusually for a woman, her character had been tempered equally by ideals, pragmatism, and rebellion.

Somewhat the same forces were at work in shaping Amity, but it was too early to tell what the effect would be, especially since Amity's experience with the outlaw had added a potent factor to the equation. Amity seethed. She intuited that her aunt knew that she was attracted to Don da Riva and for that reason did not want him in the house. Zenobia would not be fooled by a recitation by Amity of the Venetian's misdeeds.

"Show Don da Riva to the room on the south end, please, Amity," continued Zenobia.

"I?"

"Yes, Amity. I've given the servants the afternoon off. It was your suggestion, you know. The groom will be along with the luggage when he's finished with my horse and carriage."

Amity clenched her teeth in frustration, no match for her dynamic aunt. It *had* been her idea to send the kitchen maid away, so as not to have to listen to her chatter on her afternoon playing truant from the tea party. Having servants about still made her feel uneasy, but at the moment she felt as put upon as any spoiled Philadelphia darling. Gathering her skirts daintily, she beckoned to him to follow her up the polished walnut stairway.

The bedroom on the south end, with a row of windows opening onto the courtyard, was the most delightful in the house. Indoor shutters were drawn back to admit the spring breeze, and big ceramic pots of lacy ruffle fern and ivy filled the sills. By the corner fireplace a pair of satinwood chairs with interlaced heart backs and upholstered seats angled cozily together side by side, and the big tester bed was magnificently hung with peach-colored brocade. It was the room that Zenobia had shared with John, but after his death she had had no more heart for the place. Though a decade had passed since, an aura of warmth and light still seemed to emanate from it, as though the joy of those years had permeated the very walls.

Amity resented the Venetian's intrusion. She resented even more that he seemed to fit into the room easily. He assessed the place, and with a look of appreciation slipped off his frock coat and tossed it onto the bed.

"Oh, pray do not undress!" cried Amity in unwarranted panic.

Now she could see just how lithe and supple he was beneath the rippling of his gathered cambric shirt sleeves. His chest seemed broad and powerful as a lion's, his guffaw unnerving her like a jungle roar as he spun on her. She had a dizzying sensation that he belonged in this room, that he completed what had always been missing when she had come here to knit socks for the soldiers and be tormented by her daydreams of Silas and the outlaw.

"My dear Miss Andrews! Are you really so innocent as you pretend to be? In Venice such young girls are kept in convents, where they can come to no harm, but surely you're the same she-devil who caned me with my own walking stick! Surely you've seen men in their shirt sleeves! But never fear. Caleb Beale recommended me to your aunt as a gentleman, and I'll remain so in this house—provided you remain a lady!"

"You're impossibly conceited! If you've come to the colonies to indulge your low nature, you've made a fine beginning," she stormed.

"I came to see what this silly furor about all men being created equal is all about," he retorted.

"Silly furor!" she gasped.

He looked at her in surprise, and she realized she'd nearly given herself away. This was supposed to be a Tory household, as he'd obviously been told.

"Surely you agree that it's the responsibility of the aristocracy to lead, Miss Andrews! Tell your aunt not to bother with an extra place at meals. I'll not be dining here, but at the taverns, where I may touch shoulders with the colonists and learn more about the city."

"You'll do more than touch shoulders, the likes of you!" said Amity.

He howled with appreciation, throwing back his head and laughing so loudly that Amity was certain Aunt Zenobia heard him below. "Well, Amity, you're a clever girl! Philadelphia's a lively place with the British occupation. Cockfights and bullbaitings and horses to run and serving women to . . . umm. Well, I've a mind to change britches before I go out, so unless you'd like to see . . ."

Amity fled, slamming the door behind her. She was breathless when she reached the kitchen, where her aunt, with a big checkered apron over her party gown, was cooing to Grace as she coaxed her to eat a snack of applesauce at the pine trestle table.

"Aunt! That man! He cannot stay here!" Amity gasped, beside herself.

"Amity, lower your voice," whispered Zenobia. "He was here alone with you, and Lord knows what happened with no servants about, but whatever, do not tell me!"

"Don't tell you!"

"No. Because it makes no difference. We must quarter him."

"Why? I don't see why. Do you owe some awful debt to this Caleb Beale?"

Zenobia smiled thoughfully. "Perhaps I do owe a debt to Caleb Beale. We might have sat on the marriage bench together, if I had not met John. Oh, I thought he would soon wed another, but he swore he never would. It was after that he set out on his travels."

"Your suitor! But even so—"

"I had not heard from him all these years, Am, so I know it's important now. And I know enough of Caleb to know that he sides with the Continentals. This Mario da Riva is some terrible threat to the cause."

"A threat? And your Caleb sent him to stay with us? But how could a Venetian nobleman threaten America's liberty?"

Zenobia shook her head. "That is not in the letter. Perhaps he thought Don da Riva would open it and discover he'd been betrayed. But between the lines, Amity." She held out the letter for her niece to read.

"Dearest Zenobia," it said, "this will introduce to you Don Mario da Riva, whom I have had the pleasure of knowing at the court of the Empress Catherine. By all we hold most dear, I urge you to give him lodging and to watch over him during his stay in Philadelphia. As always, your servant, Caleb Beale."

Amity looked up at her aunt, puzzled. "It's only a request for hospitality to a friend."

"Oh, Am. Use your head," cried her aunt impatiently. " 'By all we hold most dear,' he says. 'Watch over his stay by all we hold most dear. Freedom is what we hold most dear!' "

"You are certain that is what it means, Aunt?"

"Indeed. He's up to something that will mean no good to the colonies."

"Well, then, I suppose we will have to find out what it is," sighed Amity.

"*You* will have to find out," corrected Zenobia.

Amity stared at Aunt Zenobia, who gazed back at her steadily, but with the flicker of a smile. "Oh, Am, I don't have to tell you. You know it's true! A girl who's eighteen and as beautiful as you can bewitch a man into telling her what he would rather die than reveal!"

"Bewitch him! He hates me, and I hate him!"

"On the contrary, Am, I believe he's bewitched already. I suppose you'll not tell me how you managed it. I saw how he looked at you when he saw you coming downstairs. Maybe you're bewitched yourself, in which case you'll have to be careful. Take care not to fall in love with him. I'd have difficulty not falling in love with him myself if I were in your shoes."

Fall in love with him. The idea was ridiculous. It was bad enough that she would have to be civil to him—no, throw herself at him. But that night she dreamed of the outlaw. She was pinned beneath him in the straw as usual, but something was different. Something in the touch of his hands was more skillful, as though his fingers were more sensitive to her, and his own desire was more towering than before. She gasped in frenzy, reaching for a star of fulfillment that seemed ready to swallow her in its fire of paradisiacal light. And then, before she could reach it, before she could do more than be dazzled at its beauty, she saw the face of the man in the straw—not the dark hair of the outlaw, but fair, wavy locks; a chin, clean-shaven, and amber eyes reflecting the fire of her own passion with a mocking passion of their own.

8

"Sit down, Amity. You'll get us a dunking," Mario ordered.

Amity obeyed, sitting primly in the rowboat, adjusting her wide-brimmed straw milkmaid hat. It was May, and the willows along the Schuylkill River had turned green again. On the cliffs above bloomed golden clouds of forsythia. It had been a month since Mario da Riva had spanked her in her aunt's parlor. The Continental Army had survived the winter at Valley Forge and was celebrating the news that the French would help the Colonial cause.

It seemed to Amity that she was forever doing what Mario commanded. Not without protest, usually. She'd suggested this outing herself, or rather Aunt Zenobia had suggested she suggest it, scheming as always for her to be in Mario's company. All to no avail. They knew no more about Mario than the day he had arrived.

Certainly he had kept his word about being a gentleman, though he kept late hours, and she thought that the tavern girls saw another side of him than she. If she had been a serving wench herself, she might have learned his secrets by now. But Amity had had to behave in a manner befitting her station.

Still, there was something distinctly ungentlemanly about Mario that had nothing to do with anything overt that he said or did. The way that the river breeze rippled his hair, for example. Or the play of muscles in his forearms as he rowed, his long legs extended toward her in the boat. He had asked permission to roll up his sleeves. She should never have given it, she thought.

"I was only looking for Grace," Amity said resentfully. "She was to meet us with her officers and a picnic lunch."

"Never mind; we'll see her soon enough," Mario grumbled.

"I'm sorry if you don't like Grace, but she is my very best friend."

"Oh, I like Grace. Grace is delightful. It's those officers I can't stand," he said.

"They are a bit ribald," Amity agreed, no more glad to hear him praise Grace. "You never say that *I* am delightful," she added coquettishly.

"That's because you're not," he said flatly.

"I'm *not!*" Her purplish eyes flew open in astonishment, then dropped to her simple but elegant lute-string gown, which she had worn especially, its flimsy material seeming as romantic as the day.

"Oh, I didn't say you weren't beautiful," Mario continued offhandly. "Of course you're that, as I'm sure you don't need to be told. I only said you're not delightful. You are . . ." His forehead wrinkled as he sought for a word. "Oh, well, when I think of it, I'll tell you."

"I've a good mind to make you put me ashore at once, Mario da Riva!" she cried angrily.

"You could swim for it," he suggested.

Amity eyed the water, with half a mind to show him by jumping in. She'd pretend not to know how to swim, and he'd have to save her. That would break his reserve. The idea brought memories of the last time she'd been in a river with a man, and she had a notion it would end the same way. The clumps and bushes along the banks were inviting, and she did not want to wind up shamed by her own dark wantonness. Would he think her delightful then?

She sighed, abandoning the plan, and looked up to see him watching her with a gently puzzled smile. At such moments she was always startled to see sadness in his brilliant eyes.

"A penny for your thoughts, Amity," he said.

"Oh, I wish you thought me delightful," she said teasingly.

"Well, I do, then, after all. Don't let's quarrel. We're young, and the day is beautiful. 'Gather ye rosebuds while ye may,' as the poet says."

"I didn't know you liked poetry, Mario," she said.

"In Venice, everybody reads poetry. I suppose it's the boat that made me think of it. In the summer when the moon is full, parties row their gondolas into the lagoon and read poetry by the moonlight."

"You love Venice, Mario. Why do you always seem so sad when you speak of it? Is it because you miss it?"

Mario felt his soul float free of him as he looked into her concerned eyes, which seemed a reflection of the cerulean sky. Her eyes were a haven where it was always spring to Mario. She was unlike any woman he had ever met; unlike the women of Venice, who were either silly convent girls or brazen young matrons who vied to steal men's hearts with their lust and their naked bodies. In London, Paris, and St. Petersburg, he had found women basically alike—simpering coquettes who could drive a man insane with their sly hints, their appetite for compliments. For them love was only an elaborate parlor game, with stakes a bit higher than cards or backgammon.

But this American woman! This little Quaker girl! When she played the coquette, it made him laugh, it was so alien to her nature. She dared to be furious with him as no other ever had; she was not afraid of him. Mario was cad enough to ignite her anger more often than was necessary, for the pleasure of seeing her fire. For just this reason, he had told her she was not delightful. Now she had asked him a question, and her intent expression told him she was not just being conversational or trying to make herself interesting to him. She truly wanted to know, and it rather unnerved him. In his entire life he had had serious conversations with only one other woman—a woman wordly and experienced and all that this girl was not—the Empress Catherine.

But this was somehow better than those conversations. He spoke of things he would never have to the empress—such as Venice in the moonlight. If only he could tell her all! If only he could tell her about the mission he'd come on and the decision he had to make that would so influence the future of this young country of hers! As quickly as he had the thought, he dismissed it. Why should he wish to discuss such a matter with her? It was not the sort of thing one discussed with a woman. But he could tell her about Venice.

"I do miss it, Amity," he said with another tug of the oars, "but not so much the Venice I could return to as one I never saw. It's the Venice that used to be that causes me grief. Venice these days is an endless debauchery where men and women go in carnival masks day and night six months a year to escape the consequences of their misdeeds. The Venice my father once knew was built on indomitable human spirit. It rose almost from the very sea, into which men had been driven to escape tyranny."

"Thee sound almost like a Continental sometimes," Amity said, lapsing into Quaker speech as she occasionally did when deep in thought.

He frowned. She had a way of confusing him. Against his better judgment, he tried to explain. "There is no similarity at all, Amity. Don't you see? Rome was invaded, but the colonies have not been. They are rebelling against rightful authority."

"Oh, now I see!" she cried. "It's all right to be a tyrant if one has the authority!"

Exasperated, Mario gave up. Water gurgled about the boat as he rowed harder than ever to ease his frustration and sent them skimming along the river.

She sounded like a rebel herself sometimes, though she said she was a Tory. She presented herself as a little virgin, too, though she had about her an air that said she was more. Mario wondered if he were going to find out. When he had had her over his knee, he had been positive that she was wild with desire. When he had promised to behave as a gentleman, he had thought that she would give herself away, and he would make love to her. It was as though she fought some terrible battle within herself, but she would never stamp out her smoldering sensuality. She would tip her hand yet, and he would have her, he thought with an inward grin.

He wondered if she would disturb him as much when he had conquered her. To his own surprise, he almost scrupled at the thought of taking her, though he knew he would not be able to resist. When he had first come to Philadelphia, he would have ravished her with no thought at all, but now he was afraid that having had her, he would want her forever. And his destiny was set. It was an important destiny, one that had carried him to Russia, now to America, and it would finally take him to Venice again, to the fate already in store for him there. The future had no room in it for this Quaker girl. Perhaps that was what made him sad.

"Mario, there they are!" Amity cried. "Grace! Grace!" She waved a lawn handkerchief daintily trimmed with drawn-work, and an answering wave came from the shore. The sun-light fell on her fresh young face as he turned to the bank, and the word that he might have used to describe her came into his mind at last.

Enchanting. She was enchanting.

They made their lunch of cream biscuits, cold fried chicken, and fig cakes, washed down with lemonade for the ladies and Cyder Royall for the men. Amity and Grace ate with relish, almost oblivious of their companions. If anything were likely to give them away as having been with the Continental Army, it would have been their shameless appetites, which had never become fashionably small after their winter on the Delaware. The British officers took off their coats and loosened their cravats, becoming jovial and now and then twisting one of Grace's curls familiarly or brushing a crumb from her lap.

Mario, obviously bored, was more interested in the squawk-ing of a group of mallards that had come up on the grass to beg for bread than in the officers' conversation. The pair of them had just made their theatrical debut at the Southwark in a revival of *The Blockade of Boston*, an anti-American satire written by General Burgoyne.

"What a way to fight a war, eh, James?" one said. "I got a fine round of applause last night."

"You were as good as David Garrick," said his friend. "You can take up acting for a career when you get home. You'll do *Richard III* at Drury Lane. Won't he, Grace? Wasn't he good?"

"Oh, marvelous," said Grace between bites of fig cake.

"You should have come, Amity," said James.

"No. Quakers don't go to the theater."

"Oh, hogwash. You're a Quaker when it suits you, Amity. You've been to the theater with Mario."

Amity shrugged and pretended indifference, tossing scraps to the ducks. It was quite true that she had gone to the the-ater with Mario and found it exciting. It was also true that she was between worlds, a Quaker when she wished to be. At other times she experimented with fine clothes and worldly activity.

It would hardly do for Amity to admit that the real reason

she had not gone to the theater was that she could not bear to see the Continentals made buffoons.

"Never mind, Amity, you'll make up for it tonight with the fun you'll have at the Shippens' party. Are you going, Mario?" Grace, more facile of tongue than Amity, hurried to fill the gap with a change of subject.

"I'll make a late appearance, since I've been invited," grumbled Mario. "It's one of those number parties. The most nonsensical sort of thing I've encountered yet in the colonies."

"But the suspense is supposed to be fun, Mario," said Grace. "You get a number from the master of ceremonies when you arrive, and you must find the person of the opposite sex with the same number."

"And then spend the entire evening together, whether you like each other or not. What a silly American notion!"

"Not if you draw the beautiful daughter, Peggy," said James.

"You'd never draw Peggy, you idiot," said his friend William. "It's not all luck, you know. The majors and colonels take their pick. I drew a lady with a wart on her nose once."

"I wager it's all she had on when you were finished, Will," hooted James.

"Hush, you blackguard! There are ladies here!"

Amity and Grace were laughing. Sometimes it was hard to think of this good-natured pair as the enemy.

"Come along, Am," said Grace, "we ought to leave these gentlemen to their man talk." She led her friend away to stroll along the river. Amity glanced back over her shoulder guiltily as she left Mario with the two officers who bored him. He was watching her, not seeming to be drawn into the conversation, which she was sure centered on conquests and intended conquests of women. Amity did not doubt that Mario had made more conquests than both James and Will put together, but she was equally certain that he was not given to bragging. He was far too proud for that.

"Quit fretting," said Grace, following her glance. "Your little chick can look out for himself. Have you found out anything?"

"No. Nothing."

"But you must, Am! He's involved in something that could ruin our chances for victory."

"Oh, don't browbeat me so, Grace. I'm doing the best I

can. Aunt Zenobia and I have even gone through all his personal belongings while he was out."

"Everything?"

"Everything except one little walnut trunk. He keeps that locked. There's no way we could break the lock without his knowing it. That is where he must keep the journal he writes in every night in the parlor. He says he's recording his impressions of America, but we are certain it would give at least a clue."

"Then you must get it, Amity!"

"You're right, but I don't know how."

"The British are treating him as though he were King George's own emissary," said Grace.

"Yes, or the king himself. Did I tell you that one of General Howe's staff came to call—to see that we had all we needed for his comfort? You should see the food that is constantly being sent—and in a time of such shortage! Smoked hams, candied fruits, and even real black tea. And we were asked to do our best to make his stay pleasant in the name of the crown. We eat well these days, and the irony of it is that he rarely dines with us at all. He is always receiving invitations to dine with the most notable Tories, but he hardly gives them the time of day, either. Mostly he frequents coffee houses and taverns."

"What have you done with the British rations, Amity?"

"Oh, I've given most to the Free Quakers, who have delivered them to the American prisoners who are incarcerated on the second floor of Independence Hall or in the prison ships in the river."

"Well, at least some good has come of it, then. But we must do better. What about the great entertainment they are planning to honor General Howe when he relinquishes command? Will he ask to escort you? That would give you a whole weekend downriver at the Wharton mansion. Think of it, Amity. If *he* became a little forward and *you* became a little forward, we might solve this problem."

"Most Quaker girls aren't going," cried Amity in a panic at the thought of an entire weekend in his compelling company.

"Oh, there you go again with your Quaker routine. You know very well that all those poor Quaker girls are dying to go. And so are you, if you'd admit it. At the Meschianza, as they so grandly call it, there'll be dining and dancing and even a jousting tournament. It'll be the finest entertainment the colonies have ever seen. Not want to go! Don't tell me you don't want Mario to carry your colors, Amity!"

"Oh, do stop it, Grace," said Amity, irritated that the idea of Mario in a suit of armor appealed to her.

"Are you still brooding over Silas? Is that it?" Grace persisted. "Amity, you might as well have your fun."

Amity paused to smell the bloom of a wild yellow rose. "Is that what you do, Grace?

"Of course I do. The war will be over someday, and you must think of that. You've got to be practical. I can't marry if my husband's still alive, and I won't go back to him. So that leaves you to marry and give Gracie a father. That's how it must be, though I wish I could keep her myself. She's all I have in the world."

Amity was astounded. It hadn't occurred to her that she should be husband hunting on Gracie's account. "Dear me, Grace, I don't want to take Gracie away from you for good, though I love her, too. Couldn't we just raise her together, ourselves?"

"What? A pair of women? She needs a man to protect her, Amity! It won't do for Gracie! She's headstrong already. Oh, I'd have a man already if it were up to me. But it's not, and you'll probably never marry, you're such a cold fish! Why, you're hardly willing to smile at a man for the sake of liberty!"

"Oh! I have done my share of such things. Don't talk to me so," said Amity with memories of Trenton crowding upon her.

"I'll speak to you as I like. I haven't forgotten that you made yourself scarce while Isabel was giving birth." Grace stalked off angrily, and returning to the picnic, gathered up her officers and went off in a huff.

Amity was so downcast on the way home that Mario felt quite depressed himself in spite of the softly waning day. Pink and white clouds drifted over the sky, casting their reflections into the darkening water where she trailed her slender fingers and a white swan floated by, but Amity was oblivious of everything, even of him. Mario was unused to having a woman oblivious of him, especially when he could not be oblivious of her.

"Did you quarrel with Grace?" he asked.

"Yes," she sighed.

"What about?"

Amity shook her head, then with sudden animation sat up

straight and put her hand on his wrist. "Mario, I'll tell you all my secrets if you'll tell me yours!"

"Why, Amity, I have no secrets!" She had confused him again with her sudden flirtatious turn, but she gave him no further hints until they were home, and she gathered little Grace up and began to weep.

"Papa," said Gracie to Mario, of whom she had become fond.

"Oh, no, you little ninny. He's not your papa. God knows where we'll ever find your papa!" she said as she hurried to tuck the child into bed.

Left alone, Mario wondered about Gracie's father, not for the first time. Amity had given him to understand that she was the daughter of a friend who had left her orphaned, but now this had tumbled out about a father. *He* did not seem to be dead, certainly. Could it be possible that Amity was Gracie's mother? She loved the child enough. And that would explain her aura of womanly experience. It would explain as well why she fought so to ignore him.

Was Amity everything she said she was? An innocent maiden? A Tory? *Tell me your secrets and I'll tell you mine,* she had said. Just what secrets did she have? In a little while he went upstairs and heard her splashing in a big wooden washtub as he passed her door. Mario smiled. Maybe if he opened the door he could partake of some of her secrets right now, but Mario preferred a more dangerous plan. Going to his room, he took out paper and began to write a letter.

9

He had left the house when Amity emerged in a wrapper and peeked into his empty room. The white envelope lay tantalizingly on the desk, seeming to beckon her with its importance. To whom could Mario be writing?

Maybe it was a letter to his family in Venice. He had told her something about them all. His father, of whom Mario seemed proud, sat on the Council of Ten, which chose the Inquistors before whom all Venice trembled. Mario wasted no affection on his stepmother, so most likely the letter was not to her. It had been an arranged marriage, as most marriages were among families in the Golden Book. But Mario thought his father's first marriage had been a love match, and maybe this was the reason that the senator always preferred Mario over the younger brother, Henri.

Perhaps the letter was to Caleb Beale, merely thanking him for his introduction to the household. But maybe . . . maybe it was the clue they had been looking for. Maybe he'd become careless at last!

Going to the desk, she picked it up. He had written the address boldly, as if to cause it to leap out at her and take her breath away.

> Catherine, Empress of all the Russias
> The Winter Palace
> St. Petersburg, Russia

Why should Mario be writing the empress? Perhaps it was a love letter. Catherine had an appetite for young men, they said, though she was middle-aged herself. She favored only the handsomest and most intelligent, gossip ran, and Amity had wondered about Catherine's interest in Mario ever since that first day when he had mentioned having shared hot chocolate in her apartments.

Amity felt a rush of an emotion with which she was quite unfamiliar—jealousy. Taking the letter, she slipped down the back stairs into the kitchen, where a kettle was steaming. Taking a deep breath, she held the envelope over the spout. She bit her lip in concentration as the steam softened the seal and she tried to lift it. It gave without breaking, and Amity sighed with relief. Unfolding the paper, she read what Mario had written.

Your Most Imperial Majesty:

I have almost completed the mission on which you sent me, and which I undertook to cement the bonds between your country and mine, which must help to defeat our common enemy, the Turks. I am looking forward to seeing you again, and to discussing with you personally the advisability of honoring King George's request for Russian mercenaries to send against the colonies.

Your servant, as always,
Mario da Riva

Amity collapsed into a comb-back Windsor chair, the letter fluttering in her hand. "Amity, what is it?" said Zenobia, coming in.

"Oh, Aunt, I've found out what's he up to! Russia is planning to send troops against the Continentals!"

"Russian troops!"

"And to think they are still celebrating at Valley Forge because the French have agreed to help us! What will we do, Aunt? We must send word to the Continentals at once, I suppose. They can capture him and throw him into prison! Oh, he's a devil, as I always knew. He is looking forward to seeing her again, he says."

"My dear Amity, I believe you are as anxious to punish him for his admiration of Catherine as for his treachery against the colonies," said Zenobia, taking out a brise fan and waving it in front of her face thoughtfully. "Pour me a glass of that rum the British sent us."

"Rum?"

"There is a time for all things, and this is a time for spirits. It will clear my head."

Amity did as she was told, and poured the liquor into a waisted dram glass enameled with flowers.

"Now, then, let's think," said Zenobia, downing the drink at a gulp, grimacing at the fiery taste. Her face took on a workmanlike expression. Amity waited, sure her aunt would have the answer.

"It would never do for the Continentals to imprison him, Am. The Russian government would protest, and Catherine would probably be so angry she'd send the troops."

"What, then?" breathed Amity.

"He must be dealt with another way. It's not for us to say, but probably he'll meet with an accident. Something for which the British can be blamed. A brawl in one of those taverns he frequents, for instance."

"You are talking of murder, Aunt, and you were once a Quaker," whispered Amity in horror.

"It's war, Amity. You agree that it's necessary to prevent him from returning to Russia, don't you?"

"Yes. If . . ."

"If what, Amity?"

"If he is really going to advise that the troops be sent."

"But how can we know that?"

"I'll find out. I must. It's his life we're talking about."

Zenobia sighed. "Well, then, find out. Thee may have what time is left. But if thee cannot . . ."

"I know. I know," said Amity.

Her blue sack gown was very low in the back and fell tantalizingly away from her shoulders. She hadn't worn it before, but she must use every weapon she had now, if she were to save him. He would be there tonight, at the Shippens' party.

She turned this way and that before the mirror, not quite satisfied with her appearance. When she had bought the material, the blue had seemed to match her eyes, but now they seemed to have turned darker and more serious, not agreeing with the mood of the outfit in the least.

Triple flounces on the sleeves fell over her slender wrists and floated gracefully behind. The brocaded overskirt was worn bunched up behind by means of loops and buttons, displaying a petticoat of a paler shade worked in sprigs of embroidery. Her white Persian gloves were tied with blue strings, and her golden hair was worn simply in a chignon of curls, instead of built up with hair pads and false tresses. A little dress cap sat on her head, with wings half-extended, like a butterfly.

Amity felt nothing at all like a butterfly as she was driven through the treacherous city carriage traffic to the Shippens' grand home on Fourth Street. She was not at all in the frame of mind to bat her fan and smile at fine Tory gentlemen.

It was hard to believe that the Shippens were Quakers. Edward Shippen was a prominent lawyer and bound to nonviolent principles like Amity's own father. But how unlike her father was Mr. Shippen's interpretation! When the Continentals had been in the city, he had entertained them. When George Washington had attended the First Continental Congress in Philadelphia, he, too, had been a guest at the Shippens', always a gathering spot for the most interesting and fashionable of Philadelphia society.

Now that the Americans had left, the Shippens were equally friendly to the British. Somehow, where many Quakers suffered for having both sides consider them the enemy, the Shippens catered to both armies, and both praised them as friends.

In the marble-floored foyer, she gave her satin pelisse to an attendent in a black velvet coat and waistcoat of silver tabby. Couples were already dancing a polonaise to music supplied by a harpsichord and an assortment of violins. Across the way other guests were clustered around a huge cherrywood dropleaf table which squatted on curving cabriole legs as though bowed down with the weight of edibles. Here Amity wandered, hoping to be inconspicuous, and quickly filled a Chelsea Gold Anchor Ware saucer with spiced nuts, pâtéed pigeon, and almond cheesecake.

"Ah, will you take a number, please, Miss Andrews?" The officer bowed, smiling, and offered a silver basket.

"Thank you, sir," she said, lifting out a dainty scroll of vellum tied with golden cord. Unwrapping it, she read the number forty-one, and tucked the paper into her little bag, along with her cambric handkerchief and her ivory fan.

Immediately several eager gentlemen approached her, each with a bow, proffering their own slips of vellum. "Have you my number tonight? I do hope so, Miss Andrews!"

She looked at each number and turned them all away with murmurs of polite disappointment. It did give her some satisfaction to note that they were genuinely crestfallen.

Across the room Zenobia was dancing, poised with the assurance of twenty years' experience in city society, and farther down the table Grace was sampling marzipan and crystallized ginger, laughing at whatever her partner was saying. Grace had no business at a society party, being herself only a farmgirl without connections among the elite of the city; but her two employers usually finagled her an invitation by designating her their "cousin." Gossip about Grace was always rampant, but Grace shrugged it all aside, clinging to her own purposes with the same dedication and practicality she had shown when she used to stand guard for General Washington.

Amity thought sadly of the quarrel they had had. She could hardly blame Grace for thinking ill of her. She had never been able to bring herself to explain everything that had happened to her the night of Gracie's birth, and the matter had lain unspoken and unfinished between them, marring the friendship that had been so strongly mortared by all they had shared in the camp of the Continental Army. Grace was right about the child, she knew. Gracie needed a father.

"Why so melancholy?" said a feminine voice at her elbow. "Hasn't your gentleman come forward? You know, sometimes they don't come at all, the naughty things, if they get wind that the wrong lady has drawn the same number."

Amity turned coolly and smiled at Peggy Shippen, youngest daughter of her host. Peggy wore a gown of Italian silk, looped up in puffs all around. Her shoes had dainty, twiglike Italian heels covered in cream-colored kid, and diamond rosettes where Amity's shoes had small gold buckles. Peggy's powdered hair was lifted high, topped with a turban of red velvet in which she had pinned ostrich feathers.

Peggy smirked with mild condescension as she appraised Amity's attire and compared it to her own, more exotic outfit. The three Shippen sisters had long since worn down their father's resistence to worldy vanities. "I've a mind to give you *my* number, Amity. Dear me, that would be a treat for you. I've arranged with Papa that Major André should be my partner. It wouldn't do for me to just draw, you know. But he's late. It would teach him a lesson."

"Your gown is lovely, Peggy," said Amity easily, not bothered by the catty remarks.

"Oh, it's a wonder I've anything to wear at all, with the ships from England all wrecking on those stupid *chevaux de frises*," said Peggy, scanning the doorways for a glimpse of the major.

The two girls were the same age and had been thrown together at a myriad of events during the winter, as Peggy had been courted by almost every luminary bachelor of the occupation force. Her gaiety and skillful flirtation had won many a British heart, but sometimes Peggy felt Amity Andrews breathing down the neck of her own popularity. Amity, who was only a country Quaker! Amity, who didn't even try half the time! What was it that men sensed in her when they looked into those oddly colored blue-purple eyes? Just now Peggy's name was being linked with John André's, General Howe's most trusted aide. The story ran he had given her a lock of his hair.

"Are you going to the Meschianza, Amity?" Peggy ran on.

"I haven't decided," said Amity. More than one gentleman had asked, but Amity had declined. It was likely to be a very improper party.

"Well, perhaps you'll get an invitation yet, poor dear," said Peggy, torn between relief that Amity would give her no competition and regret that Amity would not be present to witness her triumph. "Have you heard? My sisters and I and eleven other girls are going to dress in Turkish costumes for the jousting. It's going to be the most exciting thing that ever happened in Philadelphia."

"More exciting than the Declaration of Independence, no doubt," said Amity.

Peggy blinked confusedly, then turned to tittering smiles as a hand touched her shoulder.

"Have you number twenty-two?"

"Major André! Oh, is that your number, too? We're partners, then. How perfectly delightful!" And she sailed away on his arm.

Amity gazed after her in amusement. Then in the tall pedimented doorway she caught sight of Mario. It seemed to Amity that everyone took notice of him. Even Peggy, on the arm of her major, looked admiringly at the striking figure he cut in his gold-threaded frock coat set with Bristol-stone buttons, and his soft cashmere waistcoat and tan swanskin britches. He could not prevent a grimace as he was offered the basket and required to take a number. Unwrapping it, he stuffed it into his pocket and strode purposefully to the table where Amity was standing.

Having read his letter to the Empress Catherine, she was awash in emotion. Perhaps he had worn these clothes at the court at St. Peterburg, perhaps even danced with the empress in those shoes of red morocco. And now here he was, a threat to liberty as much as the outlaw had been at Trenton.

The Continentals would have to deal with him as best they saw fit, and she knew what that would be. How could she possibly be party to it? If only she could prove that he meant the colonies no harm! But she thought most likely he did. Hadn't he called the Revolution a "silly furor"? Why did she care so much? Why was she so sick inside at the idea of his death? Was it only her Quaker scruples?

He would die if he must, she told herself. Then *he* at least would be punished as the outlaw should have been! And he would suffer as the outlaw should have, for igniting in her what was further beyond the pale of decency than looting and thieving!

"Good evening, Amity," said Mario. He looked at her curiously, and she knew her agitation must show on her face. Her saucer clattered as she tried to regain her composure, not an easy feat when he gazed at her so. He must not guess that she had read the letter.

"Do not keep the young ladies in suspense, Mario," she

said. "See over there? They are all on the edge of their chairs hoping that they have the same number as you."

He grinned, not unaware of the row of tapestry-covered ladderback chairs where four young women fidgeted, one studying the ceiling to appear indifferent, the others batting fans and engaging in nervous conversation.

"I suppose I mustn't be cruel. I'll go and ask which one has number forty-one."

"Forty-one! Why, that is my number!"

She was gratified that relief and pleasure showed on his face as he led her out to dance. "What a pity, sir," she taunted. "Why, this very afternoon you said you did not find me delightful. I am sorry that your evening has to be spoiled as well."

"It won't be if you don't spend it all fishing for compliments, Amity," he said, bowing in the minuet.

"That would be useless," she replied when she was close enough again. "I'm sure you don't know *how* to pay a lady a compliment."

"Maybe not. Maybe you'd rather spend the evening with one of those Tory swains that are always panting at your feet."

"You are right about these parties, Mario—they are quite silly," she said, breaking away and heading out the paneled doors to the garden. She took a deep breath, feeling terrified in the sweet darkness; the glow of the new moon cast in soft globes, reflecting from the big white blooms of hydrangea trees. He would follow her. He would have to. He would look ridiculous left without a partner.

Before he spoke, she felt his presence, as though it were an essence borne like the rose scent on the mild spring breeze. His hand at the small of her back sent chills to her toes as he pulled her toward him. For an instant she saw the ardor in his moon-shaded eyes, saw his lips purposeful near hers. And then she was lost in delirium, clinging to him shamelessly as he kissed her and kissed her. Passion flooded her, rising and rushing, gathering great powerful currents like a river running seaward. Oh, the outlaw had never kissed her thus! That was the bud; this, the blossom!

He released her, his breathing short and trembling like her own. "Oh, Amity, let's not play games anymore, you and I! I'll be going back to Russia soon."

"Soon? How soon?" She swayed, too overcome to deal him a proper blow with her ivory fan.

"A boat is to sail the day after the Meschianza, and the empress expects me. Come with me to the Meschianza, Amity. We'll have that time together."

The Meschianza! She knew how dangerous it would be for her to be alone with him there. It was only under her aunt's roof that he had promised to be a gentleman. And feeling as she did, she could not be sure she would be any more a lady than he a gentleman. He was counting on that, she knew. But she must go, she knew suddenly. Aunt Zenobia could break into his trunk, read the journal, and have the lock fixed. It was her only chance to save him from death at the hands of the Continentals.

It was nearly morning when they reached home and each went to separate rooms. Where they parted company at the head of the stairs, he lightly kissed her golden hair.

"Until the Meschianza, love," he said, and his voice was ardent with meaning.

10

Days had passed since the elegant invitation had arrived, showing a shield emblazoned with a sunset seascape and bearing the message "*Luceo Discendens Aucto Splendore Resurgam.*" It meant that General Howe's sun had set on one day but would rise again in splendor.

The Meschianza was the soldiers' way of expressing their appreciation to General Howe for a war waged over banquet tables, but Amity attached quite another meaning to the seascape. Mario was the sun, and it was he who would sink beyond the ocean. He would sail away from her forever—that was the very best she could hope for.

She tried not to think about the other, more likely possibility as their luggage was loaded into the carriage for the drive to the docks, where boats waited to take them downriver to the Wharton mansion.

Aunt Zenobia was still shaking her head over the Turkish outfit that the British had provided for Amity. "I can't believe you're going to wear that, Amity. It's a good thing your father can't see it. Why, even Edward Shippen blanched and would not let his daughters go."

"Yes. Poor Peggy's inconsolable. And her Major André's in charge of the entire event. Which do you suppose she'll marry, Whig or Troy? Her family's been so cozy with both."

"That will be interesting to see. But take care. You are a proper Quaker girl, and no matter what you put on your body, what counts is what's in your heart."

That idea was exactly what frightened Amity. No way existed that she could deny the passion in her heart. Even in Quaker gray, she would love Mario! She climbed into the carriage in her floating gown of French lawn and immediately caught sight of his small walnut trunk beneath his feet.

He was taking it! And the idea had been for the trunk to remain in Philadelphia!

"Oh, goodness, you won't need that!" she said. "It's your writing supplies, and you won't have time for that."

He grinned, apparently glad that she would keep him so occupied. "I'm sure I'll have a lot to write about," he said, leaning out the window to nod to the driver.

Amity looked back at Zenobia, standing in the door, and the expression on her aunt's face told her what she knew already. It was up to her now! *She* must read the journal herself! But nothing in her aunt's glance told her how she would get it.

At Knight's Wharf they boarded a galley, sitting with officers and guests, surrounded by all sorts of craft bedecked with ribbons and flags. They were on the first party vessel, right behind a flatboat which carried one of three bands. The shore was lined with spectators as the oarsmen began to row to the beat of the music. They were with General Howe's party, but Amity was no longer surprised by the special treatment given Mario. No doubt the British had never been in the dark as to Mario's mission for the empress.

Mario did not seem impressed. He sat dark and moody, staring into the sunlit water. What was it that made Mario so somber at just the times one expected gaiety? He was altogether too serious. Maybe moodiness was a Venetian characteristic, born of constantly fighting for a city and a republic which was against nature and which nature tried constantly to reclaim.

Soon she knew she was right at least that he was thinking about Venice, for he turned to her and said, "This reminds me of a ceremony we have in Venice once a year when the doge sails into the lagoon in his gilded ship of state, followed by the state gondolas with all the nobles. He throws the ring of the Republic into the water to symbolize our marriage to the sea. I always looked forward to that day when I was a child."

But he said this with a smile, and she was not sure that such a pretty childish memory could have anything to do with his darker side. "I wish I could see it, Mario," she sighed, reminded of what she couldn't possibly forget, that since she had discovered his secret, he was unlikely ever to see his home again.

"At least we have the Meschianza," he said, reminding himself that his stay in the colonies was almost ended.

That was all he wanted, no doubt, she thought. One weekend during which he could behave as he wished. He hoped to bed her, she was sure. And she must show him he could not, as she should have shown the outlaw. She must remember that she had come with him in hopes of saving his worthless life, not to enjoy more of his kisses!

They disembarked through lines of grenadiers and cavalry, and Amity went into the house with the other girls to change into her costume for the tournament. Mario was to be one of the Knights of the Blended Rose, and like other ladies accompanied by gentlemen of that team, she donned a robe of white silk, opened low and cinched with a six-inch-wide pink sash sprinkled with spangles. The other team was called the Knights of the Burning Mountain, and ladies whose champions were of that team dressed in similiar costumes of black and orange.

Team colors decorated the grandstands, too, the canopies flapping in the breeze as the ladies were led to their seats. Around the square of the tournament ground stood a scarlet fence of soldiers at attention. Amity was ablaze with excitement as trumpets blew, and the knights galloped in on gray chargers, caparisoned in red and white. Mario's silver mail glittered in the sun as he saluted her and easily caught the scarf she threw him as her favor.

She forgot everything but the game as the trumpets sounded again, and the Knights of the Blended Rose raced to do battle with the Knights of the Burning Mountain. She forgot the Russian troops and the journal she must read. Most of all she forgot that she did not long for his kisses.

In full gallop the knights encountered, shivering their

spears. She was on her feet with the other ladies, shrieking for his victory. One of the black Knights of the Burning Mountain toppled before Mario's lance, and she shuddered with delight at the heroic figure Mario made on his prancing horse. The knights charged again. Suddenly Mario was almost unseated by a dark, streaking horseman. He whirled, regained himself, and mounted combat as excited cheers rose from the crowd. Somehow the black knight seemed familiar, Amity thought. But surely it was impossible to recognize any man with his visor lowered.

The knights fired pistols, and nobody seemed to care about the anachronism of firearms. Noise was just what everyone wanted. Mario and the black knight engaged each other again and again. They had become the show now, each more skillful than any of the others on the field, but equally matched together. The ladies sighed with romantic yearnings for each of the contenders until at last Mario's classic swordsmanship unseated the black knight, drawing cries of admiration from the crowd and sighs of envy for Amity, whose favor Mario carried. Then the marshal of the field rushed in, declaring that the damsels had received sufficient proofs of love and witnessed enough facts of valor. The tournament was over.

Next came dancing in the Wharton mansion, which Major André had had redone for the occasion. The Whartons themselves were not present, and it sobered Amity to remember that they, too, were prominent Quakers like the Shippens. But unlike the Shippens, they had not fared well with the British, and they had been marched to exile in Winchester, Virginia, where they were held in custody while the English partied in their home.

She mentioned the fact to Mario. "You cannot tell me *that* is not tyranny," she said.

"No, I cannot," he agreed. "But things are as they are; and since the moment is here, let's enjoy ourselves. I declare, Amity, no knight ever had a lady as beautiful as you!"

She bowed acknowledgment and thanked him, thinking she would never understand him. When she wished to be light, he was serious, and when she wished to be serious, he was in the mood for fun. When she baited him for the compliments a girl should expect, he denied them, and when she did not, he told her she was beautiful. He was a perplexing man.

Philadelphia seemed a million miles away. It seemed the dream would never end. He was her knight, and she was his lady, and the moment was emblazoned on the stars.

Inside, the walls of the mansion were painted to resemble pink Siena marble. The great hall was hung with sky-blue draperies, and decorated with pink ribbons and artificial flowers. The floor was a matching blue with designs of golden circles.

She danced with Mario, her spirit soaring until she felt the blue floor become the blue sky into which she floated, far from the realm of wars and of nations, into a bliss that depended only on the music, on the touch of his hand, and on his eyes holding hers with a wonderful magic that made love seem as endless as though they had danced through the centuries together from the days of true knighthood. There came a pause in the dancing, and General Cornwallis begged her permission to borrow her partner for a moment. He went, looking back at her over his shoulder as he joined a conference of officers.

Amity hugged the spangled mood about her as she went for a cup of punch. It was a night to be remembered forever. She could not think of the realities just beyond the waver of violins and the glow of candlelabra. She could not think of ever not having wanted to come.

"Good evening, Miss Amity," said a voice in a tone insultingly intimate. Turning, she saw the black knight with whom Mario had jousted. He was the one, she knew, because of his height. Up close he seemed immense, an impression exaggerated by the plumed black helmet he still wore, visor up.

Still she did not know him. Still he was unsettlingly familiar. "Do I know you, sir?" she said coldly.

"Why, Miss Amity!" His tone was shocked now. "To think you've forgotten, You know me very well."

Amity studied him more closely, and a grin spread over his features as he saw the slow horror of her recognition. The beard was gone, and so were the buckskins. He no longer had the look of a forest animal, but the lustful gaze of his eyes and the sensual aura of his body could not be shaven away like his beard or changed like clothing. The outlaw!

"What are you doing here, Moses Doan?" she breathed.

"I'm the viper in paradise, Miss Amity. It's merely a whim of mine to mingle with society. I've danced with Peggy Chew, the daughter of the chief justice, and though she's Queen of the Tilt, she doesn't guess at what it would thrill her to know, that the notorious Moses Doan has held her in his arms."

"Maybe I'll tell her," said Amity. She was shivering, though it was warm, and she was afraid the outlaw would see. How she hated him! He had degraded her, overpowering her with temptation that she had never known existed; and now his lewd expression told her he would like to do it again.

"Tell her if you like." The outlaw shrugged. "I enjoy being incognito, but I do have an invitation. Oh, the British weren't too happy about giving it to me, but they couldn't refuse, since I've been so valuable. I think they were afraid I might steal the silverware or spoil some other treasure." He leered. "Tell me which room is yours, and I'll forgo the silverware."

"Never.!"

"Oh,! come, Amity. Two spies should not make strange bedfellows!"

"I am not—" she cried in confusion.

"Oh, don't bother denying it. You're a spy as much as I am, but *you* are in enemy territory, and I am not. I did hear a rumor about a golden-haired wench who so occupied Colonel Rall in Trenton that he did not pay attention to his informer. The British have hushed it up, but perhaps it was *you*. Maybe you used the lessons I taught you against me in the colonel's bed. If so, then I only hope the colonel enjoyed himself before he died for his pleasure."

"I did not . . ." Amity protested honestly, forgetting how near it had come to being the truth.

"Never mind," said the outlaw. "We'll bed together tonight, and you'll squirm with delight. You'll enjoy me as much between silk sheets as you did in the barn, you'll find. Be sensible, Amity, and we'll both profit. I'd hate to have to tell General Howe what a wild little patriot you are!"

Amity glanced helplessly across the room at Mario, who stood with his back to her, and the outlaw laughed. "So that's it. The Venetian. You'd sooner be in his bed tonight. Is he as skillful in love as I am? He's a fine swordsman, that's sure. He bested me on the tournament field. But tonight, I'll be the winner! Tut, the British wouldn't like it at all if they found that a spy was cavorting with their pampered Venetian!"

"You are merely a poor sport, Mr. Doan," she managed to say.

"Poor sport! I don't like being beaten, I admit. We'll see how good a sport the high-and-mighty Don da Riva is when I've beaten him—with you!"

He made her a bow and went on his knightly way, begging a dance of a girl in a chip hat with lavender feathers sticking up from one side, and shooting Amity a look of triumph as the maiden innocently flushed and laid her trembling hand on his rascally arm.

"Amity? Are you ill?" Mario was beside her, studying her with concern. "I got away as soon as I could. The deuced British must always mix business with pleasure."

"I'm all right, Mario. I'm afraid I'm worn out with dancing anyway." She was so shaken she felt she might faint.

"Then we'll go and watch the fireworks. They are about to start."

In the velvety darkness, crowds of people were milling on the lawn, trying to find the best places to watch the ground displays. They sat together on the fragrant grass, he with his arm about her, and she struggled to remember that he was nothing to her. It was difficult when she was never quite sure whether the skyrockets and shell bursts that lighted the spring sky had been set by the British or had come from her own heart. Each display seemed more beautiful than the last. The smell of gunpowder permeated the air, and afterglows of silver, gold, and red hung in the night. Laughter and sighs of appreciation carried on the breeze, as Mario pulled her close and kissed her. In the darkness Mario's amber eyes gleamed with fervor, the remainder of his face cast in inscrutable shadow. Her head swam, and the voices became distant.

"No!" she said, suddenly begrudging him the kiss he would carry away with him as a souvenir in his memory.

He drew back in surprise. "But the other night at the Shippens' you didn't mind."

"You took advantage of me there. Don't expect to do so again, sir!"

"Do not expect . . . Oh ho, so it's you who has taken advantage of me, Amity. You kissed me just to make me think you cared. You only wanted an invitation to the Meschianza like every girl in Philadelphia. I thought you were different! I thought you weren't so devious!"

It was so dark she couldn't see his face, couldn't see whether he was really angry or whether he thought it funny. One thing was sure. He mustn't kiss her now! She must remain clearheaded and try to think what to do. Had the outlaw been bluffing? Would he carry out his threat to reveal her when she did not bed him? Mario must not kiss her. It made her so aware of her vulnerability. But to whom was she most vulnerable? To the outlaw? To Mario?

She hadn't seen Doan again. Perhaps he had had enough sport with her. Perhaps the girl with the lavender feathered hat was experiencing the same lesson that Amity had learned in the New Jersey barn.

A large ground display of the Union Jack ended the fireworks as the band struck up "God Save the King." Supper was announced, and folding doors were opened from the ballroom to reveal magnificent tables. Two dozen black slaves in Oriental dress served cream-of-barley soup; roast pheasant; new potatoes; artichokes; and a calf's head galantine wearing a forcemeat crown and garnished with sweetmeats, mushrooms, and truffles. The tiered centerpieces of wine gelatin mold and fruit were consumed for dessert, along with rum cream pies and cherry tarts.

Where had Doan vanished? she wondered.

Mario seemed merely amused at her agitated state, which she had been unable to hide. Obviously he attributed her confusion to his kiss, which indeed might have accounted for it, had it not been for the outlaw. The time was coming when she must steal the journal and read it, whatever the price.

If she were lucky, he would never know who had broken the lock and taken it.

She excused herself to go and freshen up, passing the gaming room, where guests were already hovering around the faro tables. Grace was there, a good-luck token for her pair of officers. It was the first time that Amity had seen her, since Grace had ridden up on another barge. She looked lovely in her gown of lilac satin trimmed with beaded wreaths of flowers, but she didn't pause in her gay flirtations as Amity went past. Amity sighed, feeling very much alone. The quarrel wasn't healed, though Zenobia had told Grace the plan about Mario. If Grace had smiled or given her a meaningful glance, it would have steadied Amity's courage. But now her strength nearly failed her as she went up the stairs and turned down an enormous hall where oil lights flickered over exquisite Oriental rugs.

Quietly, heart pounding, she turned the porcelain knob of Mario's door and let herself into his room. Already the place breathed his essence, and almost imagining he would appear in all his wrath, she nearly ran away. But there on the bowfront dresser along with his silver-backed hairbrush sat the little walnut chest in full view. She pulled at the lock, then hit at it with the silver brush. Finally she tugged a long golden hairpin from her chignon and twisted it into the keyhole, yanking frantically. The lock gave so suddenly that she staggered backward.

Inside, the chest was lined with red velvet. The little leather journal lay on top, and with a sigh of triumph she lifted it out. She was about to thrust it into her bodice and retreat when she noticed that a miniature in a round gilt frame lay beneath.

To a spy's purpose, the picture was meaningless, but to Amity's womanly soul it was as important as the journal. Taking it out, she studied the portrait of a girl who seemed quite young, innocent, and beautiful. Soft brown curls hung loosely about her shoulders, as a child might wear her hair; her gentle eyes seemed to shine with love, and her mouth turned in an appealing, wistful smile.

Who could this be? Mario had not mentioned that he had a sister, but neither could she imagine that this little creature was his mistress. The direct gaze the artist had captured seemed unspoiled by knowledge of men.

While she wondered, racked with jealousy, she heard a footfall behind her. She had lost her chance for escape, and even as she whirled, arms seized her. She tottered off balance and found herself sprawled on the damask covers of the big tester bed.

The dark, grinning countenance of the outlaw hovered over her. He had followed her, and he intended to do his will!

Worse, he intended to have it be her will, too, as he had before. She intuited that he wanted her not only to satisfy his filthy lust but also to fortify his pride by making her admit her own wanton urges.

"It's a fine room they've given you, Miss Amity," the outlaw said. "Much better than where we last met, eh?"

"I won't have you, Moses Doan!" she cried. "This time you've not the advantage of my being nearly frozen and without clothes."

"No. You are warm and very prettily clad in that Turkish getup. But you are a woman, and that is all the advantage I need!"

He set himself to prove the matter, kissing her deeply and hotly, crushing her down into the feather bed with his weight atop her. He sat back on his haunches and laughed at her struggling. "There, now. I can tell you like it."

"I hate it," she vowed between clenched teeth.

Undaunted, the outlaw slid his skillful hand beneath her white satin bodice. In spite of herself the sensation rippled down to her toes, and her nipples tightened in pleasure. But

Amity continued to fight. She would never surrender again, never! She sank her teeth into the outlaw's shoulder and bit down with force much too great for a nip of passion.

The outlaw yelped in surprise, unused to a woman's offering so much resistance, not only against his desires, but against her own. He kissed her again, forcing her head back onto the pillows. She made a choking sound as his tongue made daring inroads between her sharp little teeth, rotating lazily. She felt his triumph when she was unable to will them to clamp down again in self-defense. A moan escaped her, and she was horrified at the idea that she was losing.

She struggled feverishly, her little pumps beating against his legs, her fists pounding on his broad muscled back. Perhaps she could save herself by fainting. That would not exactly be winning, but it would not be surrender. She closed her eyes, but having had the realistic upbringing of a Quaker girl, she had not acquired the knack of fainting. Worse, in trying to faint, she had relaxed and given him fresh opportunity. His hands caressed her hips and stomach, and her thighs ached with remembrance.

She must not submit!

Then, from a distance, she heard the door slam back. Mario stood there, his face dark with fury. She was aghast, not knowing whether his rage was directed more at her or the outlaw. Then Doan's weight lifted. A crested William and Mary mirror crashed to the floor as Mario slung the outlaw against the wall.

Leaping free, the outlaw found his sword and drew it, its tip no longer blunted as it had been for the jousting. Mario drew a blade, too, and Amity crawled beneath the bed, feeling it jolt this way and that as one, then another of them was forced against it. She had no way of telling which one was winning.

Then came a shattering of glass and a spine-chilling masculine scream. One of them had fallen through the long double window. To his death! she supposed.

The other one was coming for her, his footsteps drawing closer to the bed. Amity closed her eyes in trepidation as she felt herself seized about the ankles.

"I apologize for interrupting your pleasure, Amity," said Mario as he dragged her out. "But pray take it in your own room next time."

"Oh! It was not my pleasure," she cried.

"It looked so," he said in a calm tone that cost him enormous effort. Why did it make him so angry to find that she was what he had thought she was all along?

"You've killed him!" she accused.

"Nonsense," said Mario. "There's a balcony beneath. He's gone already. He won't come back for a second try at either you or me, I warrant."

"Gone!"

She was obviously stricken by the news that her lover had deserted the fight, Mario thought. Women were all like that, it seemed, delighting in having men die for them; but it surprised him a little, since he knew she had once been a Quaker.

Passion flooded Mario's veins, mixing with his anger in an explosive combination. No need for him to scruple about taking her now. He had seen her with the outlaw and was certain she was no virgin. She was atremble herself with emotion he could not define, but which made her marvelously desirable, her flushed cheeks matching her pink spangled sash. Her hair was tumbled and decorated with a dusting of lint which some careless maid had thought safe to leave beneath the bed.

She looked like someone who expected love, he thought. Atop the bed was where she belonged, not under it, he decided, and suited action to the idea. She began to kick as he kissed her, but her breath caught in her chest, and Mario knew that she did not find his attention distasteful. But he felt something else, too. And with an interest more practical than passionate, he slid his fingers into her bodice and over her breast. Even as she sighed helplessly, she fastened both her hands around his wrist and tried to pull him back.

"Oh, come, Amity, you're not so modest as all that," he said. "I am sure that the Knight of the Burning Mountain enjoyed such privileges. Can't you be as generous to the Knight of the Blended Rose? What are you hiding? More than your charms, it seems." He secured the object he had left, releasing her as he drew it out. "Why, this is my journal. That was foolish of you, my dear, to conceal it in the one place I was sure to look. Whatever do you want with it?"

"I wanted to see if you had written that you loved me," she lied desperately.

He roared with amusement, then as quickly was angry again. "You're a spy, Amity Andrew! Now I know everything about you. You're not a lady and you're not a Tory. You've read my letter to the empress. I knew leaving it where you'd see it would make you play your hand! You weren't interested in an invitation to the Meschianza so much as in getting my journal. Ah, but you *were* interested in my kisses, whatever you say!"

"Yes, you're right that I'm a patriot. But your journal was all I ever wanted!" Boldly she jerked the volume from his hand.

She had only moments, for it would be a miracle if the outlaw hadn't already alerted all the guards. A sudden burst of speed, and she was off the bed and out the door, running for all she was worth.

Mario was close behind, though her smaller size gave her an advantage in negotiating the stairs and the twists of the labyrinthine hallways. Her fingers tightened over the journal as she forced herself to slow passing the gaming tables. Now Grace looked up and took in the situation—Amity, her bosom heaving as she clutched the journal, her pink sash askew, and her Turkish veil only partly concealing her tousled hair. Amity's passage caused only a few raised eyebrows. It was past three in the morning, and most of those who had not succumbed to sleep were more interested in some scandal of their own.

A glance told Amity that she and Grace were a team again, their friendship deeper than their quarrel over Gracie's future. She saw Grace hurry toward Mario, take his arm, and entreat him to dance with her.

"Please, sir, I can't end this evening without having danced with a Knight of the Blended Rose," Amity heard her saying. Mario would not stop to dance, of course, but Grace would not be easy to refuse. Every second he was delayed was precious to Amity.

Beyond the house, the night air was the very breath of freedom. She began to run again, evading the barbered shrubbery, and here and there, the almost indistinguishable forms of couples in the grass. Her feet kept cadence to her bursting heart as she dashed for the hedgerow, a drumbeat for liberty throbbing in her heart as pure as the one the Continentals had followed from McKonkey's Ferry across the Delaware to Trenton. Down the road a horseman waited to receive the information she would bring. She would give him the journal, and then everything would be out of her hands.

Whatever happened, after tonight her soul would be free of Mario de Riva! If she had not hidden the journal in her bodice, she would have known his love. When he had touched her, she had banished the outlaw from her passions as utterly as he had ejected him from the room in the fight. She had soared at Mario's caress, her flight like an eagle's, when the outlaw had given her only sparrow's wings. Two powerful, compelling men, each capable of devastating her, but one so much more completely than the other. Two men, both the enemy. Why couldn't she hate Mario da Riva as she hated the outlaw?

The road loomed like a dusty brown velvet ribbon, and then scarlet uniforms glinted in front of her. She knew before the command came to halt that the outlaw had done his vengeful work. She would pay the price of having rejected him and be hanged for a spy. In the last instant she flung Mario's journal into the tangle of berry bushes before the soldiers seized her.

Amity had one more blow to bear. When she was flung into a coach, it already had another female occupant—Grace. The British had put things together easily enough when the outlaw had told them about Amity. The two women clung to each other on the ride back to Philadelphia, wondering what the enemy intended doing with them, wondering if Zenobia would be apprehended as well. Their only comfort was each other's company, and then even that was removed.

Amity was thrown into a cabin of a stinking prison ship anchored at the Market Street docks. Grace was put in another. Someone had decreed they should be separated. They had been, after all, a tricky pair.

Would Zenobia escape with Gracie? If not, what would become of the child? Would she be raised by some Tory lady, never knowing that her father and mother had given their lives for liberty? Or would she grow up in some squalid orphanage? Perhaps she wouldn't grow up at all without proper care. Her health had always been delicate.

Amity tried not to think of Mario, an endeavor as futile as trying not to think of her own fate. The Continentals would be forced to deal with him as an enemy, and she wished that she had concealed the journal about her person, so that *she* at least might have known the truth. But the truth mattered not at all, for both she and Mario were as good as dead. Each had been the other's doom. Each seemed to have a naturally disastrous effect on the other.

She fell into an exhausted sleep and dreamed she was once again dancing with her Knight of the Blended Rose. The fetid stench of the prison ship was again the aroma of flowers in cut-glass vases. The sway of the waves was the rhythm of music.

Once she awakened abruptly to the sound of gunfire and splashing. Undoubtedly some poor wretch had given trouble and had wound up overboard, shot to death. Maybe it was better than the lingering death in the ship's fetid underbelly, she thought with a shudder. Had she been a man, she would have been put there, too.

Sun streamed in the window, and she awoke confusedly as a key turned in the lock. The sailor in his flat cocked hat, blue jacket, and white breeches beckoned her to follow him, and she wondered if her time to be hanged had come already. Then, on the foredeck she caught sight of the man who had been the victim of the spying she had done, who by rights should have stopped a Continental bullet by now because of her meddling. Mario! Had he come to see her hanged? The fierce glare in his eyes seemed to sear her flesh from her bones. Suddenly she was more afraid of him than of the gallows.

"Is this the woman?" asked the British officer with Mario.

"That's the wench," said Mario coldly. He was pale and disheveled, dressed in simple breeches of stout everlasting, jockey boots, and a coat of brown twill.

"Then deal with her as you will, sir. General Howe's orders are to turn her over to you. Only remove her to someplace where she cannot cause more trouble for his majesty's army."

Amity shrank back as he took her by the arm to lead her away.

"Oh, Amity, you pay me no compliment to prefer quarters on a British prison ship to my company. How your attitude has changed since last night, when you danced in my arms and made my bedroom your domain, quite uninvited. Fortunate for you that the British will do almost anything to please me. Fortunate, too, that I managed to elude your Continental friends who set upon me on my way here. I suppose you can take some satisfaction that I didn't emerge unscathed."

She noticed for the first time that blood was seeping through his coat sleeve, and she gave a little cry.

"Don't fret, Amity. It's only a flesh wound, though I'm sure it's merely the sight of blood that bothers you. It's not concern for me, surely. It does mean that I can't spank you as I did once before. I shall have to think of another way to deal with you."

"Grace . . ." she began, thinking of her friend still incarcerated on the ship. Mario was furious with her, but perhaps not as angry with Grace. He had been fond of her.

But Mario did not pause as he escorted her down the gangplank. "Mario . . ." she pleaded.

"Grace is dead," he said, his jaw set.

"Dead!" She went limp against his good arm.

"Last night a sailor came into Grace's cabin. She lured him in, he claims. She tried to get his pistol to escape, and there was a struggle."

Mario did not have to finish. Those had been the sounds she had heard in the night. Amity was almost unaware that he put her into a carriage and drove with her to another pier. Then he was leading her up another gangplank and onto another vessel, a big three-masted schooner with foreign flags. Amity found her voice then.

"Mario, this is a Russian ship!"

"Yes, one of the finest of Catherine's fleet. I designed it myself."

"I can't go to Russia, Mario!"

"You heard General Howe's order, Amity. I'm to take you where you can't spy on the British again. Or would you prefer to remain on a British prison ship?"

"But Gracie! They are bound to arrest my aunt, too! What of my aunt?"

Mario did not seem to hear her above the roar of his own anger as he shoved her inside a cabin. "Are you really the heroine of Trenton, Amity? Was it your doing that the British were surprised there? You gave of your charms that night, just as you did to that outlaw in my room?"

"I didn't!"

"Doan says you did. Dear heaven, is there no end to the men you'll entice for liberty? You enticed me, too, but I did not get my full share for my trouble, and I intend to have it. You're a dangerous woman, as this wound of mine tells me. But where is my journal? Have you hidden it in the same place again?"

"Oh! That's the only reason you rescued me, isn't it? To get your journal and to use me! I haven't got the journal."

"So you say! You'll excuse me if I check for myself. Your word has been less than reliable."

He reached for the hooks that held her Turkish robe fastened down the front. She pulled away violently, and satin ripped in his hand. Her bare white shoulders came into view, quivering and vulnerable, but still held proudly.

"You've ruined my dress, you beast!" she said. "It's all I have to wear."

"Never mind, you won't be needing anything at all for a while," he said. "Now, will you hold still, or must I tear off the rest?"

Amity did not hold still. She fought him with terror and determination. He was her captor, her enemy. Yet each time his hand grazed her skin, she felt stirrings in the depth of her being, stirrings that came from inside her, yet seemed beyond her, too powerful to emanate from her own soul or body.

How was it he could be so rough and yet seem so tender at the same time? The outlaw had not been so. He had roused only her animal instinct with his wild ways, while Mario assailed her senses with the passionate control of beautiful music. She was helpless before him in a way she had never been with the outlaw. The difference was love, but Amity did not know that. She knew only that he was a man who would take her as the soldier in her father's barn had tried to, as the outlaw had done. She did not yet know that men could love women in ways finer and greater than these, and she sobbed, hating her own passion, wishing for the simple sweetness of her girlish love for Silas.

"Well, I am convinced you are not hiding anything now, Amity," he said, blowing an appreciative breath.

Indeed she was not hiding anything. Not her pert little breasts or her trim thighs, not her buttocks, round and smooth as opals, not the nest of golden hair between her legs, from which the bird of her desire took flight.

She shuddered as he touched her wonderingly, his fingers tracing every curve of her breasts. A soft glow began inside her and worked outward, until her skin shone pink and radiant.

Mario pushed her back onto the bed. Oh, she must not let him touch her, and yet it was impossible not to let him. He was not holding her down as the outlaw had done. There was no need for that. The power he had over her was greater than physical strength.

He sighed, feeling his loins near bursting with his desire as he unfastened his breeches. She was treacherous; she was wanton. Why did he want her so, more than he had ever wanted any other woman? He scarcely knew when he had begun to want her. Perhaps it had been from the very first moment she had shown him her fire, striking at him with his walking stick. Perhaps it had only been last night, when he had felt her breasts, soft and lively, beneath his hand. He had unraveled part of her mystery now. He had found that she was neither a virgin nor a Tory. She had read his letter to Catherine, which he had left for her, knowing she would open it, if she were a spy. It had nearly cost him his life to satisfy his curiosity about her. Why had he taken such a chance?

Now he would satisfy himself about her in another way. What would *that* cost him?

He touched the flesh between her thighs and felt her tremble. Strangely, a corresponding quiver began deep within his own body. Mario would almost have turned back then, for he was unused to being so utterly moved by a woman. He had loved many, lady and courtesan alike. In Venice, they said there was no difference. But never had he had a woman like Amity. The mystery that remained about her was more profound than the mystery of her allegiance. Perhaps he might never solve it.

In the moment before he took her, Amity saw his naked body above her, the hair on his great chest glowing like a field of soft, ripe wheat into which she might fall. Then he imprisoned her in an embrace, and in captivity she knew the ultimate woman's release, as her will was lost in his.

Time and eternity hung breathless beneath the North Star of their love, as they were lifted to the crest of their tempestuous passion, crashing at last into a warm lagoon of fulfillment, where they lay spent in each other's arms.

He kissed her hair, knowing that he had not solved the mystery in loving her, but only discovered a greater mystery than he had known before. She lay smiling, in possession of her full womanhood, now that *he* had been in possession of *her*.

She regained herself at last and sensed the motion of the vessel. Jumping up, she ran to the window, bursting into tears as she saw the coastline growing small in the distance. She was leaving America—home, all she had known. Somewhere there was the Buck's County farmhouse where wild daffodils grew in the spring. Somewhere there was Silas, whom she had promised to love forever, a promise broken now. And another promise, even more sacred, broken, too. The promise she had made to dying Isabel to take care of Gracie.

Amity wept bitterly, hiding her eyes with her hands, and

he asked, not unkindly, "Have I made you so unhappy, Amity?"

"It's Gracie! I've deserted her!"

He thought again of the dark-haired toddler with her bright smile and winsome ways. The outlaw had had dark hair, he remembered. Was it coincidence that this child Amity loved had the same coloring? Should that tell him something?

Mario was filled with anger for which he could find no focus. What exactly had he interrupted last night at the Meschianza? He wanted to think that the outlaw had forced himself on her, but he had not mistaken the flush of passion on her cheeks. He had tried to cool his rage against Amity by fighting with the outlaw, but when the Tory had crashed through the window onto the balcony below, Mario had known no release.

It had become necessary then for him to stamp his mark on Amity, though he had had to snatch her from the British to do it. She had been right about that, hadn't she? He had thought he was saving her only to soothe his pride. To finish what had been started.

But he thought now it would never be finished. He had hoped to get her out of his system, but instead the affliction had deepened. He should have left her to the British, to hang if they wished.

He winced, his injured arm giving him pain. She was to blame for that, too. But the sight of her naked and weeping pained him more than his wound. She wept as a ruined virgin might, and she had not been hurt. She wept unabashedly, not thinking of trying to cover herself, her breasts heaving in a way that made Mario want to touch them again. With a frown he threw her his brown velvet wrapper. Fastening his trousers, he put on his boots and left the cabin.

The door opened again, and she caught her breath, half-hoping, half-dreading that he had changed his mind and come to take her again, to shame her with her need. She tucked the wrapper more tightly around her, planning her proud but futile resistance like the general of a surrounded army.

But then a soft voice called to her, and arms too small and soft to be his fastened tightly around her neck. Her fingers touched childish curls, and her sobs were suddenly joyful.

She looked beyond Gracie, holding the little girl as if she could never let go and saw Zenobia beside Mario, who had relaxed into smiles at the sight of Amity's reunion with the child. For a moment it seemed to her that all was well. She could have swooned away with relief. Gracie and Zenobia were safe; the war and the hated British were receding in the distance of green waves. But then her glance caught her aunt's, clear and steady, uninfluenced by love, and she remembered that nothing was right at all.

The man who had conquered her could decide the fate of the colonies as easily as he had decided hers. This man whose powerful magnetism exuded from every pore was the man to whom the Empress Catherine would give her ear. And Amity did not doubt that hordes of cossacks would descend on the colonies at his say-so.

He had escaped Continental bullets, and now nothing could prevent him from carrying his fatal word to the empress.

Russia
The White Nights

11

The days were filled with sunshine and shining water as they crossed the Atlantic. Mario seemed endlessly busy with the ship. It had a Russian captain, but that burly sailor deferred to Mario, the ship's designer, agreeing to every plan to test the boat's strength and speed. When Mario was at the helm, it skimmed over the water on the lightest of airs. When the wind rose, Mario put the ship through incredible acrobatics, while Amity stayed below in terror.

At such times Mario would, likely as not, visit the cabin, and having laughed at her clinging white-faced to a bunk or table, he would appropriate Gracie and take her out to experience the thrill of the storm. Amity would protest, to no avail, and Gracie was more than willing to be carried on his shoulders out onto the pitching deck.

It was obvious that Gracie adored Mario; and he her. Her health improved on the voyage, in spite of Amity's protests about her being out in all sorts of weather. Mario would take her up a little way into the rigging when the wind was less, and she would cling there, laughing and fluttering, all petticoats and ribbons, like some special festival pennant flying aloft.

"I'd be petrified up there, Aunt," said Amity to Zenobia.

"It's her age. The young are frightened of nothing. I would be frightened to love Mario, but you are not."

Amity tried to ignore the remark about her relationship with Mario. Her aunt was well aware that she spent her nights in his quarters, emerging at dawn conquered and glowing. Instead, she continued her train of thought about Gracie.

"I think it's more than just her age. It's a heritage from Isabel." Gracie's mother had escaped the massacre of Long Island with the child in her belly. And Amity would never forget the dreadful circumstances of her birth on Christmas morning. Life had done its worst, and Gracie had survived, imbued, Amity thought, with a certain not unjustified sense of being invincible.

"She'll be a spirited woman," Zenobia said.

"Yes. Too spirited, I'm afraid," agreed Amity darkly. "Such women often end badly."

"Like you and me." Zenobia sighed.

Soon they had passed the Azores and were in the North Sea. They began to think seriously of what might happen to them when they reached St. Peterburg.

"I suppose I will ask Caleb Beale to help me," said Zenobia.

"I should think he would! It was he who got us into this, after all, sending us Mario!"

"Hush, Am. We were into it up to our necks already." Zenobia seemed nervous when she spoke of Caleb Beale. She seemed half-afraid to see him after so many years. Amity would ask her why this was so.

"Nonsense, Amity, it's not so," Zenobia would say. "It's only that I wonder what he's like now. I wonder if he's changed. People do, in twenty years."

"I'm sure you haven't, Aunt. You're still beautiful. Is that what you're afraid of? That you've changed?"

"Do stop teasing, Am!" said her aunt tensely. "I've changed, of course."

"Perhaps he's still in love with you. He is, isn't he? That's what worries you. That's why he never married. He can't forget you."

She saw by her aunt's expression that this time she had hit the truth, though Zenobia tried to deny it. "He has his calling. That's why he hasn't wed. There are Quakers in Europe. Caleb will know where. And I will ask him to send me to them. What of you, Amity? Will you come with me?"

She hesitated, and it was Zenobia's turn to play the game of guessing, but being wiser, she needed only one guess.

"You are dreaming that Mario will marry you, Amity!"

"Oh, no! He had never hinted at that. And I could not wed him anyway. Why, he is the enemy of freedom!"

"He hasn't told you what he will say to the empress, has he?"

Amity shook her head. She had tried time and again to draw Mario out on the subject, but he always became moody and angry. Amity thought often of the empress herself. Catherine, Empress of All the Russias, was no longer young herself, but she had a famous appetite for men. She was timeless, it was said, radiant with her great destiny and with the courage and vision that had made her the undoing of her own husband, Peter, whom she had overthrown to seize the throne. Catherine did not need youth to be fascinating to men. Did Mario think of Catherine when he was so out of sorts? Was he thinking that Amity's presence would cause a fit of imperial jealousy?

He would never marry her. He thought of her as a woman who had betrayed him. A woman who loved easily, who had been the outlaw's mistress and most likely the mistress of others. She longed to swear to him that it wasn't so. But how could she, when the outlaw had bedded her? When she squirmed in pleasure beneath him every night, proving that she was indeed a woman of salacious nature.

More than that, she would never marry him, not if he begged her. He who would give tyranny sway in her beloved country! When she saw her brave country crushed, when she knew that the struggles of Valley Forge had been for nothing, then she would hate Mario da Riva, surely, and deny him the ravishment of her body!

But now she lost herself to him each night, her moans and the tension of her body telling him what she would never admit.

"You are my jailer, you may do as you like with me," she would say haughtily.

Mario would dissolve into gales of merriment. "Why, Amity, I am doing as *you* like with you!"

"Don't be absurd, Mario. I can't help it if you have a power over me!"

"I think it's you who have the power over me," he suggested. "Oh, Amity, tell me what I must do to be free from your charms!" He spoke lightly, but there was a hint of desperation in his voice that surprised her.

As they drew closer to St. Petersburg, he began to tell her about the city. "They call it the Venice of the North, partly because it's built on the marshy ground of the Neva River and is shot with canals and palaces—as many as Venice."

"Is that why you seem to love it? It reminds you of home?"

"It does, in a way. But it's different, too. The light has a special quality, quite different from that of the southern light of Venice. The northern twilight lasts forever in the summer; it has a thousand shades of topaz and lavender. The poorest shack is a palace then, and the palaces seem built among the clouds."

Amity smiled, intrigued by this poetic side of himself he sometimes showed. She was far from understanding his many-faceted personality. Sometimes he loved her with moody intensity. Sometimes he was almost violent, and she clung to him as her passion rocketed to terrifying heights. At other times he was mocking, loving her as a diversion, her helpless ecstasy a thing for jokes. But those times he made light also of his own consuming need.

He loved her and was pained by it, just as she was pained by her love for him. It was a love that should not be, and yet it shouted to the universe that it would not be denied!

They left the Gulf of Finland and sailed up the Neva. Golden domes announced their arrival at St. Peterburg. The river ran as broad as an arm of the sea, enclosed by great dikes of rose Finland granite, stretching for miles. On an island in the center stood the towering, gloomy fortress, which served as a prison and guarded the city. Half-moon buttresses interrupted the quays, and majestic flights of steps led to the water's edge and to the landing places.

Beyond lay the city that Peter the Great had willed to rise from desert marsh. Before a forest of pilings had been driven into the earth and taxes of rock exacted from visiting ships, only elk had roamed here. Now a continuous facade of palaces stood ocher and pearl in the fabled white night of midnight, refracting the opaline glow of the western sky.

The ship maneuvered slowly over the shining steel-blue water, past lighters laden with wood, to a landing spot bright with summer flowers. The pale yellow gas jet flickering along Court Quay suggested the lateness of the hour, but the sun's rays still lingered in an amethyst sky. Though it was almost midnight, only a few milky stars peeked through.

Voices echoed and seemed to float. The entire city seemed to hover, a vision of mist that might be swept away by a vagrant breeze. Amity's gait was uncertain from the voyage, and the earth rolled under her feet, adding to her feeling that they had arrived, not at a definite point on a map, but had sailed into some fantasy beyond the end of the earth.

She noted how well Mario fit into the scene, as he strode easily up the great stairway, carrying a sleeping Gracie over his shoulder. He seemed at once to belong among the magnificent palaces, the mark of nobility in his features and bearing, kindred to the proud splendor of the buildings.

"Mario!" came a shout. A well-built young man in a tabbinet frock coat came bounding down the steps, his boots touching no more than every third stair.

"Francesco!"

They slapped each other's backs like a pair of brothers. Mario still encumbered by Gracie, who, roused by the commotion, lifted her head and blinked bewilderedly at her strange surroundings.

"Amity, this is Francesco Baretti, my closest friend," Mario said. "His family's palazzo was opposite mine when we were boys in Venice. We strung a tightrope between our bedroom windows to try to walk across the Grand Canal. We didn't break our necks, as you see, but we got very wet. We went to the university together at Padua, and we came to Russia together to build ships and wintered on the Black Sea."

Francesco stepped forward to kiss her hand, and she was struck by how handsome he was. He had about him the same air of masculinity that Mario had, and his eyes were a compelling blue, with an ethereal aura that matched the palaces and the river. Could it be that the northern light affected their appearance? Or had the place already cast its spell over her to make her perceive him so?

She liked him instantly, and had Mario not lessened him by comparison, she might have fallen under his spell. His nose was most certainly from the same stamp as Mario's; it was the Venetian nose, he had told her once, bold and imposing, a beacon of strong character. But Francesco's forehead was less high than Mario's, the jut of his jaw less pronounced, although perhaps that was an illusion caused by an apparently habitual merry expression.

"Mario and I do share a taste for the same things," he said with relish.

Once, when she had been an innocent little Quaker girl, she would not have guessed his meaning. Now, though she was wiser, she was not yet enough of a coquette to do anything other than blush, a reaction that struck them both as funny. Amity frowned, annoyed that Mario did not remonstrate with his friend. Apparently he didn't mind, and she remembered that he thought her any man's trinket.

"We are hardly alike in all ways, Francesco," Mario said finally. She guessed that the remark had nothing to do with her.

Francesco sobered. "No, but we will be friends forever."

They had almost reached the top of the stairs when Amity suddenly lost her balance, and only a quick hand from Francesco saved her from a fall. There in the ghostly lunar blue her father seemed to stand silhouetted in his wide, round-brimmed Quaker hat, as though he had not been stoned by Tory or patriot on the wagon train to Virginia.

She thought only of her shame, pulling her cloak more tightly around her flounced dress that Zenobia had brought aboard, along with her other fancy Philadelphia clothes. No Quaker would ever wear such a dress in her country meeting, but her clothing was only the beginning. Even if Father had not become an avenging angel, she could never hide from him the shame of her inward impurity. She swayed, and felt Francesco's arm around her.

"You should have let her rest before coming ashore, Mario," she heard him say. "The voyage has been too much for her."

"Then you carry the child, Francesca, and I'll carry her."

The idea shocked her to her senses. She had pride left and would not be brought to judgment by the man who had been her undoing. She drew a deep breath, and daring to look into the Quaker's face, realized her delusion.

"Caleb!" cried Zenobia, her face shining. Never since Uncle John had died had Amity seen her aunt look the way she did now at the sight of Caleb Beale. Was it another trick of the twilight that Zenobia seemed to be a girl again?

"Zinnie! Can it really be thee?" said the Quaker, his astonished face similarly transformed. He was a large man with intense features, dark and solid in this fanciful land. He would be strong enough to care for and comfort a woman, Amity thought. She could understand why her aunt had loved him. But did she still? "Zinnie," he had called her. Amity had never heard anyone address her aunt in such an informal way before.

"Oh, Caleb, my niece and I ran afoul of the British and had nowhere else to go. I hope we won't be too much a burden!"

"Thee could never be a burden, Zinnie!" said the Quaker fervently. It was he who lifted Gracie from Mario's arms and led them to a carriage.

They sped along the street among the primitive two-wheeled télègues laden with peddler's goods, through crowds of common droshkies and finer ones drawn by long-stepping trotters, lightly harnessed so that nothing of their beauty was concealed. Gentlemen in damask frock coats and ladies in Parisian gowns mingled among muzhiks in sheepskin touloupes and peasant women in gaudy kerchiefs and dresses of pale green. Cossacks paced on their nervous little horses with hay nets hung from their saddles, and nursemaids, released from their charges of the day, strolled together wearing the tiaras of red or blue velvet with big pearl beads that marked their trade. Priests were somber in flowing black robes and tall brimless hats covered with veils.

They passed palace after palace—the Summer Palace, home of heirs apparent, nestled in a corner of its gardens, steep-roofed, stucco over brick, painted a whimsical primrose yellow. Then came the new Marble Palace, commissioned by Catherine for her onetime lover Grigory Orlov, who had helped to lead her coup against her husband. Quarries in the Urals and Siberia had brought new wealth of marble and semiprecious stone, and this palace, with its smooth facades, was the first stone palace in Russia, Caleb said. The onion domes of churches rose with crescent and cross, and across the quay the homes of grand dukes were cast in moonlight from the east, which caused them to cast their soft reflections toward the western shore.

They reached the endless expanse of the Winter Palace, with its three stories of water-green stucco, its great ranges of Ionic and Doric columns and its host of twice-life-size statues above the balustrade of the roof. Caleb turned the carriage up a ramp beneath a portico, and in a moment the ladies were being handed down by attendants in royal livery. The equipage was led away to the stables, and abruptly they found themselves inside, treading parquet floors and gaping as the men gave directions about the luggage.

"Is this where you live, Caleb?" gasped Zenobia.

The Quaker allowed himself a self-conscious grin. "I have lived at the palace for years, since the empress likes me close about. It's hardly a bastion of Quaker simplicity, but I have tried not to be corrupted by it. I shall like it better with thee here."

"I?"

"Of course. Thee and Amity shall have a private apartment. Mario has one, too, which he shares with Francesco. Royalty builds for display, and I daresay there are rooms that have never been occupied. There's a rumor that cows are kept in the attics."

"But the empress . . ." protested Amity.

"She is at her summer estate at Tsarskoye Selo, but I am at liberty to put up a small entourage."

They had reached the foot of what Caleb said was the Jordan Staircase, so called because of its role in a January ceremony of the blessing of the waters of the Neva.

"All the court has to attend and go out onto the river to dip themselves in the river through a hole cut in the ice," he said with a shiver.

The wide, red-carpeted stair swept to a landing and divided majestically, turned again and led up to pale pink columns and arched windows framed in great amounts of gilded bas-relief. Above a higher set of windows, celestial figures gazed down, and yet more gilt edged the ceiling.

Mario had seemed moody and withdrawn since they had reached the city. She took his arm as Caleb led the way to his apartments, but Mario did not seem to notice her. Forgetting his wound, still not quite healed, she squeezed a bit, and he grimaced with pain.

"I have business to attend to," he said suddenly, as though that had reminded him, and took his leave, without telling her when she would see him again.

She felt bereft when he had gone, and not hungry for the buffet of herring, salted cucumber, and cold viands that servants had laid in Caleb's rooms. A great samovar kept water boiling for tea. That, at least, tasted delicious. Caleb said that the reason was that it came overland from China and was not spoiled by weeks in the sea air.

"Tell me what happened, Zinnie," said Caleb. "You understood my letter."

"Yes."

"It's because of that thee had to leave the colonies." He sighed. "I'm sorry, Zinnie."

"It's nothing to be sorry for, Caleb," said Zenobia. "We were spies already, and bound to be caught. Mario rescued us—Amity from a prison ship and me before I was arrested. The British let him have his way about what became of us."

"What word does he bring the empress, Zinnie?" said Caleb tensely.

"We don't know. Oh, Caleb, couldn't you have done something? The empress listens to you!"

Caleb shook his head. "It was I who persuaded Catherine to send an observer before making a decision. She is not a despot, but she is too ambitious to always agree with my convictions against war. It was the best I could do, and Mario is a fair man."

Amity was exhausted and lonely, glad when they were at last shown to their rooms. But even then she was unable to sleep. Perhaps it was the alien palace, the bed, on which maids had turned down silk sheets, set into an alcove framed by curtains.

The vaulted ceiling was painted with roses, and the paneled walls were painted with scenes of the Neva. The bed, armchairs, and chaise longue were carved and gilded, covered with striped white silk painted in tempera; and the fireplace was inset with agate and jasper.

But more likely Amity's unrest was caused, not by the strange room, but by Mario. She did not even know which part of the great palace held his rooms.

Ever since they had glimpsed St. Petersburg, she had sensed him withdrawing from her. She had been his American adventure, nothing more. He would have been done with her long ago if he had not had to bring her along like so much extra baggage to keep her from hanging.

Baggage, she thought, applying another sense of the word. Yes, she had certainly been that. Shameless baggage. He had not asked to share a bed with her tonight as he had on the ship. Was it because some other woman waited for him here? Did he warm her bed even now, the woman eager to renew the affair after his long absence? Something was dreadfully wrong between them. She became more certain the longer she thought about it, and she tossed helplessly. Their relationship had changed since they had reached the city.

Getting out of bed, she wandered into the sitting room where French chairs covered with silk apple-blossom patterned upholstery sat like flowers among white columns. Moonbeams entering through open draperies curled in and out among the pillars like ribbons.

The effect was confusing; she felt lost in a maze, and for a moment she did not realize that she was not alone. Then a soft sigh alerted her to her aunt's presence. Zenobia sat close to the windows, clad in a satin wrapper, her hair haloed in moonbeams. She seemed nothing like the competent Society Hill matron Amity had always known; but then she turned, and seeing her niece, said briskly, "This garish palace is keeping me awake. Can't you sleep either, Amity?"

"It's not the palace that's keeping us awake," said Amity.

"Oh, I'm certain it's what's keeping *me* awake," said Zenobia. "Those enormous screens of purple glass. That obscene line of naked cupids. There are forty of them, Am!"

"Caleb Beale is keeping you awake."

"Caleb? What an idea. He's not even here."

"He's in your heart. It's far from over between you—Zinnie!"

Zenobia had the grace to become flustered as Amity mentioned the pet name Caleb had used. "My dear child, that was all over a long time ago."

"It seems that time stands still in St. Petersburg. There is not even day and night."

Her aunt sighed, gazing down on Palace Square, seeing something other than the dwindling passersby, mostly elegant couples now, lingering too close together, sequins on gowns and breast buckles in the lace of gentlemen's shirts twinkling back at the conspiratorial stars.

"Caleb was my first love, Amity. A woman never forgets her first love, no matter if it's ill-advised, no matter if someday she loves another more. He is always in her heart. You will learn, Am!"

She flushed. "You are speaking of Silas."

Zenobia looked knowingly at her niece. "I've never asked you what happened, Amity. I'd never pry. Whatever, I'm sure it was shattering, or you'd be married by now, out of meeting or not. When a woman such as you desides to marry the man she loves, there is no saving him."

"Oh, that's not true, Aunt. I'd like to marry Mario, but *that* will never happen."

"Tch, Am. I did warn you not to fall in love with him."

"I didn't plan to," protested Amity bitterly.

"There, child, I know that, too. When I was your age and met John, I struggled to be true to Caleb. But it's finished between you and Mario. Why else would he not be with you tonight?"

"The thought of that is why I cannot sleep," Amity admitted.

"There, now. Caleb says there are Quakers in Prussia who will take us in. When the war is over, you may find that things are different between you and Silas."

"And for you and Caleb?"

"That is different," said Zenobia. "He has his calling, and I have had my love."

12

Amity awoke the next morning feeling utterly disoriented. It was nearly noon, and she was more used to rising with the sun. But how could you rise with the sun, when the sun never went to bed? Obviously she had fallen into step with the ways of the capital, for outside the streets were deserted, only a few seabirds strolling on the quay.

She was famished and just beginning to wonder where among all these great rooms the kitchen was when a maid in a black uniform entered with a cart bearing a samovar and silver platters of sausage and pancakes and orange juice freshly squeezed.

The oranges had come from the orangeries at the seaside palace of Oranienbaum, Caleb told them, arriving with an invitation to join him for a tour of the palace. "Come along, Amity," he entreated kindly. "You can't miss the Malachite Room or the cathedral or the fountains in the Pavilion Hall."

She boggled at the idea of a palace with its own gold-domed church, and she longed to see the pink marble galleries of the Hall of Fountains. Nonetheless, she demurred. She was scarcely so noble as to give up these pleasures because she thought Caleb Beale would like to be alone with her aunt, though she did think so. Rather, she was hoping for another invitation from a different escort.

"Please come, Amity," her aunt pleaded. Zenobia was well aware that Amity hoped that by staying she would manage to see Mario. It was wiser for her to begin to forget him, but it was not as much for Amity's sake as for her own that she urged Amity to join them. She preferred the safety of company.

In the end Zenobia appropriated Gracie, an inadequate chaperon, and Amity, well pleased with the solution, dressed in a gown of fawn muslin with a petticoat worked in gold thread beneath the open overskirt. Afterward she paced impatiently, adding a gauze kerchief over her décolletage, drawing the ends through a ring into a V with the idea of adding to the dignity of her appearance. Then with a burst of rebellious spirit she removed it and laced her bodice more tightly, so that her creamy breasts swelled over its lacy edge. There! Let him neglect such a reminder as that, she thought brazenly, observing the effect in a long gold-leafed mirror.

As she waited, she began to wish she had accompanied her aunt and Caleb Beale. Mario had certianly not told her to expect him, and every minute became agony. She should not let him find her so much at his disposal, she knew; but when the knock finally came, she leaped to answer it. The man who stood there with his tricorne hat under his arm should have pleased any girl, but Amity knew her face fell.

"Good afternoon, Miss Andrews."

"How do you do, Don Baretti." She looked past him hopefully and he laughed, well understanding.

"Call me Francesco, Amity. Summers are too short for formality here, and the White Nights are a festival themselves. I thought we might ride out to the islands. The point is beautiful, the rendezvous of the fashionable."

"Mario—"

"Mario!" Francesco feigned surprise. "Mario's long gone. He left last night for Tsarskoye Selo to see the empress."

She felt a chill. The thing was done, then. He had gone to report to the czarina and deal what could well be the death blow to the ideal of American liberty. He had been so eager that he had not even waited for morning. No wonder he had said nothing to her. He had not wanted a scene. He had been afraid that she would beg, or even try some bit of female skulduggery to prevent him in her female way, as she had at the Meschianza.

But his haste seemed beyond the call of duty. Was there another reason he had seemed so indifferent to her, another reason he had not told her he was leaving? Was he eager to see Catherine and she him for reasons other than political reports? Was he having chocolate in the czarina's apartments this very minute? Or perhaps . . .

Seething in irrational jealousy, Amity pinned on a wide-brimmed milkmaid hat and gave Francesco her arm. She wouldn't be caught pining away when he returned, she thought proudly. But when would he return?

"How long will Mario be gone?" she asked Francesco, giving voice to this new fear.

"That most likely will depend on Catherine," he answered.

"He will be guided by her wishes, since her friendship is important to Venice. Mario has such dreams for Venice, you know. Poor Venice can hardly support her own weight, but Mario thinks new empire would restore her self-respect and her courage. Russia would be the perfect ally. In Venice they say that Mario will be elected doge one day. And then Catherine's friendship will be invaluable. Her empire is larger than the Romans'!"

Francesco gave her an amused sideways glance. She saw he knew what she was feeling. He knew a great deal about women to be so quick, a very great deal, for he seemed to intuit it would not be to his advantage to offer any reassurance. Instead he paused before a portrait and said, "That is the czarina, by the way."

The woman in the painting rode a prancing dapple-gray stallion, her slender figure straight as a rod; her soldier's uniform of red and green and her black tricorne decorated with oak leaves of victory did not hide the fact of her womanhood. Her blue eyes held dazzling vision.

Amity drew in her breath. The empress was nothing like the spoiled aristocrat she had expected. The woman was beautiful, but more than that, she was magnificent.

"It's only a copy," Francesco was saying. "The original is at Peterhof. It represents the day of her coup over her husband. She led nineteen thousand men to Oranienbaum to overthrow the emperor. And then because her men wished it, she returned victorious at the head of the columns without even stopping to rest. Do you wonder that men followed her?"

Amity did not wonder. She felt reduced to helpless insignificance as Francesco handed her into a droshky pulled by fine chestnut horses. But the air was sweet and warm in midafternoon, and the sights of the city soon claimed her attention. Amity was grateful that they spoke no more of Mario.

Following a long, straight road lined with villas and gardens, they now and then crossed a canal or branch of the river, busy with rowboats, some filled with pleasure excursionists, the ladies twirling frilly parasols—a new invention. Others carried peddlers hawking fruits, vegetables, and flowers.

Francesco drove the horses at a gallop, forcing Amity to cling to her hat with both hands to keep it from blowing off, while she bounced so hard on the seat that she began to wish she had given in to the artifice of a cork bustle that might have cushioned the knocks.

The Venetian was in high spirits, delighted with himself, the day, the fine horses, and the small coup of having her for a companion. Repeatedly he smiled at her, as if sharing some special secret, which seemed to be only the joy of being alive. He seemed free of Mario's lurking moodiness, and she wondered at the difference in their natures when their rearing had been so similar. He, too, was of the nobility, with centuries of his family entered in the Golden Book. It would be simpler for a woman if she loved Francesco, Amity thought. But she was learning that love did not favor easy choices.

A tension rose inside her as she thought of the man to whom she had utterly given her love. Would to God she could appear as indifferent to him as he to her! She was still Quaker enough to realize that she was suffering from the deadly sin of pride, but not Quaker enough to be able to fight its considerable grip. Let him go to visit his beloved empress whose name he spoke in such reverent tones! Let him do his worst and convince her to ally her mercenaries with King George!

But when he came back, he would not have *her* again. A practical side of Amity told her that such a defiance might be difficult to arrange, built on the sand of her passion. If he kept his distance, she might manage to be stony, but if he touched her, he would know at once . . .

She thought miserably of the outlaw. She had not had the opportunity to test herself against him completely, since Mario had intervened. She would never be sure that she would not have let him take her again, and because of that she could not be sure that she was not the woman of easy virtues that Mario thought her. The outlaw had been a rogue, but he had been a paragon of pleasure. How much more difficult it would be to resist Mario, who put the outlaw in the shade.

It would be more than she could accomplish alone. She needed allies, just as Venice needed Russia. Once Amity would have sought assistance from a higher power, but now she sensed that faith would desert her as soon as he looked at her. Someone of flesh and blood would have to do instead. There was Aunt Zenobia, of course. She frowned as they crossed onto the islands and sped past modest houses, where occupants sat on raised platforms inside pretty gardens, drinking tea sucked through sugar cubes held in their mouths.

Aunt Zenobia had warned her about him, and that had done no good. Aunt Zenobia couldn't help her. Who, then?

Francesco smiled at her, and his black curls tossed. Amity felt glad that Catherine did not approve of wigs and thus they were never worn at court. He was pointing out a fat burgher seated on a curbing, whose face contorted as he struggled to uncork a bottle of wine held between his bulging thighs. In the instant they raced past, the cork gave, and the man toppled backward into a bed of small blue flowers, nonetheless aiming the bottle skillfully between his lips so that hardly a drop sloshed onto his collarless waistcoat.

In spite of herself, she couldn't help joining in a peal of laughter, and as his vivid blue eyes shone into hers, she thought suddenly that he might be her unwitting conspirator. It would not be hard to feign an interest in Francesco. No, not hard at all.

That would disconcert Mario, no doubt. He'd return to find her in the arms of his dearest friend! So to speak, for Amity had no intention of committing the same indiscretions with Francesco that she had with Mario. But she would let him see that she had not missed him, that she found Francesco charming. Francesco would cooperate by monopolizing her, so that she would not again be humiliatingly undone at her lover's whim.

The more she thought about it, the more perfect the plan seemed. She had seen girls in Philadelphia employ such strategy on faithless beaux, so surely it was workable. It did not occur to her that those women were more experienced than she. They had had years of practice in the drawing rooms of Philadelphia, while Amity had only begun to be aware of womanly wiles before quite literally jumping in over her head, crossing the icy Delaware with the outlaw.

Neither did Amity think that it might be more dangerous to trifle with Mario than to trifle with other men, and so entertaining ideas that would have caused a wiser woman to shudder, she chatted gaily as they drove along, the trees becoming thicker and the villas farther apart, elegant now, decorated with fretwork. Lawns sloped down to bathing beaches at the water's edge, and yachts raced together like schools of fish, with sails hungry to capture every gust of the steady southern breeze. A long bridge gave views of rolling woods of elm and fir, the birth trees mixing their slender white columns with those of green-domed garden temples peeking from the landscape.

They paused at a restaurant with massive gables for a meal of green vegetable soup with flat onion bread, topped off with a dessert of apple charlotte drenched in apricot sauce. Francesco displayed a lively interest in America and the state of the Revolution, and he drew in his breath with admiration and envy when he heard that she had met General Washington himself.

"What a man he is, Amity!" Francesco cried, bringing his fist down on the table and making the dishes jump. "And it was just before the triumph of Trenton that you saw him?"

"Yes, the very night before the battle." Encouraged, she talked on and on, telling him things she had never told anyone, unburdening herself of the events of that dreadful December. How she had seen Washington worn and worried on Christmas Eve by the fireside in the heavily beamed central room of the Bucks County farmhouse. How he had told her he would enlist her if she were a man. How he had read Tom Paine's essay to his troops as they climbed into the Durham boats, leaving behind bloody footprints in the snow. " 'The summer soldier and the sunshine patriot—' " she began, but he took it up from her.

" 'Will in this crisis shrink from the service of his country—' "

"Why, Francesco, you've read Tom Paine!" she cried.

"Yes. And Locke and Voltaire. Tell me more, Amity. What else did you see?" His intelligent blue eyes hung on her every word. Carefully omitting her moments in the haystack with the outlaw and her near-disaster with Colonel Rall, she told him about being at Trenton, how many of the soldiers had charged with only bayonets, seizing victory, though their powder had been dampened in the crossing.

"How wonderful!" he said. "To fight half-starved and in rags for ideals more precious than life! What courage, Amity!"

"You sound as though you would like the Continentals to win," she said, smiling.

"Why, of course I would. I only wish I could be there, testing my convictions with theirs, instead of idling at Catherine's court!"

"I only wish the empress had sent *you* on Mario's mission!" she said fervently.

"Are you certain? I'm sure *I* should have liked it!"

She flushed at his reference to her romance, and wondered how much Mario had told him. "I meant—"

"Oh, I know. You meant that I would have made the right decision. But that's exactly why I never stood a chance to go. The czarina knew that I could have as easily written my recommendations without ever leaving St. Petersburg. But Mario—that's different. Mario would never be arbitrary. If you asked him to settle an argument over whether the sun gives light, he'd look before answering."

"Then is it possible he might advise Catherine against sending troops?" she said hopefully.

"I suppose so. But not likely. And Catherine would like to please the British. She has always admired the British system."

They drove on, reaching the open water of the Gulf of Finland. A dirt road traced by lines of short whitewashed stakes led through the gardens of Jelaginsky Palace with its white-and-yellow walls and green roofs. In the meadows, sprinkled with ponds and trees, men in red shirts pitched hay. At last they reached a semicircular drive girdling the Point and disembarked in a crowd of droshkies and calèches to promenade by the waters.

She felt more relaxed than she had in a long while, as though she were in the company of a close friend. Her troubles seemed far away for the moment, and grateful to him for the surcease he had given her with the outing, she asked him about himself. "Why is it that your ideas are so different from Mario's, Francesco?" she said.

"Oh, that is because our lives have taken separate courses," he said, gazing off at the rose-colored clouds. "My father was very much like Mario and his father, and I would have been like him, too, but times change and things happen."

"What things, Francesco?"

He seemed somber now. He *did* have a moody streak like Mario's, after all. She shivered, feeling a chill in the breeze, and wished she had not asked.

"My father wore himself out serving the Republic, neglecting his investments and his holdings, though Senator da Riva warned him not to. He believed in the integrity of his fellows on the Council of Nobles, trusted advice not given with his best interest at heart. Still, when his fortune began to crumble, he expected gentlemanly compliance to postpone his debts. And so it would have been once—noble aiding noble, and the populace grateful and respectful for the efforts of the aristocracy to make Venice a power. But the old ways had ceased to work. The nobility had ceased to labor and to take responsiblity for the Republic. Money had become too important and people were allowed to buy their way into the Golden Book to replenish the treasury. Nobles reveled in masked balls and assignations, while my father went bankrupt for his trouble, with no one but Don da Riva to help him. The palace fell to the da Rivas at auction. My father wept with joy that it went to no other, but when Senator da Riva attempted to restore it to the family, pride prevented my father's accepting his generosity. In a month he was dead."

"Oh, Francesco, I'm sorry."

He brightened and recovered himself. "It's all right, Amity. The ideal of the nobility was flawed. What happened was inevitable. My father was a man of vision, but not of sufficient vision. He believed in the tradition of service and virtue, but he did not see that a position in men's esteem should not be handed down from generation to generation like a set of sterling silver. In the beginning men earned the right to inscribe their names in the Golden Book. A thousand years of birthright have brought decay. We must return to the idea that all men are created equal!"

She thought it a startling idea for a man of noble lineage, but he told her there were others like him. "I am a member of the Barnabotti, the disinherited nobles, and each year there are more of us. Fortunes are lost one way or another, since society attempts to support such an immense weight of luxury and display. Many of the Barnabotti feel as I do. They talk of French ideas and dream of revolution there which may shed sparks on Venice."

"*You* would be in the vanguard of such a revolution, Francesco?"

"I would like to be, but I could not even whisper such a thing in Venice without being thrown into prison! It's better for me that I am in Russia, where I will be safely out of danger and able to earn the Council's poor nobles' stipend I receive by furthering Venetian alliances."

"And if Mario were doge? Would things be as they should then?"

"I don't know. I'd like to think so. We are forever arguing, Mario and I. The wonder of it is that our friendship has stood. We are both determined that nothing will destroy it, though I am the new wave lapping at old foundations, like the sea forever tormenting and testing the palaces of Venice. Mario has his heritage, while I am estranged from mine. I have nothing in Venice now, only my sister, Giovanna, who lives in a convent."

She saw a parallel between her and him and told him how they were alike. "I am estranged from my heritage, too, Francesco. I was read out from the Society of Friends when I ran away to find Silas. My father is dead, too, and I have only Aunt Zenobia. Caleb Beale plans to send us to Quakers in Prussia, but I don't know how we shall fit in."

"We are two lost souls, Amity." He sighed, taking her hands in his. "We are not to be blamed if we enjoy each other's company. Mario has made you no promises?"

Amity's heart thudded as she shook her head.

He smiled, obviously entranced with her. Did he know she had been Mario's mistress? She was certain he suspected as much. Did he expect that she would be his, too?

"I should like to show you more of the dispossessed, Amity. Come with me tonight to see the tziganes sing and dance. You'll never forget it."

"The tziganes?"

"The Gypsies. They perform at taverns in the countryside."

"Taverns! That hardly sounds like a place to take a lady, Francesco."

"No, it's not. But there'll be others there. The most patrician women of St. Peterburg can't resist. I hope you can't either."

She cast her eyes down at the ground as she considered. Then, giving him a dazzling smile, she said, "I'd like to go, Francesco."

She had already been quite a few places that were not suitable for ladies. What could one more matter?

It was late when he came for her, but that was part of the fun, he said. Parties during the White Nights began when decent folk should have gone to bed and lasted until dawn.

"Are you sure you should go, Amity?" said Zenobia, who was just finishing a game of bezique, which Caleb had been teaching her to play. The Russians sat incessantly at cards, and Caleb had had to adjust to what was not an ordinary Quaker pastime. Now he surprised her anew by taking her part.

"I think she will enjoy it, Zinnie. The tzigane men are huge as bears and never let things get out of hand." Caleb adjusted a pair of spectacles and studied his cards, while Zenobia could only shoot Amity a warning look. *She* had not missed the intensity of Francesco's infatuation, as perhaps Caleb had.

Amity tucked covers around a sleeping Gracie and kissed her plump little cheek; then soon they were driving along the quay, past the little houses of the Faubourgs, in an iridescent dreamlight, not quite of the moon or of the sun, but filtered through shimmering veils of mist into turquoise, apple green, and lilac. The shifting of the carriage threw her against Francesco's shoulder, and she reveled in a masculine essence that quickened her breath. Sensing her excitement, he put an arm about her shoulder, ostensibly to steady her. Had Mario been beside her, she could not have wished anything more.

"In the winter, parties go sleigh riding to the inn," he said. "You would like that even better. It's wonderfully exciting with the speed of the sleighs and bells ringing and furs and brandy to keep warm."

"I'll probably be gone by then," Amity said rather regretfully as they caught sight of the lights of the tavern, isolated in a stand of elms.

Chairs and tables sat jumbled inside four smoke-stained walls, where young officers of the Imperial Guard lounged drinking rye beer. Francesco had been right—there were ladies. Champagne was brought, and Francesco paid for a performance. The troupe appeared—men with bronzed faces bearing the tranquil dignity of their race; and then the women, voluptuous breasts only half-concealed beneath shabby silk dresses, olive complexions blazing with carmine paint, eyes smoldering under charcoaled brows.

The tzigane girls sat in a semicircle as a guitar began to play. Their bodies and faces were motionless, and they seemed indifferent to the song they were singing, so lifeless that Amity wondered why Francesco had wanted to bring her. But then it seemed that they were sinking into a sort of trance. Slowly the voices became animated, heating into a trembling wall. Melodies became filled with the wildness, and melancholy, and the passion of the Gypsy nature. The ladies in the audience caught the excitement and seemed to throb with their humbler sisters.

A dancer whirled into the center of the room. The officers cheered and clapped. The pitch grew frenzied with her coming. She could not be one of the gypsies, Amity thought. Her hair was a brilliant shade of red, thick and shaggy as firebush, rippling with natural waviness, seeming to shoot off sparks as she spun, her short skirts rising above perfect ivory thighs. Only the dancer's dark eyes seemed the same as the

Gypsies', fierce, taunting, and dangerous. Her body moved with a fluid precision, so that Amity almost believed she had sprung incarnate from the music.

"Who is she?" she asked a rapt Francesco.

"Her name is Velda. She was a member of the ballet in Moscow once. She would have been a prima ballerina."

"Would have been?"

"Yes. She fell in love unwisely, and threw away a lifetime of work. The children are selected to dance when they are very young, and they spend their lives at school in training. By the time they are grown, the government has quite a bit invested in them. That's why they are watched so closely, kept almost prisoners, lest they follow their hearts. But nothing could stop Velda."

"She fell in love with one of the Gypsy men?" asked Amity. But the music ended, and she was startled that Velda came straight to their table. She took Francesco's glass and emptied its contents with a sigh.

"Well?" she demanded.

"I gave Mario your message, Velda."

"And? Where is he? Why didn't he come?"

"I don't know, Velda. I'm not Mario's keeper. He went to Tsarskoye Selo."

Velda seemed as upset as Amity that Mario had gone to the empress, and she expressed herself with abandon that Amity would never have dared.

"Oh! " The glass shattered, flung to the floor by her furious hand. "I cannot bear it! No other man would treat me so. The czarina! It's all her fault. He eats from her plate like a pet dog!" Velda clutched at her own bright hair, as Amity cringed. Everyone was looking.

"You know that's not so, Velda," said Francesco mildly. "Mario is his own man."

"The czarina would like him to be *her* man."

"And you would like him to be yours. But Mario belongs to no woman."

"He'll belong to *me*, you'll see!"

"The empress would hardly like to hear you say that, Velda." Francesco was indifferent, though Amity was shaking uncontrollably.

"Oh, I don't care. She doesn't own him. He's not even a Russian subject."

"No, but you are. Take care. If Catherine can't have

Mario as she wants him and blames it on you, you are in trouble."

"He's the only man I'll ever love, Francesco. I'll fight the empress for him. I'll—"

"Do sit down and be quiet, Velda. I want you to meet Amity. She's an American patriot and had to flee the colonies. Mario brought her."

"*Mario* brought her!"

Amity saw comprehension dawn in Velda's world-wise face, and anger swelled to rage. Amity herself felt a wild rush of hot, bracing fury, unlike any she had experienced for one of her own sex.

"I'm going to play cards," Francesco said incredibly.

"Francesco!" She could not believe he was deserting her in this situation, and grabbed at the tail of his frock coat.

But Francesco knew what he wanted to do. He was determined to remove himself from the female battleground, and Amity would have to fend for herself. Indeed he had planned the moment.

When he was gone and she realized she was entirely on her own, Amity drew a deep breath and met Velda's murderous glance with one of her own. For an endless moment each took the measure of the other, suffering the imagining of her rival in Mario's embrace.

Then Velda said contemptuously, "Don't think you can win. Don't dream I'll let you, I who am ready to take on the czarina and all her armies for his sake!"

"I'm not afraid of armies, either," said Amity. "I've already dealt with the British. But perhaps I've no need to fight anyone for Mario. Perhaps he's mine already."

The audacity of her answer took Velda by surprise.

"Do you mean that he's married you, then?" she asked in astonishment.

"Marry? Oh, I couldn't marry him!"

Velda dissolved in raucous merriment, her fiery head flung over the back of the chair, her breasts heaving beneath their gaudy covering. Her anger diminished as she studied Amity with more interest. "Why, pray tell, couldn't you marry him? Have you a husband already?"

"Because he sympathizes with the Loyalists. He's the enemy!"

Velda laughed again, a scornful laugh that made Amity uncharitably want to fling herself on the dancer and choke her. But then she would not have heard what Velda had to say next. "You call that a reason! When you love him? Then you don't deserve to have him! You deserve what will happen to you. You'll be left in the cold, because I intend that he shall marry *me*!"

"You!" Amity was unable to control her amazement.

"You think a Gypsy dancer can't marry a nobleman, I suppose, Miss High and Mighty. But such things have happened before. There's many a tzigane girl has wed herself a general. And members of the ballet marry well when they retire from the dance. When Velda decides to have a man, she'll have him! Just look at you. Do you think you are suited to challenge me, you with your dainty ways and that pale hair and wintry blue eyes? You are merely the moon, and I am the sun!"

A Gypsy man came to tell Velda that a party of officers had paid for her to give another performance. "Stay and watch," she urged Amity. "You'll see how much I please men. I'm becoming wealthy from the banknotes they throw at my feet."

Amity was eager to decline that invitation, and Francesco appeared beside her. When they were again in the carriage, riding through the gentle night, she gave way at last to the tears she had been holding back.

"You took me there to see her!" she accused.

"Yes. Usually I don't interfere in Mario's business. But this is different. I'll be in trouble with him, no doubt, if you tell him you know about Velda. She is his past, but you are not his future."

"Is Velda his past and his future, too?"

"No."

"Oh, how can you be so certain of all this?" she cried. "Velda is very convincing. She'd battle the empress herself to claim him!"

"Velda's a remarkable woman, and there's no denying she'd devote every ounce of her strength and ability to owning him. They met when Mario and I visited Moscow on our way to the south. As foreign nobility we were entertained at the ballet, and after that I saw almost nothing more of Mario. When we left, she ran away and followed us. Mario told her to go back. She didn't."

"And then what happened?" asked Amity, not wanting to hear it, but knowing she must.

Francesco shrugged. "Mario did what any man would do. She was marvelously desirable, and there were only dull-witted peasant girls to give her competition. When we returned to St. Petersburg, she followed again, with the Gypsies. Mario would never take responsibility for her. Mario abhors entanglements. But Velda doesn't need anyone to take care of her. She's managed to hang on very well. She's prospered, actually. She's in demand."

"Is she really becoming rich?"

"Yes. Money isn't one of her problems. But she's a fugitive of sorts. She'd be sent back to the ballet, if she were found out. If Mario were an ordinary man, she'd have had him to the altar long ago. But it's not the empress Velda is battling for Mario."

"Not the empress?" Amity did not know whether to feel encouraged.

"No. Many a man would savor the love of an exciting older woman, but the empress possesses her men, and Mario will not be possessed. Not by Catherine or Velda. Not by you, Amity."

"Then who—"

"Can't you guess? Venice possesses Mario. He puts Venice before any woman. He puts Venice before himself. He knows that the few like him who are left are the only hope of restoring her to her old integrity."

"And that means he cannot wed?" she asked incredulously.

"On the contrary. It means he must. His father, the senator, is most eager for it. But Mario must wed someone of Venetian nobility. Were he to marry a commoner or a foreigner, he would almost certainly lose his place in the Golden Book. His enemies would scarcely overlook it, and then he would lose his position on the Council of Nobles and all his influence. Some of the Barnabotti have already gone that way, taking wives from wealthy middle-class families and losing title to improve their fortunes. It's the sort of thing I might do myself, but only for love."

"Then he would never marry me, even if I could let myself marry him."

"My dear Amity, it's quite fortunate that he can't. The chances are that if Mario asked you, you would find yourself in a shambles of compliance. And then the two of you would battle each other to the ends of the earth! You the fiery little egalitarian, and he the unswerving patrician!"

She wept afresh, knowing finally why Mario had often been so moody, why he had suddenly seemed indifferent on their arrival in St. Petersburg. Velda and the czarina might threaten her, but it wasn't for them that he spurned her. He might think her the outlaw's woman, but that was not the reason, either.

As they drove through the glowing White Night, she heard him say to her, "Mario is engaged to be married to my sister, Giovanna."

And then he added, "I am not the sort of man that Mario is. I would not trade love for an outdated vision. You could love *me*, Amity! You could love *me*!"

He drove with one hand, the other arm clasped about her, drawing her close. She heard the clip-clopping of hooves, the sighing of trees in the night wind. She sensed his shadowed closeness—and was lost in his kiss.

13

She was the moon and Velda the sun, the dancer had told her. Ordinarily one eclipsed the other, but St. Petersburg was not ordinary. Here sun and moon shone together, the one a scarlet harridan on the western horizon, the other a ghostly maiden haunting the east, each claiming the mighty sky for her own, locked in a season of struggle.

She thought of the girl with the childlike smile and the soft fawn tresses whose miniature lay in Mario's walnut trunk. She knew now that the guileless beauty was Giovanna, Francesco's sister, who would prevail over both sun and moon. The marriage had been arranged with Mario's full agreement, Francesco said. Her Venetian lineage was impeccable, and the marriage had been the perfect way for the da Rivas to restore to solvency the proud Barettis, with whom they had stood shoulder to shoulder over hundreds of years. Francesco and Giovanna, that meant, since they were the only ones left.

Francesco had not said that Mario loved Giovanna, but it hardly seemed likely. She was only fourteen years old and was kept, like most Venetian maidens, in a convent, protected from the sullying influences of the lusty Venetian world.

Did Giovanna love Mario? That scarcely mattered either. It was the alliance that mattered. At the end of her first pearl-wearing year, the first year of marriage, Giovanna would be expected to choose a male companion, a *cicisbeo,* who would escort her to parties and the theater and rain upon her the constant compliments and attentions that women were thought to deserve and require.

Amity had been shocked at the idea, but Francesco explained that the custom had grown from the revering of women. A Venetian woman was placed on such a pedestal that it was considered too much of a burden for one man to do all the worshiping. He had his business to attend to and must sometimes delegate his wife to another. If that included his duties in bed as well, that was not frowned on.

"Would you do that, Francesco?" she had asked.

"It's not likely," he replied. "I don't care for fortune or lineage, so I've no reason at all to marry except for love."

She spent almost every day in Francesco's company. Sometimes they went to shop on Nevskoi Prospekt, taking Gracie with them along the immense hundred-foot-wide street of cobblestone and hexagonal wood blocks. When it rained, great torrents of water spewed from enormous downspouts, soaking the skirts and breeches of unwary passersby. Francesco had to carry Gracie on his shoulders then, for Amity always worried about the child's health, remembering how ill she had been when Grace had brought her to Philadelphia from Valley Forge.

Another child would have died, but Gracie had developed great will and determination instead. Francesco thought her as wonderful as Mario had and spoiled her with toys and treats of sour-cream pie smeared with jam. Amity sighed as she tried to persuade him to stop. Already Gracie had discovered she could use her cherubic ways to better advantage with men than with Aunt Zenobia or Amity. Francesco was delighted that she clapped her little hands whenever he arrived to take them for an outing.

In the evenings Gracie was left to a Russian nursemaid while Amity and Francesco jaunted over the summery islands, now by carriage, again by boat, through the channels and canals filled with pleasure boaters singing and laughing their way from villa to villa. Musicians claimed their attention, the sweet strains of a duo of *viole da gamba* caressing the night. Lighthearted operetta played at country theaters; garlands of colored lanterns swung from lacy larch trees, casting rainbow reflections in the water. Past midnight fog threw a silver canopy over the marshy land, and trees stood poised like Gypsy dancers in attitudes of giddy delight.

At such times Amity almost forgot that Francesco was merely a means to convince Mario of her indifference, to save her from being helpless at his mercy. Each night his kisses were more intense, and though her soul did not seem to dissolve beneath them, they were a balm to the pain of the knowledge that Mario would never be hers.

"Is the southern Venice as lovely as this northern one?" she asked one evening as they watched boats scud away toward the coast of Finland.

"Oh, it's better, Amity. If we were in Venice now, we would be galloping our horses through the fine surf of the Lido. Then we'd picnic in the moonlight and watch fireworks over the city. The water would be so warm and soft, we'd run into it a thousand times for the sheer pleasure of having the waves spin us around and deposit us on the white sand. We'll be going back next spring, Mario and I, when our work is finished here."

He sighed and she knew that he wished that she were going with him to gallop on the Lido. She sighed herself, wishing she were going to Venice with Mario. Next spring, no doubt, she'd be with the Quakers, leading a life for which she was no longer suited. She did not think that a thousand years of prayer could erase from her heart the longing for the transport of Mario's love or for the fantasies of the White Nights and palaces of St. Petersburg.

These days were the blossom of her womanhood, a flower which she supposed would be short-lived as any bloom of the Russian summer. Each day she savored to the fullest, drinking in Francesco's kisses, scarcely thinking that it might be easy to do what he had suggested and fall in love with him.

"Tell me about the empress," she would beg Caleb Beale as they sat around the samovar. "How do you get on with her, when you are a simple Quaker."

Caleb smiled at her, not taking exception to being called a simple Quaker, though now he was much more—an adviser and a diplomat, a polished gentleman. "It may surprise thee, Amity, that Catherine has a streak of simplicity herself. She dislikes military display and drives out in her carriage with only footmen to protect her. She hates books with fine bindings for show and she refuses to paint her cheeks like other

Russian women. She stands out like an exquisite moonflower in a field of poppies."

"Those are merely eccentricities, Caleb," objected Zenobia. "Tell us what she is really like."

"Once she declared that serfs were as good as anyone," said Caleb. "And she has banned the punishment of the knout. She sent a rich women to prison for cruelty to her servants, and she thinks that girls are as intelligent as boys. She has established schools for girls, and the students fling themselves upon her and smother her in kisses when she visits. Catherine sees herself as an example of what women can become. She began as an insignificant princess. As a wife she was treated as a brood mare and endured years of torment from her husband, before she seized the reins of the empire."

"But, Caleb, why didn't she remain an insignificant princess? What made the difference?" Amity wanted to hear.

"It was her vision. She studied and read all those years, and at last it could not be denied. She had a dream to make Russia great beyond what it had ever been. She has brought experts to study the soil to recommend the best crops for the black soil of the south and advertised in foreign newspapers to bring settlers."

"Are the settlers coming, Caleb?"

"Yes, by the droves, in covered wagons."

"Catherine sounds too good to be true," observed the skeptical Zenobia.

Caleb looked at her fondly. "She has another side, Zinnie. For all her virtue, she is prey to appetites of the flesh. These she cannot or will not control, and some thought the death of her husband, Peter, after the coup, was murder in which she had a hand."

It seemed strange to Amity that this woman who offered so much hope to one vast country, yet raw and wild, but rich with potential for human betterment, should be the one to deal a crippling blow to the hopes of the colonies, which matched the same description. She never passed the painting of Catherine on horseback that she did not stop and study it. And then one day she did not need to look at the painting anymore.

Maids scurried everywhere with feather dusters and polishing cloths, shining the varicolored Russian marble in the throne room, putting the great palace to rights. Amity did not realize at first what it was all about; then Zenobia rushed in with the news.

"The empress is coming. It's quite sudden. She'll be here this afternoon."

Amity tried to cover her agitation. "Dear me, Aunt, you're breathless. Did you run all the way up the Jordan Staircase to tell me? I'm still Quaker enough not to be impressed by royalty. And if I weren't, I'd still be Whig enough not to care for it."

"Oh, pshaw, Am!" snapped her aunt. "I'm not out of breath from running. It's excitement. You're excited, too, if you'd only admit it. Catherine would have been impressive if she'd been born a peasant!"

"So Caleb Beale says. He's bewitched by her, like any man, and *you* are bewitched by *him*! You believe his every word."

But Zenobia was right. Amity was no little bit flustered, but not so much because the empress was coming as because Mario would come with her. She stood on a balcony and watched as the procession arrived at the Winter Palace. The empress was taller than Amity had imagined. She stepped down from the carriage wearing a gown of summery cambric-muslin, alternating white and lemon stripes, cool and crisp after her long ride—or if that were impossible, her cool, decisive manner caused her to appear unwilted.

Amity could have picked her from a hundred women by her regal bearing.

Then Amity's heart pounded harder at the sight of the man who jumped out lightly after her, dashing in a suit of *pourpre du Papa*, his jauntily tied macaroni neck gear floating elegant fringes.

Black rage rushed over her as Mario offered the czarina his arm, and she laid her finger lightly upon it, as though he were a proud jewel in her crown. He was not, Amity reminded herself. Francesco had said that Mario was obedient to no mistress but Venice.

She thought of clever and biting rejections she would deal him when he came to bed her, the betrayer of her heart and her country. And then, when he did not come, she wept, and her body was racked with need. Was it possible that Francesco was wrong?

She wondered if Velda were as neglected, and mustered her courage to ask Francesco.

"Why, he spends every evening at the inn of the tziganes," Francesco told her, not seeming to relish her pain.

But she did not ask other questions that she longed to pose. She could not bear to hear the answers. How did Velda punish him for his days at Tsarskoye Selo and how did she reward him for his return to her? Did the passions of the sun blaze in ways that she, the moon, could never dream of?

She was wild with frustration. How could she reclaim him while Velda luxuriated in his love? She wanted him and did not want to want him, and her heart divided into warring armies.

If only she could be like Velda, so confident and single of purpose! She shuddered when she thought of how certain Velda had been of making him marry her. Nothing Mario had done would disturb Velda. It would not bother her to set her cap for an engaged man. Velda's love for Mario was the essence of her powerful personality. Small wonder indeed that she should think herself the sun, and Amity the ineffectual moon!

Would Velda win Mario after all?

The czarina had decided to give a court ball, and Francesco was pleased that he had managed invitations for Amity and himself. Caleb had obtained invitations for two as well and would escort her aunt. Amity wasn't in the mood for it, but she hated to disappoint Francesco. She laughed to herself when she remembered she had begun her romance with him to flout Mario on his return. There had been no need of that! Mario had been far too successful at amusing himself with Velda. She wondered if he thought that she and Zenobia had already left St. Petersburg. Maybe he had not bothered to ask.

But she was fonder of Francesco than she had imagined she could be of another man. It was not the girlish love she had felt for Silas, not the mindless passion she had given Mario. Her devotion to Francesco was quieter, based on the kindness he had shown her, his good humor that had made her laugh and brightened days that otherwise would have been intolerable. It was based on her admiration of his beliefs and goals, which were similar to hers.

Well she knew that Francesco's feelings for her were of a different nature, but she was still too unwise to understand how foolish and dangerous it was for her to accept the balm of his love and kisses.

Zenobia tried to explain. "They are best friends, Amity!" she said.

"Why should that matter, Aunt?" she said with haughty fatalism. "It's obvious that Mario's finished with me. He's keeping that Gypsy warm at night."

"And you, Amity. Do you stay warm?"

"Good heavens, I've not bedded with Francesco!"

"And don't intend to, no doubt."

"Why, you sound as though you think I should!" cried Amity.

"You know I don't. But you are leading him on, Am, trifling with his feelings because it suits your fancy. It will come to no good."

"But he thinks I'm a lady. He doesn't treat me like a tramp as Mario did. I enjoy myself with Francesco."

"Mario treated you like a tramp because you behaved like one."

"But that's over."

"I hope so. I wish it were over with Francesco, too. Someday the war will be over and we'll go home. The world will be right-side-up again."

"Oh, Aunt, it will never be right-side-up!"

Zenobia's renewal of her friendship with Caleb Beale was clouding her judgment, Amity thought. Clearly Zenobia believed in the value of first love. She had spurned Caleb for John, but now they were together again. Zenobia saw a parallel; Amity should think of Silas and the time when the war would be over. Then whatever had been wrong between them would have been healed by time, for Zenobia had known Silas and thought his love had the depth of Caleb's. Disillusioned, Silas Springer would see solace, not in the company of other women, but in the cause of liberty, just as Caleb Beale had found his peace in his work as a public Quaker.

Caleb seemed to have forgiven Zenobia for the heartbreak she had caused him, and Zenobia glowed quietly, incredulous at her new happiness. So it would be with Amity and Silas finally, she thought.

How wrong she was! Silas could never forgive Amity for what she had done or even what he thought she'd done. And while Zenobia's John had been drowned, lost to her forever, Amity's love for Mario was frenzied and unfinished. As long as he breathed on the earth, he would threaten her ability to be satisfied with any other man.

"Perhaps I'll dedicate my life to the Friends myself," she mused. "It's not unheard of, even for a woman. And you yourself will end by marrying Caleb, Aunt. You'll have a proper Quaker wedding, for it was long ago and far away that you were read out from the Friends."

"You are dreaming, Am!"

"And so are you," Amity returned. Caleb and Zenobia would welcome her into their home, of course, but she could not live as an appendage. She would have to set out by herself and find a new life among the Quakers in Prussia.

On the morning of the ball, sergeants of the imperial household rode through the streets of the city with invitations—actually orders—made by tradition on the day of the fete. Recipients were relieved of any other duty for the evening, even mourning the dead. At nine in the evening the carriages began to arrive.

On her way to the throne room Amity trod a stairway scattered with orchids and rare flowers from the royal greenhouse. Garlands of flowers adorned the balustrades, and live butterflies with brilliant markings of topaz, indigo, and emerald flitted in and out among diamond-draped ladies and soared up to the immense vaulted ceilings, fluttering around the lights of the great chandeliers.

She stopped to follow the flight of a particularly lovely specimen in blue and white, and Francesco tugged at her arm. "Do come along, Amity. Try to act as if you've done this sort of thing before."

"But I haven't! Why, it's grander than the Meschianza."

Ladies in gowns of laylock and satin, adorned with foils, spangles, and bell-rope tassels, mingled with officers in bright uniforms. Spurs and sabers clanked as guests filed between Chevalier Guards, chosen from the handsomest men in the regiment.

"Francesco, who are those very formidable old ladies?" she whispered, noticing a contingent of women past middle age who wore miniatures of the czarina in their corsages.

"The portrait ladies. They are the guardians of ancient etiquette, living chronicles of court legend. Do you see those young girls with the czarina's monogram in knots of blue ribbon on their shoulders? They are the maids of honor, the portrait-ladies-to-be."

Francesco pointed out lancers in red; cossacks in long tunics belted with cartridge cases of silver; hussars in short white dolmans bordered with sable. Black attendants in Oriental dress reminded Amity of the Meschianza.

How long ago it seemed that she had danced in the Wharton mansion with Mario, intent on stealing his journal from his trunk! It had been this very spring, but by another reckoning it had happened in another lifetime, for then she had not experienced the devastation of his love.

She raised on tiptoe to see if she might catch a glimpse of him. It was for him that she had endured a dozen fittings for a gown of pink satin, its petticoat of puckered crepe ornamented with bouquets of roses. Roses were twisted in her hair, too. She wore no jewelry, but nature adorned her though she would not adorn herself, and her eyes sparkled like gems with excitement. Pink color drifted over her milky skin like clouds in the opaline twilight sky, and buckles on her dainty slippers glinted when she walked, like stars struggling to shine in the presence of greater brilliance.

A hush fell over the room as the doors to the private apartments opened and the empress was announced. She appeared in a regal gown of satin *couleur de noisette* trimmed with feathers cut to look like fur, and giving her hand to a grand duke, began a procession to the bars of a polonaise. When it was over, the dancing began in earnest. Catherine abandoned the superannuated grand duke and gave her favor to Mario, beaming happily in a quadrille.

Of course it would be he! Amity tripped over Francesco's feet as she strained to dance and watch at the same time, and her hoops became entangled with those of another lady, who shot her a look of annoyed disdain.

"Oh, Francesco, I'm making a fool of myself," she said in distress.

"That's nothing, Amity," he said. "I'm afraid you'll make a fool of yourself in a worse way before the evening's over."

"I shan't. I'm not interested in Mario da Riva at all. It was the empress I was trying to see. She's magnificently gowned, and not all foils and glitter, like so many here." She gave him a dazzling smile and did not allow her eyes to wander again toward Mario and the empress. The czarina had danced easily in his arms, as though it were a treat for her to unbend like any ordinary woman. Caleb had been right, though. Catherine would not have been an ordinary woman had she been a peasant. The bloom of youth had been replaced by something more vital, the sense of a woman complex and experienced, as skillful in leading men to love as in leading them to battle. It was easy to imagine that any man would be fascinated. Mario and the czarina seemed delighted with each other, one the equal of the other in ways that did not depend on kingdoms and crowns.

A dashing young captain of the Chevalier Guards bowed before her, and having entreated Francesco to introduce him, begged her to dance. She accepted, her mind on other things, and instantly forgot his name. He was the first in a long succession of officers, all eager to dance with the lovely American visitor to the court. Some spoke a little English, the legacy of Russia's diplomatic connections with Britain. Some knew French, which she had studied as a child. Still others spoke more eloquently with language of the eyes.

She was about to dance for the second time with the officer from the Chevalier Guards, when Caleb Beale claimed the turn, spinning her away from the expectant young man. "You're very masterful, Caleb." She laughed. "Look, the captain seems disappointed."

"All the more reason thee shouldn't dance twice with him, Amity," said Caleb, glancing back at the crestfallen officer. "He's marked to be the favorite."

"Favorite? Favorite what?" she asked innocently.

"Must I spell it out for thee? I've been at court for years, but there are some matters on which I'm reticent to speak, especially to a young girl. I mean he's *Catherine's* favorite. She'll install him in the apartment next to hers. Now do thee understand?"

Amity did. "But . . . he seems no one special."

"No, but rumor is all over the court that he will be the czarina's next lover. Most likely her most trusted minister, Potemkin, suggested him."

"And you mean that the poor captain has nothing to say about all this? And he is not allowed to dance twice with the same woman?"

"Oh, no doubt the arrangement doesn't displease him. But he seems rash. He should be careful, and so should thee, Amity."

"Don't worry, Caleb. I won't dance with him anymore," she said.

The Quaker seemed relieved as he left her and sought her aunt's company again, his face lighting as he reached Zenobia's side. Amity watched them for a little while, smiling at their happiness, and absenting herself from the dancing to sip a glass of Tokay. In a few minutes she noticed that the captain was dancing with the czarina, his face animated, his lips busy in what she imagined must be a steady chatter of compliments and lover's nothings. Court life was much like the banks of the creeks she had traversed in her native Bucks County, she thought—overgrown wonderfully with jewelweed and flowers, but treacherously marshy beneath.

"Planning your next conquest, love?"

The voice was cold, but when she turned, she met amber eyes blazing. The wine she had drunk seemed suddenly to go to her head, and she fought for self-control at his nearness, already lost in a rush of desire and remembrance.

"I'm surprised that *you* find time to breathe between yours," she said scathingly.

"I? Why, I couldn't hold a candle to you, Amity!" he said, his voice cruel. "I've been gone no more than two weeks, and already you've turned Francesco into a lovesick dolt and trifled with the czarina's favorite."

"Trifled!" she cried indignantly. "Do you mean because I danced a polonaise . . . While you and your Gypsy dancer . . ." Her bosom heaved with fury, and dainty rosebuds on her bodice quivered in the storm of her anger.

"Are you speaking of Velda? I only did as I was invited to do with her, just as when the invitation came from you."

"Such words never passed my lips and never will! I did not invite you, you brute!"

He seized her arm as it swung back to hit him, and with amazing ease entwined it with his own, so that she was effectively his prisoner as he began to pull her along out of the ballroom. "Your lips did indeed give me the invitation, though not with words," he said.

She became twisted with the skirts of another woman for the second time that night; and while she blushed, Mario disentangled them with a bow. Then they were out in a marble hall, her little shoes clicking double time to the pace of his boots as he propelled her up a stair and through a door.

She struggled harder as she saw the enormous bed with its canopy of four gold spiral posts, thick as the leg of an elephant.

"You gave the same invitation to my friend Francesco, no doubt, and most likely to that outlaw with whom you disported at the Meschianza. Oh, Amity, once I though you were a different kind of woman; you were always so earnest, no matter what you did. I thought your love was in earnest, too. I fooled myself because I wanted to be fooled. How could I have been so blind, with the evidence right in front of me!"

"What evidence?" she gasped, her fingers clawing lace at his wrist as he began to unhook her bodice.

"Why, Gracie, of course. I suspected all along that she was your daughter or Grace's, but when I saw you with the outlaw, I knew not only who was the mother, but who must be the father as well."

"Oh!" she shrieked, beyond words, aghast as her breasts began heaving and as the insolently knowing touch of his hands made her body begin inevitably to betray her.

"Admit it, Amity! You are a woman who cannot say no to love!"

"I can say no to you!" she cried desperately.

"Ah, then prove it to me!"

"I'll be glad to. You've done with me anyway. But which are you done with me for, Mario? The empress or your Gypsy?"

The rage on his aristocratic features told her she had struck home. "Why, Amity, I'm not quite done with you at all, don't you understand. I intend to demonstrate my point to the fullest."

She moaned as her gown fell away, and she heard him add, "You must be done with Francesco. I won't stand for it."

"So you care," she murmured triumphantly, joyous that her plan to make him jealous had succeeded so well. And yet it hadn't succeeded at all. She had planned that Francesco's attentions would prevent her being at his mercy. She had much yet to learn about the ways of love.

"Care? Of course I care. Do you think that I want you to ruin the life of my dearest friend?"

She was flabbergasted. She had expected him to be angry over her romance with Francesco, but she had hardly expected him to take Francesco's part.

"Francesco lets his heart rule, Amity, as I do not. He believes in ideas as pretty and frivolous as those butterflies let loose in the ballroom. If he were to marry you, he would lose his family heritage for your sake, and then you would leave him cuckold, his spirit destroyed. Oh, you should hear him cry your praises. He's as fooled about you as I was!"

So Francesco had spoken to Mario about marrying her. She must have known he had such ideas, but she had not wanted to think about it. How could she ever accept his sacrifices of love, while her flesh writhed with a will of its own beneath Mario's arrogant caress? His hands moved in secret places, mapping roads of passion as intimately known to him as the channels of his native Venice. He had loved her before in anger, but never in such anger as this, and the excitement of his mastery lifted her to a fever of need, fueled in addition by her own resentment that he should use her thus, to illustrate to both of them her shameful weakness.

"You were never fooled, Mario!" she declared between gritted teeth. "You never thought of marrying me! You were always going to wed that little Giovanna."

"It's my duty to marry Giovanna, Amity. Marriage doesn't mean that a man can't love elsewhere."

"Or in your case a number of places," she retorted. "Men like you are not condoned in America, Mario!"

"I suppose that women like you are? The truth is, you were not interested in marrying me any more than I was in marrying you. You began to love me as a spy and kept it up for your own pleasure!"

"Yes, yes, you're right," she cried. "I would never marry you. You, who would help trample the hopes of liberty! And neither do I want your villainous love!"

But her body throbbed with impatience for him to disregard her protests as he always had and do what he liked with her, which, he had told her, was doing as *she* liked.

"So, you don't want my love, Amity?" he said.

"No!" she cried.

"Then I'll bestow it elsewhere, my dear."

He went away, well knowing the state in which he left her, and the awful ache of her disappointment told her, more surely than if he had loved her, the sort of woman she was.

14

The next morning Amity was dreadfully out of temper, snapping at Gracie as the ebullient child clambered into her lap for a morning kiss, sending Amity's hairbrush flying, disarraying the modest lawn tucker Amity had added above the neckline of a simple gray silk gown.

"Oh, bother," said Amity, trying to put things to rights.

"You haven't worn that dress in a long time, Amity," said Zenobia.

"I'm thinking of the old ways, Aunt. I hope we'll be with the Quakers soon."

Zenobia stood looking out the window, where hawkers of sunflower seeds peddled their wares to a few fishermen on the quay "You're right, Am," she said with a sigh. "St. Petersburg isn't good for us. Caleb told me about the czarina's captain."

"Aunt, I didn't encourage him!"

"I know. It only shows what pitfalls life holds for a girl like you."

"You're much more worried about Francesco and Mario, you mean."

"As indeed I should be. They are both wildly in love with you."

"Mario is not, and Francesco will forget me."

"I doubt both, but I've asked Caleb to make arrangements for us to leave quickly—in two or three days."

Amity felt stunned, though she had been expecting it. "The sooner the better for me, I suppose. But you aren't ready to leave St. Petersburg! You're only going because of me."

"Of course I'm ready to leave. Why shouldn't I be?" said Zenobia testily. "I am sick to death of all these whipped-cream palaces."

"And sick to death of Caleb Beale?"

"Well . . ." said Zenobia. Her cheeks turned pink, as close as Amity had ever seen her come to blushing. "The truth is, Amity, Caleb Beale frightens me."

"Frightens you?" Amity tried to imagine Caleb ripping apart feminine lacings with the skill of Mario da Riva and nearly had a fit laughing. "He's the gentlest and most proper of men."

"I'm afraid of love, I suppose," said her aunt. "It's been so long, and in St. Petersburg nothing seems quite real. I'm in love again and never thought I could be. It's a mere dream of the twilight, Am, that will evaporate with the White Nights."

"Caleb's love will endure the winter." Amity laughed. "It's endured many cold seasons already. You're so afraid it will end that you're going to end it, is that right?"

"It . . . would be less painful. He has had his career all these years and I have been another man's wife. We can't be the same people."

"Aunt, it is you who are always telling me the value of first love," cried Amity.

A rap came on the door, and Zenobia was relieved to end

the discussion. A palace aide entered, proffering a note on a silver tray. Zenobia took it almost absently and handed it to Amity, whose name was on the evelope.

Amity accepted it reluctantly and ripped it open. Perhaps it was a note from Francesco, whom she did not wish to face after the fiasco of the evening before. She had returned to her rooms without seeing him again, though he had been her escort. And no doubt he knew with whom she had left the ball. But the note had not been written by a man.

"Dear Miss Andrews, If you have not eaten, I'd be pleased if you'd have breakfast with me," the note read.

Amity gulped and thought it was surely a joke and felt anything but hungry. The signature was distinctive, the first letter large and looped, the rest small and neat in a very straight line, a signature that could not be ignored the length and breadth of Russia. *Ekaterina.*

"What would the empress want of me?" she demanded of her aunt as she struggled ineffectually with her hair and ended by covering her coiffure with a little wing cap.

"I think whatever it is, you had better change your gown, child. That's very plain for breakfast with the empress."

But Amity was afraid to keep the aide cooling his heels in the sitting room and went off in her gray gown that suggested her Quaker days.

The dining room was smaller than most rooms of the palace, but unrelieved by color of any sort. The frescoed walls were white, as was the ornate table; and the white chairs were covered in sparkling white brocade. Amity tried to remember she was an American and not impressed by royalty as she was shown to a chair. A cup of tea was poured for her from a golden samovar that steamed merrily in the center of the table, but the saucer clattered as she lifted it. She was making a fool of herself again, she told herself sternly, seeing the knowing looks of the servants. If only she could forget that Catherine was more impressive than her crown!

The empress appeared suddenly without announcement, followed by two little English pugs. Amity jumped to her feet in confusion, narrowly avoiding upsetting a tray and knocking a piece of sausage to the floor, which one of the czarina's dogs gobbled, hopefully removing evidence of her clumsiness before anyone noticed. Was she supposed to curtsy?

Instead she stood her egalitarian ground, and to her surprise the empress smiled and offered her hand in a firm grip.

"So. You are Mario's American spy!" she said, giving Amity an appraising glance that made her wish she had taken her aunt's advice to wear a fine gown. The empress wore a fashionable morning dress comprising a short jacket fastened with frogs and tassels, and a silk petticoat puckered at the hem with gauze.

"I'm an American, and I was a spy, your Highness, but I am not Mario's," she said.

"Not Mario's!" The empress looked quizzical as she seated herself and flung a big linen napkin over her lap. Servants hurried around her, seeming to bother her like a swarm of summer gnats, interrupting some interesting thought.

Amity sat again, too. Obviously she was supposed to, for an attendant almost scooped her onto a chair as he pushed it toward the table. The czarina supervised everything, ordering a pot-cheese tartlet onto Amity's plate, already heaped with sweet buns and sausages served with tongs from silver dishes. Then she clapped her hands and dismissed everyone. Apparently this was not standard procedure, because the servants became confused, and one appalled little maid ventured to ask a question, gesturing toward the samovar, so that Amity gathered she wanted to know who would pour the second cups of tea. The czarina spoke more sharply, and everyone vanished. Amity was alone with Catherine, Empress of All the Russias.

"Not Mario's!" said the czarina again, breaking off a piece of bread and tossing it to her pugs. "That is quite extraordinary. Why, I have heard you praised to the skies at Tsarskoye Selo until I found it necessary to see you myself. He is enraptured, and you will not love him? It's beyond my understanding, Miss Andrews. To think I've been envying you so!"

"You! Envy *me?*" Amity burst out and was alarmed at her own candor.

But Catherine was laughing. "It amazes you that the ruler of a great empire could envy anyone, Amity? Especially a little Quaker like you without even a spangle on her gown? Oh, but Amity! I was a woman before I was the czarina. And the riches that you have will always be denied to me."

"I? What riches?"

"To be young and in love with a man who is in love with you. A woman yearns to be cherished and protected, but when a man is in my life, the crown is always between us in the bed. There's many a man who cannot separate the czarina from the woman."

"Mario would have no such trouble," said Amity sagely.

Catherine's eyes glowed with appreciation. "That is true. Mario makes a woman know she is a woman if he but looks at her. I had such hopes when Mario first came to St. Petersburg. It was so easy to care for him, but Mario is a man who must come first in the life of the woman he loves. And Russia must always come first with me."

"And so must my country always come first with me," said Amity, trembling. "Mario da Riva is the enemy of my country."

"But many a woman would gladly trade sides for the love of such a man."

"Not I. I could never do that."

"Then tell me why, Amity. I must know what it is about this revolution that is more important than a man's love. Caleb Beale, whom I trust greatly, has advised me not to send troops against the colonists, but he is a Quaker and always against war. You are a Quaker, too, but not of the same sort. You are one of the so-called Free Quakers, are you not?"

"I am. The Free Quakers abhor violence, but believe that it is crueler for a man to lose his freedom than it is to die in battle."

"You yourself were willing to die for liberty?"

"I would perhaps have been hanged if Mario hadn't made the British release me to him."

"So he said. You stole his journal, and he could not bring all he had written for me to read, everything he had recorded that he had heard Americans say. So it is your fault that I do not have it as a basis to decide how to answer King George."

Amity gulped. "I'm not ashamed of having stolen it, and I would have died for my country, had it come to that. My friend Grace did, that very night."

"So you had a friend as devoted to liberty as you. Tell me about Grace, Amity. Are there many women in America who feel as you do?"

"There are, your Highness!" Amity began to tell the empress about the women of George Washington's camp. How they had starved and frozen with the men, enduring hardship that men could not dream of, bearing children in the snow. Her face shone with pride as she spoke of Grace, standing sentry with a musket, and tears ran helplessly down her cheeks as she told of Isabel mending shirts in the lean-to beside the Delaware and dying in childbirth in the dawn of

Christmas Day. She told of women who had cooked for the ragged troops, who had risked their lives to carry water to the wounded, who had scorched their hands on the hot barrels of cannons to keep the guns in action when the gunners had been hit. Finally she remembered the women who had managed to take wagons of supplies through British lines to Valley Forge, and those who flouted the enemy by always wearing the Stars and Stripes somewhere on their clothing.

"I have heard the British officers joke that when they have defeated General Washington, they will still have to defeat the women," she said as she finished.

"The power of women is not a joke, Amity," said the czarina with a frown. "That is why it was necessary for me to speak with you."

"I still don't understand, your Highness," said Amity, all confusion.

"We are woman to woman, Amity," said the empress. "You may begin to call me Catherine. It's a privilege I don't grant many, but I give it to you because you know as well as I that the crown does not make the queen. I myself was never intended to rule. I was merely a convenience to bear my husband's sons. If God had given me a husband to love, I would have never cared to rule. I exist in a world of men, without any to love for always, and it's rare that I am able to confer with another of my sex over anything more important than the palace draperies."

Amity was still confused, so the empress continued, "War among men is one thing, Amity. It's based on greed, the need for heroic deeds or the yearning for power for power's sake. It is no great thing to allow one's mercenary troops in such a war, if it strengthens alliances. But when women care so much, it is well to think twice. There is more to this revolution, I think, than the Intolerable Acts and the tax on tea. Mario told me I would understand the colonies better after I had talked to you. He said you would be better than the journal."

Amity's heart leaped. "Then the journal did not oppose the colonists? But it must have. Mario did not think that the colonies had the right to revolt."

Catherine tried to look stern, and gave up as a smile came through. "You are surprised, Amity? Well, I shall not allow King George to recruit mercenaries in Russia. Do you see what it means?"

"Oh, yes! Yes! Thank you . . . Catherine. It means we have hopes of winning again."

"That isn't all it means."

Amity's mind was whirling, and the empress had to tell her what else it meant. "Mario da Riva is not the enemy of your country. You may admit to loving him now."

She gasped, realizing it. "But he is still a Venetian nobleman, and he belongs to Venice. That's what Francesco says. And Mario is to marry Francesco's little sister, Giovanna."

"I'm surprised at you, Amity, willing to fight so much harder for your country than for your man. Are you really going to let that little convent girl marry him? Do you believe she will make him happy?"

The empress rested her capable hands on the arms of her chair and looked squarely at Amity. "Amity Andrews, you are an extraordinary woman, and you must dare to conquer Mario just as I conquered Russia. You must make his heart rule his head. Mario will never be satisfied with half-measures in love, and neither will you. You know that, don't you, young as you are? You know there is only one man for you, and you can have what will be forever denied to me—a love that will last."

"But Mario is wed to Venice!" cried Amity despairingly. Why did the empress insist she could do things that were impossible? Amity didn't feel a bit like an extraordinary woman. She wished that Catherine would dismiss her so that she could run away and weep. But the empress had no intention of letting her off so easily. She began to pace, hands clasped behind her back. The two little dogs trotted after her, round and round, hopeful of treats.

"Amity, I'll tell you what my life has been like," said the empress, knitting her brow as she sought for words. "It's not something I've told many, but I'll tell you because your life may be somewhat like mine, if you let your true love escape you.

"I myself never had a chance to fall in love before I was married. I had been trained to value the purple; I had had a dream in which I saw three crowns on my head. Small wonder that I let myself be wed to a man who was to be the emperor of Russia. Let myself! Foolish child that I was, I abetted it. I thought I could love Peter, though he was an unimpressive man. But Peter never even gave me the chance He thought our wedding night was a joke—and it was."

"Do you mean . . ." Amity was aghast.

"He never even touched me. He set up lines of toy soldiers and played with them in the bedroom. Year after year I endured the torment of the Empress Elizabeth, his aunt, taking the blame for not producing the heir to the throne. It was my fault, no matter that Peter wouldn't do his part. At last the empress provided us with a married couple, the Exemplary Couple, we called them. *They* procreated like rabbits, and were supposed to be an example to us and instruct us on matters of sex."

"But, ma'am, I don't think . . ." Amity was blushing furiously. She had never heard such an intimate discussion before, and did not see what it had to do with her.

"Be quiet, Amity!" There was no mistaking the regal command. "You'll see in a moment how this all applies to you. You cannot imagine how tired I became of hearing of the bedroom exploits of the Exemplary Couple. But at last they fell into disrepute. The exemplary husband, you see, became exemplary with my lady-in-waiting. The exemplary wife suggested I have an affair, and I knew she wouldn't suggest such an idea on her own. It was an order from the Empress Elizabeth! I was frightened, because if things went wrong, the empress could destroy me; but I fell in love anyway, and I became a woman at last. Do you wonder that I, who am strong in so many ways, should have this weakness for men? It is a weakness that should have been the greatest of my strengths. It can be your greatest strength, Amity, this weakness of yours for Mario! You must make it so!"

Amity understood finally. She shivered and tried to warm herself with a sip of tea that had gone cold. "Even if I could win Mario, I wouldn't be good for him," she said. "He would lose his place in the Golden Book."

"Do you want to wind up in the beds of dozens of men, like me, Amity? You've met my latest, I think. He's a dear young man, and I'm fonder of him than I've been of any in a long while. But I suppose it will never work out. It will mean grief to love him."

Amity felt ill. It was as if the empress knew about her wanton enjoyment of the outlaw without even having to be told! "Perhaps you're right. But even if I tried to win him, there is another—"

"The Gypsy."

Amity's eyes widened. "You know everything."

"Yes. Where Mario is concerned. Velda will be a difficult competitor because she is ruthless. She has no morals at all.

In the beginning that will aid her, but in the end she will lose out. Your ideals are one reason why Mario loves you so. Draw the battle line, Amity. Do it at once. You may consider it an imperial order!"

Amity was dazed as she left the czarina's presence. The empress had called her an extraordinary woman. And she had been so certain of everything she had said. Could she be right? Her joy that no Russian soldiers would go to America was tempered by her chagrin that she had refused Mario's love and given him leave to bestow it elsewhere.

Elsewhere! She did not have to wonder where he had taken it. She seethed and flung a bed pillow across the room. He thought her a tramp. Well, why shouldn't he? He had seen her with the outlaw. She had not come to him a virgin. Now he thought she was Gracie's mother as well. Let him think that, too. Let him think she'd loved a hundred. He thought she was making a fool of Francesco, but Amity did not care what Mario thought. She only cared that he admit how much he loved her!

She changed from the simple gown into something low and daring and went shopping on Nevskoi Prospekt for garnet earrings and jeweled hairpins. In the evening Francesco arrived as she had expected he would, asking if she would like to go for a drive.

"I would like to go to the inn of the tziganes," she said sweetly.

He hesitated, not wanting to take her. "But you've seen that, Amity. Mario may be there."

"Exactly," she said, her chin lifted. "Will you take me, or shall I ask one of the officers of the palace guard to accompany me? There are many who'd be glad to, I'm sure."

Francesco looked horrified. "I'll take you." He sighed.

He was morose as they rode along through the endless twilight, filtered by lacy overhanging larch. It was not as bright now as when Amity had first come to St. Peterburg. The silver lamé of the sky had a lining of smoky black on which the sequined stars twinkled more strongly. Soon the White Nights would be over.

"Amity, why must you go to the inn of the tziganes?" Francesco said finally.

The unaccustomed weight of Amity's earrings made her earlobes ache, and her hand went up to rub one as she answered, "Why, I am obeying the wishes of the empress, Francesco."

"The wishes of the empress?"

"She wishes to see the moon outshine the sun."

"You wish it more yourself," he said darkly. "You love him that much."

Her eyes, colored like a rich tint of twilight, brilliant with ardor, begged him to understand. "Oh, yes, Francesco. I can't help it. The czarina made me understand how wrong it is to deny one's heart."

"Amity, you must. I am sure that Mario loves you, but he can't marry you."

"I will make him deny everything else to have me," she declared boldly, warm with courage Catherine had instilled.

"If he marries you, I will fight him for my sister's honor," said Francesco simply.

"Do you mean a duel?" Amity was horrified. "But Mario is your best friend!"

"A matter of honor has nothing to do with friendship, Amity. He would expect it. A thousand years of tradition cannot be put lightly aside, even by such as I!"

He seemed to wait for her to tell him to turn the horses and drive in some other direction, but she could not, though her success with Mario would mean that one of them might die. Two men loved her, and she, a Quaker, must be responsible for the death of one.

In the dusky inn Velda danced, her hair spiraling, the sensual movements of her body flickering like a bonfire. In the forefront of the watchers Amity saw Mario, to whom Velda addressed her every gesture. He stared unwaveringly, seeming unmoved as he quaffed his wine. Then he saw Amity. Their eyes met and locked, and his already stormy countenance glowered dangerously.

He turned his fury on her companion as he tore his gaze from her wonderfully determined face. Those purple orbs had admitted all she had denied before. That she would never be done with him, any more than he with her. "Francesco, why have you brought Amity here?"

"Why shouldn't I enjoy her company as well as you, if she's the tart you say she is?" he replied.

Mario didn't answer, but he jerked Amity by the arm and marched her toward the door. The fire in his eyes reminded her of the day when she had first met him, and having spanked her, he had warned her of lessons he had to teach her if she crossed swords with him again. A current of fear whipped about her, and almost losing heart, she wished that she had the walking stick again to beat him to protect herself.

"I told you last night to leave Francesco alone," he raged.

"You can't bear to see any other man have me," she countered. "You want me for yourself, no matter what I am."

They were both thunderstruck at her straightforwardness. And Mario was reminded again of how deeply he cared for her.

She had a way of going to the core, a maddening way of being right—at least about him! He loved her more than he had ever loved any woman; he loved her more than was good for him. In her presence, he was oblivious of everything but his enormous zeal to have her. She was a minx, a marvelous minx, and he had been glad to leave for Tsarskoye Selo at once. He had hoped that mere distance would restore his reason, but it had not.

He had been awash with impatience to see her again; she would not be purged from his memory. At night he had paced the halls, unable to sleep, and sometimes Catherine would invite him into her apartments. There he would try to talk to her about America, but everything came out Amity, Amity. How she had seemed to be innocent and was anything but. How she had claimed to be a Tory and been a fervent patriot. He had rescued her from British justice and punished her by exacting his pleasure, and had pleasured them both again and again.

Still, it had not really occurred to him that he had fallen overwhelmingly in love. Love had always been a mere pastime to Mario—as wild as a gallop on the sand or as intricate as a game of cards—but a sport, no more than that. The wise Catherine had explained his condition to him, but Mario had continued to deny it, even after his return to St. Petersburg.

But could he deny it now? He knew she had spoken the truth. All that mattered was that he have her, no matter what she was.

He had thought to have a fling with her as his mistress, but that was not enough. He wanted her in every way a man could want a woman, and because of that she was a danger to all his dreams for Venice. She was more a danger now than she had been in America, where she had almost cost him his life. Now the price was his soul!

Mario wrestled for control. Last night when he had had

her almost naked, panting with desire, he had left her to teach her a lesson. She had lied when she had said she did not want his love; now perhaps he could turn the tables by telling her that he did not want her. He dared not touch her again. He felt incapable of uttering the words that would deal the blow she had dealt him in the palace bedroom. But actions could speak as well.

Mario had only half-noticed that behind him, inside the inn, a somewhat drunken officer was claiming the attentions of the Gypsy dancer. Velda was trying to push the man away, but he, bemused with wine, placed his hand inside her well-filled calico bodice. The czarina had made a mistake in character, Mario thought absently as he turned his back on Amity and began to walk toward the dancer. The officer was the one who was to become the favorite.

The officer objected when Velda welcomed Mario, and spoiling for violence, drew a pistol. Mario knocked it out of his hand and a fight erupted. Robust tzigane men rushed to restore order, cracking champagne bottles over heads.

"Let's go, Amity," said Francesco at her side, steering her away, into the carriage. She sank back weeping, not wondering where they were going.

"Francesco, will Mario be all right?" she asked quaveringly. "Will he be hurt?" Looking back, she saw that the inn had become only a speck of light in the trees.

"For heaven's sake, Amity, won't you ever learn? How can you waste your concern on him when you have just seen what he's like? Mario can take care of himself. I've never known Mario to need help in a mere brawl. If he had needed help, I wouldn't have left him. There, that should make you laugh. I am slow to learn, like you. When we argued ideas at the university and in the salons of Venice, I loved him. Even when his family took control of my family's palazzo, I loved him—enough to pledge my sister to cement our friendship forever. We have hurt each other in a thousand ways; he's been cruel to me, too, when I stood in the path of his vision. That's what you are doing now, Amity."

"Standing in the path of his vision? Perhaps I was, but it seems I'm not anymore." The swiftness of her defeat had stunned her, shattering her faith in the wisdom of the empress. But she had forgotten that Catherine had predicted that the first battles would be won by Velda. What did that matter when Amity had no idea how to mount another attack?

Francesco had stopped the carriage in a little moonlit grove, where a latticed garden temple shone serene and invitingly empty. She let him lift her from the carriage and lead her under its shelter. The whisper of the leaves soothed her as he put his arms around her. Clustering midges wakened and called in the trees while she leaned into his gentle embrace.

"Amity," he whispered, "you could marry me. I would like you to."

She gazed up at his earnest face, wondering at the utter devotion she saw delineated in the radiance of the moon. "But, Francesco—"

"Hush, dearest. I know you care more for him than me. I know, too, that I could not register our marriage in the Golden Book, and that I would lose my place in the aristocracy—the place my family has held for hundreds of years. But the past is not as important as the future. And the present is not important, either, the present in which you long so for Mario. It's the future that counts, only the future. The future in which I will make you care for me more and more and yearn for him less and less."

"This future, would it be in Venice?"

He smiled. "It would be better elsewhere, wouldn't it? *He* would always be in Venice. You'd be reminded of him. Venice is old, and I am fascinated by the new. I was thinking of the south of Russia. We could build a house there, Amity. Now that the Crimea has been made independent, Russia can send ships through the Bosporus and the Dardanelles to the Mediterranean. It's a new world, Amity, and settlers are pouring in from all over Western Europe. No one's past counts for anything there. Not mine—not yours. I've been there and seen."

She felt loved and safe in his arms. If she married him, he would adore her forever, and surely her heart would reward that. Surely she would love him; they would build ships and cities together. Mario would follow his vision and they theirs. She would forget in time. Perhaps. But a disturbing thought occurred to her.

"There is Gracie. She is my responsibility."

"But I would adopt her, dearest. We should simply have a start on our family. Didn't I say that it is a place where the past counts for nothing?"

The words slipped easily from his lips, and she knew that he, too, thought she was Gracie's mother. But what did it matter? She might have been the child's mother, and the outlaw her father, just as Mario thought. The past would count for nothing, Francesco had said.

Amity was deeply tempted by his offer, though part of her told her it was wrong. No matter that Francesco knew her feelings and wanted to wed her anyway. No matter that she would try to overcome those feelings. She knew she would never be satisfied, as the empress had told her. Would she have the strength to deal with that lack of satisfaction? Or was her nature, unleashed first by the outlaw and then by Mario, too wild and bold to be willed into check?

"I must think about this, Francesco," she said.

"Then think," he murmured, "but make me the right answer." He kissed her, his touch lingering and sweet, making compliance with his request seem quite possible.

15

When she returned to the Winter Palace, she was surprised to find Caleb Beale wandering in the hallway near her rooms. He had such a distraught expression on his strong features that she cried out immediately to know what was the matter.

"Why, nothing," he said with an attempt at joviality. "There's good news, in fact. I've heard from the Quakers in Prussia, and they will be glad to have thee come at once. I've tickets and the necessary papers right here." He handed her an envelope. "Perhaps thee will be so kind as to deliver it to your aunt."

"Oh, but Caleb, don't you want to go in and tell her yourself?"

The Quaker shook his head. "I have been trying to knock on the door for an hour. I cannot."

Amity was amused at the sight of him brought so lovesick and low. Kings and queens might depend on him to seek enlightenment in their behalf, but he was helpless when it came to himself.

"You can't bear to part with my Aunt Zinnie, is that it, Caleb?" she asked softly.

He sighed, stared at the mosaic floor, and nodded. "I thought I was past such things, but I find I am not. When Zenobia married John, I swore I would never be tempted by a woman again. I did not count on falling in love with the same woman twice."

Wanting the tickets out of sight, Amity stuffed them into her bag. Caleb Beale was not the only one who was faced with good-byes. Her farewell to Mario was done already, accomplished wordlessly when he had turned away from her and chosen the dancer. But now it would be done irrevocably with her departure for Prussia. That could not be helped, but Zenobia and Caleb need not separate.

"Well, Caleb, if you love Aunt Zinnie, you must tell her so," said Amity. "That's simple enough."

"Oh, it's not simple at all," he cried. "Thee cannot imagine the devastation I suffered when she rejected me for John."

"You can't forgive her, after all, for falling in love with someone else?"

"Oh, that's not it. I've forgiven her, though it took many years. I was angry then as only a young man can be."

"Well, what is it, then?" asked Amity impatiently.

Caleb Beale thrust his hands into his coat pockets with such force that Amity thought the lining would rip. "It's my abominable pride," he said. "I can't bear the thought of being rejected again."

"You're a coward, Caleb," Amity accused.

"A craven coward," he admitted, the words sounding absurd coming from such a normally stalwart, self-confident man. Amity was oddly touched by the mixture of strength and vulnerability he displayed. Her aunt could do far worse than spend the rest of her life with him.

"I will talk to my aunt, Caleb," she decided. "You go and stroll on the quay. If my aunt comes to you before the clock strikes the hour, then ask what you like, pride or no."

"I do not want thee to propose the matter for me!" he declared.

"I won't," she said with a smile. "I will merely suggest what might be."

"Dear Amity!" Hope leaped to his eyes, and he pressed her hands in his before he walked purposefully away.

The weight of the envelope seemed heavy inside her bag as she went into her apartment. Zenobia was tucking covers about Gracie, who slept with a little music box tinkling in her tiny hand.

"Gracie has been up too late, Aunt," she said, feeling suddenly cross. "You should remember how prone she is to becoming ill."

"Nonsense. There's nothing wrong with Gracie, except that she's been pampered to death. This evening the empress has done the spoiling. She asked me to bring Gracie to her apartments, and spent the whole evening playing with her. She stuffed her with candy and walnut fritters, and did wonderful imitations of cats and dogs fighting. You have heard nothing, Am, until you have heard the czarina meowing and caterwauling! And the music box—that exquisite tortoiseshell piqué work is far too valuable for a child's toy. But Gracie liked it, and the empress insisted. I am worn out myself from trying to get her to sleep. It will be different among the Quakers."

"Aunt, I am not going to the Quakers," said Amity, her voice quavering.

Zenobia straightened and looked at her sharply. "Not go! What are you up to, Amity? It's Mario, I suppose."

"No. I am going to marry Francesco." The decision was made, but she did not know at exactly what moment she had made it. Perhaps at the moment she had realized that she would have to go to Prussia without Zenobia.

"That is going a long way to show Mario how little you care," said her aunt.

"Oh, don't you see? There's nothing between Silas and me, and with Mario it can never be resolved. But Francesco will adopt Gracie and adore both of us forever."

"He will adore you forever, and you will always be in love with his best friend!"

"It's the best I can do. Please give me your blessing," she pleaded.

Tears sprang to Zenobia's eyes. "If you are determined, then. I shudder to think what your father would have said. I will miss you; God only knows when we may meet again."

They clung to each other, and Amity remembered Caleb Beale. How much of her decision to marry Francesco had been a sacrifice—to keep Zenobia from feeling guilty over deserting her for her own love?

She brushed the thought quickly away and said brightly, "Aunt, there is no reason for you to go to Prussia, either."

"No reason!" Zenobia's voice was hesitant. She knew what Amity meant.

"You should go where your heart leads—go for a walk on

the quay." Amity led Zenobia to the window and pointed out the figure of Caleb Beale leaning against the dike. He was barely discernible in the cadmium glow of the streetlamps, and he seemed out-of-place by himself, when all that was left on the street were couples twined in gentle, shadowed poses, like pairs of flowers in a seaside garden. A breeze wafted in through the open window, warm and weighted with the aroma of salt.

"Oh, Am," sighed her aunt, "you are so young. You see romance everywhere."

"I see it where it is. He loves you. You have only to go to him."

"But it would be shameless after what I did to him!"

Amity suddenly felt herself older and wiser than her aunt. "It's a fine kettle of fish. He is too proud to say he cares, and you are too ashamed. You're a pair of fools, but at least you might go and say good-bye."

Zenobia had not taken her eyes off Caleb Beale. "I might do that," she said, her voice an eager whisper, fraught with new realization of possibility.

"Go quickly, then. He's waiting for you. But only until the clock strikes the hour."

Amity watched from the window until she saw Zenobia emerge from the shadows and hurry across to the quay, her light satin cloak rippling behind from the briskness of her pace. Zenobia's form met Caleb's, and for an instant they stood silhouetted, face to face against the shimmering lilac sky and water. Then the two dark forms melded. Amity did not think they were saying good-bye. In the spell of the Russian night, innocence and youth seemed recaptured, and Amity sighed, wistfully happy with the strange turn of fate that had brought Caleb and Zenobia full circle, two hearts returned inevitably to each other.

A knock interrupted her reverie. She opened the door smiling, expecting perhaps an overeager Francesco come to plead his case further. Instead a member of the Chevalier Guard clicked his heels as he made a bow and delivered a message bearing the seal of the empress.

"I must see you at once," it said tersely. It was not an invitation or request, but a command.

Catherine, Empress of All the Russias, was angry. The force of her displeasure permeated the room like the vapors of a fumarole. The hour was so late that she was wearing a nightgown and wrapper, and her hair flowed about her shoulders as she paced, like a lioness stalking the fragile French chairs of the drawing room.

"Sit down, Amity," said the empress.

Amity sat, trembling in spite of herself like the czarina's pug, which, sensing its mistress's ill temper, hid beneath Amity's chair.

"What's wrong, ma'am?" Amity dared to ask softly.

Catherine stopped pacing, as if surprised that Amity spoke to her in such a calm, familiar way.

"When one rules, Amity, one can trust almost no one. I can trust Caleb Beale, and I think I can trust you."

"I am honored—"

"Hush and listen. I have heard that you were at the inn of the tziganes this evening."

She flushed, remembering the humiliation Mario had dealt her there. "I did go—to find Mario."

"What happened, Amity?"

She hesitated, searching for words. "He . . . did not want me there. He did not want me at all."

Catherine waved an impatient hand. "I am not interested in that."

"Then what . . . ?" Amity was bewildered and becoming more so by the instant.

"The captain from the Chevalier Guards, Amity. The one I told you was special. Was he there?"

Understanding crashed over her as she remembered the captain's drunken overtures toward Velda. Francesco had told her how possessive the czarina was, how she demanded to own her lovers, body and soul. She knew that her face must already have betrayed the answer, and she wondered what punishment the truth would bring the lusty young soldier.

"He had had too much of the wine and the rye beer, ma'am. You shouldn't be too harsh with him."

"Oh, Amity!" The czarina covered her face with her hands, and to Amity's amazement, began to weep. "I won't be harsh with him. I can't. He deserves my reprimand, but he's beyond it. He was such a dear boy. He sat a horse so beautifully, and I loved his smile. I had only to call when I was restless at night. What a comfort he was!"

"Then you'll forgive him?" said Amity, feeling a chill.

"Forgive *him*. Perhaps. But not his murderers. He's dead. Dead, my lovely boy! Tell me who killed him, Amity. You were there."

"But I did not see—"

"He fought with Mario," the empress accused.

"Yes, but without pistols or swords."

"Come, Amity, come!" The czarina was impatient now. "Why do you protect Mario? Isn't it true that he and my captain fought over the dancer, Velda? He spurned you for her?"

"Yes, but Velda did not want the captain's attentions. And when he would not desist, the Gypsies were quick to join the fray."

The czarina sat down and looked intently at Amity. "I cannot quite believe this, Amity, though I suppose I should have expected it. I depended on you to give me an unbiased version, and you have surpassed all I imagined you would say. You defend them both. Him and her. Mario and the woman who is determined to take him from you."

"I have no more claim to him than she. We are both of us wronging a girl who is in a convent and cannot defend her rights at all."

The czarina drew a deep breath. "I do not want to hear of the problems of little Giovanna, Amity. My sweet captain is dead, and I have not been so fond of any in a long while. I must punish someone, and I am not satisfied to deal retribution to Gypsies."

"Not to Mario!" Amity gasped, her stomach convulsing.

"Oh, you do love him, don't you? Nothing would dissuade you. I don't blame you. I knew it before. It's Velda we must deal with. She dallied with your lover and mine, but she has played into our hands. This afternoon she had the victory; tomorrow you'll have the final one. You and I, Amity! You for Mario and I for my captain. How shall we deal with her?"

Amity thought quickly. Revenge would be sweet, though Velda had commited no crime. "Velda is a member of the ballet in Moscow. Send her back and let them deal with her for running away. She would hate going back, and she would not be in St. Petersburg to bother us anymore."

The czarina frowned. The suggestion did not meet with her approval. "You haven't the knack for this at all. I will have her imprisoned in the fortress."

Amity shuddered as she thought of the somber blue-black mass that rose from the center of the Neva. Within its grim confines many a prisoner died without benefit of a hangman. Disease and suicide took their toll.

"For how long?" she asked.

"If her spirit breaks easily, it will not be long, but if she seems strong of spirit, longer, until she is not quite so beautiful. A year or so in the fortress, and my officers will not find her so enticing."

"Oh, ma'am, please don't! It's too cruel."

"Cruel? Some might think it that. But it's only practical. No good can come from Velda."

Amity was forced to admit it, for the czarina's mind was as keen as her passions were strong, and she made Amity entertain thoughts alien to those of the Friends. She tried again to convince the czarina, but her arguments failed to sway the tempermental empress. It was a job for Caleb Beale, Amity thought, as the empress, in somewhat of a pique, dismissed her.

Caleb Beale had had years of experience in such matters. Quiet words from him had turned whole armies aside. She herself was only a younger woman, without Caleb's powers. But where would she find him?

Reaching her apartment, she gazed down at the quay where she had last seen him and Zenobia. The space was deserted now. The oxydized silver of the river was glazed with the last glimmering of the luminous sky, and only one calèche stood by the curbing, most likely sheltering a pair of occupants too reluctant to surrender the ecstasy of the night.

There would be no help from Caleb tonight, she thought, wandering through the bedrooms to check on Gracie, and noting that the bed in the alcove of her aunt's room was empty. Amity was not certain she was sorry that Caleb could not be enlisted to come to Velda's aid. She was only human, and she could not help being a little glad that the arrogant dancer would no longer have access to Mario. She felt all at once exhausted as she began to undress for bed. Tomorrow she would tell Francesco she would marry him, and enjoy the pleasure her answer gave him.

She had her bodice half-undone when a shadow moved among the pilasters. She clutched at her clothing and called out in fright, "Who's there?"

For a moment nothing happened. She thought she had imagined it. She must have seen tree leaves fluttering outside the window. And then a figure detached itself from the murk and stood boldly in the light of the globe lamp.

"Velda," whispered Amity, astonished. The dancer still wore the gaudy calico dress in which she had performed her lascivious rituals at the inn of the tziganes. Her head lifted proudly on the slender stem of her neck and she met Amity's scrutiny.

"I've come to ask you to help me, Amity," Velda said.

"Help you!"

The dancer blew an impatient breath. "Don't pretend you don't know about the trouble I am in. Soldiers came to the inn to arrest me, but I slipped away. I'll be sent to the fortress if I'm caught."

"How did you get in here?"

Velda shrugged disdainfully. "I have *some* friends among the palace guards."

"Of course. I should have known. But why? Why did you come here, of all places? I can do nothing to help you. I've already spoken to the empress, and it hasn't changed her mind. I don't see, anyway, why the moon should help the sun!"

Velda almost smirked. "You hate me, but you're a Quaker, like Caleb Beale. You *will* help me. You'll hide me here, and you'll find a way."

Amity grew hot with fury. "I'm not a Quaker any longer! Do you expect to buy my help with the money men throw at your feet? I wouldn't touch it. The empress is right. The captain wouldn't be dead if it weren't for you. Better you should be in prison for a while, where you'll harm no one."

Velda was not cowed in the slightest. She put her hands on her hips and laughed. "You have much to learn, little moon! It's not my fault that the captain is dead. He's the victim of his own ruttish desires. A woman is not to blame for being desirable. The wonder is that Mario ever looked twice at the likes of you!"

"Perhaps he preferred a softer light. One that did not blind him with its tawdry blaze."

Velda flashed white teeth in a malicious smile. "Ah, well spoken, little moon! Someday you will be a sun yourself, I think."

"I will never be like you."

"Oh, don't be so sure! We both love the same man. Perhaps we're sisters down deep. I display myself like a Gypsy, but I am really a ballerina, well-educated in art and literature in the salons of Moscow. You, on the other hand, pretend to be a lady, but you have the soul of a Gypsy, and nothing is so natural to you as to be on your back with your knees parted beneath the man who owns your heart."

Amity reached for a tasseled bell rope. "I am going to ring

and tell the guards you are here. Run before they come, Velda. That's all the chance I'll give you!"

Velda's green eyes flickered. "Pull it, if you must. You follow your heart, and I'll follow mine. We cannot help it if the road is the same. I will endure the fortress if you sentence me to it, but I will never stop loving Mario."

Amity searched the dancer's face, and for all that she did not like Velda, she saw that her meaning was true. Velda could be spirited away to prison, and Mario would never know where she had gone. But that would not change Velda's love for Mario or the fact that he had chosen the dancer at the inn of the tziganes.

Velda laughed, seeing the change in Amity's attitude. "I knew it," she said. "You are a Quaker, Amity. It doesn't matter that you don't speak like one or wear the clothes. You will always be dogged by it."

The battle raging inside Amity subsided, superseded by resignation. Velda was right. She could not send the dancer to a fate that would likely mean her death. She reached into her bag and drew out one set of passage papers. "I am not going to use these now, so you may take them. I was going to a Friends meeting in Prussia, but I've decided to marry Francesco. Board the ship tonight; it will sail at dawn."

Velda took the envelope and tucked it into her bodice with a grimace of distaste. "I would almost rather go to prison."

"Hurry." Amity was eager to get rid of her, now that the decision had been made.

"You've given up easily, little moon; I wish you happiness with Francesco," the dancer taunted, and with a swish of calico skirts, she was gone.

Amity went sensibly to bed, but turbulent thoughts assaulted her rest. Had she done the right thing? What would Caleb Beale have done? She thought of the morrow, when she would let Francesco claim her, and she wondered just what she had unleashed on the unsuspecting Friends in the person of the Gypsy.

16

Amity did not think that she had slept at all, but someone was shaking her. She had been dreaming of the outlaw, as she often did when she was upset, and instinctively she fought the strong masculine hands on her bare shoulders.

"Amity. Thee must wake up!"

She moaned and looked up into the anxious eyes of Caleb Beale. What on earth was he doing in her bedroom?

"Caleb, what's wrong? Is it my aunt?" But Zenobia was standing behind him, in an attitude of apprehension that sent alarm careening down Amity's spine. "What is it? What's happened?"

"You are the one who must tell us what's happened. Amity," said her aunt. "That dancer has escaped, and the czarina is in a frenzy. A guard told her that Velda came here."

The last vestige of sleep fled from Amity's mind as she remembered Velda's visit. "She did come here. The empress was going to imprison her in the fortress. Catherine told me so herself."

"What did thee do?" Caleb demanded.

"She had done nothing to deserve prison, so I gave her my passage to Prussia." Beyond the window Amity saw the tints of rose in the pale summer sky. "I suppose the ship has sailed."

"It's done, then," Caleb said. "The empress already suspects you helped Velda. She'll be throwing you into the fortress instead of Velda unless we get you out of here."

Amity leaped out of bed, clutching the covers. "She knew. She knew this would happen, didn't she, Caleb?"

"I imagine she did. Velda's no fool. She knows the passions of rulers as you do not. She's lived most of her life at the fringe of nobility."

"She knew it was her or me!"

"Oh, Caleb!" said Zenobia. Amity's usually calm and competent aunt was beside herself.

"Get her dressed and pack her clothes, Zinnie. I will be back in fifteen minutes."

Zenobia seemed to regain herself, given a purpose, and yanked Amity's nightgown over her head when he had departed. Then she began to dress her in a gown with puckered round cuffs tied with bunches of ribbons and petticoats of dove pearl beneath the scalloped overskirt.

"Aunt, I'm not going to a party! Oh, I don't even know *where* I am going!"

"It never hurts to look pretty, Am. There are times when it helps," said her aunt, practical as always. "Give me your bag. I'll put money in it."

Dresses, caps, nightgowns, and shoes flew into portmaneaus. Then the rap at the door. Amity stepped into the shadows while Zenobia answered. Without a word Caleb lifted her luggage and beckoned her to follow, leading the way through the dusky labyrinth of palace halls, checking for servants wandering in adjoining corridors. Amity was grateful for the Russian habit of sleeping the morning away as they came to a little-used gateway and exited.

In the square a diligence sat unattended, hitched to smoothly muscled chestnut horses. Caleb opened the door and pushed her inside.

"Lie on the floor, Amity. Don't show yourself."

She felt the coach sway as someone mounted the driver's seat. Who was he? Who dared to cross the czarina and risk his life to save her? Caleb must have paid him well. But perhaps the money was not enough. Maybe he would betray her to the czarina in hopes of a reward. Or murder her for the money in her bag.

They traveled for hours as the sun grew brighter, rich with a quality she had not seen for some time, and she knew that they had left the mists and fogs of the gulf behind. Pungent whiffs of evergreen suggested that they were traveling through the forests of pine and fir beyond the city. But where was she going? And with whom?

A chill in the air told of the end of summer, though it was only mid-July, and sitting up, she saw that the white birches along the road were beginning to have leaves like golden coins. Here and there the carriage dashed past a little roadside shrine with figures of the Panagia, or the All Holy Virgin, but the driver never paused, never ceased to crack the whip and shout at the animals for greater speed. Had the driver been a peasant, surely he would have stopped at least once for devotions to ensure the success of such a hazardous journey. If only she had asked Caleb. But why hadn't he told her?

They slowed almost as little for the villages they began to pass, little log houses built along both sides of the road. The better ones were squared, with gables toward the street and projecting roofs. The drearier cabins were unrelieved by gardens or shrubbery and had no more than one or two small holes for windows, with rude wood carvings for decoration.

Amity's stomach rumbled, reminding her that she had not had any breakfast; and although that meal was often not served until nearly noon, it was past even that time now. Then suddenly she smelled smoke, not the sweet smoke of wood fires, but something acrid and smoldering. The carriage slowed and came to a halt so abruptly that she was thrown to the floor.

The driver's feet hit the ground, and she heard him curse. "The carriage is catching fire! Get out!"

With a scream she pushed open the door and tumbled to the ground just in time to receive a splashing from a bucket which he had aimed at the rear wheels. The beautiful dress that Zenobia had put on her because it never hurt to look pretty was ruined. Beads of water refracted into rainbows on her lashes as she sought to make out the driver who had so rudely drenched her and without so much as an apology had raced to fill the bucket again.

Mario da Riva, in a traveling cap with a round crown and turned-up brim, lost hold on the bucket and nearly splattered her again as he registered her presence.

She was astounded to see him, but he was obviously even more surprised to find *her* in the carriage. He hesitated in his endeavor, his attention jolted back to the matter at hand by a yell from a short, ugly Russian in a sheepskin jacket who leaned against the black-and-white column marking the post-house.

Mario doused the smoking wheels with two more buckets of water while she stood agape, watching. Then, inspecting the damage, he drew a breath of relief. "It's nothing that a good greasing won't fix. We'd have had a miserable time of it getting a new wheel out here. I've heard tales of carriages burning to a cinder on this road."

"No thanks to you it didn't," she stormed, all in a dither at finding herself so intimately in his company. But for the leering peasant, they might have been the last two people in the world. "You drove like a madman."

"I was told it was necessary," he said witheringly. "I was told I was saving a woman from the czarina's wrath. I thought I was risking my own neck as well, and here it is only you. Please explain yourself, Amity!"

She realized with a sinking heart that *he* had already explained *himself*. Caleb had not told him in so many words that she was in the carriage. Caleb had thought it better to let him think the passenger was someone else—someone he would more likely agree to help. Mario had thought that it was Velda he was saving.

"Your gypsy has escaped already, Mario," she said. "I took care of that myself, and the czarina is furious. I'm sorry to have deprived you of her company, but you are stuck with me. I do need saving."

"You helped Velda?" he said dazedly. Just when he thought he understood her, she confused him again. "What will I do with you, Amity?

"What would you have done with Velda?" she challenged.

He sighed and cast his eyes skyward. "I would have left her with a Gypsy caravan somewhere. But I can't do that with you. I don't know what I'll do with *you*. You had better change those wet clothes. There's a shack in back for privacy, but if you try that pine grove over there, you'll find the smell is better."

She took her valise from the carriage, hoping he would offer to carry it, as a gentleman should; but Mario only lolled against the door, keeping a wary eye on the peasant as she toiled up a little knoll.

A pleasant breeze teased her naked skin as she hung her ruined gown on a pine bough and chose another. He had been right about the pungent aroma of the pine needles. Amity's mood improved. He could not help but see her dress where she had hung it like a flag to proclaim her state of unclothed vulnerability.

He would be less than human if he did not dwell now on the wonders of her body, as he had seen them so often. She began to feel quite joyous that she had followed her Quaker principles and helped Velda escape from St. Petersburg. The empress had been right, oddly enough, when she had said that although Velda would win the first battles, Amity would win at last because she was burdened with ideals.

She remembered how the dancer had smirked with the assurance that Amity would prevent her from being sent to the fortress. But Velda had outsmarted herself. Had Amity not done as she had, Velda would be here at this minute with him.

But how could she let herself love him? How could she be so shameless, when he so clearly would have preferred Velda to be in the carriage? In such a confused state of mind, she chose a simple India muslin gown and made her way back to the posthouse.

In her absence he had ordered a meal, the hearty standard breakfast fare of any Russian *traktir*. There was sterlet and salted cucumbers, fresh fruit and a bottle of white Bessarabian wine. Fortified by the food, she asked audaciously, "Well, have you decided yet?"

"Decided what?"

"What to do with me," she said sarcastically. "Will you take me to the interior and make me your love slave? Shall you deal with me as you did when you rescued me from the British? Punish me for the trouble I've put you to?"

Instantly she knew she had gone too far, as flints within his eyes struck amber sparks. He could not help remembering the ecstasy of taking her the first time, but she could not tell whether the memory had made him more passionate or merely more angry. Without answering, he went out and checked the fastenings of the newly greased wheels. She followed haplessly, and as he handed her inside he gave her his scathing reply.

"Make you my love slave? I will not do that, Amity. You have made it plain that you don't want my love."

She knew she had done nothing of the kind. Oh, she had flaunted herself with Francesco, and she had objected to his advances on the night of the czarina's ball, but he had not made it plain that she didn't love him. Indeed it had been plain that she did love him. When he had left her half-naked on the big bed in the Winter Palace, he had been entirely aware of her humiliating need.

She spent the rest of the afternoon in frustration, scarcely noticing the scenery that ran past. About eight versts from St. Peterburg, they reached the ancient city of Novgorod with its moldering walls and ruined churches with steeples that bore the cross unaccompanied by the crescent, proudly proclaiming that the Tatars had never conquered it.

Once they passed a caravan of wagons driven by unsavory teamsters with large sand-colored mustaches and beards, half of the drivers, the relief, snoring atop loads of tallow and hemp bound for St. Petersburg. Later they met a procession of a finer sort—a noble with four carriages, returning from some estate in the country, the corpulent gentlemen surrounded by pillows and cushions in the rear seat of the first stately, cumbrous vehicle, followed by another with his wife and child. The third carried the nanny, and the fourth, bedding and cooking utensils and servants.

Mario stopped at another posthouse and acquired fresh horses and supplies, but his demeanor was so stern that she dared do nothing but follow his orders as submissively as though she had really been a slave. Toward evening, stars began to shine, and now and then bivouac fires glimmered, where travelers had stopped away from the road to camp for the night.

Why didn't Mario stop, too? Perhaps he didn't intend to stop at all, but to keep driving all night, through the perilous darkness, less perilous than the temptations that would wait for them in their camp beneath the fir trees.

Finally the weary horses forced him to stop their headlong flight—a flight as much from love as from the empress. He set her to gathering wood by the glow of a lantern, and soon he had started a fire, its warmth welcome in the growing coolness of the night. Water was set to boil for tea, and sausage to roasting, impaled on a stick. Amity sighed, reminded of another campfire where tea had boiled and sausage had lured her with it's peppery aroma. She had been running away even then, when the outlaw with his breakfast fire and his evil magnetism had given her the first hint of the power it was possible for a man to have over her.

Mario looked at her sharply, as though to see if her sigh had been meant to convey longing for the sweetness both of them so desired. She glanced away from him quickly and bit into a sausage so hot it burned her tongue. At last his unguarded gaze told her that he wanted her, just as he had wanted her on the voyage to St. Petersburg. Amid the velvety pillows of the forest night, she was overwhelmed by the yearning to be at peace with him. The fiery Velda and the innocent Giovanna, the two women who stood between him and her, were far away. Tonight surely was hers!

"Mario, I have never thanked you for not urging the czarina to allow her mercenaries in America," she said.

"There's no need to thank me," he said. "I saw a spirit I liked in America. It reminded me somewhat of the way the new settlers seem in the south. You'll see—by the time we reach Kiev, we'll be on the frontier. Maybe it's how things should be when a land is new and without tradition to guide it."

"I was so angry, Mario, but I should have known I could trust you to be just."

"Ah, Amity," he said tenderly, "I wouldn't know you if you weren't angry with me." He moved closer and arranged a blanket around her shoulders to protect her from the cool air. The wind had grown stronger, but it seemed to Mario that the trees hummed with the intensity of his swelling need for her.

In truth, he had been upset to find her instead of Velda in the carriage. It would have hurt nothing for him to indulge himself with the dancer. This was different, though he thought her as wanton as the Gypsy. He was a wise man, wise enough to know she was his nemesis, but not wise enough to know that that nemesis could not be avoided.

She leaned against him now, her eyes closed, and her artless expression told him he had but to touch her to be lost in the wonder for which the twinkling stars intended them. He drew back, recovering himself on the very brink. "I've decided what to do with you, Amity," he said.

"What?" she murmured, half daring to hope in the expectant night.

"Why, you can go to Quakers after all. There are a few coming to settle, and if we cannot find Quakers, we are certain to find Moravians. Everyone goes through Kiev at one time or another. I'll find a group for you there." He sat back and rested his hands on his knees with satisfaction, as though something had been settled.

It was not the sort of solution that Amity had had in mind. Her enormous disappointment made her realize that her chance to regain the old contentment had passed forever. The simple life could not satisfy her now. She lay awake staring at the sky, angry with Mario again. For the first time that day she thought of Francesco, whom she had planned to marry. But how would she ever find Francesco again? Mario certainly wouldn't help her.

Gradually the forest gave way to sweeping plains as they reached the steppe. The road, often no more than a track of flattened grasses, stretched mile after monotonous mile. Sometimes there were white-washed cottages and rippling wheat fields, the beginning of what Catherine envisioned would one day draw shipping to the Black Sea from all over Europe. Perhaps twice a day they passed a peasant in a cart or astride a droghi made of a beam across two axles.

Once Mario stopped at a farm to bargain for a horse, paying dearly for an animal that was smaller and shaggier than the one they had, which had developed a sore foot. The farmer's wife invited Amity in and tried to talk to her, her eyes filling with tears when they had no language in common. Nevertheless they communicated. The farmer's wife thought Mario was Amity's husband and indicated her approval with smiles. Then she took Amity out beneath a little willow tree and showed her the graves of her two babies, one grave only four months old. Then she tapped her stomach to say that she was already pregnant again. Perhaps she had had no one of her sex with whom to share her grief, isolated out here, and for the space of time that the men bargained, drinking frothy rye beer, the women shared a friendship. Then the farmer's wife patted Amity's cheek, and murmuring wishes of good luck, stood looking long after them as they drove away.

As the woman's form vanished against the horizon, Amity knew she could never stand to live such a life. Mario must not abandon her somewhere on this prairie! Once she had looked forward to catching the first glimpse of a house or a tiny village of peasant huts clustered among poplar trees, but now each windmill against the cerulean sky meant he might find someone of her faith with whom to leave her, and she was happier when it seemed that he and she were the only man and woman alive in this eternity of land.

They fell into a gentle comradeship. It was enough to be together in this peaceful country—to stop by the way to pick sunflower seeds from their tall stalks, or, having crossed a marsh covered with anemones, wild roses, and floating islands of orris and lilies, to refresh themselves by wading into the river for a cooling drink.

Sometimes they talked endlessly of matters they would never have thought of discussing in Philadelphia or St. Petersburg. She described her girlhood so clearly he could almost smell the wild onions in the meadows of Bucks County. He told her of his adventures in London and Paris, and of the time as a small child he had been determined to captain his own ship, and having appropriated a dinghy, had nearly drowned in the lagoon.

Other times they rode silently for hours. And she could feel her desperate love burgeoning, just as it seemed that you could hear the grass growing as the wind rushed over it. At night, when the campfire burned low, nothing could help her. She railed at the idea that had Velda been in her place *she* would not have lain alone in her blankets. Did he hate her for her conquest of Francesco? Or was he more disillusioned with her because he believed that she was Gracie's mother and the outlaw her father?

Once when she had found he was engaged to Giovanna, she had shown him her indignation at the idea of being merely his mistress—could that be it? Did he respect her scruples? Scruples long since made obsolete by the vacant steppe? But that could not be the cause of his neglect, since the dancer's aims were no different from those the czarina had urged Amity to adopt—to win Mario's heart and cause it to rule his head.

One day they passed a train of covered wagons driven by oxen, heading east, and shortly after that they came to a Gypsy encampment of a dozen white square tents where iron pots were suspended over fires. They stopped to buy bread and vegetables among the Gypsies, dressed in coarse cloth or sheepskin like any poor Russians, but with flair in the kerchiefs tied about their heads like turbans. An old crone, dry and withered as prairie dust, offered to tell Mario's fortune. Her ancient eyes gleamed as she stared into his palm and unleashed her prophecy. Amity, who had acquired a smattering of Russian, caught the word for marriage and demanded a translation from a laughing Mario.

"Oh, she says that I am to be married soon, but she cannot see the face of my bride unless I give her another kopeck." Seeing her pained expression, he was suddenly somber himself, irritatedly stuffing his purchases into the carriage.

"What she says is true, isn't it?" she cried. "You're going to marry soon."

"Yes. I am supposed to return to Venice in the fall to marry Giovanna. She will be fifteen then, and old enough."

"Old enough! Fifteen is a mere child," said Amity. She had been sixteen when she had run away to follow Silas, but the year made all the difference, she felt.

He grinned in spite of his ill temper. "Girls grow up quickly in Venice, Amity. You, of course, are an antique of eighteen. Go and let the Gypsy tell *your* fortune. Maybe she'll tell you something to make you smile."

Tears sprang to her eyes. "There is nothing the Gypsy could tell me to make me happy, when you are going to marry Giovanna in the fall!" She jumped back into the carriage and would not speak to him, even in the evening when they stopped to cook and he tried to tempt her with a piece of walnut cake he had got from the Gypsies.

They were coming to the end of the journey. At sunset Kiev burst upon their senses, the ancient Russian capital enthroned on the crest of hills, thrown up from the wild plain in a magnificent freak of nature.

"Oh, Mario, it's beautiful," she cried, quite forgetting that here she would part from him.

"The Jerusalem of the north, Amity," he told her. "The saints are buried in catacombs nearby, and pilgrims travel hundreds of miles to visit."

Convents and churches crowned the summits of the hills and hung from the green slopes. Domes and spires, crescents and crosses gilded with gold gleamed in the western sun while they traveled the long wooden road leading into the city.

Cossack soldiers in the streets made Amity clutch Mario in alarm, but he was quick to reassure her. "There's a garrison here, but don't worry. The czarina's anger won't reach this far. They know nothing of your troubles in Kiev."

"Are you certain, Mario?" The officers with their plumed hats and finer prancing horses seemed altogether too dangerous.

"Quite certain," he replied. As always, she trusted him, and relaxing a bit, she allowed him to show her the Byzantine church of St. Sophia, supposedly a replica of the great St. Sophia of Constantinople. He treated her to a meal of fried chicken cutlets and egg-noodle casserole in a little *traktir* in the Emperor's Garden, laid out like an English park, with lawns and gravel walks, arbors and summerhouses. Below its precipitous hill lay the Dnieper River, where several sloops lay at anchor on water which reflected thick forest beyond.

"Those ships were built under my direction," he told her with a trace of pride, and she noted how sleekly the hulls were formed, adrift like so many black swans at the water's edge.

Her anger with him faded to melancholy as the long Russian twilight deepened and a military band serenaded. All Kiev seemed to be taking the evening air in the garden—or perhaps all Russia. Droshkies swung past, driven by coachmen in low-crowned hats and coats with skirts that nearly swept the ground. Besides the usual peasants in touloupes of sheepskin, varnished with wear to a bituminous glaze, there were priests with black robes and long blond hair, nuns and pilgrims with trays marked with a white cross, and Tatars with high Mongolian cheekbones and shaven heads covered with cotton skullcaps. Persians and Armenians, wearing Astrakhan fezzes, strolled with majestic gait, and Tatar women in dusky veils contrasted with buxom settler women, too exhausted to remember the romance of being female.

"It's the jumping-off point for new territories," Mario said. "The city is full of travelers—people waiting for wagon trains to form or for passage down the Dnieper to the Black Sea."

She could sense the excitement in the air, and as much as excitement, anxiety—people cast up rootless, torn away from old homes and old identities. It was a world both of threat and of possibility. She felt it all in her soul, for she was no longer of any race or nationality except this universal one of dread and hope. More dread than the impossible hope that still dwelled without cause in her young heart.

Tomorrow he would find someone among these travelers who would give her sanctuary, and she would be washed with them into the vast, empty land beyond Kiev. She thought of Gracie, wondering if the child cried for her. Then, trying to comfort herself, she thought of Caleb and Zenobia and their happy love.

Nonetheless a heavy weight settled over her, and in spite of the amenities of civilization, she wished herself back on the plains again with another chance before her to make him love her. But that was over. If he had withheld his love for her where he and she had been the only man and woman beneath the horizon, he would certainly not offer it now. She drifted half asleep, her head against his shoulder, so fatigued that she hardly knew that he stroked her hair as he cradled her.

At last he nudged her and led her away. They entered a tiled lobby, and he took her upstairs to a room where leather cushions stuffed with straw lay on the floor.

"Is this a hotel, Mario?" she asked.

"The best in Kiev. We shall have a softer bed tonight than we had on the prairie."

Once she might have been angry that he had not bothered to engage separate rooms for them, but the journey across the steppe had erased the last of such modesty. She was only sorry that he saw the tears that she could no longer hide.

"Dear Amity," he whispered as he took her in his arms.

Mario was vanquished by her humiliating need as he had

never been by her wiles. His throat constricted as he held her, wanting her as he had never wanted any other. Ever since the night at the czarina's ball, he had managed to keep himself from her, denying himself the raptures of love in circumstances that would have overwhelmed the discipline of any lesser man. Even the fury he had known then had not purged him of his love for her. On the lonely steppe he had nearly succumbed a thousand times.

"You know I cannot love you." He sighed. "It is too consuming for a simple affair of the heart. I am pledged to Giovanna. And to Venice."

She heard his words, but his hands spoke more meaningfully, denying all that his lips said, as his fingers moved on the fastenings of her gown. She moaned with mindless esctasy as her breasts came into his hands. They sank together onto the cushions, his mouth seeking hers ravenously. Her body grew tense with expectation, and it seemed that her clothing could not be gone quickly enough as his familiar hardness pressed against her. Her body rose to his, welcoming him with shudders of joy. She surrendered to him abjectly, as never before, writhing with womanly triumph in capitulation that passed beyond her shame and beyond her pride. Gloriously she clasped him inside her, winding her legs about him possessing him profoundly in her subjugation. The pale Russian stars swirled close, their fire storming within her until she herself exploded into fire.

And then it was quiet. She slid toward a sweet darkness helplessly, as though in the thrall of a drug. Vaguely she knew that he held her still, caressing her, and though the force of his passion was spent, he did not remove himself, resting luxuriously in the haven of her body.

She had arrived at some ultimate state of existence, having crossed an infinite plain to reach it, as she had journeyed over the vast steppe to the golden steeples of Kiev. But as her honeyed oblivion receded, a sense of uneasiness became alarm. Opening her eyes, she found herself lying naked and alone, moonlight only enfolding her.

He was gone. For one moment she had owned him as completely as a woman could own a man. He had forgotten the gypsy. He had even forgotten his duty to Venice and Giovanna. She had made his heart rule his head as Catherine had told her to do, but now he had remembered. Suddenly she was ashamed of her reaction to his love. She had given him her all, while he had merely been telling her good-bye.

He might be making arrangements for disposing of her this very minute. Let him do as he would, but she would not be here to be handed away like a used set of clothing! But where could she go?

The answer came to her with inspiration. She could go where Velda would have gone—to the Gypsies. Yes, why not? Since she had been spoiled for the simple, virtuous Quaker life, why not live the wild, restless life of a Gypsy and smile at any man who would throw coins at her feet and soothe her hurt for a while?

She found her way down to the stable, and taking one of Mario's shaggy horses, flung herself onto it bareback. Her blond hair, tousled from love, raced behind her like moonbeams as she galloped over the tall prairie grass beyond the city. As her anger cooled, she became apprehensive. Maybe the Gypsy caravan had gone, or maybe she would not be able to find it again. She might easily lose the cart path in the night.

Then fires winked, like fireflies sprinkled on the plain. The lights came closer and she heard singing. The camp had a festive air, colorful and gay, where by day it had seemed only dirty and rude. Strings of glass beads and coral flashed over calico, as officers from the garrison at Kiev danced with dark-haired girls. Polished boots mingled with bare, unwashed feet.

Amity's arrival caused a commotion, but they remembered that she had stopped with Mario before, and the old crone who had told his fortune drew her into the circle of the campfire. Now that she had found the camp, how would she make them understand what she wanted?

Making gestures of weeping, she pointed back in the direction of the city. She saw they grasped the situation, nodding, clucking their tongues, laughing, unsurprised at the evanescence of love. They had the answers, these vagabonds. They knew that the only way to live was freely and for the moment. She would never allow her heart to bestow itself again as it had on Mario.

Taking out her bag, she showed money and indicated the wagons. The Gypsies understood the language of money as well as that of love, and before long she had arranged to have one of the vans for her private use. In the morning she washed its interior herself and shook the blankets to rid them of fleas that had annoyed her during the night. The caravan began to move, going south, farther and farther from St. Petersburg, farther from Kiev, too. She didn't know where they were headed, if indeed there was any destination. She was glad not to care where they were bound. Day followed day as Amity tried to adopt the Gypsy ways, tying her hair in a kerchief and adding ropes of cheap beads to her gowns of lawn and Indian muslin. When they stopped near farms or villages, Amity bought her own supplies from the inhabitants, cooking her meals over her own fire in the evening. At first she slept badly in the wagon, worried about the Gypsy men who roamed the camp; but no one bothered her. They seemed instead to almost scorn her, preferring the beds of their own lusty women. Her biggest concern was that her money was giving out. When it did, it would be time for her to beg and dance for her living, like the Gypsies; and the lighter her bag became, the heavier was the knot of fear inside her.

The way of life came naturally to the Gypsies. Even little girls went to beg, and they practiced the dances of their elders as they played their childish games. How could Amity ever learn as well?

One day near a little village of thatch-roofed cottages a little girl of about ten was sent to beg; and when she returned with milk and cheese, she found Amity under the shade of a willow. She giggled, opening her palm and showing Amity coins.

"Where did you get those? No peasant would give you that much. No *muzhik*."

"No *muzhik*," said the girl, her eyes dancing. She put on a little show, putting her chin in the air, gesturing at a fine make-believe hat, prancing to indicate a fine horse.

"A gentleman was there. How lucky." Amity smiled her understanding. The girl nodded and pointed at Amity. Suddenly Amity was alarmed.

"He asked about me?" she said.

"*Da.*"

"Did you tell him that I was here?"

"*Nyet.*" The wily Gypsy grinned, and Amity realized that she was awaiting her reward. Already she had the secretive ways of her kind that made the Gypsy camps good hideaways for fugitives. Amity's purse grew a bit lighter as she added a coin to the girl's hoard, and her heart saddened.

Her first thought had been that the man had been some emissary from the czarina, sent to apprehend her, but her heart had quickly dismissed the idea and decided the man had been Mario.

He had not found her, and unhappily, she had accomplished the goal she had set for herself. She was as lost and aimless as the wind.

By afternoon, black clouds had begun to build on the horizon, one round, ominous protuberance atop another like a wall of dark lava stone. They made camp early, but supper was hardly finished before lightning split the sky in golden rivers, and chilling air whipped the grasses flat. Amity took refuge in her wagon, wrapping an unclean sheepskin about her shoulders. She almost wished she had not insisted on buying privacy with her money. Even the company of smelly, unwashed persons would be welcome tonight. In the storm the wagon jolted as though a team of horses were pulling it down the road at a gallop. Hail pummeled the canvas roof, which she pulled tight all around to keep out the weather. After the hail came rain, blowing through in a spray. The lightning penetrated, too, illuminating the wagon starkly, followed by crashings and darkness where spots of red and blue danced before her eyes.

It had rained for hours when she heard footsteps outside her wagon. Who would be abroad in such weather? One of the gypsy men, bent on having her after all?

The curtain of the wagon lifted, and Mario brought the tempest inside with him, not only the cold water dripping from his surtout, but in the fury of his eyes, flashing and leaping amid the fierce thunderclouds of his face. "What are you doing in this place, Amity?" he demanded.

She bristled, shivering from the cold, from excitement, and from fear. "I am doing what is natural for me, as you should know, sir! I'm that sort of woman, like your Gypsy dancer."

Pride sustained her, she clung to it wildly, hoping it would not desert her as it had in the hotel in Kiev. The little beggar girl had been cleverer than Amity had guessed, betraying her to Mario and lying that she had not, to receive another gift of money.

"This will never do! You can't stay here!" Mario declared.

"Have you another suggestion?" she taunted. "Shall I wear the Quaker slamkin again, after you have made me as I am? I cannot!"

"I did not make you the way you are!" he boomed with new rage. "That was not my privilege. You were far from innocent when we met!"

Amity blushed, unable to deny it. "Why did you follow me?"

She sensed the torment that boiled inside him. "I don't know," he said. "Nothing good will come of it."

Then, with a soft exclamation that seemed wrenched from the core of his being, he seized her and flung her over his shoulder. She was so startled that she offered no resistance as he climbed down from the wagon with her, and setting her on his horse, mounted behind her.

Remembering she should struggle, she did so, but only for form. She would willingly go to heaven or hell, so long as Mario took her. Wherever he took her, it would not be out of the terrible bondage of her love.

The black wind spun his words away. "We will both live to regret this night, Amity. But it cannot be helped! It cannot be helped!"

17

They rode all night, at first galloping headlong across the plain, the prairie wind behind them seeming to push them with an eager hand to whatever doom he intended. The heavens unsheathed swords of lightning, plunging them into the distant earth with roars of angry foreboding, as he drove the mare, heedless of anything but his desire to reach his mysterious destination.

On and on they went, though he should have stopped to find shelter and rest the animal. They slowed to a trot before the pale sun appeared, and the drowned grasses sparkled. They reached the Dnieper again, far south of Kiev, and Mario paused to let the horse drink in the stream.

"Tell me where we are going, Mario," she pleaded.

"You will see, Amity," he said gruffly.

Before long they passed wheat fields, tall and brown in the sun. At the end of another mile a country house rose on the horizon, lime trees waving against the sky. Even from a distance she saw it was the house of a gentleman, far grander than the little whitewashed cottages of the villages. As they rode closer, she saw that it was built of brick, with a flight of steps in front and a zinc roof flanked by a conical turret.

Wild oats and thistle grew in the dooryard, and an orchard led from the house to the pond near the road, where insects buzzed over the still water, iridescent wings shining.

"Whose house is that, Mario?" she asked.

"Why yours, love."

"Mine?" He did not answer, and the peculiar set of his mouth warned her not to say more.

Servants ran eagerly onto the porch as he reined the exhausted horse to a halt. He gave instructions, and two giggling maids took charge of Amity, hurrying her into a large hall and up a flight of stairs to a bedroom. A big tub was brought, and kettles of steaming water. The chattering girls wasted no time in removing her wet clothes and putting her into the bath. The hot water erased the chill of the storm and the grime of the Gypsy camp, but the maids did not allow her to luxuriate as long as she would have liked.

They held big towels for her and seemed to find her concern over her lack of fresh clothing amusing. Was it obvious, even to these little servant girls, that clothing was superfluous when Mario was near her? Surely they would bring her at least a domestic's simple dress and cap.

Opening a wardrobe, they took out a white gown of figured satin with a fringed silk petticoat, a pair of openwork stockings, and laylock slippers with straw-colored heels. One of the maids ran to the window and directed Amity's attention below, where a man in dark robes was climbing the steps. She glanced back at the clothing again. It was a wedding ensemble, and the man was a priest. He intended to marry her! He must have decided in Kiev and had the gown sent from there. Why, he had not even bothered to ask if she would have him! He had not bothered, either, to end his engagement to Giovanna. She had made him love her beyond honor and beyond duty, beyond all loves he had known before. She knew now how much wiser than she the Gypsy had been, knowing, as Amity had not, that an unlikely match was possible. But Amity had triumphed instead of the Gypsy. She had conquered him as the empress had urged her to do.

But while she still looked out the window, a cloud of dust appeared along the road. A horse galloping. She drew a breath of horror as she recognized its rider.

Francesco!

He had followed her all the way from St. Petersburg. He

must have known she was with Mario, guessed he would bring her here. He was the man she had been about to pledge herself to. The man who would revenge his sister with a duel in the event of her marriage to Mario.

Clutching the wedding gown against her nakedness, Amity sank onto the bed, twisting her hands together and praying for enlightenment as she had never done before, even when she had abandoned her faith to run away to Silas. She thought of her father and all the Friends of her Bucks County meeting and wished they were here to help her seek God's will. But almost as quickly as her prayers began, they ended. God's will! She cared nothing for that, she realized. She would defy any force on earth or in heaven to marry him and give vent to her unbridled love!

Atremble, she put on the white gown, and the maids fastened up the little buttons and worked on her hair. Mario might be disinherited for marrying her; the Council of Nobles might deny him permission to record their marriage in the Golden Book. She had disarranged his entire life, his ideals, his visions, and his dreams. He might lose his very life because of his love for her.

"No good can come of it," he had said last night, and now she knew what he had meant. But he had said, too, that it could not be helped, and she knew that to be the truth.

Sounds of a heated argument drifted up as she sat gripping a little bouquet of wild roses that had been picked for her to carry. A man's footsteps ran up the stairs, and she was face to face with Francesco, whom she had so recently been about to wed. His handsome face grew more anguished as he saw that she was wearing the wedding gown.

"Mario told me that you and he are to be wed," he cried. "Tell me you will not marry him!"

"I must," she said woodenly. "I love him."

"Then if you love him so, give him up and marry me instead. Marry me now. The priest is waiting, and it doesn't matter to him whom he marries. Leave Mario to the life for which he's intended! I love him, too, like a brother, and I love you. But if you wed him, I must duel him. We have lost everything—but not our honor, Amity. Mario must not deal lightly with my sister!"

"Perhaps it will be you who dies, Francesco," she reminded him.

He gazed at her sadly. "Dearest Amity, do you think I wouldn't prefer it? I had sooner lose myself than my friend

. . . and you. Please, Amity! Tell him he's too late. Tell him a lie—that you were pledged to me in St. Petersburg. I've come so far! When I found you'd run away from him at Kiev, I was certain it was over between you. I paid a little gypsy girl to tell me you were with the caravan, but Mario carried you off before I could, when I lost my way in the storm. But for that, you would have been mine. You know it's true."

"It's true I would have married you, Francesco," she said in a small voice. "But I can't now. My Aunt Zenobia was right. I would always be in love with Mario."

"And you think it more right to wed Mario and sentence us to fight each other?" he asked incredulously.

"I don't know," she whispered. "But I must wed him!"

"Then think, Amity. Think what you are doing when you come before the priest!" He choked on his words and stumbled out toward the stairs.

Bloodshed, dishonor, loss of position held for almost a thousand years. All this her wedding meant, but when the maids came to lead her downstairs, she went with decision, thinking only how different her wedding would be from what she had always envisioned—with a black wedding hood and a marriage bench.

The sight of Mario in a white coat and blue satin vest, both embroidered in silver, took her breath away. She smiled up at him as he offered her his arm, her joy utter in that one instant as he acknowledged his love for her with a glance of burning adoration.

Together they walked into the little chapel of the house, where the priest stood waiting behind the altar table, set for the wedding with candles, cross, ring, and cup.

An assembly had gathered. He had invited every peasant or neighbor, and all had arrived in their best—tunics and caps for the men; for the women, silk kerchiefs and gowns of coarse linen worn with spotless white aprons.

A band of rose-colored cloth separated Amity and Mario from the altar, and Mario whispered to her, "Take care how you step on that, love. Everybody will be watching."

"Why, Mario?" she asked.

"Because whoever sets foot upon it first will rule the marriage," he said with a grin. "Shall it be you? It's true that you've ruled me far past the limits I dreamed a woman could."

She shook her head, awash with happy devotion. "I do not want to rule you, so long as I am loved."

"That shall be forever," he vowed, "past fortune and country, past life itself."

The priest beckoned, and distracted at seeing Francesco amid the crowd, she did not notice which of them trod upon the ribbon first. The ceremony was long and complicated, a Greek Orthodox ritual, the only faith represented in the area. At one point they were given candles to hold. Then they took the cross to kiss. Amity, not understanding any of it, replied as Mario told her to. A ring was put on her finger, feeling heavy and strange. She had never expected to have a wedding ring, since Quakers did not give them, but its weight rather pleased her, making the marriage seem a reality.

But even with the ring in place she was not yet his wife. There was the wine to be drunk from the chalice, called in Slavonic ritual the cup of bitterness. All the while, servants stood behind them, taking turns holding heavy crowns above the heads of the bride and groom as the ceremony progressed.

At last only one part was left. They must walk three times around the altar, followed by the crown bearers, while the priest pronounced the words that made them man and wife.

Mario gazed at her seriously now, his amber eyes boring into hers as though to see the mettle of her soul. "Three times, Amity," he said, "and we are not married until the last turn is done! Until you've taken the last step, you may change your mind, and it is as if all of it had never happened."

He took her hand to lead her. Once around, she caught Francesco's gaze, so black she could not believe he was the same gentle man she had known in St. Petersburg. Her step faltered as she thought of what must surely occur when the third turn had been made. Mario himself was obviously disturbed, his hand quivering as he urged her to walk the second round. Was it the thought of the person with whom he must duel that unnerved him more, or the thought that his opponent had right on his side?

She looked at Francesco again and was struck to the core by the grief and loss that mixed with the anger of his countenance. Even now she could put an end to this! Suddenly she thought that she would. That she must. She had been a Quaker, pledged to preserve life above all else. How precious were the lives of these two men who loved her!

She hesitated, ready to break and run, but Mario sensed her panic and pressed her hand in a steely grip. "We must face this, love," he whispered fervently. She turned her eyes to his, and lost again in her hopeless love, made the third circuit.

The peasants cheered, and men hurried forward to kiss her cheek. She was a wife! But this same day, would she be a widow?

"Mario!" Her husband turned to Francesco's voice.

"I must call you out, my friend!"

"I know," he answered. "I'm ready."

"Shall it be pistols or swords, Mario? The choice is yours."

"Swords. We are best matched at that."

The spectators adjourned into the orchard, helping themselves to rye beer from barrels set out for a wedding celebration. They had come for one show and were to have two instead. They were a noisy group, the men talking and making bets as to the outcome, the women clucking, some already beginning to wail.

"Mario," she murmured wildly. She swayed and nearly fainted, and he caught her in his arms and carried her upstairs. "Don't fight," she whispered as he laid her tenderly on the bed. If her foot had touched the ribbon first, perhaps she could sway him after all, she thought hysterically. "I am too ill, and you cannot leave me," she moaned. "Mario, it will solve nothing. He is your friend!"

He kissed her, his first kiss as her husband, a kiss with intensity enough to be remembered a lifetime. She wept as he left her, and though she thought herself too weak to move, she found herself at the window, watching as the two men walked side by side through the rich green of fruit-laden boughs to a clearing. She twisted her wedding bouquet, wondering if the wilting roses would end on her bridegroom's grave.

Then blades flashed brightly in the summer air. The sound of steel shrieking on steel reached her ears with the twitter of finches and sparrows. They were both excellent swordsmen. She closed her eyes time and again, thinking that one or the other was doomed, only to open them to see that the thrust had been parried successfully away. Nearby the dark figure of the priest waited, ready to administer the last sacrament as efficiently as he had administered the sacrament of marriage.

Then Mario miscalculated, and Francesco's blade severed the sleeve of his fine satin wedding coat. She could see their faces, each one intent and expressionless, as earnest as they must have been in childhood, playing games together. It would be easy for either to hesitate at the moment the blade must go home. She hoped it would not be Mario who hesitated.

The duel went on for what seemed hours, to the cheers and cries of the crowd. Then suddenly Francesco's sword flew from his hand, knocked away by Mario. Francesco staggered, and she saw blood spurt from a wound.

Mario stood over him, the point of his sword at his heart. "Blood has been drawn, Francesco," he said. "Are you satisfied?"

Francesco's face was dark with rage, but he answered strongly, "I am satisfied, Mario. I am glad that you were not killed, but we are friends no more."

"I wish it could be otherwise," he answered. He turned with quick stride and hurried up the steps to the house. She met him at the bedroom door, truly a happy bride now. He covered her face with kisses, and when he had kissed her lips and eyes and cheeks, he put her on the bed and removed her wedding gown to find more on which he might bestow his endless affection.

His wedding suit followed her clothes to the floor, and she gloried in touching the springy hair of his chest and in pressing her palms against the compelling muscles of his thighs. The rapture of utter possession encompassed them both on this the golden afternoon. Their lives were joined inexorably, and time after time as the hours passed, he showed her what it would be like to be husband and wife, and she laughed to think he had said that no good could come of it.

In the evening the fireflies came over the fields, and feeling ripe and mellow with love, they went out to the orchard where he had dueled. Francesco had already ridden away toward Kiev, his heart wounded more than his body. The cut had been superficial, Mario said. "He might have killed me, dearest," he told her. "He had opportunity. Francesco didn't want to kill me."

She shivered in the cooling air. "Was there a time you might have struck a death blow?"

"Perhaps. I loved him, but we'll be enemies forever, now, mark my word." He looked downcast for a moment, and she touched his hair gently.

"I'm sorry," she murmured.

He laughed, instantly in a good humor again. "There's nothing to be sorry about when I have you. Come along, I'll teach you the cossack dance!"

He took her to a circle of celebrants, where fiddles wafted vigorous notes into the breeze. Leaving her in the circle of dancers, he sprang to the center of the ring, and bowing his legs, began the *kazatchok*. Everyone applauded as he leaped and struck the ground with his boot heel again and again. Then he seized her hand, marking her as the lady of his choice, and placing his tricorne on her head in lieu of a Russian cap, he tried to show her how to dance with him.

The memories of that long afternoon and evening she would cherish forever, just as she would cherish the thought of the days that followed in the house at the edge of the Dnieper. Mario had lived here while instructing workmen in the building of ships on the river, and for miles around people thought of him as their squire.

Mornings they rode about the fields or to the village to oversee the construction of new boats. On warm afternoons they swam, unfettered by clothing in a cove of the river, and returned to their marriage bed and their love. In the evenings they sat listening to the slow, minor melodies of the sad love songs sung by peasants, ending in eerie howls that made her draw closer to his side. Once a peddler stopped, and though the merchandise was cheap, Mario showered her with gifts of embroidery and beads. The peasants seized the occasion of the peddler's visit for another party of rye beer and dancing.

Less pleasant to her was a wolf battle, when savage *muzhiks*, armed with staves, beat a litter of young wolves from a thicket of birch and alder. The cries the hunters made, imitating the wolves, reminded her what a primitive country she had made her home. When one of the hunters rose from his hiding place with torn sheepskin touloupe, muddy arms, and hairy face, she felt more frightened by the raw destruction in his eyes than if she had been confronted by one of the animals.

All in all, she was wonderfully content as the season moved to harvest. Women worked in the fields, cutting grain with graceful movements in the muted sun. Short skirts, leaving legs bare to the knee, were bright with wool embroidery, repeating patterns of wreaths and poppies and cornflowers the cutters wore on their heads. Amity had such an outfit made for herself, and when she met Mario wearing it, standing barefoot in the soft dirt road, her hair in long gold braids, each ending in a sunflower, he loved her with abandon in a fresh, sweet haymow.

She felt she could be happy forever in this place, and except for the rare instances when Mario's thoughts seemed worried and distant, she forgot that there was Venice. He had given up all that, hadn't he, marrying her?

In the evenings, cart loads of sheaves came along the roads, and purple dust of threshing rose against the saffron and cinnabar of the setting sun. Through this dust also, a postilion rode one twilight, a rare visitor from the village with the mail. In addition to a bundle of already outdated newspapers, he handed them a letter bearing the imperial seal. Reading the address, Amity saw her married name written for the first time.

"Mario," she gasped, "it's from the empress."

"Dear Amity," the message read, "So you have won and proved yourself the woman I judged you to be. The courage you showed in defying me over the Gypsy, I admired even in my anger, and since you have dealt her a punishment worse than the fortress, all is forgiven. I would be pleased to see you again in St. Petersburg."

She hugged Mario and laughed with delight, and another paper fell from the envelope. Picking it up, they found an invitation to the wedding of Zenobia Willet and Caleb Beale, the event to wait for their arrival.

"But it's too far to go back," Amity protested. "Oh, how I should love to see my aunt married."

"And you shall." He smiled at her tenderly. "No distance is too far when Catherine, Empress of All the Russias, commands."

They went back again across the plains, as light snows began to fall; but they were warm, even so, camping beneath the stars, huddling in wedded intimacy among sheepskin covers. She saw again the domes and steeples of the great capital, and tears of happiness stung her eyes as she thought of all that had happened to her since she had left, a fugitive in the bottom of a carriage.

The wedding was held in the Winter Palace, where a hall had been set as a meetinghouse, gilding, chandeliers, and columns contrasting peculiarly with the simple benches. Zenobia wore a gown of pearl-gray silk, and as she entered on Caleb's arm, she handed her black wedding hood to Amity.

Taking their places on the marriage bench, bride and

bridegroom dared to exchange smiles as they pledged themselves before a small group of Friends who had been traveling south until the empress had commanded their presence.

Then, according to Quaker custom, each person rose in turn to speak words of love and hope to the newly married couple: Amity, her eyes shining; Mario, wishing Caleb the same joy he himself had found in love; the Friends, speaking wishes of long life and happiness; and even the empress herself, admonishing them to cherish each other forever as they did this day.

The Quaker wedding was followed by a feast with music and dancing and exotic delicacies, none of which belonged in a Quaker celebration. The wedding cake was soaked in rum and rich with currants and raisins, decorated with thick, swirling icings. Tokay wine washed down jellied veal, caviar, sausages of ground lamb, flat onion bread, and swordfish on skewers.

Suddenly Amity felt dizzy and sick to her stomach.

"Why, Amity, what's wrong?" her aunt said as she reeled against a gaily festooned table.

"Oh, dear, I don't know. I feel very strange."

Zenobia took her away to bed and asked her certain questions. "Lie quiet, dear, I'll send for Mario," she said.

Amity sat up weakly. "Oh, no, don't disturb him! Let him enjoy the party, and I will be all right in a while."

"No doubt you will. But you have something to tell him. He will want to know that you are going to have a child."

She was to bear Mario's child! It seemed incredible, but she should have known.

He came in quietly and took her hands in his. She whispered her news and saw the elation in her heart mirrored in his eyes.

"Then we must go home at once, Amity, if we are to be parents," he said.

"Yes, I should like that, Mario. We must go back across the plains again to our house on the river, before the snows prevent it. But there can't be time!"

And he stunned her with his reply.

"I said home, Amity. You know what place must always be home for me. We are going to Venice."

La Serenissima

Bride of the Adriatic

———

18

Water purled and lapped against stone. Boats thudded emptily against the striped poles that moored them. Street-lamps glistened, and a breeze scented with salt darted from some arm of the ever-present sea to play around Amity's golden curls as she reclined on soft morocco cushions.

Amity intuited, rather than felt, a warmth in the breeze as the gondola skimmed through the night, graceful and silent as a black swan. "It's almost spring," she announced to her companion hopefully. "I saw a swallow today, Donna da Riva. Mario says that it's spring in Venice when the swallows come back."

"Don't be silly, child," said her mother-in-law. "It's only April, and swallows don't come until May. Ask anyone. Pregnant ladies are always trying to wish the time away. That's your problem, of course. Who can blame you? You ought to lace more tightly. You'd look better, and a woman's mood depends on how she looks." Donna da Riva patted Amity's protruding stomach with a plump hand. "You've grown quite large, you know, for such a little thing."

Amity shrank from her touch. She hadn't expected Mario's stepmother to like her, and although Donna da Riva seemed always to offer friendship, Amity had not taken to her at all.

Donna da Riva was fat, vain, and spent most of her time drinking chocolate, attending parties, and frequenting the cafés on the Piazza San Marco. She had gentlemen callers as though she were not married, and was shockingly familiar with them, stroking their hair and calling them pet names.

Donna da Riva had not taken umbrage when Amity had had the temerity to ask about such behavior. "Dear child, he's my *cicisbeo,*" she would say, "my official companion. Hasn't Mario told you about that sort of arrangement?" The next week the *cicisbeo* might be someone different, for Donna da Riva liked variety. But the *cicisbeo* need not be one of her lovers, whom she met at a little apartment called a *casino* that she kept for such assignations.

Tonight Donna da Riva wore the domino—a peculiar mask with a monster-bird beak. A hood covered her hair and fell to her shoulders, and all was crowned by a black three-cornered hat. The rest of Donna da Riva was all glitter and spangles. She looked like a huge grotesque bird crouched on the nest of the gondola. And almost all Venice looked like Donna da Riva.

It was Carnival. The costuming had begun the day after Christmas. Even servants and beggars wore masks. Since a government officer, dressed in old pantomime clothes, had officially opened the event in the piazza, all distinctions of class had been canceled by the ubiquitous mask. Every woman was a *zentildonna,* an aristocrat. Every man was a *zentildon;* and for all anyone knew, a fisherman might sit at cards with a member of the Great Council. There were stories of fortunes that had been lost just so, and some angler from Ponte Lungo might trade his humble residence for a palace.

Or perhaps the gentleman wasn't a gentleman after all, but a lady. Nobody knew, and that was the fun of it. Everybody was a secret observer. Everyone tried to guess who was who, and who was with whom. It was a fascinating game. Donna da Riva could have played it all year.

Amity had tried to get into the spirit of it, though *her* identity could hardly be concealed from anyone. She couldn't wear the domino because it made her feel faint for lack of air, and in addition to the betrayal of her gold locks, there was the growing evidence of her pregnancy. Her eye mask thus deceived no one. Still, Amity had added more than her share of spice to this Carnival season. Everywhere people marveled and whispered. She was the woman Mario da Riva had brought from America, the woman for whom he was willing to give up his inheritance and his position in the revered Golden Book.

Spies watched her. She was a foreigner, and that was reason enough to think she might be dangerous to Venice. Amity was always fueling the fires of suspicion with some unwitting remark about freedom or equality. Time and again Mario was furious with her.

"Do you want me to lie?" she cried.

"I only want you to hold your tongue," he would storm. "As my wife you are safe from the Inquisitors, but you are not helping our chances of registering our marriage in the

Golden Book. Think of our son, Amity, and do it for him, if not for me!"

Holding her tongue was unnatural to Amity's frank Quaker nature. After such an episode she would languish and protest that she didn't want to go out. But Mario would insist.

"Dear heaven, Amity, it mustn't seem that I'm ashamed of you and have you hidden away. It mustn't appear that you yourself are too much a coward to be seen! You must hold your head high and show that you have the stuff of the wife of a Venetian nobleman!"

Appearances, it seemed, were everything in Venice. She tried again and again to please him. But cutting remarks too often left her speechless, understandably so, because she had not yet completely mastered the Venetian dialect. Sometimes it was too convenient to pretend not to know the language, even when she *did* understand it. Sometimes she wore the mask in spite of its discomfort, to hide her blushes.

Some said she was a witch and had worked black magic on Mario. There was no end of lurid ideas about her. Even Donna da Riva had hinted that Amity might tell her what exotic American trick she had used in the bedroom—learned from the Indian savages, no doubt.

She had never felt so alone. It was a dark, empty sensation, a chill she constantly felt, one that could not be erased except when Mario lay beside her in the huge Florentine bed, its paneled head- and footboards looming high above the thronelike platform on which it sat.

Nothing was the same as it had been in the little house beside the Dnieper River. Nothing was the same, except that she loved him. She needed his love more intensely than she had then, needed his smiles, caresses, and assurances as well as his familiar lovemaking. Even that comfort had become awkward now, and often Mario slept in his dressing room, so she could rest more easily, he said.

Sometimes she wondered if that were only an excuse. She wondered if he found release with other women, now that she was so ungainly. Most Venetian men had mistresses, even the married ones. Mario surely had had many once. If there were not other women, would she feel so desolate?

And yet she knew there was no other woman. There was only Venice. It was the city itself that preoccupied him. What a rival she had in Venice! Now that she had seen it, she was more jealous of it than she had been before. Even through the winter, when chill, enervating fogs had enveloped the city, she had sensed the special mystery of La Serenissima, where the sea appeared at every turn, giving a feeling of endlessness, where magnificent buildings stood against nature with dignity and purpose.

But tonight the spell of Venice was light and ethereal. The gondolier lifted his voice in song, and an answering verse drifted back from some fellow in a far-off canal. A mandolin tinkled in the warm air as they passed a lighted barge of revelers. The scents of perfume and the oil of jasmine the gentlemen used on their hair mingled with the watery smell of the canal.

It was all so beautiful! But Amity felt unwell, and the sweetness made her simply want to cry. She and Donna da Riva had left Mario in a *ridotto*, playing cards. He'd offered to take her home, but his friends had all urged him to stay at the gaming house, and so had she, playing the brave wife for once. She was having disturbing little pains, of the kind that had afflicted her often during her pregnancy. It was nothing out of the ordinary, and Donna da Riva had offered to see her safely to the palace.

I wonder if Mario thinks I make up these pains so I can excuse myself, she thought. The idea went morosely through her mind, even though he had insisted that she consult the doctor time after time. *I wish Aunt Zenobia were here instead of Donna da Riva.* But Aunt Zenobia was far away in St. Petersburg. Everyone was so far away! Her father was dead, and so was Grace. Gracie had stayed with Zenobia and Caleb. That had been Mario's idea. Gracie would be difficult to explain, he had said gently, and she had known that he still thought she was Gracie's mother. She should have argued with him, but she had been afraid of taking the child with her. She would sooner trust Zenobia and Caleb to raise her as a proper Quaker. She was to blame for the separation, and she spent bitter hours weeping for the warmth of Gracie in her arms. It was her own fault that she had no friend in Venice, no one except Donna da Riva.

At first Amity had not realized the reason for Donna da Riva's agreeableness. But soon, to her chagrin, she had. The reason was Henri, Donna da Riva's son, Mario's half-brother. Henri was her pet, and it galled her that Mario stood in his way for the inheritance. But because of Amity, Mario's father might disinherit him.

Senator da Riva was spending the winter in Paris, and nothing would be settled until his return. Mario had written to him, and Donna da Riva must have hoped that retribution would be swift. But Mario's father had replied that all must wait until he and his son met face to face. So Amity had waited, dreading his arrival, and yet almost wishing for it, to be done with the worst.

The worst! That would be that Mario would be disowned. And then? Perhaps they would return to the south of Russia to the house on the Dnieper. To a life where the past counted for nothing and life began afresh. The worst! Perhaps that was what she was hoping for! Francesco's dream—could Mario ever embrace it? The gondola seemed to chase stars in the water, and Amity sighed, knowing too well that Mario had a different dream, one that somehow she must embrace.

Mario might become one of the Barnabotti, the poor nobles, living on a government stipend, but he would never give up Venice. He would teach his son to love it, too—the son he hoped to register proudly in the Golden Book. She put a protective hand over her abdomen and thought that it was the child that would make it possible for her to share Mario's dream. The boy would make it hers, too.

"Isn't he beautiful?" asked Donna da Riva. She smiled at Amity with the typical heavy-lidded greenish-blue eyes of a Venetian aristocrat.

"Who?" said Amity, her mind still on the baby.

"Carlo. I love to watch him. He's the best gondolier in Venice. He always wins the races during the regattas. And you have yet to see the Forces of Hercules."

"What is that?"

"Oh, a treat no woman wants to miss. The gondoliers play a game on Maundy Thursday, the wildest day of Carnival. They form a naked human pyramid on planks laid across boats near the Rialto Bridge. You mustn't miss it."

"I suppose they are all very strong," said Amity, vowing to avoid the scene.

"Yes, and they make good lovers. You must remember that, because someday you'll be wanting one."

"I'll never want a lover," said Amity sternly. Donna da Riva was forever saying risqué things. She made Amity terribly uneasy.

Donna da Riva laughed, and the laughter echoed from the walls of lighted palaces. Light reflected from ogee windows and rippled on the water. "I have never heard such nonsense. Of course you will. It's because of your condition. It's about this time that every woman swears she will never let a man touch her again. But nature will have its way. You'll forget the consequences. We all do."

Amity flushed. "I did not say I would not let *Mario* touch me!" She looked at Carlo, who stared straight ahead without any indication that he had heard anything that had been said beneath the white awning. *The gondolier's creed*, she thought.

A gondolier never gave away any lady's secrets, for if he did, he would be found dead in the canal the next morning, drowned by other gondoliers. But yet he knew. He knew everything. Amity shuddered, unable to imagine the things that Carlo must know.

Without the creed of the gondoliers, Venice might have been in chaos!

Ten years of secrets were locked in his head, for he had been the family gondolier that long, since he'd replaced his retiring father on his eighteenth birthday. What a grand day that must have been for Donna da Riva—to have this skillful young Adonis a fixture in her boat. In his regatta costume, with its red cap, silk jacket, white shoes, and scarlet sash flowing from the waist, he was like the figurehead of a ship for all to see.

He had steered the gondola through a thousand nights such as this—to assignations or out into the lagoon, curtains drawn over pairs of lovers. He'd ferried Donna da Riva, Henri, Mario, too, no doubt, on excursions of love.

Carlo even knew about Amity. He knew how frightened and lonely she was. Early in her pregnancy she had lost her dinner of curry and baked polenta to the canal. Later she had given way to fits of weeping as he poled homeward. Carlo had bathed her face with a handkerchief dipped into the canal and had whispered encouragements she'd only half understood, and somehow she hadn't been embarrassed. And Carlo had never said anything about it, not even to Mario.

Now the gondola slid softly into the landing place beside the palace. Carlo jumped easily to the walkway and offered Amity his hand to set her ashore. Then he offered it to Donna da Riva, but she laughed it away.

"What, Carlo? Go in before dawn on such a night as this! Do you think I'm getting old?"

"No, *signora*." Carlo smiled just a little, his mouth turning up at the corners as though he willed it to do no more.

"Row on, Carlo. There are a thousand stars in the sky, and in Venice a party for every star that shines."

"As you wish," he said noncommittally as he stepped back

into the craft. Amity gazed after them speculatively as the gondola vanished on the silvery waters of the canal, Donna Da Riva's laughter trailing like a wake behind.

A yawning servant opened the door and asked if she would be wanting anything. She didn't really, but she'd learned it was expected of her to require something. Donna da Riva always did, and Amity's austerity seemed to upset the staff.

"I'll have a pot of chocolate. Have it sent to my room, please," she said.

She went up from the ground floor of the entrance hall and boatyard where trade goods of silk, ivory, and tapestries were stored. This was the *mezzanino*, where the da Rivas conducted business. Above, the next floor, the *piano signorile*, was elegant with a long room that ran the whole length of the palace and had a balcony over the canal and alcoves with windows over the water. Her footsteps echoed on the tiles and she shivered in a chill held by the thick damask-covered walls. The fire had died to embers, but no matter. Amity did not intend to remain. Mario's chambers and hers were on the next floor.

A soft sound caught her attention—a sort of fluttering sigh. It sounded like the wings of the pigeons that lived among the frescoes of angels and lions on the roof, where Donna da Riva went in summer to bleach her hair on the *altana*, trailing it through a crownless hat.

She paused and listened. No, it wasn't pigeons. Amity's heart quickened. The ancient palace was spooky at night, and she was afraid of ghosts. She wondered if she would ever get uesd to it. In Pennsylvania everything had been much newer, while a dozen generations of da Rivas might haunt the labyrinth of the palace.

The sound came again, so loudly that Amity jumped; but now she saw what had caused it. An old gentlemen had been asleep in a chair near the fireplace. He'd been snoring gently, but her arrival had roused him.

"Zabetta?" he said, looking about confusedly. "Zabetta, are you ready to go? Have they served dessert?"

The old man and his beautiful young wife had been guests at dinner, but apparently he had fallen into a doze, and everyone had left him. He was eighty and senile, and the girl had married him for his fortune. It must have been a fortune dearly bought, for the old man leered when he spoke his wife's name, as though he were already undressing her in their bedroom.

But perhaps that was only part of his dream. Surely he could not—at his age! Amity flushed at her very wondering. What business of hers was it what he did with his wife? She would do well to be like Carlo and make her mind oblivious.

"They've all gone, I'm afraid," she said.

"Eh? Zabetta?"

"I'm not Zabetta."

"Oh, so you're not. Well, come and keep me company until she comes back." He patted the footstool beside him.

Amity hesitated. She pitied him, but the cramping in her stomach had worsened since she had entered the house. It was often this way, as if something in the establishment caused it.

It was nerves, she supposed. She didn't belong, and it made her anxious. Amity didn't relish entertaining the old man until his wife returned. Heaven knew where Zabetta might be.

"No. I want to go to bed," she told him.

"To bed?" The elderly husband lifted his ear trumpet toward her and tried to struggle out of the chair.

Amity didn't know whether to dissolve in hilarity or explode in anger at the way he had taken her remark.

"Zabetta!" the old man bellowed after her as she fled toward the stairs.

At a turn of the murky steps Amity's way was blocked by a man busily trying to do up a woman's gown. "Oh, do hurry, Henri!" hissed the girl. "Something's waked him up!"

"Hold still! Don't squirm! You're twisting the hooks out of my hands. Who cares if he's awake? He knows about us."

"Yes. But he has his ways when he thinks I've been with you!"

"What ways, Bet?"

"I don't want to talk about it. Just hurry up."

"Tell me! I love you!" he protested.

"And I love you!" she answered fervently. Kissing him, she dashed past, brushing against Amity's large stomach without even noticing. Amity was glad to have avoided an encounter, but she hadn't, after all.

"Hello, Amity," said Henri pleasantly. They might have been meeting over luncheon, except that he was breathing a little hard.

"I'm sorry, Henri. I didn't know . . . I . . ."

"Home early again, eh, Am? It's inconvenient, you know, the way you show up where you're least expected. Don't you feel well?"

"No." Tears welled in her eyes. He was always considerate of her in an offhand way, as though she had been a stray pup. Just now he was being solicitous when he had every right to be angry. His brother's escapade in marrying her amused him. More often *he* was the errant son.

No wonder, though, that Zabetta was drawn to him. He was handsome like Mario, but his features were fleshier, and he had a florid tint to his complexion that betrayed a love of drink. What matter? She liked him more than Donna da Riva, and the two of them were all she had.

"Come along, now," he said, and taking her arm, led her to her bedroom. She felt his hands on the fastenings of her dress and tried to protest, but pain overcame her.

Henri laughed softly. "It's all right, Am. I'm an expert at taking care of women. Why, I was a lady's *cicisbeo* first when I was fifteen! There, you'll feel better unlaced."

"Donna da Riva said I'd feel better if I laced more tightly," she murmured, dazed, as he tucked covers around her.

"She's all wrong," said Henri. "This will help." Sitting on the bed, he massaged the small of her back. Amity's skin tingled at his touch, and she felt disagreeably disturbed. But the cramping eased. "I'll bring a draft to relax you," he said, getting up. "It's a special remedy of Zabetta's. You'll sleep tonight, I promise."

"I've already sent for chocolate to relax me," she objected.

"This will be better," he said.

Amity frowned. His behavior had been altogether too intimate, she thought, but she supposed it was the Venetian way. And he was her brother-in-law, after all. He returned, insisting she swallow a horrid brown liquid, and laughing at her grimace.

"Henri, I'll try not to come home so inconveniently again," she said contritely, to show her gratitude.

"It may be hard for an American to understand, but there was really nothing amiss," he told her. "I've been Zabetta's *cicisbeo* ever since she finished her first year of marriage. And we've been sweethearts since we were children."

Amity was astonished. "You were sweethearts and yet she married that old man?"

"Of course, you goose. Augusto Beltrami was a godsend! It's the custom in Venice for only one son to wed; it avoids splitting the fortune in noble families. My father always intended for Mario to be the one. There was no hope for Zabetta and me unless she acquired a fortune of her own. We never expected Augusto to last so long. It's been five years, and what's worse, he's spent them squandering his money. It hasn't worked out at all."

"If Mario's disinherited because of me, you'll have your chance, then." She sighed.

"Oh, I'm not counting on that," he answered.

"Then you think Mario's father will accept the match?"

"Not at all. I think he'll have it annulled."

"What?" Amity sat up, and the room went gray under the effect of the drug he had given her. She rolled back weakly as Henri continued.

"You'll have a little bastard da Riva, then, Amity. But it won't be the first in the da Riva family. You know, Am, I believe I'm on your side. I hope the senator accepts the marriage."

"Why, Henri?" she murmured, in the thrall of the drug.

"Because if it's annulled, Mario will wed that little Giovanna, and she is not half as desirable as you. Venetian custom is fair in one respect, Amity. If they like, brothers may share the wife of the one who marries. I'll take my turn between the covers with you someday, if the senator approves this marriage."

She sat up again, disbelieving, aware that he meant his words more as a compliment than a threat. "Don't worry. I'm an expert, sweet," he said. "Ask Zabetta."

She heard his amused laugh, and then, mercifully losing her grip on consciousness, heard no more.

19

A bird sang from the garden, hidden behind stone walls on the far side of the canal. Amity loved the luxuriant, almost tropical foliage of the place, reached by an enclosed passage over the canal. Nobody else ever seemed to go there; it had become her own private sanctuary. The bird called more insistently, beckoning her to awaken from her nightmare that held her in chains of sleep.

Zabetta's medicine. "You'll sleep, I promise," Henri had said. Now she would give anything not to sleep, to be able to respond to the cheerful cry of the bird, heard through a murk.

In her dream Zabetta's old husband had been chasing her up the stairs and had inexplicably thrust his ear trumpet into her bodice. Amity had struggled with him and thrown the trumpet down the steps. The old man had tumbled after, rolling over and over.

"He has his ways," a girl's voice warned.

Amity tried not to listen and heard only snoring through the darkness—like pigeons' wings.

But now someone was crying. A woman was rocking, holding a baby in her arms. With a burst of joy, she saw that it was Isabel, still clad in the tattered gown she had worn in the camp of the Continentals. "Isabel! We took care of Gracie," Amity cried. "She didn't starve! She didn't die!"

But Isabel went on weeping, and Amity was horrified to see that the baby was lifeless. "Isabel, whose baby is that? Is it Gracie? Is it *mine?*"

The ghost sobbed more loudly as Amity fought against the dream. The ghost of Isabel drowned out the song of the bird in the garden.

"Amity? Wake up, love." Mario's voice accomplished what she could not herself. She would always heed his will; he could have coaxed her from the doors of hell.

She opened her eyes and feasted on the sight of him, resplendent in the special garb of a Venetian nobleman—breeches of printed calico and a toga of red silk. Older nobles still wore the short peruke, but Mario's hair was his own. It must be very late, she thought. He was on his way to the Great Council, which met at noon. She would be alone in the palace, as she often was.

"I'm sorry about last night, Mario," she said, remembering that she had displeased him then. It seemed she was always saying that since she'd come to Venice.

"It's all right, Am. Are you better today?" He bent and kissed her. It was almost a perfunctory kiss, but her head reeled deliciously. She looked at the pillows on the other side of the bed and saw that they were still freshly plumped. Mario had slept elsewhere. In the dressing room? He seemed so different to her since their arrival in Venice!

He blended with the city, its every nuance familiar to him. He was part of this strange watery fantasy, and sometimes he seemed more like a piece of the puzzle of it than the man she loved so intensely. Awkward and pregnant, a foreigner, she was at a double disadvantage. Time lay on her hands, and fears expanded to fill the vacuum.

Venice owned him more than she. His bearing told her as much as the ell of cloth on his left shoulder that he was meant for a special destiny. The blood of hundreds of years had decreed it, and she had dared to interfere. If only she might share a cup of chocolate with the Empress Catherine this morning and tell her how large was the task the czarina had urged her to take on!

She thought of the things that Henri had told her before she had gone to sleep. Should she tell Mario that Henri had suggested he would take his pleasure with her?

"Mario . . ."

"Yes, love?" he said tenderly.

But Amity didn't finish what she had been going to say. Suddenly she was unsure. Henri had said that sharing the wife was the custom. Perhaps Mario might tell her to accommodate Henri. Amity no longer knew what to expect; the world seemed turned wrong-side-up. Venice was a world unto itself and her husband was Venetian. She would simply have to manage Henri herself.

What of the possibility of an annulment? That was at least as shocking to her as Henri's suggestion, but she was afraid to ask Mario about that, too. She might insult him, or worse, be told unpleasant truths. She had been in Venice long enough to know that an annulment was possible. She'd heard it said laughingly that the pope was pope everywhere but in Venice. Marriage was not the serious thing in Venice that it was in America. She had heard of couples who had had their marriages annulled simply because they'd become bored with each other. Had Mario told the priest who had married them that she was not Catholic? Would it make her marriage safer if she converted?

She had mentioned the matter of conversion once to Mario, but he had only laughed. "It's not necessary, Am. I myself never go to Mass. But we will have the children baptized in the Church, of course."

Suppose the marriage was annulled. Would Mario then dutifully marry Giovanna? Would he send Amity and her child away to some villa to live as his mistress? Would she accept that role? What choice would she have? She was committed heart and soul to Mario.

She shivered, and he put a shawl about her shoulders. "Are you sure you're feeling better?" he asked.

She nodded bravely.

"That's good." He raised the blinds, and sunlight flooded in, that special Venetian glow that made the stucco flowers and festoons seem to flow on the soft green current of the ceiling. "We'll have a wonderful time today, you and I. I have plans."

"Plans! Then you aren't going to Council?"

"Today? Of course not. This is a day for Carnival. We'll spend it all together."

She struggled out of bed, suffused with happiness, and felt dizzy.

"Are you sure it's all right for you to get up, Am? It's not getting too close to your time?"

He looked worried. He was in uncharted territory when it came to her condition, but he hoped she wouldn't spoil what he had planned for them.

"I'm sure, Mario," she said. She wasn't, but she had spent far too many dreary days alone or in the company of Donna da Riva and her frivolous friends. She tottered on her feet, but surely that was only because the baby made her so ungainly. At least she hoped that was what Mario would think.

"Shall I help you dress, love?"

She nodded, glad to let him choose among the elaborate gowns that had been made for her, gowns suitable to the wife of the heir of the da Riva family, but less suitable to her simple taste. She often felt silly in layers of brocade and ruffles, but at least her condition prevented her having to wear the big side bustles; and the stays that threw the bosoms of other women high and forward had been laced more loosely—in spite of Donna da Riva's criticism.

So far she had managed to avoid painting her cleavage, as many Venetian women did, and she had refused to wear hats with stuffed birds, butterflies, and masses of flowers. Nonetheless, Amity had found things she could not resist in the display of feminine fashion and had quite forgotten her Quaker scruples against wearing jewelry in a bombardment of silver, coral, and mother-of-pearl.

She'd grown her fingernails long, too, to please Mario; and she painted them a dainty shade of pink. Her lovely hair, always freshly washed, needed no artificial tresses added to dress it in the high Venetian style, twinkling with little gems. Mario had worried about so much washing of hair in the dank Venetian winter, but Amity would have it so. She had seen lice crawling up the towers of Donna da Riva's powdered, perfumed coiffure.

Today she crushed her locks into a simple chignon and waited to see how he would dress her. He began with underthings trimmed in silver lace embroidery, fastening up the gold buttons expertly. He went about it in a workmanlike manner, but even so his touch made her flesh leap with desire in spite of her advanced pregnancy. Soon the child would be born and they would be lovers again, she thought.

In the summer they would drift into the lagoon on moonlit nights, the tentlike *tenda* pulled tightly around silken cushions. Roses and oleander would sprawl over crumbling walls, spying on their trysts. He kissed her neck when he reached the top button, and she hoped he was thinking such thoughts as well.

But the happy, tranquil mood fled suddenly, as other thoughts crept back, like weeds choking out the flowers. How many women had he dressed as he was dressing her, to be so masterful at it? American men were nothing like this, surely. She did not think that even the outlaw had understood the workings of women's clothes as well as Mario. She gazed again at the undented pillow and wondered if she were the second woman who had enjoyed these ministrations this morning.

Was she any better herself? Hadn't she allowed Henri to put her to bed? He had displayed the same sort of skill as Mario, though the unrest she had felt had been different— Henri might be as sexually venturesome as the outlaw, but he had not the outlaw's magnificent daring that could move a woman against her will and make her will his own. What in the outlaw had seemed bold spirit seemed only rapaciousness in Henri. She could never enjoy it with him, surely. But surely it wouldn't come to that—would it?

"Mario, has this always been your room?" she asked to try to hide her thoughts.

"Yes. Ever since I was a child." He looked at her quizzically.

"This is where you and Francesco strung the rope between your palace and his?"

"Yes."

She gazed out the window at the matching windows of the Byzantine palace across the canal. The Baretti mansion was falling into a state of disrepair. A scroll of seashells had chipped away, and a broken pane gaped like unfastened clothing in spite of grillwork in front of it. The stripes of red and blue on the poles where the gondolas moored had faded. Amity thought of the trouble she had already caused between best friends and decided on another count not to tell Mario about Henri. She did not want to be guilty of setting brother against brother.

"Where do you think Francesco is now, Mario?"

"Oh, I imagine he's in the south of Russia. It's the place for him, Amity."

I wish it were the place for you, too, she thought. She wondered for the thousandth time about little Giovanna, whom Mario had been supposed to marry. Was she languishing in her convent still? Perhaps Giovanna did not care; it wasn't as though they'd been sweethearts like Zabetta and Henri. But the matter rankled Amity's stern Quaker morals. She had stolen a man from a woman he was pledged to wed, and surely she would be punished for her crime.

She might be punished by seeing Mario disinherited, losing position and purpose, perhaps becoming useless and embittered.

Or punishment would be an annulment. She would spend her days raising a child that belonged to no world at all, and competing for scraps of Mario's attention.

At the very least she would be punished by Henri's attempts to get into bed with her.

"Oh, Mario," she burst out, "are you sorry?"

His laughter boomed and chased away the sobs that had been gathering in her throat. "Sorry? For my indiscretion in marrying you? I would show you how sorry I am, if it were not for that between us." He gestured at her abdomen and made her blush.

How could he be sorry, he thought, for what was inevitable? And it *had* been inevitable—from that day in her aunt's parlor when she'd caned him. What fire she'd had! What devotion to ideals! She'd hated him so, thinking him a Tory, he'd wished himself a Whig on the very spot! Those traits were missing in Venetian women, and perhaps that was the fault of Venetian men. They'd treated their women like rare jewels for centuries—creatures of beauty without minds, to be put carefully away in the vaults of convents, the sacred property of men who paid the price of arranged marriage. There had been a time when a man who had absconded with another man's woman would have been put to death by the

Council of Ten. Once a *cicisbeo* would have been rash to aspire to the bed of the woman he served. But times had changed and society was looser.

But women had made nothing of their new freedom but this farce of decadence. They had been taught nothing for centuries but to please men. Should anyone be surprised now that they did nothing but flaunt themselves in a travesty of desirability? Was the thing that was wrong with Venetian men that they had lost respect for their women?

He felt a moment of unease as he thought of Giovanna. She had been only a child, simple and unspoiled, for the time, behind convent doors. She had told him shyly once that she remembered him every night in her prayers. He had wronged her, wronged Francesco. But no power could have kept him from the shining light that was Amity.

He had a path to follow; she would illuminate it. Was that special glow of hers the Quaker inner light of which she sometimes spoke? It didn't matter. All that mattered was that she was his. He hoped the child she was carrying was a boy. But if it were a girl, he would not be too dissatisfied, for he would make of her a woman like her mother, the first of a strong new line of Venetian women.

He took a gown from a wardrobe and showed it to her. He had had it made especially just for such an occasion. "Look, Am, what do you think of it?"

She hardly knew what to think. He seemed proud of it, but it was only a dress of plain black, although of a very fine silk.

"It's the *vesta,*" he explained. "It's what every patrician woman must wear on official holidays. It's a holdover from the old sumptuary laws which were supposed to keep people from outdoing each other. Somewhat like the rule of plain dress among the Quakers, I suppose. But everyone cheats with lace on the sleeves and plenty of jewels. You shall, too, of course."

He fastened her into the gown and finally added the *zenda,* a long veil thrown over her head and shoulders and tied with a knot at the back. The *zenda* itself was exquisite, trimmed with ermine and set with gold thread. Mario added only a little jewelry before he thought the picture was complete. He knew a thrill of possession as he looked at her in the holiday garb of a noble Venetian wife.

She had such dignity about her, her little chin held with pride, but at the same time a questioning look in her eyes, hoping that he approved of the way she looked. How could he not?

She was a diamond among gems of paste, her shimmering blond hair and the soft pinks of her complexion setting off the somber black *vesta* as though it had been merely the lining of a case in which she was the jewel. The very ripeness of her figure appealed to him, too, reminding him of a past full of nights of love and a future of new life and possibility.

Mario wished his father were here at this moment. Surely he couldn't help seeing how wonderful Amity was!

Mario sighed with a resignation that made her wisteria-blue eyes turn dark with alarm. "What is it, dearest?" she dared to ask. She must look like a huge black whale, she thought. He wouldn't want to be seen with her.

"Oh, I was regretting that we shall have to mask when we reach the piazza. But we shall not until it's necessary, and I will have that much time at least to see your lovely face."

He was eager to be off, and handed her into the gondola without asking if she wanted breakfast. It was just as well, because she was still queasy and didn't feel at all like eating.

The morning air was sweet and fresh. Sunlight blazed from an opal and sapphire sky, dazzling to blinding, drenching the palaces with amber rays, caressing every molding. The water lapped and sparkled. It seemed to be laughing. Amity's spirits lifted, and Mario, noticing the change, was pleased. He wanted her to understand Venice and love it as he did. Through her love for him, he hoped that she would love Venice, too. He hoped she would come to treasure the noble values that had built it, just as she treasured the ideas of the American Revolution. He hoped she would help to teach their sons, whom he saw as a myriad of little stairsteps.

It was a pretty vision. He grinned at her, looking forward to the getting of a multitude of children, filling up the rooms of the palace with stuffed animals, rocking horses, and busy nannies.

They slid by the wood market of the Giudecca, where double rows of great Dutch-bowed boats lay with anchor chains hanging from the mouths of carved dolphins. Amity sat cozily beneath the awning, watching clusters of masked revelers on the waterside promenades. Black *veste* sparkled with jewels and fancy trim, each more lavish than the next, exuding a holiday atmosphere that nothing could contain.

Near the Rialto Bridge, wine boats were moored along the Riva del Vin, doing a furious business for so early in the morning. Bedouin mats, all gay stripes, hung in the windows of drapers, reminding Amity of the Orient and Venice's strong connections with the East, from where so much of her wealth had come.

Ducks and chickens were being sold at auction at one stall, squawking and quacking as though they understood the indignity. Children played skittles in the narrow *calle,* shouting and laughing in the bright sun.

Amity looked long at the children and smiled at Mario. He smiled back, both of them radiant with their love for each other and the knowledge of the life burgeoning inside her. Someday their child would play beside these canals, too.

Mario called to Carlo, and the gondolier nodded and brought the craft toward the shore, poised lightly in the bow, his shirt sleeves rolled up over his strong arms. She studied Carlo curiously, wondering how late Donna da Riva had kept him up and where he had taken her through the moonlit canals all alone. Maybe Donna da Riva had required a service of Carlo in addition to ferrying her about. *They make good lovers,* Donna da Riva had said. And discreet ones, Amity thought. Carlo wore a mask today, but even if he had not, his flat, hooded eyes would have told no secrets.

"It's time to eat, Amity," Mario said. "You'll need your strength today."

She started to protest, but realized that she was ravenous after all. He helped her out of the boat and led her under a little porch, through an arched side door into a room filled with marble-topped tables. A waiter came, bowing and eager to please, and led the way through a narrow stone passage into a patio splashed with yellow-green light, filtering through grape vines laced overhead.

Big japonicas grew in boxes all about, and the spike-leafed branches of oleander swayed as they leaned over tables with snowy cloths. Amity was charmed. "Why have you never brought me here before?" she demanded.

"I've been saving it. It's one of my favorite places. I wanted to wait until the weather was perfect."

"Everything is perfect today!" she declared.

The waiter brought coffee, hard little Venetian rolls, and sturgeon so fresh and delectable that Amity knew that before dawn it had been swimming in the lagoon. Dropping flat lumps of sugar into the coffee, spreading a roll with jam, she attacked the meal with relish. The nightmares were forgotten now; she felt marvelously well. It was the magic of the spring air or the magic of being so intimately in the company of the man she loved.

They were alone in the patio. Alone as they never were in the house with its ghostly aura of dissaproving da Riva ancestors. They were alone as they had been in the house on the Dnieper—the only man and woman on the face of the great prairie.

"Mario, do you suppose I could have some of those delicious eggs we had once at the café on the piazza?" she said.

"Oh, Amity, you may have anything!" He gestured to the waiter, and before long a platter of shirred eggs dressed with smoked raw Italian ham and melted mozzarella cheese was set before them. She sighed happily, but he saw that her eyes clouded.

"What is it, Am?" he asked.

"Oh, nothing. I only wish it were always like this."

"Is it that you're afraid of having the baby? Don't be. I've engaged the best doctor in the city. You will be equal to it, Amity. I believe you will always be equal to whatever comes."

"Yes, Mario," she said. It was what he expected her to say, what the wife of a da Riva should say. But she longed to tell him that there was one thing she would *not* be equal to. If Mario were disinherited, would he continue to love her? He must. If he didn't, she would not be equal to that.

"Do you like puppet shows, Am?" he was saying.

"I've never seen one."

"You shall today," he promised. "And clowns and acrobats and fireworks and dancing and confetti." He would give her the grandest extravaganzas the city had to offer to make her happy. As for him, no display of rockets in the piazza could dazzle his heart half as much as her smile. He knew she had often been unhappy since he had brought her to Venice, and though she had seemed too delicate to bear her pregnancy easily, he knew it wasn't that that frightened her. It was the future, and it made him uneasy as well.

He did not doubt that he would love her forever, but he wondered how he would deal with his father's failure to accept his wife. He could allow his marriage to be annulled, of course, and join himself in a meaningless match with Giovanna. Amity would become his mistress then, installed in a villa on *terra firma* along the Brenta River. If Amity made such a sacrifice, he would be able to carry on the work of a lifetime.

But Mario had had her as his mistress before, and he had not been satisfied. His desire to possess her utterly as his wife had won the battle with his good sense. To have her as his mistress after having married her would do even less well.

Mario's thoughts made him moody in spite of the beautiful day and the company of his beloved wife. Maybe his brother would be a better choice to carry on the family tradition after all. Henri's faults were obvious: he lusted for women, high-born or low. He overindulged in food and drink. He was lazy and almost never filled his seat on the Great Council. Henri cared for nothing beyond his own comfort, like so many Venetians these days. But no, that was not quite accurate. Henri really cared for Zabetta. If Henri became the heir, he would please their father by marrying her, and she, though impoverished, had a proper lineage. Henri would not bring glory to the da Riva name, but he would not create a scandal, either, as Mario had done by marrying Amity.

Mario had always been the senator's favorite. The rebellious streak that had caused him to fall in love with a little Quaker girl in Philadelphia was a surprise to everyone, much as it was to him.

If only the child she were carrying turned out to be a boy! That would go a long way toward winning his father's approval.

Mario looked up in irritation as another couple entered the patio, spoiling the idyll he had been enjoying with Amity. His ill temper increased as the masked pair advanced familiarly, and the gentleman called out, "Oh, there you are, Mario. I've been looking for you."

"Good morning, Henri," Mario grumbled.

Henri gazed around the empty little patio and shook the beaked mask off his head. "What do you see in this place, Mario? All the fun is on the piazza. There're plenty of cafés with chairs left on the pavement so you can see everything. *You* can do even better. The doge wants you to join him in his box."

"Oh, well, then, we should go at once. Come along, Amity."

Henri laughed. "I do believe that the invitation is for you alone!"

"Alone! I'll not go without my wife!"

"Venice will say she's your wife when the marriage is registered in the Golden Book," said Henri, unable to hide a trace of glee in his voice. "You'd better hurry, Mario; it won't help matters to have the doge angry with you. It's unheard of to refuse such an honor."

Mario's chin jutted. "Convey my regrets, Henri. I've promised to spend the day with Amity."

"Mario, please go!" Amity's eyes told him she meant what she said.

"There's no need to be concerned about Amity," Henri said jovially. "Bet and I will take care of her."

Suspicion flickered over Mario's features as he glanced at his brother. Why should Henri want to do him such a favor?

Had Amity not been so pregnant, Mario would have known what base motive to assign to Henri's suggestion. But that could not be it. And Zabetta was along. Her mask hid whatever feeling she had about adding another woman to their party. Perhaps Zabetta's husband was becoming too jealous. Amity would be a sort of chaperon to soothe him.

Mario felt more relaxed now that he thought he had figured it out. "Are you sure, Am?" he said guiltily.

"Oh, yes, Mario." She was close to tears, but she managed to keep her eyes from filling. She was glad to have the opportunity to show him she understood his duties, glad to make up for some of the times she had failed in courage in Venice. Thank heaven she had *not* been invited to share the doge's box with Mario! Then she would have been one of the sights of Carnival, with everyone staring at her and snickering.

The four of them shared a gondola to the Piazza San Marco, the canal becoming more and more crowded until the boats were practically touching. A rope had been strung between the slender steeple of the campanile and a group of four bronze horses above the entrance of the basilica, beside which was the beribboned box of the doge. An acrobat would perform the annual *volo* down the rope to deliver a bouquet to the doge on his arrival. The piazza was crowded, and where people did not fill the white geometric design of the pavement, flocks of pigeons did. A winged lion, the symbol of Venice, gazed down from the basilica, majestic against a background of gold-starred blue. A twin lion reposed on the clock tower, where two darkly patinaed Moors stood ready to strike the hour by hitting a bell with their hammers.

"I'll meet you at Florian's at three," said Mario as he jumped from the gondola. He had masked like the others, and she felt a twinge of alarm as he vanished into the crowd, indistinguishable to her from any of the other patrician gentlemen.

Clowns wandered past: Harlequin with a face of tar and a many-colored tunic. One called Mattacino, with a feathered hat, was dressed to look like a chicken. Dr. Graziano and Dr. Balanzon wore the black garb of university professors and roamed about expounding nonsensical speeches. Everyone made sport of the *guaghi*, who were men dressed as women. Confetti sparkled in the sun, falling like a gentle multicolored snow from the tops of buildings.

"Duck, Amity," Zabetta said. But Amity did not move quickly enough and was splattered by an egg which someone had thrown. But the shell did not have egg inside at all, only sweetly perfumed water.

Henri excused himself to buy whipped cream and wafers at a *latteria,* and in a moment vanished into the faceless multitude. "Dear heaven, we've lost him!" Amity cried out in panic.

"He'll find us," said Zabetta calmly. "Sit down here and rest."

They took a table at one of the cafés with chairs stretching out onto the piazza, and a waiter brought them water flavored with raspberry syrup in glasses filled with ice. Amity found it refreshing, but Henri didn't appear. In his mask, he could pass easily without their knowing it, she thought.

Not seeming worried, Zabetta tipped up her mask to sip her drink, displaying dark, canny eyes, a nose that was large and strong in the Venetian way, and a wide, lush mouth. Impressive breasts strained against her black gown as she leaned forward. The cleavage peeking from beneath a *vesta* was painted with red roses.

Zabetta had painted flowers on her wrists and forearms as well, but the blossoms seemed an odd color. Studying the decorations more closely, Amity realized that they covered purple bruises. Amity shuddered and thought of Zabetta's husband. *He has his ways,* Zabetta had said.

What ways?

Zabetta followed her companion's gaze to her wrists and smiled ruefully. "It's all right. It's nothing I'm not used to."

"But he's hurt you, and if I had not come in and waked him . . ."

Zabetta lifted her chin proudly. "Don't feel sorry for me. I can stand anything but pity. Pity is much worse than being bound hand and foot in the nude for Augusto to do whatever he likes with me."

"Bound . . ." Amity gasped.

Zabetta laughed unpleasantly. "Didn't you guess? Or did you have some other novelty in mind? Would you like to hear how Augusto takes his pleasure? I'm sure you'd be amused."

"No . . . really." Badly shocked, Amity wondered how she could change the subject. But Zabetta didn't seem to want to leave it.

"Are you really so innocent? Venice says you are not. Venice says you must know every trick to have enticed a man like Mario da Riva from duty."

"Is *that* what they say?" cried Amity in dismay. She was wearing the grotesque Carnival mask and glad for it, for once, to hide her consternation.

Zabetta laughed again, this time more kindly. "Why, you really are! You're quite artless! But Amity, there's nothing to be ashamed of if you know how to please a man. I myself can even please Augusto, and I'm proud of it. It's not easy, pleasing a man in his dotage. Of course, there's no reason to please him, now that he hasn't any money. So I don't try. That's what makes him so furious. Before, he didn't care if I loved Henri. Do you know, Amity, I'm rather glad that Henri's got himself lost. We've never talked before, you and I. We have a lot in common."

"I can't think what," said Amity. Her blushes having subsided, she lifted her mask to partake of the welcome coolness of the raspberry-flavored water.

Through the winter she had seen Zabetta now and then when she had come to the palace in the company of Henri or her husband. She had learned quickly that Henri was Zabetta's lover as well as her *cicisbeo*. But that was almost the extent of what she had learned about Zabetta.

"What we have in common!" said Zabetta. "We are in love with brothers."

"Yes, I suppose that is something," said Amity, somewhat interested now. It seemed to her to make little difference, since the brothers themselves had almost nothing in common. She scanned the crowd, looking for Henri.

"I expect he's not coming back," said Zabetta suddenly. "He's been waylaid by some woman."

"But he promised Mario—"

"Mario has no claim on Henri. And neither have you, and neither have I. That's why I can't complain if some other woman catches his eye. I can dismisss him as my *cicisbeo*, that's all. And I don't want to do that."

Amity felt appalled, grateful not to be in Zabetta's position, but the dark-haired girl went on, apprising Amity that she was indeed in a similar situation. "You haven't much hold on Mario, either. Even though you call him your husband, Venice calls you his mistress."

Amity saw the point at last. They did have something in common. She drained her glass and felt a little faint. The sense of well-being she had had while she was with Mario was deserting her.

"Are you ill again, Amity?"

Amity nodded, her eyes filling with tears. A puppet show had begun nearby, but Amity was not enchanted as she might have been in Mario's company. All at once it was more than she could stand—the square full of people in strange costumes, all happy, dancing, and shouting. The crowd was full of foreigners; thousands of them came to the city for Carnival. English and even French seemed conservative among the exotically garbed Venetians. Here and there an Arab burnoose fluttered in the breeze. There were no Americans. Amity wished she might see just one. Irrationally she knew which one she wished she could see; Silas Springer, who had loved her so well. If only she could have gone on loving him forever and never loved this powerful Venetian, who had made her life so wonderful and so miserable and complicated all at the same time!

"Did Henri give you my draft last night?" Zabetta asked.

"Yes, but how did you know I would need it?" she said, surprised that Zabetta seemed so well-informed about her physical state of being.

"I didn't. But I guessed you would sometime. So I gave it to Henri to offer you when you'd want it. It's what I use for my monthlies. Augusto can be very upsetting, so I thought last night might have been the time."

"It made me sleep," said Amity. It seemed ungrateful to say that she had had nightmares. She was touched that Zabetta had thought of her, and she regretted all the uncharitable thoughts she'd had about her. Why, Amity wasn't so much better herself! She had been Mario's mistress before they were married. And of course, there was always the matter of the outlaw in her past. At least no one in Venice knew of that—no one but Mario, who undoubtedly suspected the truth.

Amity had been wishing for a friend, and here was one, providentially. She wondered vaguely if Zabetta would still be her friend if she knew the designs Henri had on her, but she pushed the idea to the back of her mind.

"Signor Beltrami *was* rather disconcerting," she admitted with a conspiratorial giggle. It was a wonderful relief to share a confidence with another woman of her own age.

"You're lucky if he let you off with a pinch, even in your condition," said Zabetta.

"My dear, I don't believe he noticed my condition!"

The pair of them went off into a gale of laughter. It was marvelous, but Amity gasped as a spasm of pain struck her.

"Do you feel worse, Amity?"

"No. The baby kicked, that's all." Mario must be right, Amity thought. She was making up the pains. She had been perfectly well until he had left her. The malady was her way of making sure that she did not have to deal with Venice without him, an outgrowth of her fear of facing the consequences of having married a man who was not free. It did not occur to Amity that her child might be about to make its appearance. It was not due for another month, and her feelings of discomfort were no greater than they had been a dozen times before. Amity decided to exert her will over it. She would summon the sort of spirit Mario would admire. If only he were here to see it!

"Let's walk about, Zabetta. I'm tired of sitting," she said.

"We might as well. We've certainly lost Henri." Zabetta led Amity into the piazzetta, the small square of St. Mark's. A fresh breeze blew in from the wharf as they wandered past one side of the Ducal Palace with its endless balconies and galleries of Gothic arches. Pigeons cooed and flapped their wings, soaring to the height of two red granite columns on either side of the water entrance to the square; and opposite the Ducal Palace cherubs gazed down on the merrymakers from the roof of a magnificent Renaissance building with lines of Florentine pillars.

"It's almost as crowded here as in front of the basilica," Amity observed.

"Yes. It's the one day that everyone is determined to be in the same place. Maybe the square will sink on Carnival day from the weight of all of us. We'll all be sucked down to hell then, no doubt. All their frivolity dumped to damnation. But we are young and in love, Amity. What do we care about the future, eh? We live for today, you and I. Soon all that will change. Augusto will die, and I'll be free to choose any husband that I like—any that can afford me without fortune.

What will I do then, do you think? And the senator will return to Venice and be livid to find that his son has not tired of you. But let's have a good time now. There'll be fireworks soon in the piazza."

"What? In broad daylight?"

"Yes. Isn't that wasteful? Venetians adore waste. But let's don't waste a moment. I'm bored with this. What shall we do in the meantime? I know. Let's pretend we do care about the future after all. Let's go to see the fortune-teller. I know where there's one."

"No, Bet, I don't want to," Amity said, but her companion was already leading the way, and Amity had to struggle to keep up. She panted after, too out of breath to protest, shuddering at the memory of the Gypsy on the steppe who had predicted that Mario would wed.

Why should that be such a terrible memory? Only because Amity had thought that the gypsy had meant that he would marry Giovanna. That had turned out well. The prophecy had come true in a happy way.

Still she did not relish the prospect of a fortune-teller today, and her fear told her how uncertain she was of all that lay before her. But Zabetta had pulled her into a small side street now, and Amity was not certain that she could even find her way back to the piazza through the labyrinth of little *rugas* lined with shops.

Dark green awnings shaded the windows of narrow buildings of ancient brick, and vines with red flowers cascaded from windowboxes far above the blocks of gray paving stone. Masked musicians strolled past, and here and there confetti fluttered down, a sparkling multicolored snow in the shafts of sunlight that penetrated the tunnellike lane.

Suddenly Zabetta stopped and jerked her inside a door. A Gypsy emerged from behind a curtain at the sound made by a bell hung on the door. She might have been one of the Russian gypsies, she looked so much the same, but when she spoke, it was in the Venetian dialect.

"Do you wish to know the future, young ladies?"

"Yes." Zabetta's eyes were glittering. Her breath came quickly.

"Give me a sequin, then."

Eagerly Zabetta put money in the old woman's palm. The Gypsy, unsmiling, lifted the curtain. "Now, Amity, we'll find out! Will I marry the man I love, Gypsy?"

The woman's eyes had an odd intensity. "I see an old man."

"You see? That's Augusto," Zabetta said to Amity. "Augusto is my first husband, Gypsy. Tell me who my second will be."

"I see darkness," the Gypsy said.

"Here. This will turn on the light again." Zabetta threw more coins on the table.

"The darkness won't go away," the fortune-teller said. "The darkness is in your life."

"What is the darkness?" Zabetta whispered, suddenly fearful.

"I can't see. But wait—there is a man. He is the man you love."

"Henri!" Zabetta clapped her hands. "Am I to marry him, then?"

"I don't see a marriage. The man is crying."

"Why is he crying?" cried Zabetta, suddenly in panic.

Amity thought it had gone on long enough. It was only a game, but Zabetta was too superstitious. "Tell my fortune," Amity said, and put down money.

The Gypsy sighed and told Zabetta that she could not see why Henri was crying.

"Oh, that is only because you have offered her so much more money to tell *your* fortune, Amity!" cried Zabetta.

"It's all silliness. You'll see when she tells mine."

"What do you want to know?" the Gypsy asked. "Shall I tell you if your child will be a boy?"

Amity felt a shiver of fear in spite of her brave front. "Tell me . . . tell me if my husband will always love me," she said.

The Gypsy caressed her ball with long, bony fingers, and it seemed to glow. Amity trembled, suddenly held in thrall. The Gypsy whispered guttural incantations until Amity was ready to leap from her seat. Finally the fortune-teller gave an exclamation of disgust.

"What's wrong, Gypsy?" Amity breathed.

"I can't see your husband."

"But I have one!"

"Pay her more money," suggested Zabetta.

Amity, caught up in the moment, tossed out another sequin, though she had already paid more than she should. But still the Gypsy could not see Amity's husband. All at once she sprang up and thrust something around Amity's neck. An amulet.

Sickened by a reek, Amity fought to remove it.

"Leave it there," the Gypsy ordered. "It unites us. Now the spirits admit me to your secrets."

There were more words that Amity could not understand. She needed desperately to leave the confined little room. The pain had returned, more intense than it had ever been before. Her abdomen had gone rigid, and her head swam. But she could not leave, not before she had heard the Gypsy's answer.

"Tell me if my husband will always love me!" she cried.

"I do not see your husband. That is, I cannot tell if one of the men is he."

"What men?"

"There are three men. The ball shows three men who will always love you."

"Three! I am only interested in one!"

Zabetta recovered from her own fright to laugh at Amity's. "Three lovers, but no husband, Amity! It's because you haven't one, really."

Amity sobbed, afraid that Zabetta was right. "Please! Tell me something else that you see!"

"There is something that looks like fire. It is far away, but it is coming closer. It's a woman with red hair. You must be careful. She is dangerous!"

A woman with red hair! "Velda!" cried Amity. The idea propelled her out of her chair at last. The movement sent a storm of pain through her body, but somehow she staggered for the door. She had to be away from the Gypsy, away from Zabetta, whose voice seemed to follow her, saying over and over, "Three lovers, but no husband! It's because you haven't one, really!"

In the street she bumped into a clown with striped stockings. A noise like gunfire sounded above the piazza. In the blue sky, rockets showered stars of gold. Amity kept going, trying to find her way back to the piazza, to Florian's, where Mario had promised to meet her at three. But now Amity was not walking or running as much as being dragged along by the crowd.

"Mario," she sobbed. Too late she realized what she would have known before if the baby had not been her first. If only she could see a friendly face in this sea of monster masks, this parade of merriment and unconcern!

Then an arm went around her. "Amity!"

It wasn't Mario, but she knew the voice nearly as well. "Franceso! Can it really be you?"

He swept off his mask and showed her that it was. "I've come home for Carnival. It's my favorite time of year."

She had never been so glad to see anyone. She saw him drink in the sight of her, saw him struggle with his emotions at finding her so, ripe with the child of his friend.

"I do not look my best today, Francesco," she muttered in confusion. It was not a time to be worrying about appearances, but confronted with him, she could not seem to help it.

"You are always beautiful, Am," he said. She was only half-aware that he was lifting her into his arms, enlisting other revelers to clear the way; but she felt sudden relief. She need not be responsible for herself anymore. Francesco would take care of everything; she trusted him. She clung to his neck as if clasping him would ease her awful pain, and then she fainted. Francesco, frightened though he was himself, was thrilled to hold her so intimately and know she depended on him completely.

When he had conveyed her to Mario's palace, he left without learning the outcome of her confinement. If she died, he did not want to be there. But neither did he feel up to handling the news that she had given birth to Mario's son. Francesco put on his mask again and went back to the piazza. Confetti beneath his feet rustled like autumn leaves as he walked, and the music of wandering bands was no more than unwelcome racketing in his ears.

I would never have left her alone like that, he thought. He had seen Mario in the doge's box. He knew where his erstwhile friend had been while his wife had nearly been reduced to dropping their child by the side of some canal.

The wound Mario had dealt him when they had dueled still ached when the weather was damp, but it was not that that angered Francesco.

If she dies, it will be Mario's fault, he thought. Mario did not love her enough. Not as much as she loved him.

For a while he tortured himself with such musings, and with musings of what might have been. At last he felt himself in such a state of distress that he could no longer remain abroad in the Carnival. He thought of someone who could understand. Someone who, like him, had a grief to bear. And he turned and headed for the convent to visit his sister, Giovanna.

20

"Mario," Amity whispered. "Mario."

Her voice was hoarse, her throat burned dry with her gasps. It seemed that no one would give her anything to drink. Amity could not remember if she had asked. She had only asked for Mario. It might be night now, since the blinds were drawn shut. They had been drawn a long, long time. Amity felt that she would never see sunlight again. Her body was racked as the doctor bent over her. She was aware that Donna da Riva had come into the room.

"Dear me, I'm exhausted. I danced until nearly dawn in the piazza. The moonlight was beautiful, and I had dozens of partners. One was a priest, I'm quite certain, but even a priest should have fun, eh? A domino hides everything. But I wouldn't go away with him to the lagoon. I've scruples, you know."

"No," said Amity, moaning. But Donna da Riva wasn't talking to her after all, but only to the doctor.

"A pity *you* missed all the fun," she went on. "That's the price of a noble calling. You'll have your reward in heaven, I suppose. But dear me, can heaven be anything like San Marco in the moonlight?

Donna da Riva waited for a moment, and getting no answer, went on. "I don't suppose there's any progress? Nothing I can tell Mario? He's quite beside himself."

Amity felt a surge of strength. Mario was in the palace at least. If only she could see him. The doctor lifted her legs and parted them; she screamed with agony and outrage as she felt his hand in the depth of her. "Go away! I don't want you here! I hate you!"

"There, now, he's only doing his duty, Amity," said Donna da Riva soothingly. "It hurts, of course. Pain is the opposite side of pleasure. What a pleasure Mario must have been, eh? We women pay, men don't."

"I want Mario," Amity said.

"Want Mario? What an idea. Would you have him see you like this? He won't think you so appealing in bed after this if he has to see the consequences. Men have weak stomachs. They can't be allowed to see women in childbirth."

Amity sobbed, wondering if Donna da Riva were right. She didn't want to do anything that might make him love her less. He must go on loving her!

"It's just the same," the doctor said in a hushed tone. She knew she wasn't supposed to hear. "She's very small," he went on, "and the child is in backwards."

Churches rang the matins, and she knew it was nearly sunrise. She always loved the cacophony of bells in the morning, and sometimes she had liked to slip from her bed and open her window to listen. The deep voice of the bell of St. Mark's, the *marangona,* sounded a mezza terra. Amity rejoiced at the arrival of the day. Daylight and Mario—those were the things she needed. Outside a clamor began: people going about their business, barges coming up the Grand Canal laden with goods for the marketplace of Venice.

Ordinarily she would be having a morning cup of coffee, watching the parade with interest, waving now and then to some gondolier or boatman who had expressed approval of her by sweeping off his hat and making her a bow.

If only she could partake of those simple pleasures now! But the day excluded her, churning on, unaware of her ordeal. Donna da Riva had gone. She must be sleeping peacefully, dreaming of her conquests after her night of revelry. Amity was sorry she had gone. Donna da Riva was better than no one. Now she had only the doctor, and even he did not stay all the time, stepping out for chocolate or a cigarette. Why should he remain, after all? There was nothing to do. No way to save her. She became convinced that she would die. She must. She could not endure the pain.

She thought of the child, who must die with her, whom she loved so, and somehow she held on. She prayed, trying to remember the Quaker meeting house she had left far away in Bucks County. Eternity slid by. The shadows became long, and there were bells, again, the bells that closed the shops.

Something heavy shifted against her throat, choking her breathing. Amity's eyes opened in terror. She expected to find the hand of death about her neck. But no, it was only the amulet of the Gypsy. She had been wearing it when she had left the fortune-teller's. She was wearing it still. She hated it, hated the memory of the place; and exerting herself, she tore it away and flung it across the room.

Strange, she thought, that the Gypsy had not seen death in the crystal ball. Perhaps she would not have told if she had. But no, she had told Zabetta about the darkness. The Gypsy had not minded delivering bad news. Three men who would love her forever! And she did not know if one of them was Mario!

Beyond her door she heard a commotion. Voices were raised in protest; then the door opened, and someone came in. She closed her eyes, hearing a man's footsteps and not wanting to communicate with the doctor. He might examine her again. She could not bear to think of that. She could not bear, either, to hear him say again, "Nothing's changed."

"Amity," said a voice softly. "Can you hear me, Am?"

"Mario!"

He managed to smile as she looked at him. She could tell that it cost him an effort. "Do you mind that I am here? I couldn't stand to stay away. I ought not to come in, I know."

"Oh, Mario!" Her eyes were glistening with happy tears as he gathered her into his arms. She quite forgot the admonitions of Donna da Riva as she rejoiced in the fervor of his love. It was enough to last her for eternity. She did not mind dying now. Maybe it would be better after all. He would marry Giovanna in time and fulfill his destiny. Their love would be enshrined in his memory—those days in Philadelphia, rowing along the river with the forsythia in bloom. The months on the golden steppe of Russia.

She felt a cataclysm. He read it in her face and shouted for the doctor. Amity dug her fingers into his arms and screamed.

Bells began to ring. More bells, dragging Amity back from a long distance. She dropped her hand to her stomach. The familiar bulge was gone, and her abdomen was strangely limp. She gazed down at it, filled with a sense of loss.

"Amity?"

Mario was still at her side. A growth of beard on his chin told her he had not left her.

"Why are the bells ringing, Mario?"

"It's the morning bells, Am."

She wondered if he were telling her the truth. Were they sounding a dirge instead? There was another sound Amity wanted to hear. Even in her exhausted slumber, she would not have been deaf to the cries of her child. She was afraid to look at Mario and have his expression answer the question she couldn't ask.

"Do you think the name Chiaretta is too fanciful?" he asked. "I would like to name our daughter after my mother."

Amity's heart leaped. Her child had survived its birth! She would have preferred a name from her own heritage, like Faith or Constance, but this morning, with all the Venetian bells ringing, Chiaretta seemed perfect.

"It's a lovely name, Mario." Suddenly her happiness dimmed. "A girl! But it should have been a boy."

"Yes, but I wouldn't exchange her, even if I could. She's beautiful, and . . ." Mario grinned at his inability to express the wonder of the baby. "Wait a moment, and I'll bring her to you. You'll see yourself."

When he returned, he brought a bundle that waved fists like unopened flowers and was crowned with a soft down of golden hair like Amity's own. Amity was only too joyful to agree with him that Chiaretta was marvelous.

It had been a peculiar birth, everyone agreed. The doctor had seen no way to save her, and when he had allowed her husband in, the household had known that it was a deathbed Mario had been admitted to sit beside. Then everything had changed, and the child had been born alive and well, the mother saved.

Amity had her own idea of what had happened. "It was because you came," she told Mario.

"I wish I thought it were so simple, Am," he said with a shake of his head. The event had unnerved him, and it grew more obvious how deeply with every day that passed. He attended her constantly, leaving the house only to go to the flower market to bring her spring blossoms from the islands.

"You could go to the Council today, Mario," she would say. "I'm quite all right."

"Oh, not today. Tomorrow perhaps." But the next day he would say the same thing.

She loved having him with her. During the long hours of her convalescence, he read to her, introducing her to the plays of Goldoni. Their down-to-earth common sense delighted her, and she found herself laughing merrily at the foibles of the characters. Mario would tell her all the latest news—how the gondola was being repainted for the summer, that Zabetta's husband had had a fit of apoplexy and was confined to bed but was certain to recover.

They would lunch on dishes he ordered prepared especially to tempt her—asparagus mold sprinkled with cheese, or fried crepes stuffed with white truffles. Even when she napped, she knew he was nearby to heed her call.

The weather was warm and golden. Donna da Riva, like most of the patricians, was getting ready to leave for the June season at the villas on the mainland, along the Brenta River. The first season would last until mid-July, and there would be another in the fall, when storms pounded Venice. Amity longed to go, too, to see the trees and fields of grass, but she was judged not to be recovered sufficiently. That was Mario's idea more than the doctor's, she thought.

At least she was allowed to walk in the garden, where roses and oleander were in bloom. She should have been reminded of the first days of her marriage, with Mario so attentive; but she knew it wasn't really like that at all, and the matter weighed on her heart.

It was not that the senator would return soon, though he most likely would. It was something else that made Mario seem different. Too late she realized that for all her silliness, Donna da River understood men. Mario had seen her nearly die with the baby, and he was racked with guilt at having been the cause of it. Worse, she saw that he wondered how he could ever put her through such a trial again. He must, if she were to be his wife. She had not yet borne him a male heir. Perhaps she couldn't. Next time she might die trying.

Amity had such doubts herself. Would the second time be any easier? Amity wished she had someone to ask. But Aunt Zenobia, who had sent gifts of infant clothing from St. Petersburg, wouldn't know, since she had remained a spinster for so long. The empress might give her advice, but Amity knew what that advice would be: to endure whatever she must for Mario, as she had once been willing to do for her country.

Amity sighed, leaning against satin pillows as she read a note from the czarina that had accompanied a silver mug sent as a baby gift. Once she had thought the empress wise, but the empress had not loved as Amity had. Catherine would advise her to fight to keep Mario forever, but if Amity could not bear a son, perhaps that was not the advice to follow. Would it be better for the marriage to be annulled so that Giovanna could bear him the son Amity couldn't?

Henri, of course, was delighted with Chiaretta, and rather unexpectedly played the doting uncle, attempting to amuse the infant with ridiculous faces and sounds. Often he made Amity laugh instead. He seemed so completely harmless with dribblings of milk on his shirt that Amity could hardly remember he was the same man who had vowed to exercise his "rights" with her in bed.

Zabetta came to see Amity, according Chiaretta only obligatory attention. She had other things on her mind. "Why did you run away that day?" she asked. "I would have helped you, and wouldn't have had such a time of it."

"I don't know, Zabetta. It was foolish."

"It was because the Gypsy saw the woman with red hair, wasn't it? Who was she, Amity?"

"She was someone who tried to hurt me a long time ago. But she's far away and can't do any harm now. It wasn't because of that silly Gypsy that I ran away. I was ill, and I couldn't breathe in that place."

"You're lucky that you don't believe any of it, Amity," Zabetta said with a shudder. "I still have nightmares about what she said to me."

"That she saw Henri crying?"

"Yes. And the darkness. I have always been afraid of the dark. What did you do with the amulet?"

"The amulet?"

"You remember. The Gypsy put it around your neck when you asked her to tell you if Mario would always love you. You were still wearing it when you left."

Amity had blocked the matter from her mind. "I don't remember what I did with it, Bet."

"Maybe you put it in a drawer. Would you like me to look?"

"Why? I don't want it."

"That's the thing! You shouldn't have it. Who knows what powers it has! It's bad luck to keep a thing like that."

"Oh, Bet! That smelly little pouch hasn't any powers!"

Zabetta wasn't convinced, and Amity wasn't as certain as she sounded, so they searched the big carved chests and the wardrobes. "Maybe Mario's seen it. I'll ask him," Amity said.

"No!"

"But why not?"

"He'll be angry that I took you there. He'll think it happened because you were upset, and he'll blame me."

"That's silly. But you're right that he might think so. I won't tell him."

Zabetta waved an ivory fan and looked relieved. She admired the baby with more enthusiasm. She would have to go and tend to her husband now, she said. "It's a bother. But Augusto makes a fuss if I'm gone too long. He throws things, and a bruised forehead or blackened eye would be too embarrassing with Carnival over."

"There's no end to the sorts of things a domino hides," agreed Amity with the wisdom the season had taught her. "I don't know how you stand him, Bet!"

Zabetta wrinkled her patrician nose disdainfully. "I put up with what I must, Amity. But I'm afraid that next time he'll throw his chamber pot. And to think he has no money, the old fool!"

By the time Donna da Riva left for the villa on the Brenta, Amity declared that she was well enough to venture out. Summer had come to Venice, and the world was enchanted. Amity could not bear to miss any of it.

There were fewer parties in the city, with so many people gone, but Amity had never liked the parties. Mario did not seem to mind their absence either, but was content to be alone with her. They frequented the piazza, drinking flavored ice water and spiced fruit drinks, eating whipped cream and wafers at the sidewalk cafés, with their endless lines of marble-topped tables encroaching on the pavement. Inside the cafés, rows of cordials sat in glass bottles with silver stoppers. There were white napkins, iced carafes, little porcelain pots of coffee. Now and again Amity was intrigued by some Turkish entourage or a Spanish grandee who, having taken a palace for the summer, arrived with an attendant in scarlet livery to pull out his chair.

These were the cafés of the rich. She wondered if that were the reason they never saw Francesco. Did he prefer to take his refreshment elsewhere, up some twisted *calle* where the egalitarian gathered? She wondered if Mario knew that Francesco had brought her home that day.

When it grew late, they floated out into the lagoon. Sometimes friends of Mario's halloed from other gondolas, and they turned the boats together, passed wine and cheese back and forth, and sang. Other times Mario and Amity went to the Lido and took off their shoes to wade in the crashing starlit surf. These times Amity liked best of all: the sand rushing out from around her feet as the waves receded made her feel as though she were floating as she tasted his wonderfully salty kisses.

On these occasions Amity forgot to wonder if she would be

able to bear him a son; she forgot to think of the disasters she had led him into with her love. She knew only that she loved him and wished for the time when he would once again grant her the splendor of intimacy.

On Sundays there were regattas. Carlo always competed with the best gondoliers of Venice, wearing the colors of the da Rivas, a white shirt with a broad yellow collar, a yellow sash, and yellow ribbons flying from his hat. Mario and Amity would go down to the public gardens to cheer him on, sometimes with Henri and Zabetta.

In July, Donna da Riva was back to accompany them, and even Zabetta's husband felt up to an outing in the sun. Augusto dozed on a bench while Donna da Riva, Henri, and Zabetta discussed what a nuisance he was. Mario merely found the old man amusing, but then Mario didn't know things about him that the rest of them did. Amity shivered and kept her eyes on the sparkling water, where boats of every description formed a pathway for the racers, ending at the stake boat. The day was sultry, and white clouds lay lightly against a turquoise sky. Flurries of soft winds romped playfully into the lagoon, ruffling Amity's wide hat, covered in white satin and worn gaily, with brim turned up behind and streamers hanging over.

The wall of San Giorgio, fronting the barracks, was fringed with yellow legs of uniformed soldiers perched on it, and even the roofs and towers of the Basilica San Marco were dotted with daring onlookers.

"Do you see them yet, Mario?" Amity asked, standing on tiptoe.

"No. Nothing yet."

"Carlo will win today," said Donna da Riva determinedly.

"Maybe. If you haven't spoiled him with too much cake and too many chocolates. He's grown fatter." This from Henri.

"Fatter! My dear boy, if you were half as sleek, Bet would have to lock you away."

"Well, I wouldn't mind, if I were locked away with her and the cake and chocolates."

Mario laughed and gave his brother a look that was almost fond. Amity frowned, wondering why she could not quite decipher the relationship between the half-brothers. Mario did not approve of Henri; Henri resented Mario. But beyond that was something else. A friendship in which each had his own position and each kept a wary distance, knowing that circumstance conspired to make them enemies.

"Here they come," cried Zabetta, waving a yellow flag. "Carlo! *Viva Carlo!*"

Everyone spotted the racers at once, and the place racketed with a thousand voices shouting the names of the favorites. The sound bounced from the walls and seemed to rise from the water like the roar of a great tidal wave, where the lines of spectator-filled boats bobbed and shifted with excitement.

The racing gondolas were no more than specks as everyone strained to see the colors. "Carlo's ahead," said Donna da Riva.

"No, it's blue," said Henri. "Blue's ahead. It's just harder to see blue against the water."

"I suppose you're telling me that my eyes are bad, Henri," snapped his mother.

"Well, you must face it. You're not as young as you used to be," he said. "Which was it, Mario?"

"I believe it was yellow," Mario shouted above the din as the boats disappeared in the dip behind San Giorgio.

Donna da Riva shrieked at the confirmation and attached herself to her son's arm, flapping her yellow flag vigorously. Amity thought that even in the heat of the moment Henri took time to be displeased. She understood the relationship between mother and son better than that between the brothers. Henri was the favorite, and he did not need to court his mother's good graces. Usually he displayed the opposite inclination, badgering her and poking fun at her weaknesses, which he saw with clarity.

Amity imagined that Henri resented his loving mother as much as he resented Mario. Had *his* mother been the wonderful Chiaretta, whom his father had adored, he would have had a better chance at the senator's affections.

But of course Henri would have been a different person himself. His weakness for romance and personal indulgence was the same weakness he saw in his mother. He had only inherited it.

Suddenly the boats hove into view again, and the air was shattered by more shouts. Carlo was in the lead, his lithe body swaying in springing curves, water rushing in frothy waves from his oars, while behind, his partner bent in perfect rhythm.

Yellow flags broke out all around the lagoon—on the island of San Giorgio, on the boats lining the race path. But the blue boat was close behind, and then abreast, the oarsmen beating the water with sharp, quick strokes, as though they were spurring a horse.

Blue took the lead, and flags of that color melded aginst the sky. Donna da Riva paled and leaned on Henri's arm. The boats came closer. Amity could see the surging of Carlo's mighty chest. Only five hundred yards from the stake boat, Carlo took the lead again, lashing the water—past the red tower of San Giorgio, past the channel of piles off the garden, between the lines of cheering spectators on the boats.

The judge dropped his flag. It fluttered to the water, and the race was won.

Donna da Riva squealed ecstatically. Mario waved a yellow flag and cheered, and Amity clapped her hands with excitement. Henri seemed bored, though Zabetta's face was alight with happiness.

"I'm going to the piazza for a drink," he announced. "Are you coming, Bet?"

Zabetta looked reluctant. "What about Augusto?" she asked.

"Oh, leave him. He'll be all right."

The old man gazed about him vacantly, awakened by the noise. "What's happened?" he asked.

"Carlo's won," Zabetta said.

"At the casino?" said Augusto. "I lost all my money at the casino."

"Don't remind us," groaned Zabetta.

"Run along, Henri," Donna da Riva cooed to her son. "We'll take Augusto with us in the gondola."

Unpleasantly Amity found herself wedged next to Zabetta's husband, who blinked at her and put his hand on her knee. Mario removed it and traded places with her. "He's disgusting." Amity shuddered.

"Perhaps we should have left him," Mario answered lightly, teasing her with his eyes.

Her Quaker rearing surfaced. "No. But was he always so obnoxious?"

"There was a time, I'm told, when he was handsome and girls liked him. But he's an example of the worst of Venice. A failure of the system. His family bought its way into the Golden Book when the Republic needed money for war. He was never really nobility. He never understood."

The ride back to the palace was a triumphal procession, with Carlo rowing and pausing to acknowledge cheers all along the way. People threw flowers into the boat. Amity and Donna da Riva had lapfuls of roses. Amity herself felt flushed with victory, and Donna da Riva basked in the congratulations of her friends on the quay or in passing gondolas.

"Carlo was wonderful!" The women's voices were full of lazy envy.

Suddenly Amity caught sight of a familiar face. "Oh, there's Francesco!" she said impulsively, and wished she hadn't, as Mario's face darkened.

The garlands of blossoms draped from the doorway of the da Riva palace delighted her, and the moment was forgotten as she murmured her own congratulations to Carlo. He, subservient as ever, put out his hand to help her ashore.

Amity and Mario watched the sunset from their balcony. He had supper sent, announcing that he thought her too tired to go down to dinner. Amity did not protest his protectiveness. She was too pleased to be alone with him.

"I'm not sure you should have gone to the regatta, Am," he said worriedly.

"But I had such fun! It would *make* me ill to miss summer in Venice."

She could have said nothing that pleased him more. Was she beginning to understand why he loved Venice so? A music boat drifted past in the darkening canal. Other boats followed its bright wake, like moths darting after a candle. A cool breeze wafted in as he bent and kissed her.

"Mario, where has everyone gone tonight?"

"Oh, to the piazza. There'll be music and dancing. Carlo has gone to a party for the gondoliers."

"Don't you want to go out? You needn't stay in because of me."

"But I want to stay."

She thrilled as his hand dropped to her breast, resting lightly against her bodice. At her quick intake of breath he loosened her fastenings and slid his hand beneath. She almost wept at the sensation. It had been so long! He kissed her again, his eyes seeking hers in the darkness. The kiss lay sweet and lingering, charged with meaning, declaring his intent beyond any doubt.

"It's getting chilly out here; we'd better go inside," he said.

"Yes," she agreed.

He left the doors open behind them; she could feel the

breeze from the canal playing over her body and smell the scent of trailing roses growing on the balcony.

His hands traced their way over her body like a homecoming. She was utterly naked now, tensed and trembling as he moved down her back to cup her buttocks in his tender grip. She throbbed with expectation as he slid around to the part of her that ached most with remembrance. Helplessly she threw her head back against the pillows, stifling sobs of passion as he found his way, touching her flesh in a firm, gentle way that told her of his love and his need. He knew what she wanted, and stripping off his clothing, slid into bed beside her.

Somewhere in the palace, little Chiaretta wakened and cried, as if aware of her parents' pleasure. Mario paused and raised up on his elbow.

"Don't stop, Mario," she cried in panic. "There's no need. The nurse will see to anything she needs."

"Yes, you're right." He sank back, but it was not the same as before. She was trembling in a different way than she had been before the baby had cried. She was still helpless to deny his will, but the infant had reminded her what the outcome might be. She turned her face away from him, hating herself for her lack of courage to face her woman's fate.

Mario sighed. "You are not well enough for this, Am."

"Oh, I am perfectly well!" she said. She was terrified of another pregnancy, frightened of another labor more than she was of dying itself. But more than anything else she was afraid of losing Mario's love. She was afraid of alienating her husband. Her husband! Was he that? Surely that had become another part of her fear.

She opened her arms for him. "Come back, darling."

"I'm not in the mood any longer," he said tersely.

She could not understand why. Had she transmitted her fear? Was he afraid himself? But what matter? He was a man and bound by nature to do what a man would do.

"Why, Mario?" she demanded. A thought occurred to her. "Are you thinking of Francesco? I should never have said that I saw him. Oh, but I do wish you and he were friends again. Isn't there some way things could be mended?"

"No, Amity. The loss of my friend was a price I knew I would pay when I married you. It was not all the price, either. But Francesco is a fool to come back to Venice. There'll be spies watching him. He's too critical of the powers and is too honest to watch his tongue."

"And too brave," Amity said, hoping to promote reconciliation by reminding him of Francesco's qualities.

"You don't have to tell me what I have lost," he said angrily.

"I suppose you think it wasn't worth it," she said, hurt.

"Dammit, I did not say that," he cried, forgetting his language in front of his wife.

Amity wept. "Your actions speak for you, sir! You are sorry you married me!"

Mario blew a breath of frustration. "You will have it as you will, Am. I believe I will go out tonight after all."

Amity wept harder when he had put on his striped linen waistcoat and his breeches of Florentine silk and left the palace. Fear worked on her until the substance of her body seemed to dissolve in doubt. She had put her life into his hands when she had married him and come to Venice. That had been easy in the first flush of love that had decreed it. She had believed their love was strong enough to stand against anything, but now she had begun to wonder. It might have been different if her child had been a boy. Irrationally Amity felt to blame for Chiaretta's sex. That would not please the senator, and Amity had wanted to please Mario's father as well as Mario.

Why was it that Mario had not made love to her after all? Was it because he was struggling with the possibility of allowing their marriage to be annulled?

After a while Amity finished weeping and made her way to the nursery to hold the baby fiercely. She thought of the Gypsy and wished that the crone had been able to see that her husband would always love her.

21

Mario da Riva was furious. He was furious with his wife because she made him furious at himself. Tonight he scorned a gondola and walked the little *calli*, breathing the scent of flowers and the aroma of damp, moss-covered stone. In the tiny canal a gondola drifted past with drawn *tenda* and muted light. A laugh drifted to his ears. Moonlight trickled on the water, and the soft sky was dusted with stars.

Up near San Rosario, people of all classes lined the edge of the marble quay, taking the air; children ran shouting at play in the cool night. The piazza blazed with light, and Mario's eyes strained to adjust after the dusky lanes. The deep coves of the basilica, lost in shadow in daylight, were illuminated from below, displaying jewels of mosaic, and pigeons roosted on every molding, little dots of gray and blue.

But tonight the beauty of the city was wasted on Mario. What had happened in the palace he could only interpret as failure on his part. He had left his wife unsatisfied, and he wasn't certain why. The child had cried, and it had taken no more than that to distract him. In that instant the scene in which she had lain almost dying in childbirth flashed before him.

Mario had lost his courage to do what he must if he were to be her husband. To make matters worse, she had had more courage than he. She was willing to face it all again for his sake. She had touched him and disturbed him with her compliance, and in the moment of her opening her arms to him, she had shown him the qualities of a dedicated woman. To his horror, she was stronger than he!

If she had turned away, it would have been easier on him, he thought. He would have blamed her recent illness and understood. But she with her love and courage had shown him his own cowardice. He admitted that he loved her more deeply than was wise for a man to love a woman. If he could not face the possibility of losing her, how could he father a son by her?

Mario kicked at a loose paving stone, angrier than ever. What had she done to make him love her so? He glowered, thinking of the hotel in Kiev, where he had taken her for what he had planned to be the last time. But no sooner had she vanished from his life than he had been riding hell-bent over the steppe to make her his. Perhaps gossips were right when they said she had cast some sort of spell over him. There were witches in America, Venetians whispered. *She* must be one. Such gossip Mario was always careful to defend her against, explaining that the witchcraft had been in Massachusetts and that Pennsylvania was not the same place.

Venetians were a superstitious lot, Mario knew. Venice had its own witches or supposed witches. Now and then someone brought charges, and the three Inquisitors that formed the judicial arm of the government would investigate. The hapless person might be led off over the Bridge of Sighs to the prison, known as the "Leads" because of its lead roof.

There was no appeal from the decisions of the Inquisitors, because they were elected by the Council of Ten, which presided over the Great Council of all Venetian nobles. The unfortunate person wasn't always a woman, either. Jacques Casanova had once walked the Bridge of Sighs, not for any of his celebrated exploits with women, but for possessing books on cabalism. No wonder Mario took care of Amity's reputation on this point!

Mario chose a table at Florian's, ordered a cordial, and sat staring out at the piazza. A band was playing and people were dancing, but Mario hardly noticed.

"Good evening, sir; are you alone?" said a woman's voice at his elbow.

"I am as I seem," he replied uninterestedly.

"Then may I sit with you?"

He exerted himself to look at her. He was not in the mood for company, but his depression had wearied him. Perhaps it would be better not to be alone. He did not think he would mind her company. She had a tremulous voice, wavering as though it had been difficult for her to muster the nerve to approach him, and Mario found her hesitation quaint. But if her voice were quaint, it was the only thing about her that was.

Her gown was blue, and the bodice was cut so low that he could feast his eyes on all but the nipples of her soft, ample breasts, painted with dainty birds and fishes. Her waist was tiny, but he could hardly judge about her hips, since the dress was stretched over great side bustles. He imagined that they were wide and accommodating to match her bosom.

Mario had to judge her beauty by these means alone, because she was wearing a domino, which prevented his seeing her face. He found it surprising, because most of Venice had given up masking for the season. The weather was too warm for it, and Carnival was over. Still, he was only slightly intrigued. No doubt she was being naughty, and she did not want to be recognized in the piazza.

Perhaps she did not have her husband's permission to be abroad. Perhaps she was married to someone like Augusto and was in search of adventure. Well, if she were looking for adventure, why shouldn't she find a little with him? he thought, suddenly feeling unbearably lonely for Amity. She wouldn't do as well as Amity, but she might do.

He rose and pulled out a chair. "May I order you something?" he asked.

She shook her head vigorously, and Mario grinned. She did not want to expose as much as her rosy mouth. She would not find much adventure that way!

"Are you fond of dancing?" she asked.

He shrugged. "Sometimes."

Why not, after all? He might as well please her. It was part of his upbringing as a Venetian gentleman to be attentive to women, and giving her his arm, he led her out to join the revelers. It did not cross his mind that Amity, whom he had left weeping, would be hurt or angry to see him in the company of this lady. He was simply doing as any gentleman would. But he had not danced with her long before he realized that she wanted to do more than dance.

This was no problem of morals to Mario, either. Why shouldn't he please the lady further? He was vaguely aware of Amity's American ideas of faithfulness, but it wasn't because he adhered to them that he had never strayed from her before. He simply had wanted no other woman. He'd been consumed with need for her. Beside her no other woman had been worth the lifting of a skirt to have.

But this girl danced lightly, her body sending messages of turbulence with each time they touched. Mario's own body remembered the anticipation that had been crushed during the encounter with Amity. He tingled pleasantly, his male instincts responding to her excitement.

"It's a beautiful night," he remarked. It was a silly comment, since all summer nights were beautiful in Venice, but it was something to say, a safe subject, since she obviously did not wish to reveal anything about herself, except for a lust unusually ravenous for one so young as he judged her to be. She was not the ordinary Venetian matron, languorous and casual about her moonlight affairs. Someday she would be, perhaps, but not now.

She had a touch of innocence, he thought. The idea wafted through his mind and was gone, dismissed as though it were a trick of the shadows. She could not be innocent. No woman was innocent in the warm merriment of the Piazza San Marco.

The girl was quick to confirm his assumption. Taking out a brise fan, she waved it enticingly down the cleavage of her gown and said in a tone fraught with promise, "Yes, it's a lovely evening, but so warm. I'm sure it must be cooler on the lagoon."

"Ah, let's go and see," said Mario.

He strolled with her into the piazzetta, the small square of St. Mark's, and down to the water steps, where he found a gondola for hire. Soon they were drifting in the silvery sea, the waves lapping gently to the rhythm of gondola oars.

Mario slid his arm about her. His hand traced the swell of her breast beneath her gown. Through the silk he felt her heart throb wildly with the beat of her desire. It *was* cooler. A sea breeze swept over them, bringing pungent scents, adding a caress of its own. Mario became eager, almost impatient. He wanted to have her and have done with it, relieve his aching, thwarted needs before his heart could remind him that this was not the woman he wanted, before he forgot how senselessly angry he was with Amity.

Amity had done nothing to anger him, nothing but offer herself to him, nothing but what this girl was about to do. But Mario was angry nonetheless. She had caused the foundations of his life to shake; that was the thing that she always did.

"Take off your mask," Mario demanded of his companion.

She demurred and turned her face away.

She was being coy, Mario thought in irritation. But he really didn't care. If he made love to her while she wore the mask, it wouldn't be the first time he had ever taken a woman that way. It had been a sort of game of Carnival, and if a partner did not remove her mask, she could pretend she had never been seduced at all. But Mario had always known what face lay behind a lady's domino. He had been a selective lover. Ladies who had lain beneath Mario had always *wanted* him to know; they simply didn't want to admit it in the light of day. Many women had wanted him, and the method had spared blushes the next time Mario had come to sup with their husbands.

This Carnival season no lady had had any reason at all for blushing because of Mario. This girl wished to change that. For all he knew, she was acting on a dare. He would not put it past the ladies of Venice to arrive at such a mischievous scheme to try to break Amity's exclusive hold on one of the most-sought-after men of the city. Was that why she did not want him to know who she was? The escapade would be the best-digested morsel at Venetian tea tables tomorrow if that were so.

Mario drew the awning shut. The canvas flapped and protested, the breeze sighing as it was banished from the sweetness of the girl's perfumed skin. Now she reclined on cushions of morocco while Mario's hands slid under her gown, beneath the structure of fashion, to the place where she became more than a doll-like creature of style, her well-formed limbs writhing with arousal. He found where she was hot and moist and sighed himself, like the breeze, happy with the chance encounter, so fortunately timed when his problems seemed worst, when he was at war with himself, his wife, and his future.

Her breasts welcomed his lips, the nipples swelling and hardening as they lay outside the smooth silk of her gown, from which he had freed them. His lips found the tender spot behind her ears.

She was shivering with expectation. Her little slippers had dropped into the bottom of the gondola, but other than that he did not try to undress her further. The task could not be accomplished easily in such small quarters, but a woman of any experience knew how to arrange her clothing so that she might steal a moment of ecstasy and return to a party without telltale wrinkles in her skirts to betray her.

This girl did not have such expertise. Either that or she was too overcome to exercise it. Lace and whalebone crunched as Mario moved to possess the marvels they encased.

He should have been warned. But he was not thinking of such things. He was hardly thinking of the girl at all. He was thinking of the future. Of the son Amity was so willing to bear him. Of the destiny he might surrender if his father refused to accept her.

"Mario," whispered the girl. At first he thought nothing of that. It did not surprise him that she knew his name. "Oh, my love," she murmured. Her tears trickled onto his forehead as he lay with his head on her bosom. He drew back, shocked at her fervor.

She had removed her mask after all. He saw soft brown eyes with curls to match tenderly framing a little heart-shaped face. It was a face that Mario had seen before, but that had been long ago, and the figure that had gone with it had been much different. The contrast was so great that Mario felt disoriented. He could hardly believe that the face and the lush form belonged to the same woman. They might have been welded together demoniacally, part of a nightmare from which he must wake.

Intent on the notion, he sat up abruptly. Neither the face nor the figure vanished from his vision. "My God!" he cried. "Giovanna!"

She smiled through her tears. "Forgive me for tricking you, Mario. I had to."

"Had to! Why? Francesco would be livid if he knew. Why aren't you in the convent? You are supposed to be in the convent!" For the second time that night he was enraged at a woman who loved him and whom he had caused terrible anguish.

"Oh, Mario, it was the only thing to do! I was only a child when you left! Now that you see how I've changed . . . now that you know I'm desirable, not just to some men, but to you, nothing else matters. I can never love anyone but you!"

He was moved to pity as he took her chin in his hands and kissed her lips, salty with tears. "Don't say such things, Giovanna. We were never in love. It was to be a marriage of convenience. You know that. There will be other loves for you."

She pulled away from him. "*You* were not in love! You don't know about *me!* You don't know what I felt, Mario! You never asked. Nobody ever did. I loved you, Mario. I've loved you since you were only a boy and used to come to the palace to get Francesco to play skittle!"

"What!" The idea made him laugh. "Why, you were a baby in your nanny's arms when Francesco and I first walked to Council together as pages!"

"I was barely more than a toddler, I admit. But I adored you even then." She clutched his sleeve, not bothering to cover her naked breasts, displaying them boldly to further her cause. "Mario, you know that the senator will ask you to accept an annulment. You must take it, Mario! Not just for me, but for Venice. You will be doge someday!"

"What of Amity?" he said coldly. "What of my wife?"

"Can you imagine her the dogeressa? Of course not! But she and your daughter would always be well-cared-for. And I would not mind if you made her visits. I would be understanding. I would even be her friend, if she would let me!"

Mario was beside himself with this feminine logic. How could she sound so righteous and reasonable as she offered herself to him wantonly, begging him to desert the woman he loved?

Amity the dogeressa? In some ways he thought she would be magnificent—if Venice would accept her. But he envisioned trouble, too. She might decide to wear her Quaker bonnet in the gilded rooms of the Ducal Palace or invite the entire fishing population of Ponte Lungo to tea in accordance with some democratic notion.

Suppose Giovanna were right? The possibility unnerved him more than anything else this night. He had to acknowledge that the idea had merit. He need not worry about Amity's having his son. The senator would be pleased, and Francesco, whom he missed sorely, would be his friend again. He would undo the wrong he had done the innocent Giovanna.

Innocent. Was she that? She held open her arms, begging him to take her, to explore the wonders that could be his. She smiled, confident that he would find pleasure in his discovery.

"Giovanna, I cannot make love to you," he said sternly.

"Why not, Mario? I am a woman, and you are a man. That is all it takes."

She ran her hand along his thigh, and Mario felt his body surge, ravaged with need held too long in check. Still he fought for self-control.

"I've wronged you too much already, Giovanna! You are a virgin from a convent, and your brother would do well to kill me if I robbed you of the treasure that should be saved for your wedding night."

She laughed, showing pretty little teeth. "Dear Mario! Do you think I did not consider that? Do you imagine that this is the first time that I have been with a man? If I slip out of the convent one night, why do you think that I have not done it many times? I am not the only girl who has lost her virtue by escaping through the bars of the convent in which she has been placed for safekeeping! I would not burden you with being the first."

He was amazed. He had underestimated her. She had taken care of everything. When he had been betrothed to her, she had been only Francesco's sister; now he gave her her due as a woman in her own right. Still he held back, knowing that her plan was to be his wife, his heart filled with Amity, Amity.

Giovanna, remarkable girl that she was, read his mind. "You don't have to decide now, Mario," she said. "Only love me. It's the least you ought to do. Then I will have it always to remember."

Mario's scruples crumbled as she urged his body against her and brought her lips persuasively against his. He took her with a violence that surprised her, beating into her body with savage desire. Valiantly she met his thrusts, dealt with the unprecedented sensations that raced through her being, finding glory enough in his gift to make it the pinnacle of her life.

He drew back, spent, aware finally just how much he had underestimated her. As he had begun to love her, she had not quite been able to stifle her cry of pain. Mario had felt the impediment to his entry too late to stop. He stroked her hair and looked at her in wonder. The gondola rocked harder on the water, and the awning flapped with the warning of a summer thunderstorm.

"What of your wedding night, Giovanna?" he murmured.

"I shall not have a wedding night, unless it is with you," she vowed, her eyes shining. "I will never ask any more of love, since I have had you."

22

Through the sweet summer days and nights, Mario was distracted. There were midnight picnics on the Lido. The warm breeze fluttered feathery hats and light lacy dresses, as picnickers consumed lobster and stuffed pheasant, melon and figs and almond macaroons set out by torchlight. Seabirds shrieked above the waves, their strident cries mingling, indistinguishable from those of the merrymakers. Daring young woman ran into the surf wearing flannel bathing gowns. In the water the gowns floated on the surface like the white blooms of exotic sea lilies. And beneath where the light of stars did not reach, enterprising young men dived darkly to search for the tender stems.

The Lido was the best place from which to see the fireworks that so often burst over the piazza. Dozens of parties would line the beach, gondolas drawn up in the sand. Donna da Riva, with her current *cicisbeo,* would stroll from group to group, exchanging all the latest gossip. Amity wondered how much of it concerned her and Mario.

Other lovers wandered hand in hand in the edge of the waves, but Amity, more often than not, found herself alone. Sometimes Mario walked or swam away from her, not seeming to notice her existence. When he stayed dutifully beside her, the strain of polite talk was worse. But all in all Amity was glad when the outing lasted until dawn. Then she could pretend that he would not have left her to sleep without him in the big carved bed.

Misty summer nights, the scent of blossoms trailing from garden walls and balconies, the song of gondoliers on the soft air—all seemed to mock the growing chill in Amity's heart. Nothing Amity could do would tempt Mario to her bed. When she grew seductive, he grew wary. Their love seemed a dream from which only he had awakened.

Once she tried to talk to him about it. "Mario," she said bluntly, "why won't you love me anymore?"

"Oh, you aren't well enough. There's time. Don't be impatient, Am."

"But I'm lonely. Couldn't you at least lie here beside me?"

"No. I don't trust myself."

"Then trust *me.* I know what I'm doing. If I don't prevent your loving me, then it is all right."

He sighed and put an end to the conversation by stalking away. If she had been anyone else, if she had been Giovanna, he would have agreed with her. She must do her wife's duty and be mourned for it if she died. But she was not Giovanna, who these days enjoyed what Amity did not.

Mario wondered if Amity's troubled childbirth was his fault. He had subjected her to a great deal, bringing her to Venice. If only he had stayed with her in the south of Russia, as she had wished! Poor Am! She had never aspired to be the wife of a doge, she had simply had the ill luck to fall in love. He should have stepped aside and let Francesco wed her. She would have been better off building the frontier with Francesco than in her ambiguous role as wife to a noble of a crumbling empire.

But the very idea of Amity with Francesco made Mario seize a pot of trailing begonia and hurl it against a garden wall.

The routine of the household was shattered one morning when Zabetta rushed in flushed and out of breath. Donna da

Riva fanned her as she dropped into a little French chair at the breakfast table, where they were all having coffee and rolls in a bay-windowed nook overlooking the canal.

"Have you been *running*, Bet?" said Donna da Riva disbelievingly. "You'll have the vapors in this weather."

"I didn't wait for the gondola," said Zabetta, accepting a glass of water. "It's Augusto. He's done it at last."

"Done what, Bet?" Henri said tensely.

"What he ought to have done long ago. Died."

"Are you certain?" he cried.

"He's quite purple. And he isn't moving at all. He tripped on the sash of his dressing gown and fell down the stairs."

"How dreadful!" Amity said. Everyone looked at her curiously, and she realized she was quite out of kilter. Nobody thought it was dreadful. Quite the contrary. Augusto's demise had been violent, but not undeserved, perhaps. Why, after all, had his sash been untied?

Her eyes asked the question of Zabetta, and she received the answer she had suspected she would.

"We mustn't grieve," said Donna da Riva philosophically. "He was old, and his time had come."

Nobody did grieve. In fact the funeral procession had a holiday air. A gilded barge led the way with the earthly remains. Four boatmen in black tam-o'-shanters rowed, while at the bow a carved lion wept wooden tears into a wooden handkerchief. At the stern a bearded angel kept watch over the sunny froth of water. Roses tumbled from wreaths on the barge and fell into the canal, to be plucked up as they floated by ladies on the black-and-gold-draped gondolas behind the funeral barge.

Well-wishers called from the banks as they swept into the lagoon, and the day was so fresh and bright that one gondolier forgot himself and burst into song as they rowed for the cemetery island of San Michele.

Zabetta's husband was laid to rest in a crypt among shady cypress trees in a graveyard lavish with domes and sculptures and wrought-iron gates. The church was cool and austere, tended by quiet Franciscan monks. Amity went with Mario to visit his mother's tomb and saw the confusion on his face as he laid flowers there.

"She would have liked you, Amity," he told her.

"Maybe. But she would have wanted you to be doge." Amity sighed.

"I shall be if I am meant to be," he said, staring off across the lagoon.

Amity studied the rows of da Riva tombs. Why, there were as many of Mario's family as the entire graveyard of the meetinghouse. Some were entombed in a mausoleum, where portraits lined the walls. Mario pointed out the various ancestors—one who had helped to lead the first attack on Constantinople in the thirteenth century and had helped to bring home the four bronze horses that stood above the portals of the basilica. Others had manned the galleys of the Venetian navy against the Turks in the sixteenth century, commanded the great trade routes to the Orient, bringing back silks and emeralds, ebony, indigo, spices, and brocade.

"We were born dangerously from the sea, and we lived dangerously. What times, Am, when Marco Polo walked among us!"

"Times have not changed as much as you think, Mario," she said. "Even now La Serenissima defies the world by refusing to be ordinary. And the world knows it. Why else do people from all over Europe flock to spend their summers among her palaces and cafés? The columns and frescoes of Venice are more than art; they are an expression of man's spirit. Venice reminds people of their own mystical souls!"

He looked at her in surprise and admiration. "But what about the decadence you see around you, Am?"

Amity frowned. He knew her too well. She had been trying to understand his love of Venice, but she had not yet entirely succeeded. "I suppose Venice has been dazzled by its own beauty until it has lost its common sense," she said.

He laughed with pleasure. "You have thought about this a great deal!"

She felt a little patronized. "Shouldn't I think about such things, Mario? I have a mind to use, even if I am a woman. And if I think, it's no wonder that I think about Venice."

"It *is* a wonder, Am, but it's one of the reasons I care for you so. My little Quaker, you are still seeking enlightenment, as much as though you still sat on the bench in your meetinghouse. I am lucky to have you, and so is Venice."

The ancient cypress trees hummed in the sea wind as he held her close and kissed her fervently. She knew the secrets of the ages as he held her. All life since time began had amounted to no more and no less than this—this passionate, deathless love that went, like Venice, beyond what was mundane or explainable.

And in that moment Amity knew that she had no need of the Gypsy's crystal ball. She knew that her husband would love her forever.

He drew back and looked at her, and the anguish on his face told her that there were problems that love did not solve. He studied her for a long moment, his amber eyes burning into her cool blue ones, as though to find surcease from the heat of his dilemma, a dilemma that she could never fully know or understand.

"When you seek enlightenment, seek it for both of us, Am," he said finally. "I have never had faith in a god, but only in myself. That has been enough, until now. I have a new faith now."

"What faith, Mario?" she asked, puzzled, knowing he was not a religious man.

"Faith in you, Amity! Faith in you!"

Amity wished the hours on the island would never end. She wanted to walk forever arm in arm with her husband at the edge of the beach, the surf turned to a golden lace by the rays of the setting sun. She felt as she never had before the substance of the man she had married. She realized how heavy was the rudder that still held his life toward his natural destiny.

With evening Venice rose from the blue mists, her lights sparkling brighter, beckoning over the hollow roar of the waves. The gondolas went homeward with lanterns swinging, the lights blinking like fireflies as the boats hove up and down the hills and valleys of the sea. Rocked by the waves, soothed by the sea wind, she fell asleep against the shelter of his shoulder. She was unaware when they reached the Grand Canal and were once again embraced by the city that was her only true rival. She remembered vaguely that he lifted her and carried her from the gondola so as not to disturb her sleep. The kiss that lingered on her lips roused her finally. Half-dreaming, she imprisoned him, her arms around his neck. Wild sensation raced along her spine and made her dreaming bliss. Her slumberous visions imagined the touch of his hands on her body before indeed it was there. As he undressed her, her silk gown slipped away from her as gently and sensuously as the water from a gondola's oar.

She moaned as she felt his hands on her bosom. This time he would not deny her, and when he tried to pull away, she locked herself about him and gripped him tightly, knowing he would not have the strength to overcome her, to overcome the thundering passion that welded them like the magnetism that held earth to sun.

She felt her triumph in the booming of his heart, lying against the trough of her breasts. The warm hardness of ecstasy pressed against her stomach, and her body shivered as she thought that it would soon desert that sweet cushion for the channel of her desire.

"Mario! Mario!" she murmured, weeping with relief at this longed-for proof of his love. The things that he did with his hands unnerved her. She trembled and shuddered, out of control. Unable to bear the wonderful torment any longer, she shoved herself shamelessly upward in the bed, spreading her legs as she tried to guide him between.

But somehow they had got into an unusual position that was not at all what she wished. Amity began to struggle, but suddenly she was jolted by incredible caresses between her thighs. She was scarcely able to think what must be the truth as her body writhed in helpless response to the very touches she had enjoyed in a different way when he had kissed her mouth.

A convulsion of astounding magnitude rushed over her. She lay drained and weeping.

He did not wait to hear what she would say, but quickly retrieved his clothing and left her alone in the room. He had been unable to deny her, unable to deny himself, and he had dealt with their mutual need in the only way that his fear for her would let him.

In the dark, Amity assessed at last the completeness of her defeat. She had thought to make him her love slave, when after all it was she who was held in passion's bondage, just as she had been from the beginning.

She had not guessed how innocent she still was. He had weapons of love, undreamed of, against which she could never marshal any defense. Her body still throbbed where his skillful lips had kissed her so intimately.

She sighed to remember how the czarina had urged her to conquer Mario as Catherine had conquered Russia. But even an empress could be wrong. It would be easier to conquer an entire country, she thought, than to conquer a man like Mario da Riva.

Three times around the altar she had walked with Mario, sealing their union and their destiny. But it had not been sealed at all. Tonight had proved it.

She thought of the women of the committee of her meeting

who had come to explain the sexual act to her to prepare her for her union with Silas Springer. No doubt what had happened in her bed tonight went far beyond their knowledge. They might have said it was the devil's work she and Mario had done there together. Was it? Amity's quick mind told her that what they had done had not been evil. But neither could they go on so.

If only Mario had not been allowed into the room during Chiaretta's birth! But she would have died had he not come! Amity persisted in believing that somehow he had saved her. Why else had everything changed so? Why had her body seemed to grow strong and to take charge of the task at hand? Why else, when everyone, including her, had thought she was going to die?

She slept, and when the clamor of church bells and the cries from the vending boats awakened her, she lay watching the reflection of the canal swirl like watered silk on her ceiling.

She dressed in a simple gown of India muslin with only a single row of lace on the flounce of the elbow-length sleeves, and brushing her golden hair into a chignon of curls, she went down to the breakfast room. The hour was late, but usually Henri and Donna da Riva dawdled long over their morning coffee. She was not surprised when she heard a clatter of dishes in the room. But this morning it wasn't Henri or his mother who stood gazing down at the activity of vegetable barges and gondolas in the canal.

The man's toga of black silk marked him for a nobleman—a very important nobleman, for the sleeve of the toga was long and wide. Amity had learned such distinctions. The doge himself wore the longest sleeve—to the ground—made of cloth of gold.

Before he was aware of her presence, she studied him, noting the fine Venetian profile, the deep-set eyes, the patrician nose, and the way he held his head with unselfconscious pride beneath his short peruke. He emanated assurance, but at the same time wore a worried expression. Amity did not have to be told the cause of it, any more than she had to be told that this was Mario's father.

He had about him the same aura of leadership and command as Mario, but he seemed tired, as if only great will kept his shoulders from sagging with the weight of years and dashed hopes. *She* was the reason for his ruined dreams, she thought, and trembled. If the senator had spoken to his son, then Mario had given him no reason to think that he would allow the marriage to be annulled. And the grandson that should have been in the cradle was a golden-haired girl instead. He would have heard of her mother's troubles in childbirth. No wonder the senator was downcast!

She made a sound, and he turned and saw her, gazing at her with as much intensity as she had looked at him. "You are Amity," he said simply of the woman for whom his son had endangered so much.

"And you are Mario's father. I'm glad we've met at last."

His mouth turned in a wry smile. "Indeed?" He thought she was lying, paying unfelt obeisance. He would not have expected such a trait in the woman his son had described to him. And he had hoped his son had been deceived by his passion into believing her more than she was. She would be easy to send packing.

"Yes," Amity continued. "I am weary with living betwixt and between, and I am ready to have things settled. I will pour you another cup of coffee, and we will talk."

The senator was taken aback. Flattery would not have surprised him; neither would begging or tears. He would not have been astounded to find her cowering in her room. He was aware that his was an imposing presence.

But imposing presences were nothing new to Amity, who had faced George Washington and Catherine, Empress of All the Russians. Amity poured the senator's coffee and then her own. Without invitation she seated herself, and then met his eyes evenly, making it impossible for him to do other than be seated himself.

"You are quite as beautiful as Mario said that you were," said the senator wonderingly, as though noticing it for the first time. She was undecorated by jewels, and yet it felt as though he would like to sit here looking at her for hours. If she were so beautiful so simply done, how would she be not adorned in anything but her own nature? Thus his son would have seen her, the senator thought, beginning to understand why Mario had risked his career and inheritance to have her.

"It doesn't matter that I am beautiful," said Amity sternly.

The senator burned his tongue on his coffee. Never in his life had he heard a woman suggest that her own beauty did not matter.

"It matters that I am not Venetian, and it matters even more that I nearly died in birthing, not an heir, but a poor girl child."

She was right, of course, but the senator found himself oddly on her side. "Chiaretta's a lovely baby, Amity. I've seen her."

"But not a boy. And maybe I'll never have another. You'd be foolish to agree to petition Council to register the marriage."

"That is my decision to make, Amity," said the senator. She was right again, and for some reason he did not like it.

"I am sorry to differ with you, sir," she said, "but it is mine." The senator's eyes were very nearly her undoing, for they were the same unusual shade as Mario's, and the reminder of him made tears sting her own eyes. It was almost enough to make her change that decision. "I am going to leave," she said, choking on the words.

"Does Mario know?" said the senator, startled. He had come back to Venice dreading something that had turned out to be no problem at all. The girl was enormously sensible, he thought with a touch of regret. Such a level head would have been valuable in his son's wife.

"No," she answered. "It is between you and me."

"I'll arrange for you to move to a villa on *terra firma*," he said. "You'll have an allowance, and Mario will visit you. It will be pleasant, you'll see."

"No," said Amity. She had been Mario's mistress once, and it had not been sufficient. She must cut every bond between them, as painful as that would be. He had said that he had faith in her, and she must be equal to it. She must do what she believed right. She must destroy everything so that it could not be put back together.

"You don't want a villa?" queried the senator.

"No."

"Then you are tired of my son already?" The senator could not believe his luck, and yet, looking at her, he did not feel lucky at all. "I suppose, then, you want money."

Amity's throat constricted. She had been ready to play out the charade, but her pride rebelled against taking payment for leaving Mario. She struggled for humility, and said, "There is a gentleman waiting for me to be free." The lie fell awkwardly from her lips.

The senator might have recognized it as such, except that he was overjoyed that he understood her at last. She was no different from other women. She was the victim of foolish passions like all of them, and not as guileful as some. How silly of her to forgo all that he offered her for another affair of the moment! But that was the way that women were. One was no different from the rest. Had he not thought that they were all alike, he never would have married his present wife.

But when Amity had hurried from the room, the senator felt uneasy. Deep inside, memories stirred, memories that he had thought he had extinguished forever. The senator dumped the remainder of his coffee out the window into the canal and took an early-morning cordial instead. Once, a very long time ago, the senator had been young and in love himself; and the woman he had loved had borne the same name as the baby that lay in the cradle upstairs. That itself had aroused his memories. But it was something more that that.

It was his son's wife who had disturbed the memories. She had not resembled that first Chiaretta in any way he could name. That Chiaretta had been dark, whereas Amity was fair; shy, whereas Amity was forthright. And yet in some way they had been the same.

He had tried to forget that his Chiaretta had been different, too, from the frivolous ladies of Venice. He had told himself that it had been only illusion, a young man's dream of love.

The senator shook his head as though to dispel his musings, and thought instead of the generations of unbesmirched patrician blood that ran in his family, and of his brilliant hopes for his favorite son.

23

She decided to go back to St. Petersburg. If she left quickly, the responsibility would be hers, and her departure need not come between father and son. If she hesitated—but she did not have the courage to hesitate—and if he asked her to stay, she would never be able to deny him. But worse, if he did not, the heartbreak would last her all her life.

Why, after all, hadn't she taken the senator's sensible suggestion of a comfortable mainland palace with security for herself and her child? Perhaps she was simply too American.

It would be easier for her to lose him altogether than to share him with another woman. If she weren't his wife, then Giovanna would be. She told herself that she was leaving for Mario's good, when in fact she was only too terrified to stay and lose him to his one love, Venice. She was taking the coward's way out. She was not strong enough to stay to dine on the crumbs of his life, though those might be the tastiest morsels on the table.

Choking on tears, she went out to the steps and found Carlo. "Do you know the convent where Giovanna Baretti lives?" she asked.

"Yes, *signora*," said Carlo, and his eyes did not even flicker. He gave no indication that the name meant anything to him, no hint that he understood the reason for her distress.

"I would like to go there, please," she said. She sat tensely in the gondola while Carlo rowed. Water lapped past. Carlo sang, some song with a melancholy sound. If she told him her problems, he would make a good confessor, she guessed. She was certain that Mario's stepmother opened her heart more often to Carlo than to the priest. She looked at him questioningly as the boat skimmed in beside a frescoed palace. Surely this wasn't a convent. But Carlo told her it was, and handing her out on the waterside *riva*, settled himself to wait.

A white-clad nun answered the sound of the heavy brass knocker. Amity asked for Giovanna and was led into the parlor, its walls covered in delicate damask, its slim windows flooding the room with distilled, water-reflected light. Ivory-inlaid tables, chairs of satin and velvet, a painted ceiling trimmed in stuccoed flowers, gave lie to any notion of austerity. The nun herself wore a festoon of pearls across her forehead. It was a charming, flowery place, but Amity should have expected it, even of a convent, in Venice.

The nun brought her chocolate and *diavolini*. The special tranquillity of the place calmed her enough to eat, and remembering that she had not had any breakfast, she fortified herself with the delicious Neapolitan sweet. Amity almost wished she were Catholic. Then perhaps the nunnery would be a solution for her. Surely there could be worse fates than to stay in this entrancing place and serve God, protected by her vows from her passion for Mario or for any man.

Amity sighed regretfully, knowing that such a solution would be more ill-fated than her marriage. She was meant for desires of the flesh. The memory of the outlaw assailed her, and she shuddered, realizing that without the solace of Mario she would be prey to other men, and she did not dream that any of them could satisfy her as he had done.

Then Giovanna appeared, and Amity forgot all else as she gazed on her rival's beauty. Giovanna wore a gown of yellow and apple-green stripes trimmed with feather flowers; and her hair, no longer the soft brown of the miniature, had been bleached in the sun in the manner of sophisticated Venetian women. Amity had been expecting a child. This, without doubt, was a woman. But she was a woman in more than her fashionable gown and grown-up hair. There was something in her manner, an assurance in her bearing.

She had the confidence of a woman who had been loved. Amity did not have to wonder by whom, and awful jealousy thundered over her as she became certain where Mario had spent the nights on which her own bed had been empty.

They stood awkwardly apart, each woman consumed with her own envy and misery, and then Amity stepped forward and seized Giovanna's hands warmly in her own. "We mustn't hate each other, Giovanna. We must think of what's best for Mario, since we both love him so."

"I suppose you think *you* are what's best for him," said Giovanna. "But I can never give him up!"

"You won't have to. I am defeated, and I am going to leave him. But you must love him with all your heart and dedicate yourself to no one but him, since he will be yours now."

Surprised joy registered in the girl's eyes. "Has Mario asked you for an annulment?"

"No. I am going because I am not a patrician and I am afraid I can never give him the son he needs. Mario's marriage should be without a cloud, and he should have sons to follow after him, all like him and registered, as they should be, in the Golden Book."

Giovanna looked confused. "Then the senator has refused to petition the Council. You'll become Mario's mistress."

"No. It's my own doing. And I won't become Mario's mistress. I'm leaving altogether. But Mario mustn't know where to find me, and you must help me see to it that he doesn't."

"I? How can I help?"

"Help me leave Venice, Giovanna. Send to your brother and ask him to be my boatman."

"Francesco!" Giovanna's eyes lighted. "He loves you, Amity. You will make him a happy man!"

Amity shook her head. "I will never love anyone but Mario, Giovanna."

"Are you certain? Francesco——"

"Don't talk to me of loving Francesco!" said Amity with a shudder. "That was a foolish flirtation. I've learned from it, I hope!"

"You shouldn't be hasty, Amity. He loves you so much. And you are suited to each other, just as I am suited to Mario. He's told me all about you. He talks of nothing else. You will need someone when your marriage is over. You could do no better than Francesco."

Amity silenced her with a wave of her hand. "Giovanna, you must promise to love Mario, and try to bear his sons, and help him fulfill his dreams for Venice."

"I will!" said Giovanna fervently. "Wait tonight in the garden by the canal at Ca da Riva. I will send Francesco to you."

"Thank you, Giovanna," said Amity, and her voice broke.

Outside, Carlo waited to take her back to the palace. She trailed her hand in the sunny water, thinking how quickly the city had become full of memories. She could never love Venice as she did the green meadows and hills of Bucks County, but she had come closer than she had ever thought she would.

In the shallowness of frivolity of the city, she saw a last feeble expression of the mighty spirit that had built great monuments against the teeth of the sea. Refugees from the savagery of Attila the Hun had founded the secluded city between the Alps and the sea, protected by the shelf of the Lido from heavy seas and the fleets of invaders. Greeks, Arabs, Armenians, Turks, and Jews strolled on the *calli* and *rive,* their contributions apparent in palaces with ogee windows and flagged courtyards from which rose wide staircases like those in the houses of Damascus and Baghdad.

Many peoples had shared the dream of Venice, just as many were beginning to share the dream of America. His land and hers were not so different, after all, each built by people defying tyrants. Venice had become more than a refuge. With such men to lead, it had become a power with a great navy and two million colonial subjects. So would America become a power, she thought, when it had won its independence.

Venice was the old, America the new. Amity did not think Venice could be saved. She prayed that America would never become like Venice today. But there was one great difference that might save it. America would have no nobility, no Golden Book.

A shadow passed over the prow of the gondola, and she glanced up into the branches of a gnarled olive tree, noticing that Carlo was taking her home a roundabout way. She thought that might be to confuse the spies who always watched her as a matter of form. As the wife of a da Riva she'd been quite safe, even though she was a foreigner, and she wondered why Carlo was bothering to throw them off her trail.

Did Carlo guess that she was leaving Venice? What else could a visit to her husband's former fiancée mean but capitulation? But another interpretation might occur to the spies. She was an American patriot, and Giovanna's brother was known as a critic of the government. If two such egalitarians got together, might it not mean a plot against the state? Perhaps she'd put Francesco in danger by asking that he ferry her out of Venice. Would he come? Should she have asked?

The palace seemed empty when she returned. Everyone had gone out to enjoy the day. Not even any servants were in sight. The afternoon was endless. Again and again she heard footsteps along the walk outside and hurried to the windows, heart thudding with fear and hope that Mario might be returning. He had been gone for a long time, and she wondered miserably if it were because of the thing that had happened between them during their strange night of love.

She trembled when she thought of it, little chills running up her spine and blushes rising to her cheeks, though no one was there to see. What things were there that she did not yet know of love? She had not dreamed that she, a married woman and a mother, could have been so naive. Whatever she didn't know, she would not discover it now, not with Mario.

Perhaps, then, with the likes of the outlaw, who had been her first teacher? No, she told herself emphatically. Not that either. Could she be sure? It had happened once. It had almost happened twice.

She wondered if Mario knew that his father had returned to Venice. Had the senator informed his son of their conversation? She remembered the lie she had told—that there was a man waiting for her to be free. Mario would most likely recognize the untruth if he learned of it. All the same, she marveled at the pride that had prompted her to tell it; it would serve her right if Mario did think that she was fleeing to her lover.

Every minute that passed, every tick of the bracket clock, said that it was not too late to change her decision. She could still become Mario's mistress, even if the senator had her marriage annulled. She didn't have to leave. Was she going truly because she thought it best for Mario not to have the loyalties of his life divided?

No, she admitted with her devastating Quaker honesty. It was pride again. She was hoping that she could prove he was her slave more than she his. In every particle of her soul she was praying that he would appear and undo what she had done, that he would swoop down upon her and tell her she was more important to him than his heritage, dearer to him than Venice or the son she had not borne him. In her vision he cried out to her that she was his wife, she had no other, and that his existence was impossible without her.

That was the commitment she had thought he had made when they had walked around the altar together. It had been a commitment he had been willing to die or to kill for, but that had been in another land and in the first flush of love. Now the dreadful choice lay before him in all its starkness. And the absent rival, Venice: was absent no longer, personified not only in the winged Lion of St. Mark, but in the ripe beauty of Giovanna. All summer Mario had bedded her, Amity was certain. Giovanna had had the self-assured glow of a woman whose love had been requited.

He had loved Giovanna when *her* bed was empty!

Amity did not bother to ask herself how it was possible that a girl locked behind convent walls could be her husband's mistress. In Venice nothing was remarkable.

The senator had not thought it remarkable that Amity had a lover eager for her to be rid of her husband after only a year of marriage. He would have thought it more surprising, most likely, had she told him the truth: that in her unreasonable American way, she would have Mario all to herself or not at all.

It seemed it was to be not at all, she thought as the pink glow of sunset glinted on the steel-blue water of the Grand Canal. A gull flew overhead, its strident cry seeming to ask direction. Amity sighed, feeling the city in a mournful mood as the first touch of fall hung in the evening air and bells echoed, ringing to close the shops.

How could she blame Mario for falling in love with

Giovanna? She was what he had always been meant for. Amity had been only the indiscretion of his youth. She wondered where he was; and her heart went out to him as she imagined him wandering the city, perhaps along the tiny Canal of Thoughts, or gazing into the water from the Bridge of Paradise. Amity was sure that Mario would not be found in more public haunts. Florian's would not see him this evening, nor would he be found lolling about the bright, flimsily decorated gambling establishments. He would be alone somewhere, struggling with himself, admitting with awful finality that the prediction he had made when he had carried her away from the Gypsy caravan had come true.

No good will come of it.

Soon the moon would rise, low and large, with the promise of harvest, drenching palaces in honey-colored hues, reflected from the dark, shining mirrors of canals, the great city preening herself like her own self-indulgent *zentildonne*, smiling into a pier glass before a ball. The mosaics of the piazza would sparkle back at the sky like earthly stars, and link boys with lanterns would wander the labyrinth of *calli* and canalside *rive* like fireflies in the murk, lighting people from place to place on secret errands where moon and streetlamp did not reach. So Amity would see Venice for the last time.

She packed a portmanteau, carefully sorting out what she was likely to need—simpler gowns for traveling, patterned linen or embroidered muslin, more elaborate ones for the court at St. Peterburg.

She would see Gracie again, she thought, her heart a little lighter as she packed a length of Venetian lace to trim a gown for the child. Then, with a frown, she unpacked it, remembering that Caleb Beale might not approve such an un-Quakerish gift. Glancing into her oval giltwood mirror, she wondered if anyone would ever guess that she had been of that faith. Her father would not have known her, and perhaps Silas Springer would not have recognized her either. She packed sweets for Gracie instead. Had the child forgotten her? She had been away for more than a year, an eternity in Gracie's young life. Indeed it seemed an eternity to Amity as well, so remote did her days in Russia seem.

Footsteps banged on the stairs, almost drowned out by the sudden racketing of Amity's heart. She sank into a lacquered chair, her body quaking and her breath coming in gasps. The steps did not have the sound of a woman's slippers or clogs, but it might be only Henri on his way to his apartments. Perhaps it was the senator.

She knew it was neither of these. The very fury of the booming feet told her of the tempest whirling up to engulf her. The paneled door crashed back against the delicate damask of her sitting-room wall, and there was Mario.

"I've seen my father, Amity," he said. He tore off the fringed *velada* that covered his silk cutaway coat and flung the cloak angrily to the marble floor. "I understand I am to be a free man," he continued so coldly that she forgot her quaking and went as rigid as though she were one of the pilasters.

"Mario . . ." she breathed, and the whisper carried all the pain of her tormented love.

She saw confusion and hurt in his amber eyes as well. The thing that was happening was beyond his comprehension. He could not fight it with his sword, and he did not know what to do. "Amity, I will make my father record the marriage in the Golden Book. He will listen to me."

"Perhaps he will, but I will not," she said, knowing all the while that she would give in to him, that one touch would destroy her already devastated will. "You asked me to seek enlightenment for us both, and I have found it. It matters only that our marriage doesn't belong in the Golden Book. It was never meant to be."

He drew a shuddering breath and would have spoken, but she pressed her fingers against his lips to silence him.

"I am going because I am not truly your wife. I took a man who belonged to another, and I should not be surprised to have to suffer the consequences. I have wondered why you have not been a husband to me since Chiaretta's birth. Today I visited Giovanna, and I know now."

"Giovanna! She told you!" She heard his sharp intake of breath, and his lips seemed to burn her fingertips as he pulled them away to speak.

Amity's heart sank as he thoughtlessly confirmed what her own judgment had told her. "No, Giovanna did not tell me. I felt certain that she had become your mistress, but you are the one who has confirmed it." He had not given the answer she had prayed that he would. He had not even tried to lie to her. She would have believed a lie, since she wanted to so much.

Amity's chin tilted up as she tried to keep tears from coming into her eyes. If he would not lie to save her pride, she would lie to save it herself. "It's quite all right, Mario. Didn't the senator tell you that I have a lover, too?"

"No, Am, not you," he said, and she saw at once that he didn't believe her. Suddenly it was important that he did. She could not crawl away beaten because her husband had fallen in love with the girl who rightfully should have been his wife in the first place. She would not be pitied.

Mario would never have turned to Giovanna if it had not been for Amity's awful experience in childbirth—if he had not been at her side when she had seemed to be dying. He had abandoned her bed from concern for her, but he could not have humiliated her more. Now, desperate to keep him from knowing the depth of her mortification and her grief, she taunted him with his anxiety for her.

"Why shouldn't I have a lover, after all? I've been in Venice all summer, and Venice is made for love. Why should you be surprised that I have found a man with a charming little *casino* in which to pass the nights? *You* are rarely here yourself to see that I am in bed alone, and who would tell? Perhaps your stepmother and Henri are even in league with me to deceive you. They have nothing to gain by pushing you into the arms of a woman who meets your father's approval."

To her satisfaction, she saw doubt register on his features. "Not you, Am," he said again finally. He had been certain of her since he had married her, since their time together as man and wife in Russia. She was steadfast in love, as her nature meant her to be, and that had communicated itself to him without need for words. For a long while after they had met he had been as suspicious of her as he had been captivated by her, but that was a time he had almost forgotten.

His face darkened as his fury deepened. He had been angry before because she was leaving, angrier because he knew he had not done his part as a husband, angry at his own indecision about the future. Now his wrath reached a culmination as he remembered all that he knew about her. He remembered that he had found her neither a virgin nor a Tory at the Meschianza, and that he had surprised the outlaw, the notorious Doan, beneath her skirts. He had almost ceased to think of Gracie, having blotted out his suspicion that she was the daughter of Amity and Doan, but now he recalled that he had not wanted to bring Gracie to Venice for that reason. Of course Amity had a lover! How could he have been so foolish as to think she would not acquire one? Amity was a wanton who could not do without, and he stupidly had withheld what was necessary to bind her to him.

Amity sobbed as she saw that he believed her. She felt her world collapsing, everything sliding away in the loss of his trust. But it was too late to turn back, too late to fling herself upon him and plead that she had told him an untruth, too late to be humble and selfish instead of proud and generous.

She had done what was right for Mario, after all, and for the rest of her life she would have to be satisfied with that. But it was a moment too terrible to endure passively. She could not simply watch her life being swept away. She must finish it by delivering the coup de grace.

"When you were in America, did you ever hear of the Belle of Trenton, Mario?"

He blinked in astonishment; then she saw him put everything together. "The tart who distracted Colonel Rall until Washington was upon him! I heard rumor of it. They say that Moses Doan sent a note, but Rall was too busy with the temptress to read it. Moses Doan! But he was your lover!"

"Yes, yes. And I betrayed him. You might ask Silas Springer, if you think it's not true. He was the boy from my meeting whom I was engaged to marry until he found me in Colonel Rall's bedchamber."

Mario felt as though he'd been hit in Washington's cannonade. He was sickened at the idea of his wife's body beneath that of the lecherous Rall. And she'd admitted that the outlaw had been her lover, too.

"And now you've a lover in Venice, Amity," he said with awful calm. "Tell me his name. I want the names of all your lovers. Are there too many of them to engrave on the blade of my sword? Who is your Venetian lover? Is it Francesco?"

Amity's head spun as she remembered the duel the friends had fought on her wedding day. "No, Mario! It's not Francesco! It is . . . someone who is not afraid to love me as you are!"

"Afraid! I am not afraid, Am!"

She gasped, thunderstruck at the expression of bitter passion in his eyes. She had gone too far, she knew, and almost before she had made that assessment, he had pushed her to the floor. She fell on her knees, then toppled backward as he flung himself atop her.

"No! No! You cannot have me and Giovanna, too!" she cried, but her body said otherwise. She fought for breath, her lungs heaving with need for oxygen as he pressed himself into her. Mario was in too much of a hurry to loosen her stays, and whalebone crackled as her flesh strained for freedom. Helplessly she clung to him as he took her with frightening violence. She was reminded of another time he had loved her so brutally—at the Czarina's ball. Then she had been determined to resist him, and he had punished her by leaving her in unendurable need. Amity had learned the lesson well, and she did not resist as the storm of his desire lifted her like a feather and blew her against him until she lost all sense of where she quit being and he began. The oceans of their passion crashed and mixed indistinguishably, and one did not exist without the other.

She wanted it to go on and on, because as long as it did, she could forget about her failure as a wife and his as a husband. She could forget the lies she had told him and those he should have told her. And yet at the same time she could not slack her ascent to the pinnacle, a journey no less grand and spectacular for its sweet familiarity. She felt her anger and his dissipate into bliss as they traveled the homeward road of their love, and sobs burst from her pent body. She wept with joy for the perfection of the moment and with agony for the reality they would return to face.

If only she were freer, she might manage to control the tumult that was racing too swiftly with her toward the precipice. She tried to guide his hands to her lacings, but he was too engrossed in his own urgency to notice what she had in mind. Suddenly they reached the limits of human felicity and catapulted over the brink into clouds of oblivion.

And then they remembered their terrible, consuming anger. It was irrational anger, since they were in Venice. Mario should have expected his wife to have lovers; most Venetian noblewomen did, especially when neglected by their husbands as Mario had neglected Amity. But Mario was too much in love with Amity to be reasonable. Amity, in spite of her American upbringing, realized that things were different in older parts of the world, where values were not so fresh and uncorrupted. If only he had not had the poor taste to take his former fiancée as his mistress, she might have dealt with it.

But Venice itself was what neither of them could subdue. Venice, with its thousand years of tradition and its awesome demands, was the thing that stood between them more than Mario's infidelity or Amity's supposed paramour. Venice had become too much to live up to, and perhaps that was what had crumbled that great society.

"Am," he said.

She listened and heard only a sigh instead of whatever he might have said. She half thought it was just the whisper of the olive tree that grew in the walled courtyard beneath her balcony.

Each was too proud to beg forgiveness. She ached to tell him that she had no lover; but how could she, when he had shown his preference for Giovanna, who could offer him her fine Venetian heritage for the sons she would bear?

He could not beg her to stay, not when she had made it plain that other men were so desirable to her, not when he felt himself at fault for failing to love her and loving another instead. But in spite of the guilt he felt, he directed his enormous wrath at his wife.

She, minx that she was, had cast a spell over him, blinding him to his destiny and his duty. He had mistaken his condition, imagining himself part of a love beyond anything he had dreamed of. She, with that Quaker simplicity and those frank American ways! He saw clearly the value of the Venetian custom of sending young noblemen about the world before they settled into their duties in government and in running the Republic. Certainly nothing in Venice, not the most devastating *zentildonna* or courtesan, would ever have prepared Mario for a woman like Amity!

But now he knew. And the pain of knowing was so intense that he would never allow himself such an experience again. It had been on the tip of his tongue to ask her to stay as his mistress, even though she would not remain his wife. Wretchedly he knew that the idea had been in the back of his mind all the time, ever since Giovanna had suggested it. The wife that was proper for him, and the mistress of his dreams! Even his father had thought he should persuade her to it. But no, he would never recover from the madness of his love for her as long as she remained to taunt him past his better judgment, as she just had when he had made love to her.

It was over. Mario stood up and fastened the buttons of his breeches, retrieved his jacket, and went away. Amity, still lying dazed on the floor, pressed her ear against the boards and heard his footsteps going farther away, until the percussion of a slamming door told her that he had left the palace.

Too overcome for tears, Amity put herself to rights and fastened up her portmanteau. Mario had been returned to his destiny as though none of it had happened. He would have sons, and his sons without question would be registered in the

Golden Book. Giovanna would have Mario as it had been meant to be.

But neither Mario nor Amity had yet found the englightenment that he had asked her to seek for them both. Amity had been wrong. Neither was wise enough to guess that no destiny held sway in the world like the destiny of love.

24

Darkness came at last to match the blackness of Amity's soul. Chandeliers glistened in the rooms of Ca da Riva as Amity made her way through the halls in search of a bit of the maize bread called polenta on which to make an evening meal. A man's figure loomed up, and her breath caught, as for an instant she thought it was Mario, returning after all to make amends.

"Good evening, little sister," came the salute.

"Oh, it's you, Henri," she said.

"Why so mournful, Am! Ah, never mind telling me. I know. It's because I'm always second best. Second best with my father; second best with you. You hoped I was Mario."

"No."

"Then you were *afraid* I was Mario. That's more like it."

"Whatever you say, Henri. Let me pass." He'd been drinking, and there was a glassy gleam in his eyes. Suddenly, "afraid" was an appropriate word.

He blocked her by leaning his hand against a wall. "We never had our fun, you and I," he said with a sigh.

"It wouldn't have been *our* fun, Henri," she returned stiffly.

"Oh, I know. You think it would only have been mine. But I hear that I will have to make do with little Giovanna now, though rumor is that she's quite enchanting these days."

"Perhaps Giovanna will be more amenable than I as a sister-in-law," said Amity with a trace of bitterness.

"Maybe. Give me a good-bye kiss at least, then, Am. We are both losers in this."

He leaned close to her, reeking of liquor. It was unusual, because Henri, like most Venetians, held his drink gracefully. This occasion was different, Amity thought, and was touched by compassion. Poor Henri. He had hoped, more than to bed her, that Mario would be disinherited because of her.

"You ought to marry Bet anyway," she said irritably. "You could manage on your allowance."

Henri stared at her as though she had gone mad. "I, Henri da Riva, live in such circumstances! Like a Barnabotti! My dear child, I could scarcely buy Zabetta's gowns on my income! No, she must take rich lovers now, and I must make do as I can."

Amity saw that it was pointless to continue along this line. Zabetta and Henri did love each other in a way, but they could not conceive of themselves without the trappings of Venetian splendor. And perhaps the fate to which they went was suitable.

"Really, Henri, I haven't finished packing," she said, trying to squeeze beneath his arm. It was a mistake. The arm left off merely blocking her passage and wrapped around her.

"Don't be so righteous, Amity. You're not an innocent Quaker girl now, if you ever were. You have a lover. Are you surprised I know? You told the senator, and he told my mother, and she tells me everything. So why don't we have our fling before you go. I should like you to have fond memories of Ca da Riva."

"Henri!"

Her protests served no purpose. He was already kissing her. She was locked in his embrace so tightly she could feel the throbbing inside his satin breeches.

She managed to pull away. "Henri, help me with my luggage while I get the baby," she said in such a tone that he desisted. Having crumbled, he carried her portmanteau downstairs.

The scent of roses lingered among myrtle and palms as she waited in the dark shadows. She wondered if the last roses had died already and had left only their scent behind in petals crushed on the ground. At any rate, if they were not gone, they soon would be, and so would she, and she wondered if her passage would leave behind some ineffable scent in her husband's heart to remind him of her. Autumn storms would soon wash the last of the roses from the garden, but they at least would have another season. Amity never would, and the finality of it closed over her at last.

A distinctive scrape of wood against stone roused her from her reverie—a boat thumping the edge of the canal. Francesco came through the gate, which she had unlocked. She hesitated for a moment; then, sensing the warmth and gentleness that had always been his nature, she ran to him and buried her head against his chest.

"Oh, Francesco."

"There, Am. I'm not surprised it turned out badly. I did warn you against him."

"I'm so miserable, Francesco. I wish I could die." She whispered this last in a quavering voice, admitting it for the first time. She had been taught that the most worthless life was sacred, but hers seemed worse than worthless to her.

"Don't say that, Amity. The last time I saw you, I thought you *were* going to die."

She looked into his eyes and saw how deeply that occasion was marked on his memory. "I was about to have the baby, and you were there to help me," she remembered. "Dear Francesco, you are always close when I need you."

He raised her cold hands to his lips and kissed them. "So will I always be, whenever you will let me."

"I should have not let you tonight. You are taking a chance, Francesco. The Inquisitors—"

"Hush. I'm not worried about that. Oh, it's true that my opinions are known, and they are frowned on by the Council, but I've done nothing. I've stayed away from treasonous meetings, and I haven't embraced revolution. I've the ideas of a Freemason, nothing more."

She took his word for it, since he seemed so certain. Chiaretta began to cry, and Amity took her out of her basket to rock her to keep her from giving them away. Meanwhile Francesco loaded her belongings into a *burchiello*, a floating house with a dining room, sitting room, kitchen, and bunks for servants. Amity had seen these little establishments before, but she had never traveled in one. Sometimes nobles used them for traveling up the Brenta Canal to their country villas.

Francesco had thought of everything: there was a cradle for Chiaretta, and a servant girl to tend her. Dinner was laid on a linen cloth beneath silver candelabra.

"Have you eaten?" he asked.

She shook her head, thinking of the meal she had tried to take from the kitchen. She wasn't hungry, but she had been going to eat from duty. She had insisted on nursing the baby herself, instead of having a wet nurse. She told herself she must eat to keep up the flow of milk.

But after all it wasn't necessary to eat from duty. Francesco seemed to know all her favorite dishes—grilled shrimp with oil and lemon, browned diced potatoes, romaine salad, almond macaroons. The first glass of wine went to her head. She felt her cheeks flush as she downed another. Francesco reminded her of the good times they had had together in St. Petersburg, and as they drifted out into the lagoon, where the moon reflected like a huge brooch on the dark throat of the canal, she managed to forget for the moment that she wanted to die.

Pleasure boats drifted past, the occupants huddled close against the sharp air off the water. Now and then there was a boat with a red beacon lighting its prow, which meant that the lady beneath its *tenda* would bestow her favors for a price.

"It hasn't been easy for you, Am," said Francesco, glad that her mood had improved a little.

"No. At least your sister will be happy, and you and Mario can be friends again."

But Francesco removed that consolation. "Friends!" he bridled. "Giovanna will marry him without my blessing. A wedding now does not make amends for what happened!"

Francesco's pride was as great as Amity's, which had prevented her staying in Venice as Mario's mistress. She realized that Francesco had no inkling of the new relationship between his sister and Mario. She shuddered to think what might happen if Francesco discovered that they were lovers.

"There's a place in the mountains I should like to take you to, Amity," he said. "It's a lovely spot for you to rest and spend the winter."

"Spend the winter! But I am going to St. Petersburg! You needn't take me all the way. Simply tell me how to accomplish the journey."

"Accomplish the journey! It cannot be accomplished this time of year! By a man, yes. But a woman—and with a tiny baby. Only think, Am! There are mountains to be crossed, and the Baltic will freeze before we get there."

He was right, she knew. She had not been thinking clearly. She had only wanted so much to flee to the kind arms of Aunt Zenobia. "But, Francesco . . ." she said lamely.

He laughed at her discomfiture. "I know that you do not

want a lover just now, and I am willing to be a friend, which is what you need. Someday . . ."

"Dear Francesco! There will not be any someday. I almost married you once. My aunt told me it would be a mistake, and I know now that she was right. I will always be in love with Mario."

"I am sure of that. And he with you. But what matter? Mario is devoted to a cause that is doomed, a society in which men forsake women they love so their sons' names may be written in a silly book that will one day be thrown into the sea. You could have stayed with him, but you made the break. You know it cannot work between you and him. You may love him forever, Am, but I will love you forever, too. And you are an American and know the way in which the world is going. We'll go that way together, you and I, someday. Someday will come, Am. Someday will come sooner than forever!"

She saw that she could not dissuade him, and in truth she wasn't sorry that he was so devoted. Deep inside, she wondered if he might not be right after all. She had tried to embrace Mario's dream as her own, but she knew that it wasn't the sea eating at the foundations of ancient palaces that endangered Venice. It was the self-indulgence eating at its once rocklike values. How easy it would be to return to the ideals of her American girlhood with Francesco! Could she be certain that the someday he spoke of would not come?

She slept that night on a little velvet-cushioned couch in one of the cabins, and in the morning she awakened to find they were at Padua, where Francesco and Mario had attended the university together. After their morning coffee, laced with cream, they left the boat for a carriage, which Francesco procured, and drove out across the plains into the hills. At midday they paused at an inn where copper utensils hung from whitewashed beams and a huge fire burned cheerily in a hearth of white marble, open on every side, with a great black soup kettle hanging from chains.

The soup proved delicious and warming, and during the afternoon Amity, snuggled in a comforter, dozed as the carriage jounced along. Francesco studied her, pleased that she slept, but a bit worried that she had not wept at leaving Venice. Her golden hair caught the lowering rays of the sun and shone as though it had been dressed with rainbow-colored sequins. Her face lost its sophistication, and was even more beautiful, all rose and cream with the serious, unplanned expression of the child she had been when Silas Springer had stolen her bonnet from the grass so many summers ago. The baby waked and cried, and since they had left the servant girl behind with the *burchiello*, Francesco took Chiaretta himself, holding her awkwardly while still driving the carriage and managing to his great satisfaction to lull the child back to sleep so that Amity would not have to be disturbed to nurse her.

Toward evening the September sky was so spectacular that he awakened her to see it. In the distance the bare peaks of the Austrian Tyrol rose against a deep expanse of blue. Clouds of pure white streaked from horizon to horizon, twined with delicate threads of gold spun of windswept vapor.

The road had risen steadily, and it was colder. They passed through a fir wood, and then out into a high meadow where cows with black muzzles and switches grazed on bright green grass. All along the road blue gentian bloomed in masses, so that they felt as though they were floating between two cerulean skies. And here and there was a patch of gray-green of edelweiss or red Alpine roses.

At evening they found another inn, and having taken separate rooms—surprising the innkeeper, who had thought them a young family—they supped on a simple meal of cheese, gray bread, and Asti wine. Francesco watched as the place worked its spell upon her. He had been right to bring her this way, he thought. Venice already seemed incredibly distant. A winter in the mountains would teach her contentment, and contentment was all that he asked.

He did not expect that she would ever be wildly in love with him, as she had been with Mario, but Francesco did not need that. He had a greater faith in her than did Mario; he knew that whatever love Amity gave would be steadfast. He had never thought, as Mario had, that Amity was a woman of many appetites. Oh, it had occurred to him that Gracie might be Amity's child, but he had not been treated to the sight of her and the outlaw sprawled together in the bedroom of the Wharton mansion at the Meschianza, and certainly he had never heard of the Belle of Trenton.

He thought instead that Gracie's conception had been some innocently tragic occurrence. Amity had fallen in love with some brave soldier of Washington's army and had given herself to him on the night before battle. The soldier had marched away to die heroically before a marriage could take place. In so thinking, Francesco came close to the truth about the circumstances surrounding Gracie's beginning, though poor Isabel had been married already when the British had skewered Gracie's father to a tree at Long Island. But Francesco was less canny than Mario in his judgment of Amity's character. Where one refused to admit her stalwart devotion, the other did not see the ungovernable cravings unlocked by the wily outlaw.

Amity seemed more relaxed the next day than she had been before, and she even thanked him for bringing her to such a delightful spot.

"It will become more delightful, Am," he promised her. He searched her face for traces of tears that she might have washed away in cold water drawn from the swift-flowing Piave River, but he did not think she had wept, and was discouraged that the wound Mario had dealt her was still too deep for weeping.

He must give her time. They would have all winter, for no one knew of their whereabouts, except his sister, Giovanna. He had told only her, trusting her judgment, and he could think of no reason why Giovanna would tell anyone where they had gone. Certainly it would not benefit her to tell Mario. It was just as well that Mario did not know that he and Amity were together, though he had no more claim on her. Jealousy wasn't a reasoning thing, and Francesco was certain that Mario would be jealous.

He wished she would talk to him about the reasons she had left her husband. He knew only what Giovanna had told him, and Giovanna had seemed confused about the facts. Francesco knew that Senator da Riva had returned to Venice, but according to Giovanna, he had not demanded that Amity leave. Amity had turned tail, and that was unlike her. But Francesco did not know about Amity's empty bed or about her suspicions about Giovanna, which Mario had confirmed.

They took the road again, past village after village of gray stone houses. Men worked at sawmills, and burning resin made the air rich with its pungent smell. Women carried baskets of stones on their backs and sang in spite of the load. Francesco said that the stones were required for the maintenance of shoots in the river through which the logs were driven.

"Those stones are not so heavy as it is possible for a person's heart to be," Amity commented. "I used to dig stone from my vegetable garden by the hundred pound when I was a girl. But I had learned to think of every task as a sacrament, and so the burden did not seem difficult at all."

"I wish *you* felt like singing, Am," Francesco sighed as the horses jogged along the narrow road.

"Perhaps I *should* sing. I might be better at it than at languishing." She treated him to a chorus of a ditty she had learned in Washington's camp, and then confessed, "I thought of throwing myself into the canal to drown, since I had heard so many stories of lovelorn ladies doing so, but I'm too good a swimmer. I would never make a proper Venetian woman; I could not even do *that* right."

She smiled wanly as she told him this, her mouth twisting up at the joke on herself, and Francesco's heart lifted. She had begun to laugh at herself, admitting that her spirit was too strong to be destroyed by the vagaries of love. Amity had courage. If she had not had, she could never have done the things she had, never have married Mario to begin with. She would survive, but Francesco wondered if she would ever begin to love him instead of Mario.

Finally they traveled by water again. This time they took a sloop that carried passengers up the Lago di Garda, the longest and bluest of Italian lakes, piercing the mountains like an arrow to point the way to the town of Riva at its northern end. The day was golden, the weather chill enough for the fur-trimmed winter pelisse she had brought along. On the eastern shore, villages, monasteries, and chapels clung to the cliffs, nestling among vineyards and chestnut groves.

They came ashore where lemons grew in tiny orchards at the foot of the mountains. The orchards, which belonged to Italian nobles, were studded with tall brick columns supporting a framework of roof. Workmen were already busy lifting boards into place to protect the trees from the approaching winter. Soon the space between the columns would be shut with long panes of glass, the roof covered completely. The town itself was graceful and vine-grown, with red-tiled houses and terraces. Here, to Amity's surprise, Francesco had a house.

"It's the one thing my father saved," he said. "I suppose his creditors didn't know that it existed. My family used to come here in the summer. My sister and I played in the lemon gardens, and my first sailboat was given to me on the lake."

She was struck by the strength of his memories, as if only here in all the world did things remain as they ought, the sweet past undisturbed by the present in which his family and all that it stood for were destroyed. She noted, too, the love in his voice as he spoke of his sister. Through the whitewashed rooms of the cottage, among the rough beams of the low ceiling, Amity seemed to hear the laughter of children—a boy who had sat here on the cushions of the bay window and thought of his dearest friend in Venice. And a girl, much younger, but perhaps already in love, dreaming of the day when she would marry her brother's friend.

And suddenly Amity wept.

Francesco was beside himself, thinking that she did not like the place. After all, it was too simple, and the idea of staying here after Ca da Riva appalled her.

She wept and wept and was too racked to tell him why. He put her to bed in a feather bed supported on a frame of finely carved chestnut from the neighboring slopes, and turning the lamp low, he sat beside her until at last, in the depth of night, she shared her sorrows with him.

"Oh, Francesco, you are so fortunate to have this to come back to. I have nothing. The British took the farm, and I never had a brother or sister to care about. I think I loved Mario more than most women ever love a man, and now he is gone, too. He was all I wanted, and now I have nothing!"

The baby cried and gave lie to her words. She stumbled across the room and took it to nurse with fierce devotion.

"She should have been a boy. Then you would not have left Mario. That's it, isn't it, Am?" he said.

"It would have made a difference, but it isn't all of the reason."

"Tell me the rest."

Amity shook her head. "I'm not sorry that she's a girl," she said. "At least she won't grow up to be a man and give a woman the sort of pain I've had from Mario. Thank heaven I have her to love."

He kissed her on the forehead and went away without saying, as he longed to, that she could have him to love, too.

They passed the days in quiet companionship. Sometimes she spent hours in tears, but Francesco was always patient; and as time passed, she smiled more often. He took her to see the great waterfall of Ponale, where water plummeted to the lake, shattering the serene surface with a thunder of spray. They went for drives over the cliffside road that wound through tunnels in the mountain like a thread strung through beads. They did the marketing themselves, with only an old woman who had used to cook for the family to help set the kitchen to rights and show Amity how to make Francesco a treat of fried cream or a soup of peas, tomatoes, and chicken, covered with Parmesan cheese.

"She thinks we're married, Francesco," Amity told him worriedly.

"Yes, of course she does. We look like a family, don't we?"

"Don't make jokes, Francesco. We are misleading people and living a lie."

"Then I shall inform her that we are not man and wife. It will be a scandal, though you sleep in your bed and I in mine. Nobody will understand."

Amity frowned. He had reminded her that she was not sure that she understood it herself. She was unused to a man who could be so obviously in love with her and yet refrain from attempting to accomplish a physical manifestation of his passion.

He had not been at all this way in St. Petersburg, when he had taken every opportunity to kiss her as they drove about the islands of the Neva. What sort of game was Francesco playing? She was coming to depend on him. What would she do without him there to share her pleasure at the changing season, her observations about people going past the steep street, her distress when the baby was fretful? It was a cozy arrangement, as quiet and comfy as the calico cat that had come in from the cold to take up residence on the warm hearth.

It was altogether too cozy, she thought. What would come of it? Sometimes she remembered that Giovanna had urged her not to be hasty about rejecting the idea of marriage to Francesco. *He loves you. And you are so suited to each other.*

They *were* suited to each other. Every day it was clearer. In the evenings they would roast chestnuts that they had gathered during a pleasant afternoon and read together—sometimes from the French philosophers, who were her favorites and with whose works he had stocked the library, sometimes from English novels, which Amity, being a Quaker, had been denied in her girlhood. Their frankness rather shocked her, but she agreed with Francesco that honesty was laudable. Once Amity wrote a poem about the mountains, and Francesco translated it from her English into Tuscan, and she was delighted with the effect.

But it wasn't only in such things that Amity and Francesco

were suited. She sensed how much he liked life here, as she did. He would have been content with a farm on the Russian frontier, to live with roughly but unfettered.

How different from Mario! Even during their time near the Dnieper, Mario had never been content. His heart had been always straining toward his heritage, his dreams. Francesco had his dreams, too, but if she married him and set out for some new land, all *his* dreams would come true. She had never had the capacity to make Mario's dreams reality. Indeed she had been a drag against them. Had their marriage been annulled yet? If not, it soon would be. They would hear someday that Giovanna and Mario were wed, and then . . . What then?

One morning as she put her feet from the bed onto the cold floor, a wave of dizziness washed over her. It was just because she was still unused to the altitude, she told herself. But she had been in the mountains for more than a month, and it had not bothered her before. The next morning it happened again. Amity skipped breakfast and was sick to her stomach instead. Once in the past she had experienced such symptoms, in St. Petersburg, when Zenobia and Caleb had wed. Then it had taken her aunt to explain to her what was wrong. Now she was wiser. Her mind skipped back to her tumultuous encounter with Mario on the floor of her sitting room at Ca da Riva. At that last stupendous moment his seed had taken root in her womb, and now she was to bear his son!

His son! She was altogether certain that the child would be a boy. She was elated, but confused. What was she to do? Return to Venice and tell Mario the news?

There had been more wrong between them than her failure to bear him a son. The matter of her supposed lover. The affair he had had with Giovanna. Her utter inability to mold herself into the sort of Venetian wife he wanted her to be, glib and agreeable in that slothful, self-gratifying society. No, she would never be the wife Mario needed, never be able to accept the idea that lovers like Henri and Zabetta should not wed or that lineage in a book was more important than what was written in the heart. Eventually she would probably get into trouble, as he had warned her she would. She'd embarrass him and bring him low. Some night at someone's salon she'd forget to be a mindless beauty and give vent to some outrageous American idea.

Was it even possible to return to Venice as Mario's wife?

She could not bear to face the reality of seeing Giovanna in her place. And Mario would gently consign her to some villa to await his secretive visits. She could not raise her children so! She could not bring her son into the world to live as the bastard son of a da Riva, while his half-brothers basked in public approval at the palace and took their places as young nobles on the Council.

Amity grew strong with purpose. *She*, not Mario, would decide their children's future. She would give them a better life than that they would have in the decadence of Venice.

"Amity?" She turned and saw Francesco come into the room. "The coffee's gotten cold."

She was still wearing her nightdress, and she started to grab up a quilt for modesty's sake. But she changed her mind and allowed him to gaze on the curves of her body beneath the thin silk. She trembled as she saw that he was at last driven beyond the limits of his self-control.

"Am . . ." he breathed. Not moving, she waited for him to cross the room. His lips were warm as they met hers, and unresistingly she let herself be lowered down into the feather bed.

25

Mario stood in the piazza and gazed up at the winged lion that was the symbol of Venice. Above its blue, gold-starred backdrop the two Moors of the clock tower began to toll the hour, striking the bronze bell with their hammers. Beyond, white waves were churning, splashing over the water steps. Big gulls flew overhead, driven in by the ocean wind. A storm was coming. It was going to rain any minute, to judge by the dark clouds overhead. Mario would be caught in the downpour, but he didn't seem to care, in spite of the fact that he was not even wearing a cloak over his toga.

As the drops splattered down, Mario continued to stand in the rain, too intent on his thoughts to notice that he was getting soaked. He had just come from a session of the Council.

He had put a petition before that body, and it had been acted upon favorably without procrastination. No one had had anything to say against it, not even Mario's brother, Henri, who had been present at Council for the first time in months. Henri's appearance had disconcerted Mario, and he'd wondered if his brother had some trick in mind. But when the matter had been opened for discussion, Henri had only grumbled and shifted in his chair. Mario told himself that he was relieved when Henri had nothing to say, but actually it had rankled. Mario was used to being opposed or at least harassed by his relation, and just this once he would have welcomed it.

If Henri had found a way to prevent the Council from approving the annulment of Mario's marriage to Amity . . .

Mario wasn't a man to do anything halfheartedly, and he'd been sure that the annulment was the thing that should be done. He'd been bewitched by her, imagined that she lighted the way for him, when all along, the road she'd illuminated had only been the way to faithlessness and deceit. He'd done what he'd had to—amputated her from his life. But the pain was at least as great as though he'd hacked away an arm or a leg.

"Mario . . ."

He saw his father coming toward him. The senator took him by the arm. "What are you doing out here? Come along, we'll have a brandy." Soon they were seated in Florian's, where a fire drove away the dank of the rain.

"To your freedom, Mario," said the senator, and lifted his glass.

Mario smiled thinly and joined the toast.

The senator looked worried. "You are still in love with her, my son," he said.

"What does it matter?" said Mario. "She loved me once. It's my fault if she doesn't anymore. I tried to make her into something she was not. If I had been an ordinary man, it would not have been important for her to bear a son or understand Venetian ways or have her name in the Golden Book."

"If you had been an ordinary man, she would never have loved you at all," said the senator with such insight that Mario stared at him, wondering how his father came by his wisdom.

"I will never be able to forget her," Mario sighed.

"Of course not. But choose the good to remember and let

the bitter die. She will be a memory to comfort you all your life, wherever duty may call you."

"You are speaking of my mother," said Mario suddenly.

The senator did not answer, but finished his drink in a swallow. "Will you serenade Giovanna tonight?" he asked.

"Serenade?" said Mario wearily. "It's too wet for that kind of foolery. Besides, it's silly. It's not as though Giovanna and I were not betrothed before. I've been through all that nonsense."

"It's not nonsense to a young lady, Mario. They quite dote on it. I'd advise you to accommodate Giovanna's girlish illusions. It will cause her to be accommodating to you when the time comes."

Mario smirked, thinking how accommodating his bride-elect had already been. "I am not worried about that side of things, Father," he said.

"Ah." Mario's father was quick to grasp the fact. "Perhaps you're right, after all. We might arrange to have her to dinner this evening. The nuns will surely agree to it, since your stepmother will be present to chaperon. These are modern times, after all. It's not like the old days, when a young man and woman might not see each other between the betrothal and the wedding."

Mario wasn't in the mood for a festive meal. "That's not necessary, Father. I'm going to the convent tomorrow. I'll see her then, when I give her the betrothal ring to wear again."

"I'm glad, Mario. It's time to get on with things. But why not tonight?"

"I'm tired. Tomorrow will be soon enough."

"But," said the senator, "she's already been invited."

Mario left the café assuring his father that he would take a gondola back to the palace.

"Don't be late, Mario," his father called after him.

Mario was annoyed. He was being pushed into Giovanna's arms like a schoolboy, and it did not set well. He had made his own decision to return to her and revere his family duty above his foolish love for the little American Quaker. Wasn't that enough? Did his father think that he couldn't be trusted to fulfill the bargain he had made? Tonight was too soon. He needed time to be alone and soothe his wounds.

Did his father think he was likely to run after Amity? He wouldn't. He'd had enough of chasing that woman down. Mario thought of the grueling days he'd put in when she had left Kiev with the Gypsy caravan. He'd been like a madman when he'd found her. Yes, a madman—insane with love for her. What but that could explain his actions? He'd even dueled his dearest friend because of her! But then . . .

Memories of the Russian steppe suffused him. He thought of fireflies over fields and the love songs of peasants. He remembered her swimming naked beside him in the river, and enticing him in short embroidered skirts and long golden braids tied with sunflowers.

Mario did not take a gondola home. There were none to be had, which suited him, anyway. The piazza was almost empty. Most families had already departed for the autumn vacation season at the villas up the Brenta. Everyone went away to escape the weather; there had scarcely been a quorum to hear Mario's petition at the Council. The boatmen were huddling in the wine shops tonight, drinking sweet garba. Even the pigeons had deserted the pavements, taking shelter beneath the eaves of the basilica. Cats crouched miserably behind grilles in the alleys.

Venice was his city, and Mario had always enjoyed such times as these, being alone with its great presence. Always the city seemed to speak to him, whispering of past glories and of a possible future. Mario had expected the same tonight; the square seemed more vacant than simply unpeopled, more lonely than private. Why was it, he wondered, that rain seemed wetter in Venice than elsewhere? It was not a healthy place now; he'd catch his death. But Mario did not walk any faster, idling along, staring at the water, murky from sediment stirred up by the rain. Before he had reached the Rialto, with its shuttered shops, a heavy fog had marched in from the sea. Had Mario not known the streets so well, he would have become lost. As it was, he went blindly, his feet leading along paths he had been accustomed for many years to travel.

Then, to his surprise, his brother emerged from a *calle* to walk beside him. Mario could not remember when they had ever been together by choice. They had learned long ago that avoidance was the best policy.

"It's a miserable night," Henri offered.

"But not as miserable as I am," Mario agreed.

"Nor I," said his brother.

"It's too bad," said Mario of everything in general. Alone with Henri in the fog he felt an unusual kinship to his half-brother. Mario had thought Henri a spoiled, pleasure-loving fop ever since they'd been children, but suddenly he thought that he really hadn't been fair. He'd missed his mother horribly when she'd died of malaria, which was epidemic each summer in the city, and he'd resented his father's new wife from the beginning.

It was natural that he'd resent the new child as well, the proof of union between her and his father. But what was more peculiar was that Mario and his father had united and shut out Henri and his mother. Don da Riva had married again because it had been expected of him. Henri perhaps had been too real a reminder of the degeneration of Don da Riva's passions for his first wife into his carnal lust for the second.

The senator had never given Henri a chance, either. Mario remembered when they had both served as errand boys to the Council, as the sons of nobles did, bringing coffee and carrying the ballot boxes with their golden and silver balls. Even then the senator had smiled only on him, the elder son, who was heir to love and approval as well as fortune. Ah, it wasn't fair!

Why was he thinking these things tonight? Perhaps it was because he and his brother were sharing something at last—a mutual grief in love. The annulment of Mario's marriage had sealed Henri's fate as well as his own. There was no chance now that Mario would be disinherited.

"It's a shame it isn't the other way around," Henri was saying.

"Eh?"

"I mean, Mario, if I were in love with Amity and you with Zabetta, we would have no problem," Henri went on. "Amity would hardly care that her husband wasn't rich. She'd make do with a bowl of stew and a slamkin, though it'd be a crime to hide those charms of hers under a piece of calico. And Zabetta would make every bit as acceptable a wife for a da Riva as Giovanna."

"It's no use wishing things were different," said Mario with a frown.

"No." Henri sighed. "At least we'll each have a woman to warm our beds on this cold night. Bet is coming to dinner, too."

Mario grimaced, and his fond feelings for Henri evaporated. Henri chuckled, and then burst into guffaws that echoed unpleasantly in the fog. Mario thought to defend the honor of his future wife and decided against it. He'd only look a fool. It wasn't surprising that Henri knew the state of things between him and Giovanna, though the senator had not, Henri and Donna da Riva were terrible gossips. He imagined that half of Venice knew his indiscretions with a convent girl.

Francesco didn't know. At least there was that. Francesco would have murdered him by now if he had found out, perhaps not even in an honorable duel, but with *bravi*, hired assassins. It would be no less than he deserved.

Nonetheless, Mario supposed he would sleep with Giovanna tonight. Why not? She had pleasured him on other nights, surely she should not cease to do so simply because they were about to be betrothed once more.

Mario smiled to himself when Giovanna arrived wearing a mask, though it was not the season for it. It was the custom that a girl who was engaged should mask until she was wed, and he guessed she'd had no choice. The shivering nun who handed her over to his stepmother at the palace door would have insisted on it.

Giovanna herself felt a bit silly in the mask. She'd known Mario since she was a tot. Certainly he knew what her face looked like. These days the custom was outdated. Even the nun wouldn't object if Giovanna removed the mask, now that she was no longer outside where her blushes might be a matter of public attention. But Giovanna kept the mask in place.

How else could she hide her unseemly elation? Henri led her to her place at the table, his hand warmly at her waist. Even through her satin gown, sprinkled with garlands of flowers and trimmed with thick mignonette ruching, his touch transmitted unmistakable meaning. But unlike Amity, Giovanna was only mildly disconcerted. Rather, she was flattered that her future brother-in-law had designs on her. Like any young aristocratic Venetian girl, she had not had the experience of admirers. That was reserved for after marriage when, her virtue safely disposed of, little harm could come of it.

Giovanna's virtue had, of course, been disposed of already by Mario; nonetheless, Henri's admiration made her feel grown up.

"Pray remove the mask, dear sister," Henri entreated close to her ear.

Giovanna had never so much as exchanged a kiss with any man but Mario. She was still unlearned in flirtation, her seduction of her husband-to-be more the result of a simple unfettering of passion than of skillful wiles. She took out her fan and waved it briskly in response to Henri's appeal.

It was much too late in the season for a fan, which was carried merely for form, and the motion set up a current of chill air between them. Having no desire to conduct a dalliance in a draft, Henri stepped backward. The palace had heating problems, and Henri had not got thoroughly warm since his walk in the rain.

If only he were on *terra firma* now, as all sensible aristocrats were! He was missing a lot of good parties, where there were always plenty of high jinks and practical jokes. Why had he stayed in Venice, after all? When Mario made up his mind to something, almost nothing could change it, certainly not Henri. Well, thought Henri, it would surely not turn out completely bad. Next year at the villa, he'd disguise himself and chase Giovanna through the boxwood maze. Then, at a turn in the path, he'd reveal himself, and appear, presumably in response to her screams, to save her. She'd be so grateful she'd fall into his arms. It was a ploy Henri had used countless times, though sometimes he thought the girls weren't really fooled. What did it matter? The result was the same. Henri cheered up as he became aware of Giovanna's fingers pressing into his arm a little more deeply than necessary. He caught a stern look from Zabetta as he helped himself to a big slab of warm polenta and a piece of tunny. Mario was staring into space, obviously unconcerned about anything that Giovanna did.

Henri's spirits lifted still more. He wouldn't be surprised if he managed to get a string of little bastard da Rivas on Giovanna. The next child to be heir to the da Riva fortune might be his, and not Mario's, and that would be a good joke on the senator.

It was a peculiar meal. Even the senator was morose. Mario wondered why. He and Giovanna were the only ones who had benefited by the events of the day, and ought to be in a good mood, as she obviously was. But Giovanna seemed too overcome for conversation, and it was only Donna da Riva who saved them from silence, chattering on about closing the palace and the entertainments she intended to give on *terra firma*.

"I shall outdo everyone this year," she declared. "I shall have a costume party that will last for twelve days."

"My dear, I thought ten was more than enough last year," said the senator.

"Oh, pshaw! That was last year! This year must be better! A person would think you didn't care at all about our social standing! You don't want to spend a ducat!"

"Nonsense. I've spent a fortune already." The senator sighed. "There was your new milkmaid's outfit to wear when we visit the peasants, and the new trappings for your four pairs to draw your carriage, and——"

"But the food! We must not be parsimonious about the food!"

Here Giovanna piped in, eager to ingratiate herself with her mother-in-law, who would rule the household over her. "I know how to make a number of wonderful soups using only a bit of chicken or fish and plenty of spices. After your guests have gone through the soup tables, they'll not have too much appetite, and you can save on roast and mutton."

But Giovanna had misjudged, and everyone glared at her, even Mario. Everyone knew why Giovanna knew how to make fine soups. She'd learned to make do after the Barettis had lost all their money, and her comment reminded them that in the uncertain economy of the Republic, it was a fate from which none of them was quite immune. The Barnabotti class was growing, filling up more and more of the houses that were available to them rent-free in the San Barnaba district of the city. It seemed that every week someone else went bankrupt, and it was for precisely this reason that it was so important to spend lavishly on the vacation session at the villas. It proved to everyone that one's fortune was still intact.

Giovanna realized her mistake, and overwhelmed with embarrassment, fled the room.

"You had better go and see to her, Mario," said the senator.

"I suppose I should." Mario sighed and threw down his napkin.

When she knew that he was coming, Giovanna ran up the stairs, making sure that her blue kid slippers tapped loudly on the steps for him to follow her. When she reached the top, she paused, her heart pounding from more than the climb. Giovanna knew that he was missing Amity bitterly tonight, and she wanted to soothe him with her love. She wanted to press his head against her bosom and put her arms around him and whisper, "Never mind, dearest, I am here."

But Mario had not given her the chance. Since Amity had left, he had come to the convent now and then and shared a cup of chocolate with her. To her disgust, he had become a perfect gentleman. Why was it so different now that it was understood that they would become engaged again? Was a man's attitude toward his mistress really so different from his attitude toward his wife? Giovanna had tried to arrange meetings at the *casino* Mario had kept for years to receive his ladies, but he had pretended not to understand. Tonight she would make it impossible for him to do that! She would make things as they had been before!

His soft, sand-colored hair appeared above the landing, and Giovanna remembered that she wished he would wear the peruke as so many nobles did. It would look so elegant—so much more civilized than natural hair. Perhaps when they were married she could convince him. . . .

Giovanna gave a sob and flung herself against her intended, clinging to his neck as he topped the stairs. Poor Mario nearly fell backward down the whole flight.

"There, Giovanna, there's no need to be upset," he said. "Keep clear of my stepmother, and you'll be all right."

"But I wanted her to like me, Mario," said Giovanna with true innocence.

Mario laughed. "There's not the slightest chance of that. You ought to give up."

"Give up? But I've scarcely started," said Giovanna in surprise. And to Mario's annoyance, she started to weep.

"Don't cry," he urged. "Come along, now. You'll miss dessert, and it's chestnut pudding."

"Oh! Don't treat me like a child!" she stormed, and pushing away from him, fled off down the hall.

Mario frowned. He *had* treated her like a child. What had possessed him to do so? He hadn't thought her a child when he'd made love to her in the gondola or in dozens of subsequent meetings in secret at his *casino*. Then she had been an exciting woman—with her ripe breasts, her sun-bleached hair, her native female skill in loving him. She had been forbidden, more dangerously illicit than any other he could have taken to his bed. She was not forbidden now. She was not the mystery woman who had waylaid him on the piazza. Here in his palace she was Francesco's little sister, by whom he was doing his duty.

Doggedly he trod after her. She had gone into his sitting room, he thought, but no lights shone in there. Mario entered the doorway and waited for his eyes to adjust. Streetlamps cast a pearlescent glow over walls with rococo designs of shellwork and flowers, and chairs and tables in Chinese style, all gold and green. Her skirts rustled, and the sound drew him toward the sofa.

"Mario," she whispered. Reaching out, she pulled him off balance. He fell atop her and crushed her against him. Giovanna's arms imprisoned his neck, and he felt his head being pulled down. Instinctively he met her kiss, languorous and long. Her tongue teased his lips until he parted them and met it, too, with his own.

"Mario, I don't care about the chestnut pudding," she murmured.

"Nor I," he agreed, working at the fastening of her gown. Her nipples came into view, hard and tight with longing. He touched them lightly with his fingertips and felt her body lurch, her thighs surging up against his. Mario's body responded, straining to be released from its buttons.

Giovanna knew the effect she had on him, for she opened his breeches and freed him. Her tender caress inside his clothing struck him suddenly. He moaned and went wild with desire. Giovanna a child? What nonsense! In a moment he had her naked beneath him. Lifting her compliant buttocks, he raised her to him and thrust into the soft, ready flesh that waited for his love.

Giovanna writhed, her breath quickening, her passions rocketing. But now something began to happen to Mario. He felt an ennui, a peculiar boredom. He thought of how she would be waiting here for him day after day for the rest of his life with her surfeit of unbridled devotion, and all at once his longing for Amity became unbearable.

Amity, who had always had the daring to stand up to him and whose love was challenging to his soul. How could he do without her?

He pushed harder into Giovanna's luscious body, making her gasp with a mixture of pain and frenzy. She was like other Venetian women—no more than an embodiment of fashion and sexuality, with no purpose beyond entrapping the male to make love to her and perpetuate the species.

Mario felt a lack of air; he couldn't breathe! He'd have to open a window. But he couldn't stop his endeavor with Giovanna. She was wound about him, seeming herself to choke with pent-up breath as she reached for ecstasy.

Mario wanted to escape. Perpetuate the species—that was why he was marrying her, why he was not still married to

Amity, who had made him happy, but who had been no good at creating da Riva sons or at dealing with the culture.

Giovanna would give him sons who would grow up and marry other Giovannas out of duty. . . . He realized incredulously that he was having doubts about Venice.

The woman beneath him cried out and released him. He blinked and looked down at her, thinking how meaningless it was to have brought her to her climax while he had been meditating on other things.

For a moment she lay stunned with her bliss. Then, noticing that he had not reached the same level of contentment, she drew him back to her. "No, Giovanna," he said.

"But, Mario, I would like you to," she insisted.

He heaved himself into a sitting position and felt the last of his desire drain away. Giovanna rose onto her knees and studied him. Her soft brown eyes were limpid with love, and her hair streamed prettily over her provocative breasts, which she made no effort to hide, resting her hands on her slender thighs. The fluff between sheltered her intimate channel like fern veiling an enchanting little forest den.

He felt sudden pity for her, giving herself to him so openly and utterly, he who would never be able to give as much in return. "It will never work, Giovanna," he said. His voice was flat and mechanical.

"You're silly, Mario. Of course it will work." She laughed as she tried to make love to him.

He held her away. "Not that. It's not that that won't work. It's our marriage that won't."

"Pray tell, what's the difference?" she demanded, puzzled.

He looked at her perplexed face and thought that the difference was that she didn't know the difference. Soul and body might be inseparable, but they were not the same thing. She loved him, but she would never confound him as Amity did, never would a beautiful glow shine on his life because of her.

"You *are* a child, Giovanna," he said, at a loss to explain it to her.

"Oh! How can you say that when we have just done what we have done? When you are looking at all the evidence to the contrary?"

Mario smiled in spite of himself. "Dear Giovanna, you will be a child when you are forty," he said.

She wept. "I am not so much a child that I don't know that you are still in love with Amity!"

"Tell me where Amity is, Giovanna," he said, feeling inside him a great unstoppable flood at the mention of her name.

"Tell you! So you can run to her, just when I have you all to myself! Just when everything is as it should be at last?"

"Everything is not as it should be," he cried, beginning to pace the floor. "I was informed that she came to the convent to visit you before she left Venice. You helped her leave. You are the only one who knows where she has gone!"

She gazed at him warily. "You are right, Mario. I know where Amity is. But Amity did not want you to find her. That is why she confided in me. She knew that I loved you, too, and that I would think of what was best for you, just as she did. I can't tell you where she is. That would be breaking a trust."

Panic filled him. Knowledge was rushing into every pore of his being, a certainty that everything he had done so far in his life had been wrong, everything except for the night he had carried Amity away from the Gypsy caravan. Thunder rumbled outside, muted by the fog, and reminded him of that other stormy night. He knew with conviction that whatever else his destiny was, it was first of all to love Amity. He experienced a sense of liberation; he could have taken flight, as confusion vanished from his mind. He wondered if this were similar to what Amity described as the "inner light," for at last Mario was not listening to the voices of duty or of generations, but only to the voices inside himself.

But what if Giovanna would not tell him where Amity had gone? What if it were too late?

"Giovanna . . ." he said, half-moaning, and he sank beside her on his knees.

She gathered him to her and felt his trembling, matching an awful trembling in herself. They stayed that way a long time, his head against her bosom; and she knew that she had him in her power as she never would again. She was not a child, no matter what he said. No child could love so overwhelmingly as she did. But could any love be strong enough to carry her through the pain of doing as he asked? She must tell him what she knew, because she loved him, and she understood now that he could never be happy without Amity. She must love him enough to give him happiness, but she did not answer until she had savored the moment and put the bittersweet memory away to last her a lifetime.

"Giovanna, you will be a bride yet," he promised. "I will

see to your dowry, and with your beauty you will have a husband of fine standing."

"I'm sure I shall," she said finally. He was relieved that she smiled at him, but there was a serenity about that smile that unnerved him, that made him think that somehow she had been right about herself. She was not a child. He wanted to ask her if she had someone in mind, but it did not seem proper. Instead he simply caught his breath and waited for her answer.

"She went with Francesco," Giovanna said at last, "but only as a friend. The house on Lago di Garda. You know where it is."

He sighed and kissed her forehead fervently and went away to find his father.

26

Through the chill night Mario raced, his own boatman in a long black gondola. In the lagoon the waves were high and choppy, making the going difficult, but that didn't matter. Mario was a strong oarsman, as strong as Carlo. He had been fascinated by boats since childhood, not only by the big navy ships that he and his father before him had sailed from the arsenal.

The interview with the senator had gone better than Mario expected. His father had scarcely seemed surprised to see him. Don da Riva was alone, taking his ease with an after-dinner brandy, dressed in a chintz smoking jacket, worn with a white dimity waistcoat and velvet breeches. Even on such a stormy night, Donna da Riva had gone off to a card game with her *cicisbeo*, and Henri and Zabetta had disappeared together.

"Ah, Mario, have you left your intended to fend for herself?" the senator wanted to know.

"She is not my intended, Father. I did not give her the ring."

The senator nodded, his face looking old as he stared out

at the rain-splattered window. "Because of Amity," he said. It wasn't a question.

"Yes," Mario affirmed.

"She doesn't love you, Mario. She went away with a lover," the older man protested. But his heart wasn't in it. He knew the cause was lost.

"I don't care. I was a fool to let her go. I'll go after her and bring her back."

"Take heed, Mario. Watch your blade. This lover of hers may be an excellent swordsman."

"Perhaps. But I don't intend to fight him."

"What? Not fight? But the gentleman himself will surely insist!"

Mario shrugged. Well, if he insists. But I am interested in winning Amity back, not in winning a duel. Oh, I know. A Venetian lady would give herself gladly to the winner of the duel. But not Amity. Amity doesn't approve of killing."

The senator shook his head in wonder. The woman was undermining the most basic of his son's values. Perhaps, after all, she was a witch. He had heard tales of the incantations of Quakers. More than one Quaker had stood trial in England for withcraft. Long ago, the Quaker founder, George Fox, had cried out at a hanging and cast a spell over the jailers so that they had been unable to carry out the execution. There was precedent. It would be easy to whisper in the ear of the Inquisitors—he could have Amity got rid of quite simply.

Could he possibly do such a thing? She was hardly a proper daughter-in-law, with those American ideas. Neither was she of aristocratic blood. Those drawbacks might have been overlooked had she seemed better suited for a woman's main function—breeding children. But still there was something about her that moved him. Perhaps she'd cast her spell over him, too.

"I concede, Mario." He sighed. "When you have married her again, we will petition the Council to have the marriage entered in the Golden Book. No doubt it will be more difficult than the petition that passed so easily today."

Then Mario did the most astounding thing his father could have imagined. Surely the girl *was* a witch! What else could have prevailed on his son to say what he did—to turn his back on everything that had ever had meaning in his life.

"Father, I do not wish the marriage to be registered in the Golden Book. I resign my right to the inheritance and to pass the family name through my sons."

"Mario . . ."

"Are you all right, Father?"

The senator felt as though he might have an attack of apoplexy. He wondered about his heart. If anything could fell him on the spot, surely this would. "Pour me another brandy, Mario," he said.

Mario did, glad to have something with which to occupy himself. "You see, Father, it's Venice and the Golden Book that have caused all the trouble. I might have stayed happily in Russia with Amity, but I was obsessed by Venice. I don't want Amity made unhappy by it anymore. I don't want to have to worry about having an heir."

"Mario, the da Rivas must have an heir!"

"So they shall, Father. You have another son, and he will most gladly furnish a proper wife and heir. I've been talking to Henri, and I've decided that he's right. Things ought to be reversed. Give Henri a chance. You know you never have. Let him marry Zabetta!"

"Henri! No. No, Mario, he is not half the man you are. It's you that Venice needs. When her dark hour comes, you must be there to lead!"

"I will always do what I can to help Venice, Father. But who knows? Henri may rise to his opportunity." He turned on his heel and left, with the senator dumbfounded, holding his brandy and having forgot to drink it.

Out on the lagoon, Mario thrilled to freedom he had never before experienced. The cold night seemed like spring to him. Droplets of fog that clung to his paduasoy mantle were like sweet June dew. Mario sang a gondolier's song. He might have been a boy again, racing Francesco across to Mestre.

Francesco! Suppose after all he were her lover? Would it be necessary for them to cross swords again? She had left Venice in his company, but Giovanna had said only as a friend. Would she say that just to protect her brother? He had to admit it was likely. Amity, too, had denied that they were lovers. She would be likely to protect him, too.

He himself had done a wrong, bedding Giovanna. But she had been there, so eager and compliant, and too late he had realized that his appetite for her had been only an outgrowth of his hunger for Amity. Now he renounced the pressures that had driven him to it. Now he would set everything right! Mario rowed on and saw a star peek through the clouds to guide him on his way.

On those same fog-cloaked waters another boat made its way over the choppy waves—a *burchiello* headed for the city. The mist was so thick that the lights of the palaces couldn't be seen at all. The boat might have been a hundred miles at sea, for all the sense its occupants had of the nearness of civilization.

"Are you sure that the boatman knows the channels?" Amity asked.

"Relax," Francesco advised her. "Every Venetian knows the channels. It's a birthright. Only invaders are ever run aground."

"It's difficult to relax." She sighed.

"Here, Am, drink this and try not to worry. Worry is not good for the baby." He handed her a cup of chocolate from the little stove and watched as she drank it dutifully. Still the tension did not go out of her body. How could it?

She and Francesco had not become lovers in the pretty pastel house on Lago di Garda. No sooner had she felt his lips on hers, his fingers on her breasts, than she had known she could not become the dissolute woman Mario already thought she was.

"You deserve better than this," she had told Francesco.

"Let me decide that, Amity," he had said. But Amity had decided herself. She had decided that she must return to Venice to tell Mario about the child she was carrying. She was glad at least that Francesco had persuaded her to leave little Chiaretta with his old family retainer at the house on the lake. Snow had fallen as they had come down from the mountains; the child would have undoubtedly caught her death.

Suddenly a dark shape loomed up out of the fog. A light flashed, bouncing off the walls of the cabin. The boat heaved with a crunch and grind and Amity tumbled off her chair. Chocolate splattered onto her skirts. "We've hit something, Francesco!" she cried.

He was peering out the window, unable to keep anxiety out of his expression. "Keep your wits about you, Am," he said. "It's a constable and his men."

"Well, we've done nothing wrong," she said, examining her ruined clothing.

The boat lurched again as heavy footsteps came aboard. Burly figures in black capes and round hats with broad brims flipped down to obscure faces were silhouetted against the fog.

"Are you Francesco Baretti and the American woman, the Quaker who was once wed to Mario da Riva?"

There was no use denying it. Their identity was known. But Amity didn't even think of denying it. "Once wed" was all she heard. So he had had their marriage annulled. Was he married to Giovanna?

"Come with me," the constable said.

"You will have to give us a reason," said Amity with American irateness. The man reached out for her, and Amity began to struggle, sinking her teeth into his wrist and gagging at the contact.

"Am, stop!" She obeyed Francesco's urgent tone and heard him say, "You must be careful with her; she is in a delicate condition."

To her surprise, she felt herself released. "By whose authority are we to go with you?" Francesco was saying.

"By the authority of the state tribunal, sir," came the reply.

"We will have to go, Am," he said gently, and he helped her gather her belongings and climb into the waiting gondola. It was obvious that they had no other choice. Francesco would be badly outnumbered in a fight, and he did not want her left to their mercy after he had been killed in a useless fight to defend her. Francesco knew where they were being taken, but he hoped Amity did not. He hoped that somehow he could be of some use to her, more than if he had ended the night floating dead in the lagoon.

Water purled about the craft as they slid quietly into the city. Vaguely Amity could see the shapes of buildings, and she looked eagerly for some familiar, comforting landmark. But in the fog everything seemed strange and distorted. She put her hand in Francesco's and racked her brain as to what this could mean. Were they being arrested? Before they had left Venice, Francesco had seemed sure that nothing of the kind could happen.

She saw something she recognized, and her heart leaped. Then just as quickly it froze. She had caught sight of the prison quay. The boat landed, and they were taken ashore. The constable led them up several flights of narrow stairs, and then they crossed an enclosed bridge. She glimpsed the water of a tiny canal, the Rio di Palazzo, and knew that they were crossing the notorious Bridge of Sighs that connected the prison with the Ducal Palace. Over this bridge unfortunates passed, often never to be heard of again.

They crossed a long gallery where a man in patrician dress

sat at an imposing desk. A torrent of protests rose to Amity's lips as he looked them up and down, but this time she took her cue from Francesco and said nothing.

"Take them away," the man said at last. She had decided that she recognized him. He was the secretary of the Inquisitors. He turned them over to a jailer with a bundle of keys, who led them up two more flights of stairs and down another gallery to a locked door. Beyond this, another door opened onto a dirty garret, dimly lighted with night glow from a window in the roof.

She thought at first that this was their destination, but the jailer opened an iron-barred door and pushed her through. The door was only about three and a half feet high, and she hit her head painfully on its frame as she twisted around in panic to see if Francesco was following. She heard him cry out to her as the door slammed shut, and then she was alone, without any protector.

At first she was aware of nothing except the total darkness, like the void beyond creation, where there was nothing, not even God. Then came a moaning. She was almost glad to hear it, for it meant some fellow creature was in earshot, someone who was suffering, but who might give her comfort anyway.

"Are you here?" she called. "Is anyone in this cell?"

The moaning had stopped. She thought for a moment she had frightened some mad soul, and then she realized that she had been the one who had been moaning. Her cheeks were wet, and her body was still heaving. Now a scuttering answered her call. She was not alone, and she wished she were. Rats. Large ones, by the sound of them. She hoped it was only the awful silence that magnified the sound.

She stood stock-still, afraid to move, afraid of whatever horrors lay in the darkness. But that was nonsense, she told herself. Things could hardly get any worse, and if she remained motionless, the rats might be tempted to run up her skirts. She began to feel about the cold walls. Finally she located a bench, screwed into place, where she might sit on an old mattress. But a chill of revulsion ran through her, and she could not bring herself to lower herself to it.

If only there were light. Suddenly her fingers met something hard and cold. She jerked back with a scream. Human bones! She was convinced of it.

For a long while she was petrified, but at last she became less sure of what she had felt and touched the place again.

This time she discovered that it was a latch, and pulled it eagerly. A small shutter swung back. The barred opening was not more than a foot wide, but the place was lighter, and fresh air came in. Beyond was a view of the leaded roof, quickly obscured by gables. She was completely disoriented, wondering which side of the prison she was on—did the cell front on the sea or on the piazza?

As her eyes adjusted, she looked around the room. There was nothing there at all. Just a wooden floor and stone walls, no human bones or visible rats. The rats must have been in the passage outside, after all. If it were not for the silence . . .

It was the quiet that unnerved her. If only there were some sound of human life! But she remonstrated with herself. Silence wasn't evil. Silence was good. Hadn't they always sat in silence at meeting? Or course, then she might have heard a bird outside, or some naughty boy shuffling his feet. Nonetheless, she would have meeting now, here by herself. She would imagine herself back in the old stone meeting house, and she would listen for the voice inside her that surely must be there, even after so many years away from home.

She sat down on the bench and closed her eyes. She must have fallen asleep and been dreaming, when she thought she heard the inner voice. "What would you like to eat?" it said.

She was rather surprised to be spoken to on such a mundane subject, but her stomach rumbled as she sat up and opened her eyes. A grate in the door had been opened, and a jailer was looking in, not the same man that had brought her here. His eyes were marvelously gentle, and Amity almost wept. He was huge and unkempt, and a certain look about him told her that he hadn't an ordinary complement of intelligence. His enormous bulk must have secured him his position. He could easily crack the bones of any prisoner who tried to escape.

Poor man, she thought, to be brutalized because of how he'd been made! The stupid eyes pleaded for a little warmth or friendship as he asked her again, "What would you like to eat? It's supposed to be bread and water, you know, but there's no need for that. Old Jacques can get you anything at all. I know the kitchen. Why, I can slip next door and bring you food from the palace, intended for the table of the doge himself!

"Well, I'd like a cup of coffee with milk, Jacques," she

said. "And some rolls and maybe some cheese. Could you manage that?"

The jailer gave her a grin, twisting up his ill-formed face, and snapped the grating shut. She felt more alone when he had gone than she had the night before. She hoped at least he'd bring coffee. She was chilled through and through from having slept on the wooden bench, and the pelisse she had wrapped around her was not making her any warmer.

He was gone a long while, and she began to think he had just been bragging on his ability, when the key turned again, and this time the door opened instead of the grate.

Jacques came in beaming, bringing a tray of crusty turnovers and a plate of shirred eggs with prosciutto and mozzarella. Coffee steamed in a pewter pot. The jailer spread a white napkin on the bench and served her as though he had been a waiter in an exclusive café, apologizing for the ivory spoon he gave her, instead of a knife and fork, which weren't allowed.

Amity hadn't thought she'd have much appetite, but everything was delicious. The turnovers had an unusual filling that seemed to be grape jam and cinnamon with walnuts and a flavoring of rum. Jacques stood at her elbow, and she knew she'd disappoint him if she didn't eat. At first she ate to please him, then greedily to please herself.

He stood there grinning idiotically, and at last she thought to ask if he would like some. He shook his head. "No, it's for you."

"Thank you, Jacques. Thank you very much." Amity thought the man would burst with pride. "Jacques," she said, "what happened to the gentleman I was with last night? Do you know where they put him?"

His expression turned crafty, and her heart sank. "I'm not supposed to tell," he said.

"Ooh." She made her mouth droop in a pout. "Please, Jacques!"

Jacques couldn't resist her. "He's in the cell right beneath you, *signora*."

"What's going to happen to us, Jacques?"

"Who knows? They'll decide at the hearing."

"Hearing! When will that be? What crimes are we to be charged with?"

But all that was beyond Jacques, who offered her another turnover, clutched between grimy fingers. Amity fought against desperation. She hadn't done anything; it was a mistake, and she'd be released. Yes, in a little while she'd be taken from the cell into the palace, and she'd explain—the Inquisitors weren't monsters, they were patrician gentleman of the kind that had so often came to dinner at Ca da Riva. They would be different from the constable or the moronic jailer. The hearing! She pinned her hopes on it.

Jacques left, and nothing else happened. Pigeons walked on the roof outside, and she relieved her loneliness by throwing crumbs onto the lead surface for them to eat. The dreadful night came, and somehow she lived through it. In the morning Jacques came again.

"Is the hearing to be today, Jacques?" she asked.

But it was hopeless to get any more information out of him about her situation. She tried to play on his sympathies by telling him she was a mother, and chatted away about the child she had left at Lago di Garda. "I must get back to her, Jacques!" she said. "You understand. You have a mother, haven't you?"

He almost wept, and shook his head. His mother had died of malaria long ago, like Mario's. Jacques had been left on his own while still a child.

"What about your father?" she asked. But Jacques shrugged and said he'd had only a mother.

She confided that she was to have another baby as well, and Jacques lighted with smiles. "Ah, *signora*, that is fortunate. Then if they are to hang you, they will perhaps wait until after the child is born. It is innocent, after all."

"Innocent of what?" she screamed, but Jacques was only upset by her outburst and scurried off like a frightened animal. For the first time Amity was unable to eat her meal. She hadn't thought of hanging. She had thought only of harassment and inconvenience. She'd done nothing, and nothing could be proved against her! Jacques was wrong; he wasn't bright. But another voice told her that intelligent or not, Jacques had experience in these things. He'd seen these cells fill and empty many times.

The next day he brought her a bearskin rug to wrap herself against the dank nights. He gave it to her worshipfully, in tribute to her approaching maternity, she thought. He couldn't have afforded to buy it, she knew. He'd stolen it. But Amity didn't care. She thanked him profusely, and his eyes shone.

"Jacques, do you think that you could send word to my husband that I am here?" she asked. It was time to alert

Mario to her situation. She hadn't wanted to. Pride again, she supposed. He'd had their marriage annulled, and that, most likely, was that. No doubt he was betrothed to Giovanna again, and would do no more than suggest she become his mistress. Seeing him would be painful, but he would have her released from here; and that had become more important than the pain of seeing him. She hadn't thought it wise for him to learn that she had been arrested in Francesco's company, either. They might do each other violence. But Jacques made matters seem serious enough that she must take the chance.

"Your husband, *signora*?" Jacques said.

She remembered that she couldn't call him her husband anymore. "I mean Mario da Riva. He has a palace on the Grand Canal."

"I will try," Jacques promised.

She was beside herself with impatience until his next visit, and occupied herself by jumping on the floor to try to get a response from Francesco, whom Jacques had said was incarcerated below. It was an endeavor she had tried every day without luck. She had decided that beneath the wooden floor there must be another of terrazzo, formed of bits of marble, the most favored floor paving in the city. The sound of her jumping didn't carry, she thought, and wondered why it should matter anyway. Francesco couldn't help, even if he could hear her.

Having exhausted herself, she sat down panting on the bench, and immediately heard a sound. It was so faint that she thought it was the pigeons on the roof. But she couldn't see any birds walking there, and the scratching sound came again. She threw herself onto the filthy floor and put her ear to it. Yes, it *was* coming from beneath her. Amity jumped up and down until her feet stung. Again came the faint answer. Someone was beneath, but maybe not Francesco. He might have been moved—or even hanged! They weren't really communicating anything except human presence. Amity wept with frustration.

"Did you send the message?" she asked Jacques when he brought her evening meal.

"I tried, but Ca da Riva is closed for the season. They've all gone to the villas."

"Oh! You fool! Couldn't you send someone after them?"

An awful look came into Jacques's eyes, and she thought that his overly large orbs transmitted emotion better than most people's, perhaps since they had so little else to convey. She saw woebegone hurt mixed with anger, and felt both pity and fear.

"I'm sorry, Jacques," she amended. "Thank you for trying."

"I'll send to the mainland tomorrow," he promised.

She waited several days until Jacques brought her word that the message had been delivered. "But your husband wasn't at the villa," he reported.

"Where is he, then?"

"Nobody knows."

"What of his father, Senator da Riva?" She had no reason to hope for aid from Mario's father, but she had a feeling about him. He was a man of high standards, and she thought he might have understood the sacrifice she'd made, even though she'd told him the story about the lover. But the senator perceived her as a threat to Mario, and well might not help her.

"The senator has gone to Milan," said Jacques.

"Who *is* at the villa?" Amity said despairingly.

"Only Henri da Riva and his mother. They received the message of your confinement here."

Henri! They had not been enemies, but she wondered if he would exert himself in any way. She almost wished that she had given him his "fun" on the night she'd left Venice. He'd feel differently, then. But it took nerve to confront the Inquisitors, and Henri had little to gain by mixing in. Amity suspected he was a coward.

Her delight at hearing the noises below diminished, but later in the evening they came again—a steady scraping and tapping that went on for a long time. Amity didn't try to answer. She wrapped herself in the bear rug and went to sleep on the floor, to hear the sounds more clearly for a lullaby.

In the morning Jacques arrived with her coffee, but this time as the little door opened she saw that he had someone with him. "The abbess has sent someone to attend to your spiritual needs, *signora*," he said, entering and laying places for breakfast for two.

Amity turned away to hide her tears. A nun! She had been praying for days for Mario, and a nun came instead! How could a nun help? She had needed a powerful man!

The door closed, and she was alone with the sister. "I know what you're thinking, Amity," said a familiar voice, "but the Lord's ways are sometimes strange."

Amity stared at the young figure in the garb of a novice. "Giovanna!" she cried, stunned. It was the most amazing turn of events she could have imagined. The woman whom she had supposed had taken her place in her husband's bed was instead in the service of the church!

"You expected that Mario and I would be wed," said Giovanna gently. "But you see, I've become betrothed to another. I will be a bride of Christ when I have completed my novitiate."

"And Mario?" Amity breathed.

Giovanna's eyes clouded, betraying that he was still in her thoughts as a man shouldn't be in the thoughts of a bride of Christ. "Mario couldn't stop loving you, Amity."

"You told him where to look when you knew it would mean losing him? When you promised not to?"

"There was nothing else to do. I had tried every way to make him forget. And he gave up his inheritance. He stepped aside for Henri, even though the senator agreed to register a petition to enter the marriage in the Golden Book."

"He went to Lago di Garda?"

"Yes. I've sent a message after him, but who knows when it may reach him. It may be snowing heavily in the mountains by now."

"The old woman will tell him when he reaches the house," said Amity.

"What old woman?"

"The one who used to cook for your family. I left Chiaretta there with her."

"The cook? But . . ." Giovanna paused, thinking better of what she'd been about to say.

"But what?" cried Amity, feeling a chill.

"Don't worry. It may be all right. It's only that the cook doesn't live in the village in the winter, when there aren't any tourists to cook for. She'll have gone into the mountains, where her husband has his vineyards."

"Then Mario is unlikely to find her? He'll go on looking until your messenger catches up with him?"

"I'm afraid so."

Amity tried to quell mounting panic, but her mouth felt dry and furry, and blood seemed to drain from her as though she had holes in her feet. "What about Henri?"

"Henri paid for the messenger. That's all the help we'll get from him."

"Giovanna, what's going to happen to me?" Amity whispered.

Giovanna hesitated, her eyes troubled.

"Tell me, Giovanna! I must know the worst, so that I can prepare myself for it. Jacques says I may be hanged, but of course, he's simpleminded. I can't be hanged, since I haven't commited a crime. This will all be cleared up soon, won't it? Francesco and I will be released." Amity waited for Giovanna's confirmation.

"You won't be hanged, Amity. If you do as they wish, you'll be released."

Amity went weak with relief. She leaned against the stone wall and felt no coldness from it, so cold was she inside. She waited for the natural warmth to seep back into her limbs, now that she had heard the good news, but something in Giovanna's tone prevented the warmth from coming. She gathered her strength and sorted out what the novice had said.

"If I do as they ask? What do they wish me to do?"

"They want you to testify against Francesco. You're to say that he is a traitor and was engaged in recruiting Swiss mercenaries to help overthrow the Venetian government."

"That's ridiculous. Francesco and I didn't even go to Switzerland."

"They don't care. Francesco is one of the foremost of the Barnabotti. All the Barnabotti listen to him. The government would like him silenced, but they need a witness to make it official."

Amity shuddered. "Oh, I could never testify against Francesco—even if it were not a lie!" Silenced? How? she wondered, but was afraid to ask.

"I knew you wouldn't agree to it, but Francesco wants you to. I've been to his cell before I came here. He worries more about your welfare than his own life—and he says there is a child to consider. He would confess to save you, but it would be a blot on the Baretti name. Honor is all the Barettis still have, and he cannot do that to the memory of our father. Besides, to have Francesco appear a coward would weaken the Barnabotti. Francesco believes that a new order is the only thing that will restore Venice. But he would like it to come peaceably and from within, instead of violently from invaders."

"I cannot do it, no matter what he wants!"

Giovanna looked miserable. "I ask you to do it, too. Amity. You might as well. They'll break you down, anyway. It will save you grief."

"I will have truth behind me, Giovanna! How can you ask me not to stand up to them, when it's your brother whose life may be at stake? I have been the cause of your losing Mario; how can you want me to be the reason you lose Francesco as well?"

"I ask you to do it for Francesco, so that he will not have to confess to save you!" She wept. "The result to my brother will be the same; only, if he dies, his honor will be intact."

"And I will have his blood on my hands!"

"There's the child, Amity!" cried Giovanna desperately.

Amity was puzzled. "I am eating well, and Jacques takes me for exercise in the corridors. You said I wouldn't be hanged, and even Jacques said I wouldn't hang before it was born."

"You won't be so lucky as to hang, a beautiful woman like you. It will be worse. If you won't testify, this is the only gift I can give you." She unfastened the cord that tied up the waist of her habit and handed it to Amity. Then she banged on the door, weeping and speechless, and Jacques rattled the lock and escorted her away.

Amity stood incredulously holding the cord. Each woven strand seemed to sparkle in the rays of wan sun that filtered in, heavy with dust motes. She had no doubt of the reason that Giovanna had given her the rope.

Not so long ago she had petulantly thought of ending her life in a canal because of her ruined marriage. She had been willful and immature, then, wanting Mario as her love slave, wanting him on her own terms or not at all. How foolish she had been! But he had loved her anyway—loved her enough to sacrifice everything for her! If she cooperated with the Inquisitors, they could be wed again, but only with the ghost of Francesco between them.

That was her choice: To do as they asked and be free, or refuse and suffer the consequences, perhaps to be driven to using the "gift" Giovanna had given her. She tried to be calm and forced herself to sit with folded hands and hold her lonely meeting. But the light inside her seemed to have gone out, the God of comfort had fled. There was only Jacques to give her solace, and sensing her distress, he brought her a lovely hot wine custard from the palace kitchen and offered it to her humbly. She began to cry and was unable to thank him, taking his big, meaty hand and squeezing it in her own.

Now each day she dreaded morning, experienced palpitations of the heart at every footfall along the corridor outside her cell. Anytime they might come for her to make their "request." At first she wondered why they were waiting so long, but after she had thought about it, she realized they were playing a crafty game. The longer she was kept in debilitating dread, the easier she would break. There was nothing she could do to combat it; all the weapons were in the hands of her tormentors.

One afternoon Amity saw a second shadow behind Jacques as he unlocked her cell. But it was only Giovanna again. "I've brought you some books to read," she said, and handed over some musty-looking tomes. They're from the library at the convent. I suppose you'd rather have novels, but only books for spiritual enlightenment are allowed in the prison."

Amity was unable to hide her disappointment at the reason for the nun's visit. "Has anything been heard from the messenger who was sent to find Mario?" she asked when the jailer was out of earshot.

"No, I'm afraid not."

A silence fell between them, and then at last Giovanna went on, revealing what she had come to say. "Francesco is working on a hole in the ceiling of his cell, and he asked me to tell you to work in the same spot on your floor."

Amity was confounded. "How can Francesco work on a hole in the ceiling? Don't the guards see it? It's not possible to cover it with a rug or chair."

"It's covered with something better," said Giovanna with a hint of a mischievous smile. "It's a picture of Our Lady. I brought it to him, and he put it up with a paste of bread and water—to meditate while he lies in bed, he told the guard. The archers wouldn't dare disturb a sacred object."

"Those are the sounds I've heard, then!" Amity whispered, her heart leaping. But quickly she sank into despair again. "Giovanna, I am certain that there is stone between my floor and Francesco's ceiling. That's why the sounds are so muted."

Giovanna looked discouraged, too. "But it's the only chance," she said. "Perhaps you're wrong. Perhaps there isn't any stone." She stepped off a distance carefully and made a mark. "Here is where you should work."

"But what will I use to work on the hole?" said Amity. She was bursting with anger now. How dare Giovanna come and ask this of her? It was too cruel when there wasn't any hope.

Suppose, after all, there was no stone, and she could enter Francesco's cell or he hers? They would only be punished for their cleverness. There was still no way out. She flew into a rage and heaved the books at the feet of the offending nun. "Get out! Get out!" she cried, all the pent-up defiance of her imprisonment threatening to engulf the startled Giovanna. The nun called for the jailer and fled, while Amity screamed hysterically after her. She had no idea how long she kept screaming, but at last she grew too hoarse to scream anymore.

Slowly she regained herself. She tried to look at the books that Giovanna had left, as a means of regaining her reason. There was *The Mystical City* by Sister Mary of Jesus and *The Adoration of the Sacred Heart of Our Lord Jesus Christ*, written by a Jesuit priest. Both were unthinkably dull, even to someone as starved for reading matter as Amity was. She tossed them aside and sat listlessly, drained of all thought and will, drained even of regret and despair.

As she sat, staring down, she gradually became aware of the buckle of her shoe. She must have been looking at it a long while before she began to see it in a different way. With a start she recognized that the buckle was the instrument she needed. The spiritual light inside her had rekindled, and the inner voice was calling to her to have faith and begin to work on the hole.

She greeted the voice joyfully, as an old friend returned; and pulling off her shoe, she jerked at the buckle until it came loose. She worked most of the night, scraping away at the larchwood floor, using the buckle as the chisel and the shoe as a hammer. Every chip that came away seemed a promise, and she hid all the tiny promises inside her straw mattress. In the morning, before Jacques arrived, she pulled the bearskin over the edge of the bench, so that it covered the spot where she had been working. She was ravenous for breakfast and even asked Jacques if he could bring her another plate of eggs. Then, exhausted, she slept until it was night again and it seemed safe to work on the hole.

Her life had purpose again. Every day she caressed the hole, smoothing the ragged edges of the slowly growing cavity, while she dreamed of a reunion with Mario. Their love had overcome other great obstacles, why not this? There would be no stone between the floors; and when the hole was completed, Francesco would know how they could escape. Her mattress grew thick with wood chips, and when Jacques came, she was careful to keep her hands hidden, so that he wouldn't see the blisters.

Having fallen asleep one morning after hours of work, she was annoyed to be awakened by a rattling of keys in the lock. Jacques had brought her breakfast earlier. What could he want now?

"Come with me," he said.

"Oh, I'm too sleepy to go for exercise."

"That's not where we're going," he said, pity in his eyes. "We're going to the tribunal."

She was led down stairways and through hallways that became progressively less prisonlike and more palacelike, the ceilings adorned with stuccoed flowers and angels, and flowing ribbons of putti swirling about the chandeliers. At last she was brought to the tribunal chamber, where three men, all masked to hide their identity, lounged in easy chairs about a table set with decanters of liqueurs and little crystal glasses.

She tried to stay close to Jacques, feeling protected by the familiar presence of the jailer. But then even that bit of security was removed, and she was alone with the dreaded Inquisitors. Amity trembled and was angry with herself for her cowardice. They looked inhuman in their white beaked masks, like vultures of prey dressed up in tricorner hats and velvet breeches. Except for the secrecy, they would probably be assassinated by friends or family of their victims, she thought, and the idea made the dominoes even more abhorrent.

"You are accused of consorting with an enemy of the state," one of the Inquisitors intoned. She knew that he calculated his voice to strike terror to her heart.

"You will have to tell me who, then," she answered. "I am not aware that I have been friends with anyone of that description."

"I am speaking of Francesco Baretti, of course." Hawk's eyes seemed to glare at her through the mask. "Tell us the plot he was hatching against the government when he was arrested."

"I cannot. It would be untrue," Amity said.

"Then we shall have to press the charges against you," said the Inquisitor chillingly.

"What charges? I've done nothing," Amity contended, feeling the breath of peril. Was she, too, to be accused of plotting against the state? Had she been loose-tongued once too often about her love of democracy? But instead the Inquisitor took a different tack.

"Do you deny that you are a Quaker?"

"Certainly not. Is that against the law?"

"It is not against the law to be a Quaker. But witchcraft is against the law."

"Witchcraft? I?" It was ridiculous; if that was the best they could do, they could never make it stick. Amity almost laughed with relief.

The Inquisitor's voice sounded bored with self-assurance. "We have heard that Quakers often practice witchcraft in their meetings. They speak in tongues, and they dance naked."

"Quakers do not deal in witchcraft, sir!" she replied. There had been a time when Quakers had been persecuted for witchcraft in England and Massachusetts, but that had been a long time ago. The Inquisitors were only trying to scare her. Why, that had been the seventeenth century!

The Inquisitor took something out of his pocket and tossed it onto the table. "Do you recognize this?"

"No," she said, but the object did look familiar. Where had she seen it before?

"It's an amulet," the Inquisitor supplied for her. "Do you deny that you wore it in the streets of Venice? It was found in your bedroom at Ca da Riva."

Amity remembered. "That is easily explained. A fortune-teller gave it to me. She said it was necessary to tell the future."

"You don't deny it, then?"

"No, but fortune-telling isn't against the law, either."

"The amulet qualifies as witchcraft. Anything is against the law when it is mixed with witchcraft."

"Then *she* should stand before you, not I," said Amity stoutly, more annoyed than terrified. If Mario were here, they would not dare continue this farce.

"The charge has been lodged against *you*," said the spokesman, and the others nodded and sighed assent, like grotesque birds on gilded perches.

"By whom?" she demanded, and shivered in spite of herself.

"That is not for you to know. Can you guess the penalties for witchcraft? Are you willing to tell us now the crimes of Francesco Baretti?"

"No," she cried, and wondered at her own strength. She

thought of the lion's-head boxes she had seen all over Venice, mouths open to swallow the charges of citizens against each other, all that was vindictive and destructive. Someone had written a note about her and slipped it inside. But they were not really interested in her; it was Francesco they wanted.

The Inquisitors conferred. Then Jacques was called to take her away. Soon she was in her cell again, pacing the floor in a frenzy. Asking her to guess the penalty for witchcraft had been worse than telling her. She guessed it must be death, of course. But death in what manner? Could she really be convicted on the evidence of the amulet? Why not? Who was to stop it?

Amity understood now why Zabetta had been so upset when she had come looking for the amulet after Chiaretta's birth. Venetians were a superstitious lot! Without waiting for darkness, Amity began to work on the hole again. She had made it wide enough for a person to squeeze through, and she thought she must be nearly finished. Perhaps before sun-up she would be able to see into Francesco's cell!

But before midnight the buckle struck something harder than larch wood. Amity pounded again, and this time by the night glow from the window she saw mosaic peeking out. Stone! There was stone between her cell and Francesco's! This was the reward of her faith!

In the morning she was dispirited when Jacques opened the door of her cell. "Where is my breakfast?" she asked, missing the rich smell of coffee.

"I cannot bring you breakfast today," said the jailer mournfully.

"Why not?"

"We are going somewhere."

"To the tribunal?" she asked in dread. "It's no use. I won't tell them lies about Francesco Baretti, and I won't confess to witchcraft."

"We aren't going to the tribunal," he said. Amity didn't ask where. She hardly cared as long as she didn't have to face the Inquisitors again.

Jacques led her through corridors to what seemed to be another cell. She experienced a moment of panic then, for if her cell were changed, they would discover the hole she had been making. This room did not have a bed, to her relief, but relief lasted only a moment as he showed her a contraption built into the wall.

"When their excellencies order someone to be tortured, the

person is seated on that stool and that collar is put around his neck. A silk cord goes through the holes at the ends and then over a wheel. When the wheel is turned . . ."

Amity grasped the idea and tried to run. Jacques caught her easily and flipped her onto the stool. She tried to struggle as she felt the collar tighten around her neck, but she had had the breath knocked out of her when he had flung her onto the stool. The collar tightened about her throat, and then she felt the cord.

"Jacques!" she managed to scream. She wanted to tell him that he couldn't do this. He had been her friend. She had come to depend on him. But the collar choked off all that she would have said.

Jacques looked at her impassively. "Do you wish to tell the tribunal about the crimes of Jacques Baretti? I would if I were you. If you do, they won't ask you to confess to being a witch. You'll be expelled from Venice, that's all."

Amity shook her head, and then did not think about anything but the cord tightening and tightening against her throat. Dimly she heard Jacques sobbing as he turned the crank, and she thrashed wildly, trying to bring her hands up to pull the cord away. But her hands were chained, and she remembered iron rungs in the wall. He had orders to torture her, not execute her, but Jacques wasn't strong in his mind and might easily turn the crank too far. Mario's face flashed into her mind in a burst of colors as she lost consciousness.

Amity heard a sound. It was a sound she had heard so often that she did not have to think what it was. It was the sound of Francesco working on his ceiling. He, too, must have reached stone by now. Did he really hope to break through it? Or was his continued working to signify to her that he hadn't given up on their situation? Why hadn't he? She had. She sat up and rubbed her throat, thinking that Jacques must have carried her back to her cell and covered her with the bearskin. She had survived the torture, but she doubted if she could give testimony now, with her bruised throat.

Her supper sat across the cell, placed thoughtfully on a small table, the dishes covered to keep the food warm. She poured a cup of water and swallowed it painfully, all the while listening to Francesco's pounding. Morning came and brought her jailer. She turned her face and would not look at him.

"Please, *signora*, I brought you some nice coffee," he said.

"You betrayed me, Jacques," she accused. "You're not my friend."

"I only did what they told me to do," he protested. "I thought of the baby and didn't pull the cord too tight."

"Please, Jacques, help me escape. Then I'll know you're my friend," she begged.

He looked horrified. "I *am* your friend. I saw the hole you're making when I brought you back. And I haven't told anyone. Tell the Inquisitors what they want to know, and everything will be all right again."

"No, Jacques. I've seen how bad it can be, but it can't get any worse, unless I'm convicted of witchcraft. They'll be careful about doing that, since I can't implicate Francesco in some treasonous plot if I'm dead."

"Please, *signora*—it *can* get worse!" She saw pleading in his eyes. He seemed to be begging for his own soul.

"Poor Jacques," she murmured. "I forgive you."

"Are you certain you won't give the testimony?" he asked.

"Yes," she said, putting herself into the hands of the fates. She fell into a stuporous sleep, and when she awakened he was still there, or rather he had come again, since the deepening shadows told her that hours had passed.

"Hello, Jacques," she said. It wasn't time for him to be here; perhaps he'd changed his mind about helping her escape. But before her words were out, she sensed something different about him. He was not the same man who had brought her treats to eat, or even the same one who had wept as he tortured her. Evil emanated from him, filling the cell with a suffocating miasma. She had seen that look before in a man's eyes.

Somewhere inside, she knew what it meant, but she did not have time to think where she had seen it or what it meant before he had crossed the distance to her and put his big hands over her breasts. The face of the British soldier rose to memory, and this time she did not hesitate to scream as she had hesitated that day. But this time there was no Silas to rush in and save her. Today there was only Jacques, moaning as he kneaded her breasts in his rough hands and began to tear at her bodice. With a cry she brought her knees up under him to unseat him, as he wallowed astride her body; but this only worked in the jailer's favor. He forced her knees apart, and his hand went under her skirts, up between her thighs. One of his thick fingers penetrated her inner channel, and she retched and vomited what little she had eaten.

Jacques was not deterred from his task, and she realized that this was what he had meant by worse. He had been ordered to rape her by the tribunal, and once unleashed, his feeble mind could not control the weeks of lust for her.

He removed his fingers and grunted as he forced her tissues apart to make way for what was larger and more powerful as well as infinitely more disgusting. She willed her body to lock against his entry, but his will prevailed and the dreadful invasion wrung another scream from her still-aching throat.

Jacques looked at her to see if she were hurt, but even when she began to moan to him, "Jacques, my baby, please think of my baby," he thundered on, his enormous weapon seeming to leave no room inside her for her own cringing organs. Again and again he thrust until she felt his hot, sticky seed running between her thighs. They lay together, she too weak to crawl out from under him, he too deep in the aftermath of passion to think of moving.

When he did think, it wasn't of moving. Instead desire overcame him again, and she endured what she did not think she possibly could. When it was over, he left her moaning in pain, her body convulsing with what she knew was the beginning of a miscarriage. And then she knew no more.

27

Giovanna's voice called to her. "I tried to get them to let me take you to the convent," the novice said.

Amity opened her eyes, and Giovanna's habit swam into view. She looked like an angel in flowing robes as she put a cup to Amity's lips.

"Jacques . . ." Amity murmured fearfully.

"There, now; he's gone. They'll keep him away from you for a time until you're better; then they'll send him again. You must get out of here!"

"There's no way. There's stone beneath the floor."

"I know. Francesco told me. He's hit it, too, but he's chipping it away little by little."

"That will take forever. There's not time. I'll use the cord you gave me before Jacques comes again."

The loss of the baby and the degradation of rape had destroyed Amity's spirit more profoundly than the annulment of her marriage. She lay without will, listening to Francesco's frantic hammering in the night, and wished she could tell him not to tire himself. She would do what she had to do before Jacques came again.

Giovanna visited her every day, but no words of hope from her had any effect on Amity. Giovanna's words were only kindness.

"Francesco is going to confess," Giovanna said finally. "You won't be raped again."

"No!" Amity cried.

"You must think of Chiaretta," said Giovanna sadly.

She did not want to leave her child motherless; she did not really want to die, but she made a noose of the nun's cord to be ready when the time came. It was unthinkable that Francesco should confess and go to *his* death to save her.

She was able to walk about her cell, but she refused to leave it to walk in the corridors with one of the archers who had taken Jacques's place. She was too afraid she might cross paths with her former jailer.

Then one morning the archer said to her, "I will not be the one who comes tomorrow. Their excellencies wish me to tell you that you may still give the testimony."

She knew the time had come when she must have the strength to extinguish her own life. If she drew breath when Jacques came, she was sure that she would not have the courage to refuse to give the testimony against Francesco.

"Tomorrow is the day," she said when Giovanna came in. "Pray for me."

"I've already been praying," said the nun. "I've brought you something." She took out a jug that had been half-hidden by her robe. "I said that I needed this to care for you. They let me bring it in."

Perhaps it was poison, Amity thought. Poison might be easier. But when she unscrewed the lid, she knew immediately what it was. "Vinegar! This is nothing but plain vinegar!" Amity stared at Giovanna as though she were mad.

"It's a chance, Amity! It may be insane, but on the other hand, it may work. The tale may be true."

"What tale?"

"The story that Hannibal used vinegar to soften the rock to make a passage through the Alps. Pour vinegar on the stone, Amity. I'll keep watch to see that no one's coming near."

"Giovanna—"

"Pour it," Giovanna ordered. "You had faith to make the hole. Have faith again!"

Have faith! Amity seemed to hear her father calling to the Quakers in the old meetinghouse to have faith as the British marched toward Pennsylvania. She remembered how his words had moved her, how she had longed for the challenge of being tested. As she poured the contents of the bottle over the stone, she thought that she had never known the full meaning of her father's words until now.

Darkness fell on what Amity felt was the last day of her life. She could not have faith! It was one thing to put oneself into the hands of a mystical God in meeting, quite another to have faith in the Almighty through a jar of vinegar! She knew she should try to work on the stone, adding her efforts to Francesco's, whose tapping could be heard below. But instead the shoe buckle lay unused while Amity sat on the bench, focusing her courage on the nun's cord in her lap. No pain it could give, nothing that lay beyond, could frighten her as much as what she must suffer at the hands of the lust-crazed jailer.

The sky grayed, and pigeons began to coo. Amity wondered irrelevantly if the official pigeon feeder had arrived in the piazza with their breakfast. She let her thoughts wander back over her life and regretted nothing, except that Mario would never hold her in his arms again.

She thought of Grace and Isabel, the three of them huddled together in the lean-to on the banks of the Delaware, each enduring more for a cause than ought to be endured. Of the three, two were dead. Soon all would be. She prayed for the ability to die as well as each of the other two. Then she noticed that the tapping beneath her had grown much louder, and seizing her shoe buckle, began to work furiously. She could not accomplish nearly as much with her instrument as Francesco with his iron bolt, but chips of stone flew away beneath her blows. It had worked! The rock had softened. She was gasping for breath when the first crack of light appeared.

"Am! Am!" came Francesco's voice.

"I'm here!"

Large hunks of stone began to fall away all at once. They seemed to thunder as they dropped to the floor of Francesco's cell. She was terrified the noise would bring the guards.

But nobody came. It was too early, and they were all dozing. The morning bells had not yet begun to ring. "Give me your hand," he said, and she did, tying herself to the bench with the nun's cord to keep from plummeting into the hole herself. Then miraculously he was in her cell, embracing her. He was thinner than he had been, having had no Jacques to pamper him. He seemed so frail that she felt she ought to assist him, rather than he her.

But she knew no way either could assist the other. It had seemed so important to make the hole, she had all but forgotten that once it was completed, they would still both be in prison. Francesco would be no match for Jacques. He'd be murdered trying to defend her when the jailer arrived.

"Francesco, you mustn't be found here," she whispered. All her efforts to save him by refusing to give testimony would be for nothing if he came between her and Jacques.

"Neither of us will be found here," he promised, and showed her the iron bolt in his hand. And then she heard the sound she dreaded—the thudding of boots along the corridor, the rattle of keys at the jailer's waist, like the rattling of a coiled snake.

"Francesco!" she whispered, pleading for salvation she could not hope for.

Francesco pushed her behind him and stood to the side of the door. She saw the jailer's eyes, glowing with lust as he entered, and read in them the things he planned to do to her. And then the expression of lust changed to surprise as Francesco, bracing the bolt with both hands, brought it down on his head. Blood spurted as the eyes went dull and vacant and, she thought, almost innocent, as they had been when she had first met him. She stepped over his inert body with disgust, but not without pity. He was almost certainly dead.

"Hurry, Am, there's no time to lose," Francesco urged, bending to remove the keys from the jailer's belt. He dragged her along as they fled through the corridors. She stumbled after him, her legs stiff after her inactivity. Outside her cell, it seemed more dangerous than within, and she almost wanted to scurry back. Did Francesco know where they were going?

A door loomed in front of them, secured by a huge lock. Francesco searched among the keys. "If we get past this, we'll be in the palace section. There won't be anyone about, and we'll hide until they open the doors to the public for the day."

Footsteps running somewhere behind them alerted them that their escape had been discovered, but the lock opened, and they were through to the palace. But they were in a gallery, and the door at the other end was locked also.

"The keys, Francesco!"

"No, these are only prison keys."

The sound of pursuit came louder, and she pressed herself against him, bracing for their recapture. Impatiently he shook her off. "The window, Am!"

It wasn't barred, and Francesco flung it open. Outside, the gray of predawn was heavy, with a thick, damp fog. The lead roof was slippery with dew as Francesco pushed her out, and following, closed the window behind them. She lost her grip and slid, expecting to plummet into the canal. But her heels found a hold on the marble gutter.

Francesco spared a moment to grin at her as he slid down beside her. "We're out," he said triumphantly. "We're free."

"We are on the roof, and we cannot get off," she corrected.

"Don't say 'cannot,' Am! Remember all that we've done already."

She thought of the softened stone and was remorseful. "I can't seem to keep faith, Francesco."

He laughed. "Faith? Is that what you call it? I call it determination not to be hanged. We came out one window, and we'll go in another."

"Go in!" She was aghast at the idea of returning to the gloomy interior of the building. Here the air was fresh. She didn't even mind the cold autumn wind.

"It will be daylight soon, and we will be a sight, perched on the roof for everyone to see."

She knew he was right and fought her revulsion as they inched across the Leads. It seemed hours before they were atop a gable. Francesco was sure that the window below it would lead into the palace again. She held on to his boots to brace him as he leaned over and worked loose a grating.

"It's a long way down inside," he said, panting as he pulled himself back up.

"Too far to jump from the sill?" she asked.

"Yes. This is the top of a loft."

"Then how will we get down?"

"With a rope. We'll make sure. Can you rip your petticoats?"

They worked together, she ripping, he tying the pieces with sturdy knots, using the nun's sash, which had been tied about Amity's waist, as part of the construction. She was astonished at the length of the rope as it lay like a fantastic kite's tail over the lead tiles.

"You'll go first," he said matter-of-factly when the job was finished.

"How will *you* get down?" she asked.

"I'll find a way," he said in a tone that didn't brook argument. Amity knew she had to obey. It was getting lighter by the moment. Soon the bell tower would begin to chime, and the *calli* would fill with people on their way to the wells.

She allowed him to toss the rope into the opening and climbed down it into the dark hole of the room, her fingers whitening as she swung precariously. At last her feet touched the floor, and she looked up to where Francesco's face was framed in the glow far above her.

"Hurry, Francesco," she said.

But he had nothing to attach the rope to, and no one to hold it for him. "I'll find a way," he said again. "But don't wait. Go on without me."

"I'll wait," she said emphatically. For a moment she thought he hadn't heard, but she was afraid to speak any louder. Then his answer came drifting down to her.

"You must go on, Amity. I love you more than life! *You* must escape. It will do no good for both of us to be caught."

He was trapped on the roof unless he found some other route, and every instant came closer to the moment when the matins would ring. When that happened, guards would leave the piazza and the Ducal Palace, and that would be to their benefit. But the square would fill with people and he would be discovered on the roof.

"Go, Amity!" he whispered again, his voice desperate as it echoed down into the dusky room.

"I don't know the way!"

"Find it!"

Amity went, running down a staircase into a gallery filled with shelves. The archives, she thought, but the knowledge helped her none at all. She took another staircase and came to a room which must be the ducal chancery. The door leading out was locked, and Amity sank against it, drained of her last energy. She had not fully recovered from the effects of Jacques's assault and her miscarriage, and now her weakened limbs refused to support her. She was safe for the moment, but soon someone would come. Someone must work here every day, so she would be found, even if the archers failed to trace her path to this room.

Perhaps she could throw herself on the mercy of that person and ask for safe conduct to the piazza. But her good sense told her that was wishful thinking. She could not conceal that she was a foreigner, and most Venetians were suspicious of foreigners. If he guessed that she was the one accused of witchcraft, he'd give her away at once!

Her eyes roamed about the room and fixed on a tool on the desk, a slender chisel which was used to pierce parchments before attaching the lead seal of the chancery. She seized it, delighted that fate had caused it to be left outside the locked desk. It was a perfect instrument with which to force the lock.

Beyond it she entered a section of the palace where she began to remember the way. Mario had brought her to receptions here, but Amity had been too bewildered to take much note of anything. If only she had had her wits about her then! Her heart gladdened as she recognized the door of the royal staircase. Beyond that was the main door and freedom.

It didn't surprise her that the door was locked, but she expected it to give way to her chisel like the door of the chancery. It had to. She couldn't have come to the very last obstacle to be thwarted! She had kept faith when she had pounded her hands raw and bleeding, working on the hole. And she had kept faith pouring the vinegar onto the stone. She had even managed to find faith when she and Francesco had been trapped on the roof. She couldn't be stopped now!

But the heavy door didn't understand the part it must play. She could not work the chisel between it and the frame. It stood rocklike as she beat on it and frantically tried to chop a hole in it with the little tool.

Amity knew the effort was ridiculous. It was only that her instinct for life was so strong that she couldn't stop herself. She heard a faraway sound like the dripping of water on stone, but it came closer, and she admitted the truth. Footsteps! She would be found and taken back to her cell to be ravished—by Jacques if he hadn't been killed. By others if he had. Archer after archer would have his fill of her until she did as they wanted. She no longer had the nun's cord to hang herself, but there was one last service the chisel might do. It could not unlock the door to the royal staircase, but it could unlock the door to another world.

Footsteps thundered, and her breath seemed already to have stopped as she crouched beside the door and, eyes closed, lifted the chisel to aim it at her heart. But her courage faltered and she hesitated an instant too long. She felt her wrist in a man's grip. She struggled and tried to turn the weapon on him, utterly forgetting her Quaker scruple against killing.

"Amity, stop!" She thought she heard the voice from the depth of her soul, calling her back to the values of her youth. But it was the voice that she always heeded, even before that of God.

He spoke to her again. "Amity open your eyes. You can't hate me so."

She did as she was directed and saw a wonderful apparition in a travel-stained surtout with a fall of wide collars. His French turned-over top boots were caked with mud and grime, and his amber eyes were anguished.

"Mario!" She flung herself into his arms without thinking of all that was wrong between them. But after all, nothing was. The touch of his lips, his crushing embrace, told her that. None of it mattered anymore. His failures as a husband and hers as a wife were swept away in the power of their love.

"But how?" she said finally. How was it that she was with Mario instead of in the lecherous clutches of the archers of the prison?

"Giovanna's message came to me, and I rode day and night to return to Venice," he told her. "I arrived only an hour ago and went to the convent and made the abbess let me in. Giovanna told me what was about to occur here. We've no time to waste. I know a way out. There's a passage onto the canal. It was built hundreds of years ago as a secret exit for the doge in case of invasion. My father showed it to me when I was a child."

He took her hand to run with her, but she drew back. "Mario, you must save Francesco, too. He's trapped on the roof!"

He seemed not to hear, and pulled her after him, his hand gripping hers so tightly that she had no chance to break away. "Mario!" she protested.

"Hush. Do you want the guards to find us?" he whispered.

"You cannot leave him there!" But Mario paid no attention, his mind on navigating narrow little halls and stairways on his route to the secret door. Amity wept. Francesco and

Mario had loved each other until she had came between them. How stupid she had been to encourage Francesco in St. Petersburg!

The wet morning air touched her face as she was propelled into the open, where a gondola waited with drawn *tenda* beneath the Bridge of Sighs. Carlo was ready to help her over the side and hide her beneath the awning.

The bells began to clang as she sank onto the cushions. She covered her ears at the sound. But Mario was with her no longer. "Carlo!" she cried in alarm.

The gondolier grinned at her. "He will be back. Be quiet and don't let anyone catch a glimpse of you."

The truth dawned on her. He had taken her to safety before returning to the palace to look for Francesco. But it was too late. The bells were ringing, and there would be people in the piazza. Already there were vendors' boats and movement on the quays. It was impossible for her to remain under the *tenda*, blind to all that was happening, and she peeked out and located Francesco's dim figure clinging to the roof.

Suddenly she saw him turn his attention to a certain window, and she knew that Mario must have called to him from there. A grate fell away from the window as Francesco inched toward it, and dropped, narrowly missing the barge of a vegetable vendor. Mario must have broken it loose from inside.

The startled vendor looked up at the roof and gave the alert, pointing and yelling. For an instant she saw both of them utterly vulnerable as Mario climbed out to give his hand to Francesco. Francesco slipped, and the crowd gathering gave a gasp as his feet plummeted over the marble gutter.

But Mario, clinging to the window frame, still held his hand, his own feet braced haphazardly on the lead tiles. Amity heard a discharge of muskets. Mario might make safety yet, if he released Francesco; but Amity knew he wouldn't. She hardly knew whether to hope that he might lose his hold in spite of himself. Francesco's legs thrashed, and he managed to hoist himself back up, where he lay exhausted in the gutter of the roof. Mario half-dragged him to the window, and there was a shout from the onlookers as they disappeared inside.

"They will be safe now, *signora*," said Carlo reassuringly, but she didn't believe him, even when they emerged on the *calle*, Mario with drawn sword, exchanging thrusts with two archers.

He shouted something to Carlo, and to Amity's horror,

Carlo began to pole away from the bank. "Carlo! Don't leave them!" she begged.

Then Francesco hit the water with a splash. She thought at first he'd been shot, but instead he was swimming. In another instant Mario dropped his sword and flung aside his great-coat, and he, too, swam toward the gondola.

The craft heaved as Francesco scrambled aboard and turned to pull Mario on. As they collapsed on the cushions, she understood why Mario had told Carlo to row away. He hadn't wanted the guards to be able to jump into the boat at quayside. Behind them their pursuers had hesitated, disdaining to plunge into the cold water. Instead they were shouting at the citizenry in general to stop the escape and looking for gondolas in which to continue the chase.

It was easy to see that the endeavor was hopeless. Mario had taken an oar, too, and he was as strong an oarsman as Carlo. Together they could outrace anyone in Venice. Already they were far enough away that the fog had begun to close around them. Now and then the gondola surprised a fisherman or maneuvered skillfully around a lazily moving barge of firewood. Shops and cafés were opening their shutters, and in the squares women were engaged in morning gossip. Nobody paid any attention to the speeding gondola, and Mario and Francesco began to laugh uproariously and sing old Venetian songs like a pair of young blades returning from a night of revelry. They were friends again; the rift between them was forgotten, the daring escape as exhilarating to them as any exploit of their boyhood.

Amity, tucked tenderly in blankets by the pair of them, felt left out of it all. As they rowed into the lagoon, she fell asleep smiling, listening to the sound of their singing.

28

Before noon they arrived at the da Riva villa on *terra firma* up the Brenta River. It lay at the end of a great garden, ornate and artificial, with pools and fountains, bushes trimmed into the shapes of animals, and statues of sea horses and tritons. Enormous columns adorned the stucco facade of the house, and Amity looked it over with a great deal of curiosity. She had never had the opportunity to come before, though Donna da Riva and Henri were rapturous about the good times to be had.

The gardens would be the work of Donna da Riva, Amity thought, imagining Mario's stepmother in an elaborate gardening outfit, supervising workmen, adding shapes and statues until she was certain she'd outdone everyone.

The inside of the villa had been more difficult to spoil. The rooms were too vast for intimacy, but the ceiling paintings were beautiful, lighted by long windows; and the chandeliers, of wood and gilded copper, curled into delicate rosettes, with little crowns for candle bases.

The bedroom upstairs was a different matter, made cozy by a terra-cotta parlor stove. The bedstead had a design in tempera putti, and the bed itself took up most of the little room. Sliding doors led to the *retrès*, or side closets. One of these was the dressing room, and another, down a tiny corridor, was a secret sitting room, with rococo patterns of twining stems and flowers adorning its walls.

Amity allowed herself to be bathed and powdered, her hair washed free of the grime of prison. When all was done, she slept again, drifting off in the luxurious feather bed. It was dark when she awakened. Mario, having parted the bed curtains, sat watching her from the foot of the bed, his expression in the lamplight full of love and awe.

"Where is Francesco?" she asked.

"Safely gone."

"They won't catch him? What had he done that was so wrong?"

"Nothing, dearest. He only wants to save Venice from its decadence, as I do, but his ideas are different. They are afraid of different ideas in Venice, these days."

"They wanted me to say that he had gone to Switzerland to recruit troops for revolution."

"He did nothing against the regime. Francesco's not a revolutionary, at least, not yet. Oh, Amity, Francesco told me all that happened to you in prison."

She dropped her eyes, and a sob rose in her throat. "Everything? Did he tell you about Jacques?"

"Yes," he answered. "Francesco told me what you endured to save him. How you refused to swear to lies and how you made the hole with your shoe buckle, though the stone was underneath. I am proud of you, Am."

Amity's voice choked. "I wasn't brave, Mario. I lost courage. I would never have succeeded if it had not been for Giovanna."

"Giovanna!" Mario was astounded.

No wonder, Amity thought. Giovanna had begun as a lovestruck convent girl and had ripened into a passionate woman. But since Mario had left Venice, Giovanna had undergone other changes. Amity believed that the experience of the prison had honed Giovanna and sharpened her dedication to her new calling. But she would never be free of her love of Mario. She would struggle against it and say her rosary in penitence for her carnal thoughts for the rest of her life.

But Amity had more on her mind than Giovanna. Her eyes filled with tears as she remembered the wonderful surprise she had had for Mario when she and Francesco had come down from the lake. "Mario, did Francesco tell you about the baby I lost? I would have borne your son if it had not been for . . ."

Apparently Francesco had not broached the painful subject, for it was obviously news to Mario. A good thing that Francesco had killed the man, Mario thought. Otherwise he'd have done the deed himself. He gathered her into his arms and let her weep against him, tears of his own mixing with hers. But his tears were not so much for the lost child as for everything that had happened to them.

"It was my fault, Am," he told her ardently, "but I've broken the spell of Venice now, and I will never allow that to hurt you again. Will you go back to Russia with me and walk three times around the altar again?"

"No, Mario," she whispered, clinging to him.

"Zounds, woman," he cried, thunderstruck. "Do you mean to say you won't marry me again? You can't refuse me when I have learned that loving you means more to me than all the world. You can't say no, though it's what I deserve!"

"I will marry you," she said.

"Thank heaven!"

"But I will not go to Russia."

"Not go to Russia! But you adored our house there. I've always known that you wanted to return."

"So I have. But not now. Mario, you must stay here. *We* must stay here! Because of what happened, you must stay and fight for your vision, until Venice is no longer a place where women are imprisoned and raped, and men are put into irons for their ideas. You can't give up, Mario! It will be my dream, too, that someday Venice will be as beautiful again in soul as she is in palaces and canals."

"Are you certain, Amity?" he said.

"It's what you must do and what I must do, Mario," she said simply. A glow shone keenly in her eyes, and his heart leaped as he realized that he had not overestimated her mettle when he had fallen in love with her and married her. No, if anything, he had underestimated it.

"Will we be safe at the villa?" she asked.

"Yes, dearest. There are eighty rooms, and acres and acres of woods and mazes in which to hide you, should the Inquisitors come after you. But they won't come. Francesco is the one they wanted. Witchcraft was only a convenient charge to frighten you and justify whatever they did to you. They gambled that I wouldn't court scandal by defending you, since we were no longer married."

"But who accused me, Mario?"

"I don't know. I have been working from reform of the judicial system and the prison, but the custom of the lion's head boxes is entrenched. I have an enemy, perhaps. Someone who wanted to discredit me through you. When I find out, his name will be marked in blood with my sword!"

He expected her to protest his intended mayhem, but she only leaned against him and sighed. He was reminded of another with whom he had been expected to cross blades. "What have you done with your lover, Am?" he said gently. "Have you sent him on his way?"

"I have no lover," she confessed. "I told you so from pride."

"Ah. And were you the Belle of Trenton?"

"Yes, but I didn't bed with Colonel Rall," she said with a shudder.

"The outlaw?"

"Yes," she assented. "But I didn't know . . . I didn't guess . . ."

"He was your first." Mario was still jealous of the man who had known her before him, but he understood her better. She had been, not a wanton, but only too innocent.

"There will be no more telling of lies between you and me, Am," he said.

"And you will have no more mistresses."

"No, not one. You shall have your American way about

that, though it would make me the laughingstock of Venice if anyone knew."

He felt an overwhelming urge to tenderness as he parted the fastenings of her nightdress and touched his lips to her bosom. He glanced up at her inquiringly to see if she wished him to love her, and found her eyes were closed, her lips parted in a breath of pleasure.

They remarried several days later in the chapel of the villa. Amity's hair, held in a jeweled coronet, flowed down like a Venetian bride's over her bare-shouldered wedding gown of silk damask and gold brocade. At the end of the ceremony the guests shouted "Kiss! Kiss!" to the bridal couple, and it didn't seem to matter to anyone that it was not the first time they had been united as husband and wife. Donna da Riva was especially pleased, since it provided an occasion for a magnificent party. How many families could boast a wedding during the season? Donna da Riva made a great to-do of batting her fan and exclaiming how exhausted she was.

"Imagine! I have not one son marrying, but two!" she would say, for Zabetta already wore the betrothal ring given her by Henri. Donna da Riva was even maternal toward Mario, since he had abdicated his inheritance to his half-brother.

Henri leered pleasantly at Amity as they drank the wedding toast, but she did not think that she had anything to fear from him, since he was about to have a wife of his own. She smiled and raised her glass in his direction.

Zabetta, glowing with happiness, laughed about the predictions the Gypsy had made for her. "Just think, Am, that old crone didn't see a wedding in my future, the fake! We'll neither of us have anything to do with the likes of her again, eh?"

"No, never!"

"Oh, Amity, I am sorry about that day! I'm sorry for all the unhappiness I've caused you! I shouldn't have taken you there!"

"You couldn't have known, Bet," said Amity warmly. When she had been in the Leads, she'd come close to hating Zabetta for her part in it. But Zabetta had gone out of her way to show remorse, even insisting that she wear a brooch on her wedding gown that Zabetta had intended to go on her own.

A cloud seemed to settle over Zabetta's joy, and Amity wondered if she were remembering the Gypsy's other predictions for her—the darkness, the man they'd thought was Henri, weeping. But why should those predictions come true, when the other hadn't? Amity dismissed the thought and wondered instead about the three men who would always love her. One was Mario, Francesco was another, but what of the third? Then she became annoyed with herself for thinking about the Gypsy at all.

The celebration seemed endless. Food was served in three dining rooms. The soup room boasted Roman consommé, consommé with poached eggs, soup with custard drops, fish soup with tomatoes, asparagus soup, and a dozen others. In the second dining room the revelers found veal chops with cheese, roast Genoa duck, guinea fowl in casserole, stuffed poached partridge, pork chops with vinegar, and braised Lombardy beef. There were vegetables of every description: onions baked in white wine, baked artichokes, stuffed zucchini, and fricassee of new carrots.

But Amity, with her love of sweets, visited the third dining room most often. Never, even in the palace at St. Petersburg, had she seen such a surfeit of fritters, macaroons, chocolate truffles, tortoni, and cakes.

The serving rooms were open and filled with people at almost every hour of the day. She marveled to find the Spanish ambassador and an Austrian duke engaged in a game of cards on the terrazzo floor at four in the morning, stuffing themselves with spaghetti and sausage.

Practical jokes abounded. She became used to screams in the night. Once a young woman raced stark naked through the halls, horrified at having discovered a dead rat in her bed. Amity wondered if Henri were the culprit. But surely there were plenty of other suspects. Amity wondered if there had been a naked man who had resisted chasing after the girl as she rushed from the bed he had anticipated sharing with her. She was almost certain there had been. It was that sort of party.

Donna da Riva was in her element. This entertainment would be talked of all winter in Venice. She wore a different gown every morning, changed by noon into her various shepherdess or milkmaid outfits, and finished the day in low-cut gowns embroidered with layer on layer of gold brocade. The skirts boasted enormous side bustles on which more lace billowed, and her hair was dressed with precious gems and flowers into a tower, which was held together with wire hoops and powdered over by means of a little powdering bellows.

She was especially fond of a hairstyle known as *pouf à senti-ment*, in which she wore locks of her admirers' hair or per-haps portraits of her son, Henri, or even of her pet dogs.

Some evenings the great hall became an opera house with a proscenium arch and curtain. Usually they heard the music of Baldassare Galuppi—gay arias with well-modulated rhythms, each quick and fascinating, with pizzicato accompa-niment or an accompaniment of mourning strings.

Amity was familiar with much of the music. The composer had been a favorite of the Czarina's and once had been em-ployed at her court. Later there would be dancing, gambling, midnight rides in hay wagons drawn by horses grandly buckled and reined. Only a few guests rose early enough to go hunting. Not many even went for rides over the beautiful fields.

"How long will it go on?" Amity asked Mario.

"As long as my stepmother can cause it to," he said with a grin. "Are you having a good time?"

"Oh, yes!" She was, but not so much because of the extrav-agant entertainment as because she was glad to be among people who were enjoying themselves again. She relished the sound of laughter and thrilled to the sight of trees, which had been so absent in Venice. Most of all, she was jubilant to be with Mario. She fell into the spirit and painted her breasts with daisies, some tucked even beyond the edge of her bod-ice, for Mario to discover when he unfastened the silver but-tons of her undergarment of Holland linen. What happened after that in the privacy of their bedroom made her more joyful than all else.

"When will Henri and Zabetta be wed?" Amity wanted to know.

"In a few days. They are finishing the gown. And Zabetta is going to Venice tomorrow to visit the convents in a wedding gondola."

"I'm glad for them," she said.

"Yes." Mario sighed, and she wondered if he would ever quite make peace with what he had done for the sake of sav-ing their marriage.

"Mario . . . ?" she said to bring him back from wherever his mind had wandered.

He smiled at her. "Let's hope Henri will be equal to his new position."

In spite of his smile, she was afraid he might become moody. He seemed in danger of it every time he was reminded of the uncertain future of the Republic. It rankled that the da Riva power was mostly in Henri's hands, now that he was the favored son with the proper marriage arranged.

"Mario, let's leave here for a while. We haven't had a honeymoon yet."

"So we haven't. I know where there's a wine harvest. Would you like to go and see it?"

She packed a reticule and they drove off together in the sharp, fresh air. She was delighted with the vineyards and threw in her lot to help pick for a while. They stayed to share a meal of fish stew and polenta, and Amity went to admire the animals, and as evening came on, surprised everyone by expertly milking a cow.

"You're better at that than I," said Mario, amused. But Amity was suddenly sad.

"What are you thinking of, Am?"

"Of my farm in Bucks County. I wish you'd seen it, Mario."

"Would you like to go back someday? The colonies will have their independence soon, since the British forces have just surrendered to General Washington."

"Surrendered!" Amity was exultant.

"I heard the news only yesterday when the papers came from Venice. I've been waiting for the right moment to tell you." He withdrew the clipping from his pocket and read to her about the Battle of Yorktown and the defeat of Cornwallis. How the French under Lafayette had sailed into the mouth of the James River to put siege to the enemy, who had been driven to Yorktown by the Quaker General Greene. The Venetian paper was sour about the victory, calling it a triumph of dangerous ideas.

She walked away from him and stood looking into the dusky distance. He watched her, moved himself as he let her savor the moment. She seemed to be on the River Road again. A voice demanded the password, and she called out, "Boiled stone," and a girl in thin calico stepped from the trees with a musket. Grace. And in the lean-to was Isabel, staunchly loyal, mending the lace of General Washington's shirt, though her husband had deserted her for the comforts of the Tory camp.

Amity tried to experience the victory for the three of them. And Silas? Had Silas lived to see the colonies free? She wondered if she would ever know.

Freedom, she thought, remembering the ring of the word when Silas had spoken it in meeting.

Finally she returned from the past and threw her arms about her husband to thank him for the part he had played in the winning of independence when he had advised the Czarina to refuse mercenaries to the British.

"Well, Am," he said, "you haven't answered my question. Do you want to go back to America? I offered to take you to Russia. I would take you to Bucks County again as well."

"Oh, Mario," she whispered. She wanted more than anything else to go home and be a part of victory, but even as she spoke, she knew that she couldn't go home to America, any more than she could go to Russia. He would go where she wished, but she couldn't allow it. He must stay where *he* belonged. That was what mattered. She belonged where he belonged, and Venice was his battle, even though he was no longer the da Riva heir, even though his marriage to her would make a political rise difficult.

"We will stay and make Venice great again," she said.

"Sometimes I think that's impossible." He sighed. "There seem to be so few who care."

She had never heard him voice such a thought before, though she was aware that doubt had been working on him for some time. In altering his future to remarry her, he had also altered his vision of the Republic, and he seemed to see it in a different light. Just the same, she knew he did not want to leave.

"Anything can happen, if it's right for it to happen, no matter now unlikely," she told him. "No one thought that the Continentals could win. And I surely did not think that the vinegar could soften the terrazzo."

"You're right, Am," he said. She could always renew him. It was a special quality she had, like the quality that made his body run rampant with desire. The one feeling awakened the other, and he found it necessary for them to stay the night, snuggled in the fresh-cut hay in the loft of the farmer's barn.

It was the next night before they returned to the villa. The party was still in progress. As they entered the hall, a candle raced across the floor, seemingly on its own power, fluttering eerily in the darkness. Amity shrieked and grabbed Mario's arm.

"Don't worry, it's an old trick," he said. "The candle's fixed to a crayfish. Come on, let's find it before it sets fire to the house."

Somewhere madrigals were being sung. In the dining rooms, dishes clinked. Shouts came from the gaming tables. But the room into which Mario and Amity followed the ghostly candle was empty and dark.

A moan that was half a sob floated on the air, and Amity wasn't sure after all that the candle had been a mere trick. Mario put on a lamp, and Amity saw the grotesque creature about to skitter beneath a sofa. "There!" she cried.

Mario caught it and snuffed the candle. The crayfish emitted an acrid odor, half-burned itself from hot wax that had dropped onto it. Amity turned away from the sight and met another as vulgar. Henri, hopelessly drunk, slumped into a wingback chair so that his head rested on its seat and the rest of him sprawled haplessly over the needlepoint footstool. Amity felt a chill of foreboding and thought Mario felt it, too.

"Henri!" Mario shook his brother. Drunkenness was unseemly, even at a party like this one. Venetians were not given to it.

"Go away, Mario. Go and find the senator and tell him I don't want the inheritance anymore. I shall only be badgered to attend Council and to marry someone, and I don't want to marry anyone but Bet."

"What are you talking of, you nincompoop?" said Mario.

"A lover's quarrel," Amity guessed with a rush of relief. "They've had an argument. It's nerves, most likely, just before the wedding."

"We did *not* quarrel," said Henri with effort. "I went to Venice with Bet and sat in Florian's waiting for her to finish her round of the convents. But she didn't come. I waited past dark before I learned what had happened. She's been arrested."

"What?" they chorused, but Henri fell over and began to snore. Mario removed a bouquet of chrysanthemums from a vase and dashed the water into his brother's face.

"Why?" asked Mario as Henri spluttered.

"For witchcraft, like Amity. I tried to help her. I talked to everybody. But I haven't enough influence, even if I am the da Riva heir. It's no small thing to deal with the Inquisitors. She is in the Leads, and women do not last long *there*." Henri collapsed again, and Amity prevented Mario from yanking him to consciousness again.

"It's kinder," she said. Shaking, she sought the comfort of his arms. "Why has this happened?"

"I don't know. In your case the reasons were simple. You

were a foreigner and a Quaker and that made you an easy mark. Perhaps someone hoped to discredit me, and there was your friendship with Francesco. But Zabetta is a *zentildonna*, and about to be Henri's wife. They cannot expect that the da Riva family will allow her to be imprisoned on some trumped-up charge."

"It's the amulet," Amity said suddenly.

"Amulet? What are you talking about?"

"It was at Carnival. You had gone to sit in the box with the doge, and Zabetta and I lost Henri in the crowd. Then Zabetta wanted to go to a fortune-teller. The Gypsy put an amulet around my neck, and I began to feel ill and ran into the street wearing it. After the baby was born, Zabetta came looking for it, and she seemed frightened. They used it as evidence against me. They had searched my room at the palace and found it."

"It was foolish of you to go to a fortune-teller, Am. They often engage in sorcery."

"Well, I didn't know!" she cried, tears starting. "You talk as though you believe in it."

"I don't, but it's against the law, and the law is to be obeyed. Cabalism is of no benefit to anyone; it only frightens and coerces. But it's my fault. I should never have left you that day. It was stupid ambition. A woman of worldly morals like Bet was no proper chaperon for you. But at least I know what's caused the trouble. I'll go to Venice at once and see what can be done."

She watched him ride away and then went to find Donna da Riva. The hostess was engaged in cards, and since she was on a winning streak, it was an hour before she would allow herself to be drawn away so that Amity could tell her what had happened.

"But the wedding is set for tomorrow night!" she cried, falling onto a chair and fanning herself with her ivory-handled fan.

Amity waved smelling salts under Donna da Riva's nose, but she seemed intent on swooning away. "You will have to stop this party. Make an announcement and then see what can be done for Henri, since you are closest to him."

Donna da Riva recovered dramatically and sat bolt upright in the chair. Amity thought it was because of the way she had spoken to her. Venetian women did not command their mothers-in-law. But it wasn't that at all.

"Stop the party!" Make an announcement! Not on your

life! Nothing must stop the party now! Mario will bring Zabetta back, and we'll have the wedding. I'll go and organize a treasure hunt in the garden, and that will keep everyone busy."

"But—" said Amity.

"Go and order more champagne sent out," ordered Donna da Riva, suddenly a rock, filled with the courage of things to be done.

Amity went to her room, knowing that her face would give away the disaster to everyone if she stayed among the guests. As dawn approached, there were shrieks and shouts. From her window she saw figures dashing about from bush to sculptured bush. Girls ran giggling, teetering on the brittle heels of little laylock slippers, the hoops of their gowns bouncing up to display gold clockwork stockings. Men loped after them, their wigs, set with tight rows of "buckles" on each side, glimmering in torchlight, the queues jouncing against frock coats of fustian or silk.

Now and then one of the gentlemen paused to dip snuff from a silver jar, and a lady might have to secret herself behind a boxwood fish so that she would not be too far away when he began to pursue her again. Amity didn't know what "treasure" had been hidden in the garden, to be located by unscrambling intricate clues, but the event was a great success. The searchers had become the "hunted" themselves, which was infinitely more satisfying. Once, having dozed, she was awakened by splashing and screams as guests toppled into one of the pools.

Unable to sleep again, she decided to pay a visit to the dining rooms. In the dim hall something creaked behind her. Amity gave it little attention. She had grown used to such proceedings. The party had gone on for two weeks, and at late hours guests could always be discovered skulking between rooms. Better to pretend she heard nothing.

It didn't occur to her to be frightened. Whatever else the men were, they weren't dangerous. Suggestions and advances were made in abundance, but they were easily turned aside. No one made a boor of himself; there was no reason. If one charming girl rejected a man, there were plenty who wouldn't.

As she crossed a long gallery, her eye was drawn toward the windows. Something seemed to move there behind the draperies. But Amity still wasn't frightened, only curious. Then a long, horrible sigh floated across the corridor. Amity felt her blood go cold clear down to her feet. The sound hadn't seemed human. She was impelled to run, but she held her ground instead, remembering the crayfish with the candle. This was only some trick. Some sort of device must have been attached to the window to make that sound when the wind blew. If she looked, she'd find it. Amity took a step toward the windows.

The sound came again, and something separated itself from the draperies, rising whitely, floating toward her, stretching as though it would fly, fluttering, vague extensions that might have been wings reached for her.

Amity did not wait to think again that it might be a trick. Seized by primal terror, she fled, screaming. The shape pursued her. She turned down another corridor, realizing that she was becoming lost. The hall dead-ended and forced her to turn again. And then there was no escape.

She had entered a little sitting room which seemed to have no other exit. But it must. It had to be part of a bedroom suite, and somewhere in the paneling there would be a door. She could find nothing in the darkness as she ran her hands frantically over the wainscoting.

The shape had followed her. The sound of its flutter made her heart drop. It *was* a ghost. She'd been told that all these old palaces had them. Some ancient da Riva ghost? What did it matter *whose* ghost it was? She turned to face the apparition, nothing seeming worse than to allow it to creep upon her from behind.

The instant she turned, it seized her, wrapping her in its gauzy, mummylike folds. She screamed again, hoping uselessly for aid in this distant part of the villa, and felt her breath squeezed off in its grip. Then, mystically, the whiteness rippled away.

"Hello, Am. Now we'll have our fun!"

Face to face with Henri, she whiffed the oil of jasmine with which he coiffed his hair. She was so confused that her first reaction was to cling to him and thank him for having saved her from the terrible specter. But of course he had been the specter. He had herded her into his pen, and now she was at his mercy.

"It's time we knew each other better," he said, not releasing her. "It seems, after all, I'm not to have a wife, while my brother has you. It's time for Mario to share and share alike."

He'd slept off some of his drink, but he was far from sober, and Amity felt an alarm quite different from her alarm over the "ghost."

"Henri, this is silly," she said in what she intended to be a voice of reason. "You are sure to have a wife—tomorrow, most likely. Mario will bring Zabetta back." Her words sounded more like pleading than calm reason.

"He won't, mark my word," said Henri. "Why should Mario exert himself for me?"

"If not because you are brothers, to avoid scandal," Amity said.

"He'll only make a scandal of himself trying to save her, and there are those who would make capital of that. Why should he fuel their cause?"

"Do you mean the same people who had me arrested, Henri?"

"Oh, don't play so innocent, you little idiot. You know who had you arrested."

"Who?" she cried blankly.

"Ha! You really don't know. Why, the senator, of course. You ought to remember, sweet sister, that while the senator fathered the likes of Mario, he also fathered a scoundrel like me. How do you know which one of us he resembles most? Is he the noble statesman you see in his toga, exhorting us all to be true to values that are long dead? Or is he practical underneath, like me? Don't you suppose he would risk anything to see Mario in his rightful place? You are the only thing preventing it. You are what upset everything." Henri chuckled as he saw her concede the credibility of the idea. "With Mario safely out of the way, chasing after you, why shouldn't the senator have you arrested?"

"And then leave the city, so that he couldn't be held responsible for not helping me!" Amity said. "But who is to blame for Zabetta's arrest? Is that the senator's doing, too?" asked Amity confusedly. She hardly knew what to think about—what he was saying or the threat he presented.

"Why, that is your doing, of course. You needn't play innocent. You had only to prevail on some gentleman here to take a message to Venice to drop into one of the lion's-head boxes to alert the Inquisitors to Zabetta's crimes."

"I! But why?"

"Because with Bet gone, I'll become a sot, as you see me at present. I'll be obviously unfit to be the heir, and the senator will have to accept Mario and you with him!" declared Henri triumphantly.

He lifted her and tossed her onto a couch. His hands worked feverishly on her bodice as he held her down, his knee pressed between her thighs, ready to force them apart when the moment came. She struggled and fought to pull his hands away as they succeeded in clasping her breasts.

"Amity, be sensible," he said, sounding more reasonable than Amity. "It's going to happen. Why not enjoy it? We ought to be friends, you and I."

In response, Amity kicked, catching him under the ribs as he tried to hold her. Her shoe flew off and clattered across the room. His grip loosened, though he still had hold of her undergarments. She struggled harder and felt them tear away. A rush of air told her how much more she would be at his mercy if he caught her again. She herself had been a party to removing one obstacle to his purpose.

He was still blocking the entrance, and she had nowhere to go but against the wall. She found the shoe and heaved it at his head, missing entirely. He laughed and came for her, and she sank to her knees, as if that would help her.

Then suddenly the paneling gave. She had found the door, and she tumbled though, discarding the other shoe as she ran.

Henri did not follow Amity back to her room, and by midmorning she dared to venture out again, driven by pangs of hunger. Here and there guests slumbered in the French brocade armchairs. A few bleary-eyed revelers, having got bravely out of bed, were drinking coffee.

Donna da Riva looked exhausted but magnificent, decked out for the day's battle in a gown showered with rich Mechlin lace. Filled with determination to save face no matter what, Donna da Riva suddenly did not look frivolous at all. Not even her customary layer of pink rouge or the little jewels in her tower of hair or her dagger-length fingernails could accomplish it. This very circumstance—her not seeming frivolous—might give her away in spite of all she did, Amity thought. If anyone bothered to notice.

"Isn't there any word of Mario?" Amity whispered.

"No," said Amity's mother-in-law, and allowed worry to flash across her face.

"You will certainly have to call off the wedding soon!"

"No. Not yet. Zabetta is a widow, and widows must be married on the stroke of midnight, veiled and dressed all in black. It's an old custom, but no one will be surprised if the da Rivas adhere to old customs." She gave a rueful little smile as though thinking that for once her husband's attitudes could be put to good use. "I will organize some activities for the afternoon. The gentlemen can play cards, and the ladies will enjoy croquet or perhaps an expedition to visit some peasant farms. The peasants will be glad to welcome us. We always throw them money as we drive past."

The day seemed to pass slowly. Nobody remarked on Zabetta's absence, assuming she was busy with fittings. Amity walked in the gardens and saw a group of women depart on the expedition to the farms. Some very young women undertook to make Henri's last day as a bachelor memorable, and having made him a crown of corn husks and berries, rowed him about on the canal with much hilarity. Henri looked sheepish as he saw her watching, and she wondered how much he remembered about the night before.

He'd been very drunk. Did he recall what he had done? Or the accusations he had made about her? About the senator? Amity could think of little else. Was Henri right that Mario's father had been the one who had triggered her arrest? He had made a good case for it. She shivered and wondered if Henri really believed that she had been the one to implicate Zabetta. It would have been easy enough, since Zabetta had taken part in the episode that had incriminated Amity. Revenge would have been motive enough, after all Amity had suffered.

Dusk came on quickly, and it seemed that no one was about. Everyone had retired to their rooms to make their lengthy toilets for the nuptial event, and the midnight-to-dawn partying that would inevitably follow. Amity locked her door and tried to sleep, but she could only listen for the sound of horses in the drive and watch the hands of the clock move—past ten . . . past eleven.

Now the hallways began to fill with expectant guests. Music and laughter drifted up. Donna da Riva had not yet cancelled the event. What could she be hoping for now?

A knock came on Amity's door. She hesitated, thinking of Henri. With his nuptials spoiled, he might come to finish what he'd started with her. "Who's there?" she called.

"It's I, let me in," came Donna da Riva's voice, and Amity flung open the door to admit her mother-in-law, carrying an armload of dark clothing.

"Mario hasn't come back, Amity," she said in agitation. "Henri was right. He said that he wouldn't."

"But I'm sure he's done all that he can," Amity said.

"It doesn't matter. When men have done all that they can,

it is time for women to step in. It is we who must protect the da Riva name tonight and prevent scandal from touching it."

Amity was impressed. In some peculiar way this silly woman reminded her of the women of Washington's army. She brushed the thought away. "But how?"

Donna da Riva held up a black gown. "You must play the part of the bride, Amity. No one will suspect if you don't appear at the wedding. It will only be said that you are jealous of Zabetta's position as the wife of the new heir."

"I? Marry Henri? Never!" The idea of standing in for Zabetta repulsed her.

"Don't worry. It won't be a real wedding. The priest will know, but I'll bribe him."

"Bribe a priest!"

"Why not? Just a gift for a favor. It's done all the time. And no one will know the difference. You'll be completely veiled."

It seemed to Amity that half the problems of Venice must be caused by masks and veils. If only everyone had to show his face and take the consequences for his actions, the city would be a different place, and of course, many would say, not so much fun. Perhaps Donna da Riva's plan was as innocent as it seemed, but something rooted beyond reason would not allow Amity to accept it."

"I can't," she said.

"Won't," said Donna da Riva angrily. "Henri said that you wouldn't do it. It's true, then, that you implicated Zabetta in your witchcraft!"

"I'm not a witch!" cried Amity.

"Then prove it! Prove it by helping Zabetta! When you were arrested, we managed to keep word from leaking out, and the family was protected. But this! All these people will ferret out the truth when the wedding doesn't occur. It will be a disaster for the da Riva family."

"You are exaggerating to get what you want," Amity countered. "You can't stand the embarrassment."

"Maybe I can't. And Henri is like me. He won't stand up under the derision. Henri doesn't have the strength Mario would have. He'll become dissolute; he'll be irresponsible. He's never cared about anything but pleasure and Bet. Maybe he'll gamble away the fortune—like Zabetta's husband, Augusto."

With a sinking feeling Amity recognized that Donna da

Riva was close to the truth. "All right," she said. "I'll do it for the family."

Donna da Riva kissed her effusively. It seemed strange when a moment before she'd been calling her a witch. Amity put on the black gown before a thought struck her. "I will not go on a wedding trip with Henri," she said.

"Tch, don't worry about that. You'll leave with him, and I'll send a carriage to the first crossroads to wait for you and bring you secretly back."

"All right," Amity agreed, but she wasn't satisfied. Henri might very well bribe the coachman to "lose his way." If a priest were to be bribed tonight, why not a coachman? They'd wind up at some inn together, and Henri would suggest "fun" again. She would simply have to handle him, and if she couldn't . . .

Amity shivered and tried not to think what the consequences might be. As the clock moved toward midnight, a rap came on the door. She opened it, thinking someone had come to take her down to the chapel. The person who stood there made her draw back with surprise. It was the senator.

"May I come in, Amity?" he asked.

She nodded, remembering that Henri thought him to blame for her arrest.

"Mario's right behind me. We've just come from Venice," he said.

"You've brought Zabetta," Amity cried with relief.

"No. But neither are you to go on with this charade."

"Donna da Riva says . . . The scandal . . ."

"Scandal can't be avoided this time, I'm afraid. Mario and I have come to the conclusion that she is guilty as charged."

"What? But she can't be! I was there, and it was nothing but a silly visit to a fortune-teller."

"The Gypsy has confessed, Amity. There was more to it than that. It was arranged that she would bring you there, and the Gypsy would cast an evil spell. The curse was in the amulet she put around your neck."

"Why?" Amity recalled how Henri had disappeared that day. Zabetta hadn't seemed to want to find him.

"Because of the baby. Zabetta hoped to curse the birth of the child so that it would die. She hoped that would cause a rift between Mario and me. Mario was insanely in love with you, enough not to desert you if I disapproved the match, she and Henri hoped. It was their only chance to be wed."

Amity was amazed that a man of the senator's stature

could take such a thing seriously. But she remembered with a chill that she had had the amulet about her neck and thrown it off in the crisis of childbirth. It had been after that when things had begun to go right. She had thought it was because Mario had come to her side, but perhaps that hadn't been the reason. Perhaps . . .

"I nearly died," she said wonderingly.

"Yes. I don't think that was part of the plan. Mario might have done his duty and married Giovanna then."

Amity wept with disillusionment. "I thought Zabetta was my friend. She even had Henri give me a special draft when I wasn't feeling well. Was Henri in on it?"

"I'd like to think he wasn't." The senator sighed.

"I suppose we'll never know." Amity shuddered. "The draft was part of it, wasn't it? I had such terrible nightmares!" Now she was talking like the senator, she thought, frowning, and corrected herself. "I don't believe any of this. There is no such thing as witchcraft. It is a bugbear that has caused many people useless suffering."

"You think so because some of your own people were accused of witchcraft, falsely. That sort of thing sometimes happens when new religions challenge the old. But that is not enough reason to believe that witchcraft doesn't exist. Can you be certain there is no black magic?"

"No," said Amity honestly, thinking of all that had happened to her. "But can you be so positive there is? Enough to condemn Zabetta to the Leads? Senator, she must be set free whether she marries Henri or not!"

The senator looked at Amity thoughtfully. "You wish me to help her, even though you know what she tried to do to you?"

"Yes. The Leads are not fit for any human, no matter what!"

"I suppose that is a Quaker idea," said the senator. To his surprise, he was beginning to feel somewhat the way his son did about her. He was starting to understand why Mario was willing to risk everything to have her. The disturbing memories she had aroused when he had first met her surfaced, and this time would not be banished. He felt lightheaded. He might have been young again and in love himself. If he had been Amity, he would have liked to see Zabetta endure the bastinado, but the strength of her convictions impressed him. Suddenly he knew that he had been gullible when he had believed that she had a lover. Amity had never loved anyone but his son, he was certain. She had even been willing to go through with the false marriage ceremony to save the family from scandal. Amity wasn't so innocent after all this time in Venice that she didn't know the price Henri might have exacted.

The senator's hopes rose, and he felt more optimistic than he had in a long while. Witchcraft! Without that to interfere, Amity might even still produce his grandson. What a man *he* would be! But the senator remembered he had a problem. Henri was the heir now. He'd offered reluctantly to register Mario's marriage when his son had gone chasing after her, and Mario had refused his surrender on the matter.

"What's to be done if there isn't a wedding?" Amity was asking. "Donna da Riva says that Henri will run amok because of the scandal."

"Do?" said the senator exultantly. "Why, Mario must become the heir again. And I will register your marriage. And there will be sons, Amity."

"But Mario—"

"You'll convince him it will work, Amity. He will do it if you say so. You know it's right."

"Yes," she murmured. It would be up to her again to provide the son. She must have faith that Mario would have a son, she thought, and heard the clocks chime midnight.

29

It was almost Christmas. Venice blossomed with decorations and shoppers. The season had sweet intimacy. All the visitors, the summer travelers, were gone, and it was a cozy, family kind of time. Venetians were returning by the hundreds from the villas, and in the warm little cafés there were countless reunions over sticky cakes and coffee. Zabetta was still in prison, and Amity's thoughts turned toward her every time she visited the piazza and saw grim walls of the Leads.

It seemed impossible that she had once been incarcerated behind them, impossible that Zabetta was there now, while people sang carols in the square. Amity wasn't sure she had really forgiven Zabetta, but she had tried. Zabetta was the product of that society, and that society had become her undoing.

Giovanna, in her convent, helped to make the crèche, and laying the doll of the infant Jesus on the straw, wondered for the millionth time whether the da Rivas had returned to their palace on the Grand Canal. There would be parties and dancing if they had. Giovanna had difficulty ridding herself of her worldly thoughts, though it wasn't so much the parties that troubled her as the idea of Mario gazing into her eyes as they danced a polonaise or minuet.

It seemed every week she had the same confession to make to the priest behind the grille. She was forever doing penitence, scrubbing a floor or staying behind to say Hail Marys while the others went for a stroll on the piazza.

With the approach of Christmas, the burden became too much. Everyone was happy, it seemed, but her. Where was the special joy she had been promised as a bride of Christ? Shouldn't she experience it especially at this season? But Giovanna wasn't feeling well. She experienced a malaise. Sometimes the chapel even seemed to spin during her devotions. Giovanna needed help, but the priest would never understand. Atonement and more atonement were all the solution he could offer.

Perhaps a woman could do better, Giovanna thought, and went at last to consult the abbess in her private quarters. "Something is wrong," she said. "I've prayed and prayed and I cannot put it right."

"It will come in God's time, child," said the abbess. She was a kindly Venetian lady, herself the daughter of a *Zentildonna*, who had chosen the convent over meaningless marriage.

Tears welled in Giovanna's eyes. "But it's taking too long! I can't endure it!"

"If it is that bad, then it is a man," said the abbess.

"Yes."

"Perhaps you have no vocation. Perhaps you should marry him. I suppose that's impossible. That's why you're here."

"It's impossible, since he's married already, but I'm sure that I have a vocation. God couldn't be so cruel to me, to deny me the solace of a vocation as well as love! Oh, I'm sure I could conquer my feelings if they only weren't making me so ill!"

"Ill?" The abbess pricked up her ears. "How are you ill?"

"Well, I'm tired all the time and fall asleep during Mass. I'm sick at my stomach nearly every day, and I lose my breakfast in the morning."

The abbess sighed. "How long have you been a novice, Giovanna?"

"Almost three months."

"And how long has it been since you've had your female complaint?"

"Oh," said Giovanna blithely, "you needn't worry about that. That doesn't bother me at all. In fact, I can't remember that I've had it since—"

"Since last you were bedded by this man?" the abbess suggested.

Giovanna flushed, and her mouth fell open prettily. "How . . . did you . . . ?" she began, astonished that the nun had guessed at her transgression. But the abbess didn't answer. Instead she gave an astounding order.

"Take off your robe, Giovanna."

"Take off—"

"Yes, yes, take off your clothes. It has been three months at least. I want to see."

Giovanna dropped her habit to the floor. The abbess was not satisfied until she stood there naked. Then she studied the gentle swelling of her abdomen and sighed again.

The evidence was unmistakable. The little novice was pregnant.

Carnival began the day after Christmas. Amity threw herself into the whirl of gaiety. She had not been able to persuade Mario to reassume his place as the da Riva heir. He had given his word to Henri, and Henri remained the heir, gambling and carousing as Donna da Riva had predicted. But their marriage had been registered in the Golden Book, and Amity had decided to make herself accepted among her peers. But on second thought, making them admire and envy her might serve better.

She'd made up her mind to become a Venetian woman, a credit to Mario, but somewhat better than merely Venetian, with the added spice of her foreign origins. Gone was her incompetence on the social scene. She altered her hair, dusting it with a reddish powder to achieve the titian shade that was so sought after. She grew her fingernails long and painted her bosom every day.

Evenings she spent at the gaming house or in the cafés; days were for sleeping or for making her toilet. It was a plan that worked well. Soon she was holding her own salon at one of the cafés on the piazza. Zabetta might be spoken of in snickering whispers, but if there were rumors about Amity's arrest, they only made her more exciting, and the doge himself often attended her salon. That suited Amity perfectly.

A few months before, she had been in prison, prey to the rape of her dull-witted jailer. That all lay behind. The Gypsy had confessed and shown Amity innocent, and the Inquisitors, who were elected at six-month intervals, had changed. Nothing lasted in Venice, nothing but the palaces, the gondolas, the piazza, the parties. She might be playing cards with a man who had ordered her arrest and never know it.

Frivolity and masks—that was the game everyone played, the game Amity must play for her own purpose. When she had refused Mario's offer to take her to Russia, when she had forgone the pleasure of returning to enjoy the victory in America, she had also formed a plan. She intended to see that he became the next doge, and then Venice would change! The Inquisitors would be disbanded, the Leads opened. People would marry for love and dance with joy instead of debauchery.

Mario smiled wearily as she told him of triumph after triumph. He didn't seem to understand that she was engaged in battle on his behalf. He didn't understand women's parts in such things. But she could have told him that even General Washington's army had benefited from its battalion of ladies in Philadelphia's drawing rooms.

Mario would kiss her absently and begin to tell her of the things that were wrong in the Republic. He was grateful to be able to unburden himself. Too many wives would be bored by it. The arsenal was in a miserable state. It cost more to run than ever before, and fewer ships were being built. The guild laws were disregarded, and most of the workers turned up only for pay day. And many stole the wood intended for building ships to heat their homes.

"Apprentices pay for their certificates instead of studying for them, Am," he told her, interrupting some gossipy tale she'd heard while shopping on the Rialto. "Why, some of the ships are not seaworthy at all. The navy is a farce, and as for our colonial defenses, the battlements are all overgrown, and the drawbridges are too rusted to be raised."

"I know, dearest, but someday it will be different. You are

working too hard. Come along to the theater with me tonight and forget all this for a while."

"Forget! I might as well. Everyone else has!" But he did not go with her to the theater. Amity was displeased, and everyone noticed what a pique she was in that evening.

"It's time you took a *cicisbeo*," one of her new friends suggested. "You're not really a bride anymore. You can't expect your husband to escort you everywhere."

The suggestion did nothing to improve Amity's mood. He was her husband. He was supposed to escort her. But that was another of her American ideas. A *cicisbeo* was *de rigueur* in Venice. If she didn't have one soon, it might begin to harm her social standing. But Amity didn't relish choosing from among the gaudy dandies who vied to dance with her. Some of them heightened their complexions with rouge. Most smelled of perfume. One or two, she was certain, wore false calves inside their stockings to improve the shape of their legs. Conversation was usually inane, all compliment and innuendo. Amity, making use of the skills she had acquired in Philadelphia, delighted them with witty banter. They didn't guess that Amity quickly tired of their chatter. She was all the rage, and they debated over their cordials at Florian's as to when she would rent her *casino* and who would be first to share it with her.

Amity would have to take the *cicisbeo*, she thought. She was lonely with Mario busy at Council and Chiaretta still in the mountains, awaiting spring to come to Venice. Any number of men would be overjoyed to be her companion, although the position did not automatically include the privilege of bed. She decided to discuss the matter with Giovanna, whom she considered to be her best friend in Venice. Giovanna would know what she should do, she thought, but when she visited the convent, she found to her annoyance that Giovanna had been sent to one of the islands on a mission. Amity felt deserted. Every time she thought she'd found a friend in Venice, something happened to leave her alone again.

There had been Zabetta . . .

Never again, Amity thought, would she be so trusting of her own sex as she had been when she'd gone to the fortune-teller with Zabetta. But she continued to urge Mario and his father to have her released from the Leads. At least Henri seemed convinced now that Amity had not been Zabetta's accuser. But he continued to insist that the senator had precipitated Amity's arrest.

"Where did they find the amulet, Amity? It was in your bedroom. In the palace."

She failed to see how that implicated the senator, but Henri told her that the palace of a patrician was sacred, and archers could not cross the threshold except by a special order of the tribunal or with permission of the owner.

"Now do you understand?" he asked.

"But perhaps there was an order of the tribunal. None of the family was in Venice to know about it."

"Oh, Amity! You will persist in trusting my father." Henri sighed.

"I suppose it's because Mario holds him in such high regard," she answered. She could not bear the thought that the senator had been the cause of her terrible suffering. What hope could there be for Venice if even staunch defenders like Don da Riva were capable of base deeds? But she knew Henri's argument was good. And if not the senator, who?

Henri himself had given her no more problems. His sexual demon seemed stilled as far as she was concerned, and he seemed more to seek her out for comfort. He was grateful for her unexpected efforts on Zabetta's behalf. Or perhaps Henri had considered the probable consequences should Amity bear a male child, even if it might be Henri's. The senator would put pressure on Mario to become the heir again. So Henri became companionable and confided to Amity his father's attempts to get him to marry elsewhere.

"Why don't you?" she asked. "No one marries for love in Venice."

"Oh, I know I should. But Bet and I had wanted it since we were children. I'll take my chances and wait for her to be set free."

He would look downcast then, because he knew Zabetta was guilty as charged, and perhaps would never be released. The sentence need not be too long to mean death to a beautiful woman in the Leads. Henri had advised Amity that the senator might be like his rascally son, but nothing argued for the possibility of the senator's innocence like the streak of sentiment in the rascal.

It had not been easy for Amity to convince Mario to use his influence for Zabetta, but he saw how much her imprisonment upset her and one evening came home with the news that she had been released, thanks to his intervention.

"Is she coming here? Will Henri be allowed to marry her?" Amity cried.

"I doubt that the senator would agree to it," he said, unwinding her from him. "But it doesn't matter. Zabetta's not coming back to Ca da Riva."

"Then where will she go?" Amity didn't really want to hear. The expression on Mario's face filled her with foreboding.

"To the lunatic island," he told her. "She's gone quite insane."

Amity went with Henri to see her, shivering as Carlo rowed them across the gray winter water of the lagoon. The asylum sat white and barren on its little island, austere as the monastery it had been centuries before. Zabetta, in a simple white gown, her eyes wild and staring, was unrecognizable as the competent woman of the world Amity had first known. She began to scream when she saw Henri, and would not let him approach her.

"You mustn't take it personally," the matron advised him. "She's frightened of all men. It's the things that happened to her in prison."

Amity shuddered, remembering. Zabetta had been strong enough to bear the abuse of her husband, Augusto, but even that had not prepared her for the Leads. Amity thought that she, too, might be here insane if she had not had Francesco to help her escape before it was too late. She spoke gently to Zabetta and at last persuaded her to eat the sweets they had brought her from the city. But when Amity tried to brush her tangled hair, Zabetta became frenzied, lashing out at her and drawing blood with her long nails before the attendants rushed to subdue her.

On the ride back, Amity covered her ripped dress with a cloak, and Henri advised her to keep it shut tight. "Most Venetians know what to think when a lady comes home in such condition after an expedition with me," he joked, and then wept with his head in her lap.

"Mario and my father are right about Venice," he said woefully. "I suppose I've known it all along. I haven't wanted to admit it. It's easier to make fun, when I know I'm not the man either of them is. I can't help save Venice like my brother."

Amity's spirits lifted a little. If Henri realized the sorry state of the Republic, then maybe others would awaken to it.

"Of course you could help, Henri," she said. "You could go to Council meetings and support reform. You could talk about the needs of Venice in the cafés. You're as much a da Riva as Mario."

He brightened for a moment, then went glum again. "It's no use, Amity. I've no discipline. I'd get halfway to the Council and stop for a game of cards or to admire some pretty face. I've no flair for oratory of any kind, and no courage to be laughed at."

"Mario isn't laughed at. He just isn't listened to. If there were more voices—"

"Not mine. There's even the matter of the toga. I haven't worn mine for so long I'd have to have a new one made. I've gained weight from riotous living."

"Will you marry someone else now, to please the senator?" she asked to change the subject.

"No. I've no wish for the complications of an arranged marriage. I am perfectly suited to being a second son, but Mario isn't. I know what I must do."

Henri did what he thought he must the next day and gave up his right to the da Riva fortune in favor of Mario, who would become more powerful with the wealth behind him again. Henri did it in part because he was too lazy and ineffectual to take on the responsibility it entailed, but more, Amity thought, as his contribution to Venice and his brother's cause. Amity supposed this put her in danger of becoming the communal wife again, but for the time being he seemed too grieved over Zabetta to be interested.

Henri and Amity were both delighted when Mario was elected to the Council of Ten. He had become one of the most powerful men in Venice, in spite of his marriage to a foreigner. Mario was elated, and Amity felt satisfied, certain that her embracing of Venetian society had been worth it. She had mounted something of a campaign for him, batting her tortoiseshell fan and prevailing upon her admirers to vote for her husband to please her.

"Perhaps you're even one of the Inquisitors now," she reflected, congratulating him.

"Perhaps I am, since they are elected from the Ten."

"You would never tell me, I suppose."

"No."

"I might be sleeping beside a man who has sentenced someone to be hanged that very afternoon," she mused, only half-teasing.

"Do you find the idea exciting?" he asked.

She shook her head, but she touched her bodice in a way that electrified her senses. She fell back on the bed, pleasantly helpless as he unfastened buttons too difficult for her to reach, his fingers massaging the small of her back disturbingly, and straying over the smooth mounds of her buttocks.

"Mario, we must think of having another child," she said. "It was only Zabetta's witchcraft that made the first so hard."

"Do you really believe that, Am?"

"Yes," she said, telling half an untruth. "And the second I would not have lost had it not been for—"

"Don't speak of that, Am!" he commanded.

"Then love me as I wish to be loved, and I will never so much as think of it again," she promised. "We must have children, Mario."

She pressed her naked body against him and made her request difficult to refuse. When she felt his seed hot inside her, she knew a surge of jubilation. She had helped to seat him on the Council of Ten, and soon she would produce his son, to lead the next generation of da Rivas. And her sense of power filled her as deeply as had his love.

At the beginning of June it was time to leave for the villa on *terra firma* again, but Mario wasn't eager to go. "I've work to do, love," he said.

"But, Mario!" She was childishly disappointed. She had hoped they'd have such a wonderful time, a shining pair, each in a position of increased prominence.

"You could stay here with me," he suggested.

"Stay here!" The thought was preposterous. "Why, I'd lose touch with everything and everybody! Donna da Riva has wonderful parties planned. There's to be a costume ball which everyone will come to dressed as Quakers in my honor. I can't miss that!"

"I wonder if you will have anything to wear," he said with an edge to his voice. She had become different since she had returned from prison and taken on his dream, since their marriage had been registered in the Golden Book. But how could he complain? She was only making possible what he had always wanted. Venice was coming between them again, but in a different way. Once she would have been aghast at the sort of party she spoke of with such anticipation.

"It's not clothes that are the problem; it's the lack of an escort," she said angrily.

"Well, I will come now and then, of course," he replied with equal ire. It was unfair of him to expect her to remain in the city; nevertheless, he was hurt.

"Now and then!" she repeated jeeringly. "Now and then!"

"Perhaps it's time you took a *cicisbeo*, then," he said. It was the usual solution to this sort of husband-wife dispute, but Mario wasn't sure that he liked it.

"Oh, I should be bored to tears with a foppish *cicisbeo*," she declared, to his relief. "It's you I want."

He kissed her and ended the argument. "Try to understand, dearest. You won't be as lonely as you think in the country. I've arranged for a surprise for you."

The idea of the surprise appealed to her. Had he bought her a new horse to ride? She had told him how much she had loved to ride as a girl. But the surprise was even better—a dark-haired beauty of six in the company of Aunt Zenobia and Caleb, coming shyly to an "Aunt Amity" whom she hardly remembered.

"I am glad to see thee," she said gravely, and offered her hand.

"And I you, Gracie. It's been a long while. May I have a kiss?"

The child pressed rosy lips to Amity's cheek, and Amity, choking back tears, gathered her into her arms. "I wish you could stay forever, Gracie."

"Oh, but I can. Aunt Zenobia and Uncle Caleb say thee are to be my mother. And they say thee can tell me about my real mother."

Zenobia confirmed Gracie's report. "Caleb and I will be sorry to give her up, but the Russian winters are too harsh for her, and Gracie has a delicate constitution."

"Yes, I remember. Grace Turner and I worried about her so much when Grace brought her to Philadelphia from Valley Forge. Oh, Aunt! She is charming and I would be ecstatic to have her, but Mario . . ."

Amity remembered that Mario had always thought that Gracie was her natural daughter, the child of the outlaw, whose coloring she had. He would not like having her about as a reminder. He hadn't wanted to bring her in the first place, when they'd left Russia.

"Oh, but he's already agreed to it," Zenobia assured her.

Her gratitude toward her husband washed away the ill feelings of their parting in Venice. His acceptance of Gracie was a very special expression of his love for her. She felt almost guilty about her joy at having Gracie, whom Zenobia and Caleb would certainly miss.

"Whatever will you do without a child about, Aunt? You did dote on her."

"Oh, I shall have a child, Am," Zenobia replied with a blush and a secret smile.

"But you cannot mean . . . At your age!"

"Nature does not think that I am too old. Things have come to me late, but they have been the best," said Zenobia, and Amity knew that she had not done the wrong thing to send her aunt out from the Winter Palace to meet Caleb Beale on the quay.

The reunion with her aunt did not last long enough, and during the visit Amity was distracted from the social scene. Donna da Riva was irritated. "Where were you this afternoon, Amity?" she would ask. "The gentlemen were all asking for you."

"Oh, I was talking to my aunt about the fashions on Nevskoi Prospekt and quite forgot the time," she might say. Or, "Caleb and I took Gracie to see some new piglets."

She tried to keep Caleb away from as much of the goings-on as possible, for even after his years at St. Peterburg he was shocked and wondered grumpily if Gracie should be raised in such an environment.

"But *I* am here, Caleb. You know I'll teach her values."

"I suppose so," he said. "But she's spoiled already."

"Nonsense. She's just spirited, like her mother."

There was news and gossip from America to be heard, too. Peggy Shippen, the belle who had so resented Amity in Philadelphia, had married Benedict Arnold, who had proven a traitor. Zenobia said the misfortune suited, since the Shippens had played both sides of the war, befriending Tory and Whig alike.

"And Silas? Have you heard anything of him?" Amity was almost afraid to know.

"Indeed. Colonel Springer was decorated for bravery at Yorktown and has been elected to the new Congress."

"Colonel Springer! That is hard to imagine. He was only a Quaker boy with a rifle when I saw him last."

"He asked after you, Am, in a letter to Caleb. He'd heard you'd gone to Russia. He's never married."

"Well, he will find plenty of ladies eager to wed a hero in Philadelphia," she said, hiding a blush.

"But perhaps he loves no one but you," said Zenobia mischievously, enjoying her niece's discomfiture. "I declare, Am, Silas Springer must be quite a man. He brings color to your cheeks, and no other ever did in all your days in Society Hill or St. Petersburg. Except Mario, of course."

"I am not interested in Silas any longer. Aunt. Don't be silly! I am not sure we'd even be friends if our paths were to cross again."

After that it took Amity a while longer to get up her nerve to ask about the other person whose fate interested her. Probably Zenobia wouldn't know, she thought, procrastinating, even though Caleb received all sorts of letters and newspapers from America.

"Aunt, is the Doan gang still about?" she asked finally, curiosity overcoming her inhibitions.

"Oh, yes. They're a canny lot. All but one, that is. They caught Moses Doan hiding in a cabin on Tohickon Creek."

Amity's head reeled. "And?"

"They shot him dead, after he had surrendered. It was abominable behavior, but he was a scoundrel and deserved it, if anyone ever did. Am, are you all right?"

"Yes," she said. "It's only that I'm still appalled when human life is destroyed so cold-bloodedly."

He was dead. As he deserved to be, if he had done nothing wrong except the wrong he'd done to her, awakening her passions with his evil sensuality, setting her on a course that couldn't be changed. Most likely she and Silas would have been wed finally, if it had not been for the outlaw. And then she would not have known Mario's love, or seen St. Petersburg or Venice or the wild sweep of Russian steppe. She was awash with confusion as her fonder feelings for the outlaw came over her. He had shown her the richness of life.

When Caleb and Zenobia had gone, Amity turned her attention to providing for Gracie. There were clothes to be made, for her simple Quaker clothing, decreed by Caleb, would never do in Venice. Gracie must be dressed like other Venetian children in silks and bustles and lace; and her hair should be dressed high for parties. Gracie took to the new mode eagerly, as though she had been born to it, holding still with more patience than Amity had, until every curl and frill was in place. Soon she was a great favorite at the villa, and the gentlemen would take her on their laps while playing cards, to bring them luck. They spoke of the hearts she would break when she was grown and had joined society as a married lady.

Amity engaged a *ballerino* to teach Gracie dancing and deportment, but Gracie hardly seemed to need it. She displayed a natural charm and elegance. Mario, on his visits to the villa, was even more captivated by her than he had been in St. Petersburg, and he gave her a necklace of tiny diamonds to wear about her throat.

"That's silly," Amity protested. "She'll lose them. Children always do."

"She won't," Mario said, and he was right. Gracie kept the jewels in a little velvet-lined box and wore them almost every evening.

Discipline was harder to instill. Despite having been raised by Quakers, Gracie had also been raised at court. Perhaps that accounted for her willfulness, as well as her aplomb. She was quite willing to kiss Mario's hand when she came downstairs, as was the custom with fathers, but it proved impossible for anyone to teach her to await permission to be seated.

The *ballerino* wrung his hands and appealed to Amity. Amity appealed to Gracie, who answered sensibly, "Why should I ask? You will always say that I may."

"It shows proper respect," Amity explained, but Gracie had already gone on her way, bouncing a ball through the halls and finding plenty of guests willing to engage in her illicit game of catch.

Gracie became the prankster of the season, always ready to assist with any joke that was under way. She helped to exchange the salt for sugar in the kitchen so skillfully that the cooks noticed nothing, and all the desserts were salty and the soups sweet. It was necessary to throw away mountains of food, but Donna da Riva did not mind. The waste was a way of affirming the da Riva riches.

Amity spanked the child. It wasn't easy, since Mario wasn't there to help. Henri, whom she begged for aid, would have none of it, and Amity suffered bruised knees from the child's kicks.

"Gracie needs a father all the time, not just now and then," Amity complained on Mario's next visit.

"Well, then, bring her back to the city, and I will be one," he said.

"You know I can't do that. I'm very busy here."

"Yes, it's too bad. I need a wife more than just now and then, too," he said in a tone that gave her pause.

Amity thought he might show more gratitude for all she

was doing in his behalf. It was a great deal of work being a grand hostess. But Amity didn't want an argument. The season would soon be over, and she'd be back in Venice for the rest of the summer. She could manage Gracie for a few weeks. There would be time enough to get her in hand. But there wasn't.

Gracie grew bolder in her escapades, urged on by adult tricksters who should have had better sense. Gracie was a convenience, with her small size, able to pass unnoticed where a larger person would have given the joke away. One afternoon a group of merrymakers led Gracie to the edge of the canal and showed her where a gentleman and a lady had left their clothing while bathing in the nude. Gracie was assigned to creep through the bushes and make away with the garments.

Quiet as a little ferret, Gracie carried out the task, removing breeches and shirt, silk stockings, a white crepe petticoat, lute-string gown, and a "balloon" hat covered with colored sarcenet and a large piece of Italian tiffany in puckers around the crown. Gracie was just making off with the gentleman's wig, which he had carefully draped over a tree stump, when the deed was discovered.

Much shrieking ensued, followed by threats and then by tempting bribes of sweets and money. To everyone's delight, except the embarrassed pair, Gracie could not be bought. Finally there was nothing for them to do but make the best of it and twine their bodies in the tangle of wild honeysuckle along the bank and wend their way back to the villa inadequately concealed in their carriage.

It was one of the most callous pranks Amity had seen at the villa, though she thought she'd seen almost everything. Gracie was called to account.

"Why did you do that, Gracie?"

"Oh, for fun!"

"It wasn't fun for the lady and gentleman. How would you like it if someone had taken your clothes?"

"Oh, but they deserved it. Ladies and gentlemen aren't supposed to take off their clothes together, even to go swimming. And it was a lie that they were swimming. They were doing something else."

"What?" said Amity. It was a question she didn't want to ask, but if she didn't, Gracie would tell her anyway.

"Oh, jumping onto each other and rolling about, giggling and making funny sounds. They seemed to enjoy it a lot. Do you know that game, Aunt Amity? Do you think some of the gentlemen would play it with me?"

Amity was speechless with horror, and Gracie continued in a pique. "I asked Henri, and he said he would be glad to if I were older. How old do I have to be?"

"Quite old!" Amity almost shouted, and she banished Gracie to her room, presumably as punishment for her prank, but actually to give Amity a chance to collect her thoughts. She was still feeling rattled when Mario arrived from Venice and asked Gracie's whereabouts.

"Oh, let her out, Am. I've brought her a present," he said innocently, and was astonished by a sudden flood of tears from his wife.

"Whatever shall we do, Mario?" she begged. If anyone had the answer, he did, although he had no more experience as a father than she as a mother.

"That's simple enough," he said. "We'll do what all Venetians do with young girls as soon as such problems develop. We'll send her to a convent."

"A convent! Mario, she is only six!"

"It's true she's a bit young. Most girls don't go until they are seven or eight. But Gracie has been at the court in St. Petersburg, and she is older than her years."

"That's barbaric, Mario, locking girls away like china in a cabinet. I won't stand for it."

"But the china doesn't get broken in the cabinet, Amity." he said. "What you object to is losing her, I think."

"Well, I've only just got her back," sobbed Amity.

"There, love, let's go to bed now. Things will look brighter in the morning. You'll come to grips with it then. It's what must be done to protect the innocence of her mind and her body. Think, Am. There are a few men at least who are depraved enough to take Gracie up on the kind of suggestion she made to Henri today."

Amity would not accompany him to their bedroom. She went walking in the garden and then danced the remainder of the night. She knew how he had intended to deal with her, overcoming her objections with his prowess as he always did. If she stayed away from the bed, it could not happen. As the night went on, she drank wine nervously and grew giddy and reckless. Let Mario do without tonight. She would punish him as well as Gracie. Why else did he visit the villa but to satisfy his lustful appetite? He wanted love, but not responsibility.

Perhaps that was all any man wanted. Perhaps the women of Venice were right to give it to them.

Amity grew flirtatious. She, after all, was a piece of china that had long since been broken. Before she quite realized what had happened, she was in over her head. She had accompanied several gentlemen to the boxwood maze and in attempting to back coyly away had become the fox to their hounds in a chase. The moon was full, and it was difficult to hide; the soft air echoed with their laughter and their promises of bliss should they catch her. Amity had become lost in the rows of tall shrubbery. Which way led back to the villa? she wondered, filled with the memory of Jacques. The men were unlikely to rape her, and probably any one of them would release her at the realization that her screams were sincere, but Amity had drunk too much and her fears were irrational. The summer air seemed full of the suffocating miasma of evil that she had known in the Leads.

A man loomed in front of her. She gasped and tried to run away. But at the other end of the path another shadow appeared. Instinctively she turned back toward the first, a moan rising in her throat. The first shadow raced toward her and circled her with his arms.

The second man gave a wave of his hand, and conceding defeat, wished her captor luck. Amity struggled, and to her surprise he began to laugh.

"Oh, Amity, it's only me."

She turned and looked at his face in the moonlight, patrician like Mario's, but with sea-colored eyes and a framing of raven curls. "Francesco!" she cried joyfully. "Oh, Francesco!"

She had not seen him since the night they had escaped from the Leads together. She had not known for certain that some Inquisitor's spy had not caught up with him wherever he had gone.

"But you're in danger here!" she said when she had hugged him.

"No. The three Inquisitors who charged me are out of office. Exile doesn't last long in Venice. The only danger I'm in is of loving you too much, Amity."

"You mustn't—" she began.

"I know. And everything is going so well with Mario. He's doing grand things since he's been elected to the Ten. There's less corruption at the arsenal, and he's managed to have an audit of the army payroll begun. Perhaps you were right to love him instead of me. I have not accomplished anything except to get you sent to the Leads with me for my foolishness."

"I never blamed you for that," she said.

"Are you well, Amity?" he said anxiously. "After all that happened? Are you and Mario happy?"

"Very happy," she said, though at the moment her feelings toward her husband were not as tender as they might have been. "Where did you go when you left Venice, Francesco?"

"Oh, around and about. Paris for a while. They speak of nothing but revolution there. The American colonies have inspired them, and they speak of democracy for France and for all of Europe. When I left there, I went back to Lago di Garda. I've brought you someone, Amity."

"Chiaretta!" she cried. "Oh, I want to see her at once! But which way is the house?"

He laughed and showed her, and soon she held her daughter in her arms, kissing her as though she could never stop. The baby had grown over the winter. She was a plump toddler, full of smiles and charming baby ways. Holding her, Amity breathed the fresh baby scent of her skin and never wanted to be parted from her again.

"You'll stay with me, Chiaretta," she promised. "No convent for you!"

The child's arrival cooled hostilities for a time between her parents, but finally Mario was ready to return to Venice and wanted to take Gracie with him. Amity was still opposed, but she'd been able to think of no other solution. At night she had lain awake making plans to move to another villa and create a working farm there, as all the villas had used to be. There she would create a wholesome environment for the two little girls and hopefully for the son she'd someday bear.

But that was a pipe dream. She and Mario would both have to spend too much time away—he at the Council, she with her various endeavors. In the end it was Franceso who made peace between them.

"There is my sister Giovanna's convent. Giovanna loves children, and maybe she could be assigned especially to care for Gracie. And since she's a friend of the family, she could bring Gracie to see you often."

"Giovanna is no longer at the convent," Amity objected.

"She's returned," Francesco said.

The idea appealed to Amity. She could look forward to seeing Gracie frequently, and as a bonus see her friend

Giovanna, too. The compromise was agreed on, and Mario left the villa with a tearful Gracie in tow.

"You don't love me," Gracie accused. "It's because the baby came that you're sending me away." Nothing Amity could say dissuaded Gracie from the belief.

Amity's spirits sank after they had gone, and it seemed nothing could revive them. "Venice is always taking the people I love away from me," she complained to Donna da Riva.

"Perhaps you're demanding too much from the people you love," suggested her mother-in-law.

"Too much? I only want them to be with me. Quaker families always live under the same roof. This is so different!"

"Yes, that's the thing, Amity. This *is* different. You must think of what's good for Gracie, and what's good for Mario."

"Should I? But what about myself?"

"You must make do for yourself. That's what women do in every society. They sacrifice their own happiness for the happiness of their husbands and children."

Amity's view of Donna da Riva had been undergoing a change ever since the night that she had asked Amity to take Zabetta's place in the wedding. She seemed less a frivolous woman than the victim of an unappreciative husband and son. The parties, the many hours devoted to grooming were not so much to satisfy the ego as to have some sense of purpose in her life. Was this a form of sacrifice and making do? It was a notion Amity would never have considered when she had first come to Venice, but she was beginning to understand the Venetian way only too well.

"Dear child, you are making yourself needlessly miserable mooning about Mario's absence. If you would show a little pluck, things would go better," Donna da Riva advised. "Take a *cicisbeo* and be done with it. It's a moment that comes to every woman of your standing. Some look forward to it as a release from drudgery after their first year of marriage. Others fight it. No matter, it comes, as inevitably as the menses and the budding of breasts."

Amity felt chagrined to have the likes of Donna da Riva advising her to show pluck. It wasn't a quality she had ever thought herself lacking. "Oh, but I am so bored with all the men. They are like a swarm of mayflies," she said.

"So they are. It's a problem I have myself. Most men are tedious after a man like the senator. Why do you think that I change my companion so often? But there must be one of the mayflies that buzzes louder than the rest."

"No."

"Oh, think, Amity. I can tell you who it is. It's Francesco, of course."

"Francesco!" Amity's blush told Donna da Riva how right she was. "Ask him? Oh, but I couldn't!"

"Why not?" Donna da Riva was amused. "Because you might have wed him, if you had not married Mario? Because you went away with him to Lago di Garda. *Were* you lovers there? Is that it? You're afraid it will be something more if he becomes your *cicisbeo*? Lucky for you if it does!"

Amity frowned. She and Donna da Riva would never see eye to eye in a hundred years. "I cannot ask him after I have refused him in marriage and in bed. He'd be insulted. And Mario would be furious. It was because of Francesco that he risked his life for me in a duel. It wouldn't be fair to either one of them."

"You've a great deal to learn yet, Amity." Donna da Riva chuckled. "What a notion, being fair where men are concerned! Are they fair to women? No indeed. *Life* is not fair to women. We must use whatever weapons are at our disposal. And you have a perfect one. Mario may be jealous of your new *cicisbeo* and spend more time with you. As for Francesco, I suspect he won't be insulted. If he is, he is free to refuse you in his turn, and that will be fair!"

Amity heeded her mother-in-law's counsel. It sounded wise. She was lonely, and it reminded her of the daring advice of another woman of the world, the Empress Catherine. Catherine had urged her to vie for a man who was engaged to another, and she had done it more because it was in her heart than because of the source of the advice. It was in her heart now, too. How pleasant it would be to have Francesco's constant company! Catherine had made no more success of her love life than Donna da Riva, so that was not a reason for rejecting the suggestion. But Amity did not bother to consider that there all resemblance between her mother-in-law and the Empress of All the Russias ended.

She asked Francesco the next evening and was mildly surprised to find that Donna da Riva had been right that he would not be insulted. Instead he bowed, kissed her hand, and with an impish grin proclaimed himself delighted. She lay awake all night wondering if she had done a foolish thing. What would Mario's reaction be? And Francesco was more in love with her than a *cicisbeo* should be. With a shiver of titillation she wondered if he would be able to control himself now that he had been granted such intimacies.

He was at her side before she had dressed, bringing her a cup of chocolate and discussing their activities for the day. It was he who chose her gown and helped her do up the fasteners. She shuddered at the touch of his fingers. Strange, he had not taken such liberties when they had been in the mountains together. But then he had not been her *cicisbeo*. Amity glanced nervously at the maid, who was busy making the bed and straightening the room. What would she do if Francesco decided to dismiss the girl? She could not show that she distrusted him by countermanding the order.

But Francesco did not dismiss the maid. He went about his tasks coolly, arranging pearls about her neck and imparting a tender but dispassionate kiss where he laid them. Amity's cheeks heated, and she was vastly relieved when they went downstairs. But it was not because of any fear of an advance from Francesco that she was relieved, rather because of the treacherous desire she had discovered in herself. He was her *cicisbeo*, and that itself did not call for lovemaking. He played the role with dignity, not deigning to give way to passion. She admired him for it, and his sudden unobtainability bothered her more than she would admit. He would never make love to her, she was certain, unless she asked him.

She almost hoped that Mario would put an end to it when he next returned from Venice, and she waited, all in a dither, wondering if he would send Francesco packing and vent his anger by pleasuring her violently in bed.

To her annoyance, he did neither. He accepted the situation with hardly a bobble. He would not make an issue of it, but her own guilt racked her until she did it herself.

"Doesn't it annoy you that he was your rival and that now he is in my company nearly every waking hour?"

"No, love."

"But you know he still loves me. Do you really trust me so much? He is an attractive man, and you are always away in Venice."

"Dear Amity, you don't understand at all. He is your *cicisbeo*, and he is an honorable man. I could not assure your faithfulness more if I had put you in a convent like Gracie."

She was flabbergasted. "But your stepmother makes love to all her *cicisbei*," she said. "I'm sure of it."

"Yes. But they are the decadent sort, without moral fiber.

Francesco has the old virtues, though he tries to deny them with his politics."

He was right. She was as safe as though she were in a convent, and she grew increasingly frustrated. She had no wish to be unfaithful, but she had grown used to having the constant opportunity. Her admirers grew distant, lavishing their attentions on more promising prospects, and Amity's spirits were affected. She felt almost desexed by her handsome, charming companion.

Mario's visits to the villa were fewer. "It's because he doesn't have to worry about my behaving myself," she complained to Henri.

"Maybe," he agreed. "But most likely it's that Gypsy woman."

"Gypsy woman?"

"Well, they say she was a Gypsy woman once. She's not these days. She's had plenty of . . . umm . . . benefactors, to judge by her gowns and jewels. She's new to the city, and all the rage, but it's Mario she likes best. She holds her salon in the piazza, and the men flock to it. Mario spends almost every evening there. She's a marvelously beautiful woman with hair like fine red wine in color. I can't say I blame Mario. I wish she'd turn those dark eyes on me!"

Amity felt ill. She remembered the fortune-teller's crystal ball. She'd warned Amity to beware of a woman with red hair, and Amity had been sure which red-haired woman the Gypsy had seen. But it couldn't be!

"Henri, what is this woman's name?" she asked.

"Velda. She calls herself Velda."

Amity did not try to be rational. She packed immediately while Donna da Riva wailed that she was deserting her in the middle of the season, and taking Chiaretta, went back to Venice.

"Francesco, did you know that Velda was in Venice?" she asked along the way."

"Yes," he admitted.

"You might have told me," she accused.

"Why? You are only going to make a spectacle of yourself, sweeping down like this."

Amity had another idea why he hadn't told her. He had enjoyed having her to himself at the villa. Now he would have to share her with Mario again, though of course she was certain that he had other, more carnal liaisons. Make a spectacle! She would not!

But she did, in spite of herself. She arrived in the city in the evening and was unable to prevent herself from going down to the piazza to see for herself. If she had hoped to find Velda any less beautiful than before, she was disappointed. Velda still had a fine dancer's figure, emphasized by a gown of boldly striped peau do soie; and her hair, done in a tower, without need of any false hair being added, was even more magnificent than when it had been worn loose and natural. At the corner of her mouth perched a devastating little patch, positioned to signify *assassina,* or murderess.

No sooner had Velda caught sight of Amity than she rose and came over to greet her, trailing admirers behind her like so many little ducklings. "How wonderful to see you," she exclaimed, kissing Amity's cheek. "I never had the chance to thank you for saving my life in St. Petersburg."

She turned to her flock and elaborated, "The empress was furious with me, you see. A man had been killed over me. The empress wanted him for her lover, but he preferred me." Velda made the event sound thrilling, then disparaged it with a tinkling laugh.

A sigh ran around the group. They could all understand how the poor man had come to die. But what a glorious end!

"It was merely a barroom brawl, Velda," Amity returned, "and as for the help I gave you, I only did what my conscience told me I must. It turned out well, for both of us. I never had a chance to thank you, either."

"Thank me?" Velda's canny eyes registered surprise.

"Why, yes. You know that I would have to flee after I'd helped you. It was kind of you to take the ship and leave me to be rescued by Mario."

Amity was pleased to see that she'd struck home. Her escape with Mario was news to Velda. Quickly she followed one thrust with another. "That's when we were married."

But Velda had had time to recover. "I understand that marriages count for very little in Venice, especially after the first year."

"Mine is an exception," said Amity, lifting her chin.

"Ah, we'll see about that, won't we? Why isn't he with you, then? Why are you with Francesco? Your *cicisbeo,* I understand."

"He is not with you, either," Amity countered, marveling at how much Velda knew about her.

"Ah, we shall see," Velda repeated, and turning away, began to gossip with her beaux.

"She plans to have him yet," said Amity with a shudder. "How did she come here, Francesco?"

"They say an Austrian general brought her on his holiday. The general is long since gone; she needed him only until she established herself. For a while she lived with the Gypsis, but now she wants for nothing."

"I suppose Venice has always been her goal." Amity sighed.

"Yes. Would you like to go for a stroll on the Lido? It might clear your head. I think there will be fireworks tonight."

"No, thank you. I'd like to go home, Francesco." She felt him squeeze her hand comfortingly as he helped her into the gondola, and she smiled up at him woefully. How glad she was to have him! Only he could understand the nature of her conflict with Velda, and she was sorry for the uncharitable thoughts she'd had about him at the villa.

Mario did not come in until late, wearing a coat and breeches of sulfur-colored velvet and looking angry. "You might have told me you were coming, Amity," he said.

"I decided on the spur of the moment," she told him. She had expected him to be glad to see her. He had been urging her to come back to Venice, but she had waited too late.

"I've been the butt of jokes all evening," he told her. "People are saying that you returned to Venice to spy on Velda and me."

Her flustered expression informed him of the truth of the matter, but suddenly, to her relief, he laughed. "You were not very subtle about it, Am. But that is one of the things I love about you. You are not that kind of woman."

She wriggled like a happy puppy in his embrace. Surely he would love her forever! She had nothing to fear from Velda, but she was glad she had come back to the city anyway. Something else to thank Velda for the next time they met.

They seemed to run across each other everywhere after that. Walking on the Liston. At the embroidery shop. Once she caught sight of Velda at the theater, her shadow leaning against that of some gentleman in the murk of the unlighted boxes; and then again as they left the theater, carrying lanterns to show them the way to the gondolas through the dark opera house. Velda flashed a smug smile when she saw that Amity was again with Francesco. Amity, in spite of herself, was almost afraid to look to see who Velda's companion was.

When she did, it was not Mario. Neither of them could command his presence. Where was he so much, and why had his eyes never lost the worried look she had seen the night she'd first returned to Venice? Neither his anger nor his subsequent good humor had hidden it.

But Amity had not long to worry over Mario. Another problem claimed her attention. It was Gracie again. Amity had thought the problem was resolved. Gracie had taken a liking to Giovanna, who had been pleased to have special charge of her. But suddenly the abbess sent a message that Gracie had run away. For an anxious two days Gracie could not be located. Amity paced up and down the halls of the palace, while Mario scoured the city. It was Carlo who found her on the nearby island of Murano. He brought her home asleep beneath the *tenda* of the gondola.

Amity was beside herself. "Gracie, what possessed you?" she cried, "Where did you think you were going?"

"To the . . . the . . . I can't remember, but it was one of the Isole de Dolore."

"The Islands of Sadness!" Amity shivered. "Those are for hospitals and asylums. Why would you want to go there?" San Clemente, where Zabetta stayed, was one. But Murano was only where glass was made.

" 'Leprosy' is the word she cannot remember," Carlo advised. "She was looking for the Isle of Lepers."

"Lepers!" Amity's voice gagged. "Why?"

"Because that's where the sister has gone."

"Giovanna has gone to the Isle of Lepers!"

"Yes. She said that she had a special penitence to do, and God had given her this way to perform it. She said she was happy, but she cried and said she might never see me again. I wanted to go with her. Will you let me go there, Aunt Amity?"

"No, Gracie!"

"Well, I won't go back to the convent, if I can't be with the sister," said Gracie, and crossed her plump little arms.

"You'll do as I tell you, Gracie," Mario said. "You'll go and you'll behave yourself." For reply Gracie kicked Mario's shin.

"Gracie!" Amity could not imagine having the sort of spunk or foolhardiness it took to challenge a person as awesome as Mario must be to a small child.

Mario turned Gracie over his knee. Amity stayed out of it,

but when Gracie ran off howling, Amity went after her and cradled her in her lap.

Mario was in a fury. "You'll undo all the good I've done!" he stormed.

"Good!"

"Yes, of course. She has to go back to the convent. You've seen what it was like the other way."

"She won't go back! She'll stay here with me! She's a little child who never knew her mother, and who is getting a different 'mother' all the time. I'll be her mother from now on."

Mario started to say something, then thought better of it, but no matter, it was too late. Amity knew what he'd been about to say. He was thinking of the outlaw, about to announce that perhaps she'd been Gracie's mother all along.

"Oh! You *will* always think that!"

"I have reason," he countered, too angry to stop himself.

"Perhaps that's the kind of woman you like," she said, swiping back.

"Perhaps it is. I know one who would treat me better— whose tongue is not as sharp as yours."

Amity felt a blade of fear. The argument was out of hand. She was bereft, her bearing on the world lost, as it always was when she fought with her husband. Without Mario's steady support, the sun might as well not have been in its place. But Amity was too upset over Gracie to draw back.

"Why don't you go to her, then?"

"Since you request it, I will, madam," he said, and taking his walking stick, went out the door. He was gone all night. She felt life and will drain out of her. She was tired and beaten after so many years, and she had brought it on herself in a foolish way.

When he appeared in the morning, he gave her no hint of whether he had been with Velda, but the worried look she had noticed before had deepened in his eyes. "I hope you have changed your mind about returning Gracie to the convent," he said.

"I'm sorry about our disagreement, but I haven't changed my mind," she answered.

"Well, then, you'll have to manage by yourself, and Gracie is a handful."

"By myself!" Her voice became a shriek as rage overwhelmed her. "If you are going off with that woman you might have had the decency not to tell me! you promised you would not take any more mistresses, but I suppose that you think *she* doesn't count, since she's been your mistress before!"

Seizing a lacy bed pillow she flailed him with it, sobbing. Fluff sifted out and clung to his velvet coat as he stayed her hand. Suddenly she felt herself flung backward onto the bed. The pillow was torn from her grip and wedged beneath her to facilitate his entry, and knowing what was about to happen, her body began to seethe with anticipation.

"No!" she cried, but he had heard such protestations before and knew better than to pay them any mind. In another moment her wrapper had been pulled away, and her nightgown of silk and Honitron lace was above her waist. He took her forthrightly and shamelessly while she pulled his hair and kicked her objections, shattered that he would use her so when he had just come from the bed of another woman. Her exertions lifted both of them to incredible heights of desire. She fought until she could keep hold on her passion no longer and with a scream of fulfillment glided over love's peak, drifting helplessly into a sweet delirium of satisfaction.

Mario fell heavily onto her with a groan of contentment. Then he rolled away and began to laugh softly. She raised herself onto her elbows indignantly and saw him looking at her with fond amusement.

"Oh, Am, you are fascinating to love when you're angry. I am not going away with Velda, you goose."

"But you are going away?"

He turned serious. "I am going with the fleet to fight the Bey of Tunis. The Republic must show it can still make a stand against piracy in our colonial waters."

"War! You're going to war!"

"Yes."

"Oh, Mario, please don't! You know I hate fighting. And I don't want to have to fend for myself in Venice. I'm afraid for you and for me, too."

"You're a strong woman, Am. You'll survive whatever happens. If not for that, I couldn't go. But Venice needs me."

She saw the struggle inside him written on his features and was ashamed of herself. She regained her composure and made it easier for him, bowing to the one true mistress she could never ask him to renounce. "How long will you be gone, Mario?" she asked.

"Until the pirates are defeated," he said with calm assurance that he could accomplish the victory.

She helped him pack his trunk. It was not the first time

that a man she loved had told her he was going to war, but in this case she hardly knew whether she ought to be relieved that it was only to war he was going.

30

Months slipped by. Now and then some ship from the fleet returned to Venice. Always it brought letters from Mario, and Amity would send packets of letters in return. She looked forward to such occasions, but afterward she was always moody, lonelier than ever.

She listened to the tales sailors brought, of how his ship had clashed with the ships of the Barbary pirates, the treacherous Moors of North Africa, who terrorized the Mediterranean and swept in along the coast of the Adriatic to plunder among Venetian colonies. His leadership was competent, but not cautious. She supposed he would die before he would surrender, since Venetian honor was the most important element of victory. He was a skillful sailor, from his nobleman's youth in the navy, but it would be a miracle if even a man like Mario could guide the weakened fleet to triumph.

She feared for his life, and there was no way she could quiet her fears except to throw herself into the social whirl of Venice. She held her own salon on Tuesday nights at a café on the piazza. At other times the da Riva palace was the scene of one of the great Venetian *conversazioni*.

Velda, remarkably for an outsider without family ties in the aristocracy, had become one of her main competitors. It was rumored that she was the mistress of one of the Inquisitors, and Francesco thought the rumor was true. "That's how she gets by with it, I suppose," he said.

"Gets by with what?"

"Why, her revolutionary connections. She even holds her salon at the Café Ancilotto, and everyone knows that's where the Freemasons go."

Amity had heard rumors of the French influence in Venice. Secret societies were said to be forming, though no one had any proof of it. It was thought that many of the Barnabotti belonged to such groups, fomenting ideas of revolt. Amity wondered if Francesco belonged to such a group, but she was really afraid to know.

If he were, she would have to dismiss him as her *cicisbeo*. With her marriage recognized, she was not likely to be arrested again, but the memory of the Leads had not faded. At the very least there would be ugly gossip if she were known to keep company with a revolutionary.

Velda, on the other hand, thrived on the same sort of gossip Amity dreaded. She was playing both sides—ingratiating herself with Venetian powers and with the French as well. Before many years, revolution must come in France. Should it spread to Venice, Velda would be ready.

"Do you think that will happen?" she asked Francesco.

"Maybe. Revolution will bring a strong wind, and a mere breeze would topple the Republic. I think everyone is waiting for it. The common people would rise to defend Venice, I think, but even they know the cause is lost. And the nobles, Barnabotti or not, are celebrating a great farewell party, like a New Year's Eve ball, saying good-bye to the order of a thousand years."

It was one explanation of the revelry and debauchery of Venice, and as good a one as Amity had heard. "And you, Francesco. Are you afraid?"

"Yes. I am only human. But there's no use protecting what is worn out and useless. The new will come; it's the way of all life."

"Take care, Francesco," she said with a shudder. She did not need to ask whether he would be a part of the wind that would finally shatter the Republic, and when a "lodge" was discovered in the Riomarin district and black curtains and costumes belonging to it burned, she was relieved that he was not among those arrested.

At Amity's *conversazioni* the talk was gay and inconsequential, and that was the way that she liked it. Once, she would have been among the voices for revolt, she who had fought so for the colonies. But then she had not been a wife, with her husband's heritage of centuries to defend. Amity had changed her attitude. She believed in Mario, and that was reason enough now to believe in his cause.

Speculation was rampant about whose bed Amity shared. Some said that she slept with her *cicisbeo*; but others said she loved elsewhere, that her relationship with Francesco was too warm and genial, without the fire of lovers. Only a few, like Henri, knew the truth.

"How can you stand it, Am?" he asked over a cup of chocolate in her sitting room one day. "Love is all around you, everywhere you turn, but you live the life of a nun. Well, the sort of life nuns are supposed to lead. In Venice even the nuns—"

"Oh, don't tell me, Henri! I don't want to hear about goings-on among nuns. I need to think there are some women I can respect."

"Dear me, one would imagine you a dedicated Catholic to hear you, Am. But you know you needn't take any of those sycophants of yours as a lover to gain relief from your natural urges. That is what I'm for. Mario has been gone a long time, and he's likely to be gone longer. It's not the same thing when it's kept inside the family."

He put his hand on her knee, and to her astonishment, she felt a quiver of desire. It *had* been a long time. Instead of pressing himself on her, he drew his hand away and excused himself, leaving her vaguely disturbed. If only Mario would come home! Henri was right that she was badly in need of a man, and it was a measure of how acclimated she had become that she gave some credence to what Henri had said.

She was glad when shortly thereafter she was invited to ride aboard the *Bucentoro*, the doge's ship of state, for the annual ceremony in which the doge threw a golden ring into the ocean to symbolize the marriage of Venice to the sea. The event would take place on Ascension Day, one of the greatest holidays. There would be masking, as though it were Carnival, and Carnival activities in the piazza—fireworks and bullfights, a sea monster of glass belching smoke from a furnace inside. She looked forward to the day, expending nervous energy on the creation of her costume for the occasion.

It would be necessary to wear the official black gown, as it was on all official holidays, but like other Venetian aristocrats, Amity planned to make it magnificent with bustled skirts and a low-cut neck, which, combined with tight lacing, threw her bosom forward. Jewels could be strung about the neck and also glued to shine in the décolletage.

The long veil, the *zenda*, was trimmed in gold braid and lined with quilted satin. Over all went the mask, with its beaked nose, and the three-cornered hat, a combination she had become used to wearing.

Spring breezes washed the winter fog from the canals as the regatta traveled down the Grand Canal to the sea. The *Bucentoro*, with its gilded statues supporting the vast roof, carried dignitaries and high officials of state, all lounging around sipping spicy drinks on luxuriant morocco cushions.

Amity thought she saw a swallow overhead, and her heart lifted. Then she remembered what Donna da Riva had told her that first spring: swallows never came until May. Suddenly her attention was riveted by a figure near the doge's throne.

The man seemed to be a Quaker, dressed simply in a gray jacket and breeches, wearing the distinctive broad-brimmed Quaker hat. A wave of longing swept over her, and she moved nearer to see him better. She supposed he must be a Prussian Quaker, but he looked as though he might have come from her own Bucks County meeting. He raised his head and gazed directly at her, and a cry rose in her throat. It was Silas Springer. Now she saw the coppery queue of his unpowdered hair, the eyes, gray as November woods, steady without shadow. The face was older, the boy chiseled into the man by the conflicts of faith and of war.

It was the Silas she had loved and never quite forgotten, yet it wasn't the same Silas at all. This Silas, had she loved him, would never have allowed her to escape him. She could feel, even now, a magnetic power, drawing her to him.

But all this was happening in a dream. It couldn't be Silas, after all, for he didn't seem to recognize *her*. He was gazing off now, uninterested in her, as though she had been invisible. Then she remembered the mask.

Dear heaven! No wonder he didn't recognize her. He would be expecting a slamkin and bonnet, or at most, the fawn silk meeting dress she had carried away to Washington's camp to be married in. She had a vision of herself as she had become, and all at once she was ashamed. Hurrying below, to a ladies' dressing room, she began to strip away her jewels and wash paint from her wrists and her breasts. While other women looked at her as though she had gone mad, she loosened her corset, tore off her mask, arranged her black *zendà* to cover her modestly.

That was better, she thought, studying her reflection in a mirror. But did dissipation show on her face from her years as a luminary of Venetian society? How different life would have been if she had married Silas, she thought with a twinge of regret.

He saw her at once when she came on deck again. It was as though he'd been searching for her, and he pushed among the revelers, his intent eyes never leaving her as he made his way toward her. Her heart pounded as he took her hands in his.

"Amity! Thee art as beautiful as ever!"

"Silas! Or must I call you Colonel now?" Up close she could never doubt he was the same Silas. The turn of his mouth awakened an overwhelming memory of kisses among mayapple and Queen Anne's lace.

"You may call me whatever you please, Am," he said, smiling, and she knew that he wished it would be "dearest" ... "darling" ... "beloved."

"I am married, Si."

"I know. When someone was needed to come to Venice to establish a consulate, I asked for the assignment. I told myself it was the satisfaction of helping to forge the first diplomatic ties for the United States that interested me. But all I really wanted was to see you again, I had to see thee, Am. Thee art the only woman I will ever love."

He was the third man, she thought. The man the gypsy had seen who would love her forever. She should have known! A cheer went up as the doge, wearing his toga made of cloth of gold with sleeves touching the floor, threw the ring into the frothing water.

"It seems a waste of gold, doesn't it?" Amity said. "You'd think there would be hundreds of gold rings on the ocean floor by now, but there aren't. Men will dive for it tomorrow and vie to bring it back to the doge. It's all a sham."

Silas ignored her patter, and she gave up her attempt to change the subject. "I love Mario, Si. I cannot—"

"I know, Am. I don't expect anything. But we might have dinner together, might we not? For old times' sake?"

She couldn't refuse. She didn't want to refuse. They spent the evening together on the piazza. The hours drifted by, the morning star shining behind the last of the fireworks as Carlo rowed them home to the palace.

The next evening he took her to the theater and the next for a stroll on the Lido. Henri met her coming in late, and laughed knowingly. "So you've found a man after all, Am!"

"He's not my lover," she said with a blush.

"No? Why not? You're certainly attracted to each other. It's going to happen. You might as well not fight it. Besides, it's the talk of Venice already."

He had never said anything that had made her dislike him so much. She supposed it was because she knew it was true. They *were* becoming the subject of talk. Maybe she was jeopardizing the consulate he had come to establish. Perhaps more than that. Venetians barely tolerated foreigners. And Silas with his American ideas was courting trouble, along with Amity. In the cafés Barnabotti gathered around him. Even Francesco was fascinated by the quiet, battle-weathered American.

If someone formally accused him of having an affair with the wife of a nobleman . . . She shuddered at the thought of a note shoved into one of the Inquisitors' lion's head boxes. It would be a perfect excuse. A group of *bravi*—assassins—might come for Silas, and he would wind up mysteriously drowned in the Grand Canal.

And Henri was right, too, that the affair was bound to happen. Every time they were alone, the tension was between them. They tried to talk of other things and pretend that it wasn't there, but the sense of all that might have been was heavy in the air. Of all the men she had known, she had never known another as compelling as this new Silas Springer. None except Mario.

She was afraid she was falling in love with Silas again. As they floated together through the moonlit canals, she ached to have him touch her. With Silas, the desires of nature were strong, the passions so long unfulfilled by Mario were in danger of overcoming her. She must quit seeing him, and yet she did not.

Occasionally he spoke of the past. "I was a foolish boy then, Am. I should have married thee when thou came to find me at Washington's camp."

"No, you were right, Si," she would say. "Then I might have died like Isabel, in a lean-to. I was meant to wed Mario. It was the light, Si. We were both of us following the light. It was no one's fault."

"Thank heaven thee forgive me, Am!" he said fervently.

She knew he was speaking of more than his refusal to wed her out of meeting. He had had years to grow and consider since that December morning when he had found her in Colonel Rall's bedchamber. Perhaps he had heard the whisper of the Belle of Trenton, and if so he had come to accept the nature of her contribution to the victory there. Whatever, he had learned not to judge, but only to love.

Sometimes Silas spoke of Bucks County, how he loved the

sight of the mountains that told him he was coming home after he had been away at war or to the Congress in Philadelphia. "Each time I see home again, I am glad I fought for freedom," he would tell her. "Now a man has the dignity that God intended."

And then his eyes would cloud with the memory of the men he had killed, whose only dignity was in the markers of their graves.

Amity would talk then of the things that caused no pain: of the moon that rose with the blush of a peach on the horizon, and soft long hummocks of grass making meadows of flowing silver. Of deer that made trails behind the farmhouses and stood poised in the dawn, and the height of the corn in August.

"Why don't you come home with me when I leave, Am?" Silas would suggest. "Bring Chiaretta and Gracie. Gracie should see her heritage. And a chaperon, of course. How about Donna da Riva?"

Amity was amused at the idea of her mother-in-law embarking on a journey. "Oh, she could never go, Silas. She would never leave her position in society unattended."

Silas caught the spirit and chuckled. "But think what an impact she'd have on Philadelphia, Am! It would be another revolution!"

Such companionable moments were rarer as the strain of their feelings deepened. How long before even the strong-willed Silas lost control? She was almost certain that she could not resist if he touched her. She had been lonely and unloved for too long.

An affair between her and Silas would be of a sort not common in Venice, not a fling for pleasure, but a relationship that would someday be mortally wounding to one or both.

Nobody understood her predicament better than Henri. "You're in dangerous waters, Am," he said. "You're about to jump in deep when you ought to be content with wading, the way people do in the piazza when it floods."

"Oh, Henri. It's a harmless flirtation," she protested.

But she couldn't fool him. "*I* am still here, Am," he told her with a flicker of lust in his eyes.

Amity was almost charmed. Henri had very nearly given up his long-standing ambition to bed her. The time when she had feared him seemed ages ago. Once he'd been the lurking tiger; now he was just a puss, ready to curl up beside her on a winter day. She very nearly appreciated his company.

He still suffered from the loss of Zabetta, and his unhappiness drew her to him in a special way. Once she succumbed to his plea that she accompany him to the lunatic asylum. Zabetta was thinner; and her once-shining hair was dull, but not disheveled as it had been before.

Amity saw recognition in her eyes and was encouraged. "It's Amity, Bet," she said softly so as not to startle her.

Zabetta scrambled away into a corner, an expression of terror on her features.

"Don't be afraid of me, Bet. I'm your friend," Amity coaxed.

"You can't be my friend. Not after what I did to you. You've come to pay me back."

"I don't believe in witchcraft. You did me no harm." Amity tried hard to sound convinced of it.

"But I wished you harm—terrible harm!"

"I've forgiven you, after all you've suffered!" This time her tone held no doubt. "Look, I've brought you some lavender soap and some *diavolini*."

Zabetta's eyes glazed as Amity offered the liquor-filled sweets. "Poison!" she cried, and began to scream, throwing herself at the barred door of her room as madness reclaimed her.

Amity was appalled, but Henri was, if anything, pleased with the visit. "She's getting better, Am," he told her on the way back to Venice. "She spoke to you. She won't speak to me. It's because you're a woman, and she's still too afraid of men. Come with me again next week. I'm sure it will be good for her."

Amity could not bring herself to go again, but Henri, ever hopeful, asked her each time he left for the lunatic island.

Then suddenly Amity had more exhilarating things to think of. Mario came home with the triumphant fleet, and Venice erupted into celebrations. An atmosphere of victory pervaded the city. It was as though it believed in itself again. Mario was a hero. Everywhere he went women swarmed over him, ravenous for the attention of a real man after all the ineffectual dandies. Amity basked in the jealousy of her peers. It was obvious that Mario had eyes for no one but her.

They had been separated for two years, and each was as hungry as the other for love. She did not make the mistake of asking if during the time he had been gone he had kept his promise to take no mistresses. If he had eased his desire with the bodies of other women, he had not been able to quench his need for her. The fire of his longing had made him fierce in battle, he told her, laughing as she lay naked and rapturous beneath him. He had sent shiploads of pirates to their briny deaths with his cannon, and it seemed to him that he had done it more to get home to her than for the honor of the Republic.

The idea should have repelled her, with her Quaker scruples, but she was beyond morality on her way to ecstasy. It seemed only right to her that pirates should die so that Mario could come home to her. If anything, the idea that lives had been lost in love's conquest aroused her even more. Amity was a different woman than the one who had come to Venice, even a different woman from the one Mario had left. She had coped, but coping had had its price. When Silas arrived, she had realized how much she was sliding into the decadence of the city, but now she had forgotten again.

"You'll be elected doge when there is an election," she told Mario.

"It's possible," he agreed, and his grin told her he thought it more than just possible. People spoke of it. Victory had accomplished what his years of work and dedication in the Council had not. Tales of his exploits spread through the city. He was the hero Venice had been needing. He was what they had been waiting for.

"You'll be the next dogaressa, Amity," said Donna da Riva. "Imagine! A foreign woman in the Ducal Palace!"

"I shall be no worse than the present dogaressa," said Amity cattily. "In fact, I'm bound to be an improvement."

The present doge, Paolo Renier, had officially named his niece the dogaressa, but he kept a mistress from Constantinople. Margherita had once been a rope dancer, and when people, inside the palace or out, spoke of the dogaressa, she was the one they meant.

Mario and the Senator shook their heads over Paolo Renier. He sold state offices and licenses to beggars to solicit alms at the door of the Basilica.

"The shame of it is that the doge is a brilliant man," sighed the senator. "But he has no spirit."

"Yes, the doge is a fine speaker," Mario agreed." But what does he say? 'We live by luck, by chance.' And he's right."

"But that will not be so when Mario is doge," declared Amity. "Venice won't live by luck then. She will live by strength."

Mario's eyes gleamed with his appreciation of her confidence, and she felt vindicated at last in her marriage. He would be doge, and she had helped, if only by not allowing him to forsake his vision. She remembered a time when he had offered to, when he had suggested that they go to Russia or to America. She had had mettle then, and she had earned her place beside him in the Ducal Palace. Amity was elated. She knew that even in office, he would depend on her for his inspiration. She would be more than a mere hostess.

But being hostess in the Ducal Palace would have its satisfactions. Everyone in the city would vie to sit at her dinner table or play cards in her private parlors. Her great balls would be anticipated for weeks.

Donna da Riva was already planning the parties, and while Mario was away at Council, she and Amity spent many delightful hours over chocolate, dreaming of the future.

"It's too bad the election can't be held now," said Donna da Riva.

"Yes," agreed Amity, "but I suppose it will come soon enough."

"Perhaps not. People forget."

"Oh, but they can't forget what Mario did."

"Don't be too sure, Am. Paolo Renier is old. It would be convenient if he were to die now."

Amity was only a little shocked. She had had such thoughts herself, but she would never have voiced them. Donna da Riva was as honest as she was practical.

At night in her dreams, Amity saw the funeral procession of the doge, moving out toward San Michelle, and she saw herself beside Mario on the Basilica steps as he took office before a cheering throng. And in her dream she smiled and said to him gently, "And to think you said no good could come of it."

And then she would wake up, horrified with the knowledge that she was wishing for a man's death; and wishing it, not even to benefit the Republic, but so that Mario would love her more. He would love her then as only a man who had fulfilled his goals could love; he would love her because she had sacrificed to encourage him to pursue those goals. He loved her now, but then he must love her even more. She was greedy for his love; she could not possibly have enough.

Velda could never compete with her when she was the dogaressa, she thought, and laughed to herself. Why should she still worry about Velda? Twice now Velda had campaigned for him, and twice Amity had won.

But Amity could not quite put the thought of Velda aside.

"You've only got good feminine instinct," Donna da Riva said, when Amity confessed her lingering fear. "A man's never won forever. Velda may think that the third time's the charm. She'll find him more desirable than ever now, as do all the ladies."

"Nonsense," said Amity sternly. "When a man loves a woman as Mario does me, he can be trusted."

Donna da Riva snorted. "All the same, child, you'd best keep your sails trimmed if you want your ship to come in."

Amity chose to ignore the advice. Wasn't Mario with her constantly? Francesco's duties as her *cicisbeo* had become a joke. Once he had even come in with her morning chocolate and surprised her in Mario's embrace. Amity had been overwhelmed with embarrassment and had dashed naked for her dressing room, dragging bedclothes with her. Mario had cursed as his pleasure was yanked from his arms, but when she had finally emerged, she had found the two of them looking at her amusedly and sharing her pot of chocolate. It was a measure of how Venetian she had become that she was able to bring herself to join them.

"Tell me about this Silas Springer," Mario asked one day.

Amity's fingers stopped in midstitch as she worked on a piece of crochet. She had hardly thought of Silas in months. She'd had time for no one except Mario. But there had been talk about them while Mario had been gone. Perhaps he'd heard it. She'd committed no deed that she ought to be ashamed of, but maybe only Silas' strength of character had prevented it.

"Silas Springer?" she repeated, trying to sound innocent.

"Oh, Am, don't be coy. I know you are acquainted with Colonel Springer, and I would like for you to invite him to dinner."

"Invite—"

"America will make an influential ally for Venice, and Silas Springer is an important American," he explained. "Do you see, Am? It will be a help to me in the future to be a friend of Colonel Springer's."

"Oh, I don't agree," she hedged. "The United States is a struggling little country. And you might not even like Colonel Springer."

"The United States is founded on idealism, love. It will show, in the long run. And why wouldn't I like Colonel Springer?"

"Because he is the one I was engaged to marry when I was a girl," she said in a rush.

"Ah, I knew it all along. I remembered the name. I was only waiting for you to tell me again," he said infuriatingly. "But is that a reason that we should not have him to dinner?" His eyes looked into hers.

"No, Mario," she said, and met his gaze directly.

"Then invite him, love."

She was nervous when the day arrived, and changed her gown three times before going down to greet Silas. First she wore one of her newest dresses, fastened in front with small buckles of diamonds. She felt confident gowned at the height of fashion, but perhaps Mario would think she was attiring herself to please Silas. She chose one of the gowns she had bought for the previous season and disgarded that, too. It had been one of Silas' favorites. At last she compromised on an open robe of green satin with black velvet sleeves.

All the same, Silas looked at her more appreciatively than he should as he bowed and kissed her hand. She was certain that Mario noticed. They chatted inconsequentially over dinner and then Mario and Silas withdrew. She had gone up to bed before they emerged. Mario came upstairs and sat on the bed to remove his boots.

Amity pretended to be asleep, but in a moment she couldn't stand the suspense anymore. And he jiggled the bed as he pulled at his boots and dropped them loudly to insure that she was awake.

"Well?" she demanded.

"Your taste in men is excellent as always, love," he said. "We must see more of Colonel Springer."

She started to protest, but he was lowering the bodice of her nightdress; and the things he had begun to do to her body, she did not want to protest. She sank back, sighing, and forgot about Silas Springer.

Slowly the glow of the victory over the pirates began to wane. Venice sank back into its old ways. People began to gossip more and talk less about the building of new ships and the rejuvenation of the Republic. Daily routine began, almost imperceptibly, to separate them. Mario was frustrated in the Council again, his leadership foundering, when only weeks before he had been listened to avidly. Amity had her own problems as well.

The question of a convent for Gracie had reoccurred, proposed this time by Donna da Riva. "Gracie is developing, Amity—into a woman, I mean."

"She can't be. She's a child. She's only ten."

"She's always seemed old for her age. And you have only to look at her to see."

Amity wandered into Gracie's room as she stood in her chemise and saw unmistakably the budding breasts beneath. She wanted to cry. It seemed unfair that Gracie should be growing up so soon. But Amity was frightened, too, at the sight of Gracie's new breasts; and she tried to discuss the convent with her.

"It's not a dreary place, you know. They have parties almost every week, and all the other girls your age are going there."

"Chiaretta isn't going," pouted Gracie.

Amity felt a new tug at her heart. Chiaretta was her baby. How could she stand to be parted from Chiaretta? But in a few years Chiaretta would have to go to the convent, too.

"Chiaretta isn't old enough," said Amity reasonably.

"You only love Chiaretta," stormed Gracie, returning to an old theme; and then she threw herself into Amity's arms, sobbing, needing to be loved, unable to bear separation from another mother after she had had so many. Isabel, Grace Turner, Zenobia, even Giovanna, had all deserted her in one way or another, all without wishing to. No wonder the child was so demanding of Amity!

"What shall I do?" Amity asked of Donna da Riva.

"If I were you, I'd send her to the convent no matter what," replied Mario's stepmother. "But since you will not do that, you will have to devote a great deal of time to guiding her. And, above all, you must tell her what a woman has to know."

"You mean—but she is only ten, and I did not know those things until the women's committee—"

"But you did not grow up in Venice, Am," said Donna da Riva.

So Amity tried valiantly to explain to Gracie the delicate facts of womanhood. "Men will want to touch you, Gracie, but you mustn't ever let them."

"Why not?" said Gracie.

"It's for married people. The things that men do to you will make you have babies."

"Why do men want to make women have babies?" asked Gracie.

"They don't usually—"

"Then why—"

"Because it's fun for them!" cried Amity, becoming muddled.

"Isn't it fun for women, too?" Gracie wanted to know.

Amity put an end to the conversation, certain that she had succeeded more in arousing Gracie's curiosity and daredevil spirit than in instilling fear. She longed to discuss the matter with Mario, but was afraid he would merely force Gracie into the convent again. It was the right thing to do, but Amity couldn't do it.

Her spirits sank. It seemed that everything was going wrong again. She had hoped when Mario had returned that his many nights of loving her would render her pregnant. But it seemed it wasn't to be. He might be the doge, but she could never completely fulfill her wifely duty unless she gave him his son. She had a feeling that Mario, too, was thinking of this. In the old days he had worried about the effect childbirth might have on her health, but now that he had accomplished one triumph he was hungry for another, the getting of his son. He never spoke of it, but she knew what he was thinking. Once he had given up his inheritance for her, but now he had become ambitious again; and she was ambitious for him more than she had ever been before. He'd set Venice to rights if he became doge. Ships would be built, and young noblemen would serve their apprenticeships at sea and learn to be proud of Venice. There would be new alliances. Catherine would stand ready to share in trade and conquest, and Mario had grand ideas about friendship with America.

"America can't help but become great if she has many men like Silas Springer," he would say. Mario approved of Silas so thoroughly that he was often at the da Riva palace. Once Amity tried to tell Mario that it was unwise to throw Silas into her company so much.

"He still cares for me," she said cautiously.

But Mario wasn't alarmed. "Ah, it's no wonder," he said. "Only think, Am, if you had married him, you might have inspired him to high office and been the wife of the president instead of the dogaressa. You were destined for glory, love!"

Mario did not want to think that Amity might have feelings left for Silas, too. He wanted to think of nothing but his plans for the future, in which Silas Springer would play a part.

Gradually tension crept into Mario and Amity's lovemaking. Perhaps it stemmed from the intense but unspoken desire of each of them for her to become pregnant. Perhaps it was only that their appetites were sated, the moment of reunion passing, just as the city had eased in its celebration of the victory over the pirates.

Her sense of failure began to return, and it was a comfort to have Silas about, for he seemed to sense her need for solace. He contained himself as long as he could, and then one day when she had taken him into the garden to show him some new blossoms, he pulled her into his arms and kissed her.

The air was sweet, as it had been the first time he had kissed her, but she had not planned this encounter and was taken by surprise. She pushed him away and saw his gray eyes ardent and compelling, as they had been in the days of their courtship. She hesitated, and he kissed her again. She melted into his embrace, unresisting. They were both trembling when they separated. "Oh, Am, I should not come here again," he said.

"No," she agreed.

But he continued to come. It was difficult to make excuses to Mario's invitations.

"You had better be careful, Am," said Donna da Riva. "Kissing a man like Silas Springer leads to other things. He will not be able to make do with a flirtation like Venetian parlor flies."

"How did you know?" gasped Amity.

"I'm one of the best gossips in Venice. I know everything. Lucky for you I'll keep this one quiet. Gracie told me. She saw you in the garden. If she'd told Mario, you'd not get off so easily!"

It was a warning and one that Amity heeded. She knew she ought to talk to Gracie about what had happened, but she couldn't think what to say. There was no way her dalliance with Silas could be justified. She ought to say simply that neither of them had intended it to happen and that it would not happen again, but she was unsure that either statement would be entirely true. Better to say nothing than to say something that might turn out to be a lie. So Amity said nothing and noticed that Gracie became even more belligerent.

Why had Gracie gone to Donna da Riva with her news? Because she'd known Donna da Riva would appreciate the gossip? Or because she had wanted to cause Amity discomfort, but not the sort of trouble that would have come from telling Mario?

Gracie was always misbehaving, as though she dared Amity to love her in spite of it, or perhaps to support her oftmade allegation that well-behaved Chiaretta was the only one who was loved. Amity remembered that Donna da Riva had told her that Gracie would need a great deal of guidance if she didn't go to a convent, and she knew she was failing dismally at that task.

Mario took up less and less of her time. She found herself having her morning chocolate again with Francesco. Once, at a café, she saw her husband, animated in the company of Velda.

"It's only a coincidence," she told Francesco. "The woman pushes in everywhere. It's not possible for him to avoid her entirely."

But a week or so later it happened again. She lay awake listening for him to come in that night. He came late, and when he crawled in beside her and kissed her, she pretended to be asleep.

In the morning her fury was cold and calm. She was finished ranting about Velda. She would not stoop again to demands and recriminations. Instead, as she poured his coffee, she said evenly, "You should consider that you may harm your career by being seen with Velda. Francesco says that she is flirting with the French. She is in the thick of the secret societies, and Francesco thinks she has become a spy."

"Yes," he agreed. "On the other hand, Velda would like to be on good terms with me in case I become doge, and Venice survives. I am aware of the possibilities, but you should trust my judgment after all this time."

His calm equaled hers. On the surface they were discussing politics, but beneath that, the conversation was really about something else, and Mario bore down on the word "trust." Amity felt her composure flee. She wanted to scream at him, but that had not got the desired results before. What was worse was that she was certain that Mario knew that she wanted a fight. His coolness was patronizing. When he had gone, Amity hurled her cup at the wall in frustration, but she could think of no way to change whatever situation existed between Mario and Velda.

There was nothing to do but go on playing the dutiful wife, left, like most Venetian wives, more and more in the company of her *cicisbeo*. Month by month her mood grew more dismal. Each time he left the house she suspected him. Each time she said nothing, but gowned and jeweled herself to be beautiful for his return. She tried not to be alone in Silas' company, but sometimes it was impossible not to be. Once, having invited Silas to dinner, Mario sent a note saying he'd been detained. Her defenses were down that night, imagining who might have detained him, and again Silas kissed her.

The realization began to grow in her mind that she must get away from Venice for a while. She must go away from Silas, get Mario away from Velda. She could not think how. She hinted that she would like to travel, even mentioned Lago di Garda. But Mario was interested only in Venice. Then one day he came in happily to show her an invitation elegantly engraved on heavy, cream-colored paper.

"You've been wanting a trip, love. What do you think of this?"

"Why, it's an invitation from the Czarina!" she cried, reading it.

"Yes, to her Silver Jubilee," he said, pleased with himself. "Shall we accept?"

"Oh, Mario!" She flung her arms about his neck.

For the first time in a long while, time passed rapidly. Gowns had to be made. Hats with soft crowns of silk or gauze had to be ordered from the milliner. Fringed slippers must be purchased. She needed gear for riding on the steppe as well as clothing for court.

"Am I to go with you?" Gracie wanted to know.

Amity looked at the child. She had not thought of taking her. But obviously she would want to go. She had fond memories of her years there, and of Zenobia and Caleb, who had raised her.

The Court of St. Petersburg was no place, however, for a precocious young girl. Gracie was only eleven, but with her sophisticated manner and her rapidly ripening form, she might easily be mistaken for older.

"No, Gracie," she decided, and Gracie sulked.

Mario, his sympathies touched, thought they should give in to her. "Since you will not have her in a convent, you can keep an eye on her better if you take her along."

Amity disagreed. "She'll stay here, Mario. Donna da Riva will look after her, and she'll not get behind on her studies. I've hired a new tutor for her."

Mario grumbled. "You're wasting your time teaching

Gracie history and mathematics. She's only a girl, Am. Anyhow, Gracie has dispatched every one of those dreamy-eyed British governesses you've hired. None of them was interested in anything more than getting a trip to Venice at my expense anyway."

"This tutor is different, love," she said.

Mario looked disbelieving.

"He's a man," she said.

She hoped the new tutor would be strict. He was just what Gracie needed. She wouldn't be able to run over a man as she had the drab women who had preceded him. And as for wasting her time educating Gracie, she knew she was not. Gracie could think circles about her teachers; and Amity, according to her Quaker way, thought Gracie should use whatever talents God had given her.

But it was not fear of Gracie's misbehavior at court, or interest in her studies, that was the main reason Amity refused to take Gracie to Russia. It was that she wanted to be alone with Mario. It would be like a second honeymoon to return to the land where they had been married and spent their first innocent days. Once they were in Russia again, Mario would forget all about Velda.

St. Petersburg was glittering with balls and parties when they arrived. Amity enjoyed a reunion with Zenobia and Caleb and their small, delightful daughter, who had been born since she had seen them last. The Czarina was about to make a triumphal tour of the frontier and the now-annexed Crimea, but Caleb did not intend to go. Zenobia was expecting another child, and he wanted to stay close by. Much as Amity loved them both, their absence on this excursion suited her. She did not want to share Mario with anyone.

The frontier was blossoming with new farms, and everywhere people turned out to cheer the Czarina and her magnificent entourage. The moon and stars were as immense as the land, and nights drew Amity and Mario close as they remembered their trek across the steppe together. At Kiev there was a huge celebration, and then everyone boarded a fleet of specially-built Roman galleys, outfitted with flags and gilding, to journey downriver and along the coast of the Black Sea to Odessa.

Each night there were bonfires, fireworks, and dancing; but gradually Amity began to grow morose. It was the Czarina herself who intruded on her idyll. Mario was forever being summoned to her side, as Catherine enthused about his prospects of becoming the next doge. Mario's face glowed as she imagined it never did in *her* company, and though Amity was not fool enough to think it romance, she felt neglected. He was making plans, cementing his alliance with Catherine. Too late she realized that he had not seen the trip as a nostalgic journey, but as a political opportunity.

The Czarina was not long in noticing Amity's discontent. "What's wrong?" she asked, standing beside her at the ship's railing one morning. "Are you ill?"

"I wish I were. The last time I was ill in Russia, I was pregnant. I was hoping I might become so again here, but the past few nights Mario has been too busy talking to generals and grand dukes to notice me."

"Ah. You're worrying that he hasn't a son. But you will manage it. I still think you're quite remarkable, Amity," said the Czarina with a twinkle in her eye.

"Not that remarkable. I can't have Mario's son without Mario." Amity sighed.

"There is something else," the Czarina guessed.

"Not something. Someone. Velda."

"A most determined woman. She has not given up yet? But you'll best her, Amity. You always have."

Amity did not have the Czarina's confidence. Donna da Riva's advice that a man was never won was more on her mind. By the time the trip was over, she was only weary and ready to return to Venice. And there more troubles awaited her.

It was Gracie, of course.

"The tutor's gone," Donna da Riva told Amity.

"Oh, but I had such hopes for him!" Amity cried.

"So did he, for himself," Donna da Riva said dryly.

"What do you mean? Make sense, please!"

"I mean that he was a wonderful teacher, and Gracie has learned a great deal, but it wasn't geography or science."

"Oh, dear!" said Amity, catching on. "Did she— Did they—"

"I hope not. Gracie was only half naked and sitting on his lap when I found them. She swears she's still a virgin."

"She'll have to go to the convent," said Amity, aghast.

But Gracie wept when Amity confronted her with her transgressions and begged for another chance. "It was only because I was so angry with you for not taking me to Russia," Gracie pleaded. "You'd have taken me if you loved me.

I only wanted to have a little fun since I was missing so much!"

Amity was overwhelmed with guilt. She should have taken Gracie. Even Mario had said so. And taking her would not have spoiled anything, as it had turned out. Amity gave in and another pallid Englishwoman was engaged, while a Venetian *ballerino* continued to teach Gracie manners and dancing.

"Are you sure you've made the right decision?" Mario asked.

She knew he thought she was wrong, but thankfully he chose not to make an issue of it. She sighed and thought that only time would tell.

31

"Are you going out again tonight?" Chiaretta asked.

"Of course," said Gracie. "It's Carnival, and I'm going to the piazza."

"But Mama thinks you're too young. And this is your third night in a row."

"I'm not too young. I'm fourteen now. And these aren't the old days. I'm a modern woman. It's 1791!"

"Humph. You'd better not let Mama catch you. Or worse, Papa. He'd send you to the convent, where most girls your age are."

"Venetian girls!" scoffed Gracie. "That's different. I'm American. American girls are much more independent. *They* are not shut away like prize pigs!"

"Mama—"

"She *won't* catch me. She's already gone out herself."

"She has? With Papa?"

"No. But he's gone, too. Don't be so stupid, Chiaretta! He's got a lady."

"You don't know that," said Chiaretta resentfully. "Why would he want one when Mama's so pretty?"

"Because that's the way things are done. You might as well

learn. You'll be ten soon, and it's high time you quit being such a baby."

Chiaretta looked as though she might cry. She didn't like to think of her papa being with another woman. She had to admit that her parents went their separate ways a lot, but Mama said it was only because Papa was so busy at Council, especially now, since the revolution had begun in France. Everyone was in such a flap about Marie Antoinette and all the royalty having been parted from their heads on the guillotine. Chiaretta din't see why. It was all so far away.

When Mama and Papa were together they laughed and kissed and seemed happy. Chiaretta repeated to Gracie what Mama had said about the Council.

Gracie burst into derisive hoots of mirth. "That old story! Well, let me tell you. She is beautiful and has marvelous red hair, and her name is Velda. I've seen them together. They didn't know, of course, because I always wear the domino. It's the only way to find out the truth of things. Adults never tell you."

"I won't believe it until I see it," said Chiaretta spunkily. "Will you take me with you sometime?"

"Of course. When you're older. You'd only be an embarrassment now. And if I were to get blamed for leading you astray—" Gracie shuddered at the thought. "They really care so much more about *you*," she added.

"Oh, you will always say that, Gracie. It's not so. You only think that because you're adopted."

"I'm only half adopted," Gracie said.

"Half adopted? How can anyone be half adopted?"

"I mean I'm certain that Amity is my real mother."

"But your mother died, Gracie," cried Chiaretta, boggled.

"That's what Aunt Amity says. But I think she's my mother, and I think Uncle Mario thinks so, too."

"Well, then, who was your father?" Chiaretta challenged.

"That's easy. Silas Springer. He's insane about Aunt Amity. Did you know that they were engaged once?"

"Yes. But they didn't ever marry."

"Oh, you goose. A man and woman don't have to be married to have a baby together. But when they aren't, they are ashamed of it and try to hide it. That's what Aunt Amity and Silas Springer did."

"Mama does see a lot of Colonel Springer," Chiaretta admitted.

"Exactly. They are out with each other tonight. They're

having an affair. Aunt Amity doesn't miss out on the fun. She only wants me to. Aunt Amity doesn't love me because she's ashamed, and Uncle Mario doesn't love me because I remind him of what Colonel Springer did and is still doing with Aunt Amity."

"What he is doing?" demanded a perplexed Chiaretta.

Gracie groaned in exasperation. It was difficult to have a small sister. Especially one like Chiaretta, who never seemed to have any problems with Mario and Amity. She drew a deep breath and started to educate Chiaretta. But then she reconsidered. She'd given Chiaretta enough of a lesson for one evening. If she explained any more she'd be late, and a gentleman was waiting for her.

"I have to go," she said.

"Oh, Gracie, do be careful!"

Gracie gave her a hug. She was, after all, very fond of Chiaretta. As she slipped down to the boat landing, Chiaretta gazed admiringly after her. How exciting it must be to be Gracie and go places and know so much! And Gracie had promised that she could go along someday.

At the palace boat landing Carlo was waiting as Gracie had ordered. It was a frosty winter night, but cloudless. The stars stood like crystals of ice in the sky. Gracie breathed the sharp air and felt drunk with her youth and freedom. "To the piazza, Carlo," she said.

He looked at her disapprovingly, but he said nothing. She was the daughter of the household, and he was subject to do-ing her bidding. Gracie had discovered this wonderful fact during last season's Carnival. At first he had tried to dissuade her from her excursions, and that had been a bother. But now he knew it was useless. And Carlo never told tales on her, not even to Mario or Amity. That was the gondolier's creed.

"Wait for me," she said as he helped her out at her des-tination. Carlo nodded resignedly. She might have told him a time to return for her, and he might have gone to warm him-self drinking *garba* in a wineshop. But Carlo was used to Gracie's inconsiderateness. She was young and hadn't learned to be thoughtful.

Gracie's gentleman moved to her side as she entered the cafe where they had arranged to meet. She allowed him to buy her a blackberry cordial and was excited by the burning taste of forbidden liquor. The gentleman was an aristocrat, a student at the University at Padua. She had met him only the night before, while gambling away her pocket money in a game of faraone.

The young man supposed her to be a married lady of seventeen or so, who, having put in a year or so of wedded confinement, was ready to begin cheating on her husband. Certainly he hoped she was. Gracie knew exactly what her escort was thinking and was intrigued. It was for this reason that she had told Carlo to wait for her.

In spite of her adventuring about Venice, Gracie was still a virgin. Her tutor might have ended that situation for her two years before, but they had been interrupted. Since then Gracie had had plenty of opportunity for sexual experience, but she had steered carefully away from it. Most of the propositions had come from older men—worldly, jaded exploiters of feminine flesh. Gracie wanted someone more her own age. She wanted romance. She wanted to fall madly in love with the man who deflowered her and he with her. Perhaps this gentleman was the one. He was an aristocrat, and she was sure he was unmarried. Maybe they'd have an affair. She'd let him think their passion was hopeless, and then she'd confess that she, too, was free. Mario would arrange the match for her. What a commotion that would cause! Mario would be livid, but Gracie would get her way. Aunt Amity would be horrified, but that only showed what hypocrites people became when they had children. Gracie was certain Amity had had a fling with Silas Springer before she had wed Mario.

The company this evening was rather intellectual, a group of the gentleman's fellow students and a few of their mistresses. They were having a lively debate as Gracie joined them.

"I say that there is no stopping the French," said one. "They'll conquer Europe, and we'll be reading our own street signs in French before many years."

"That's true," said another. "Unless we appease the tyrant we'll all wind up without our heads like the French aristocracy."

"But even appeasement may not do the job," shuddered someone else.

"We'll just have to do the best we can. What other choice do we have?"

"We could defend Venice," said Gracie. Everyone looked at her. The women had not been taking part in this masculine discussion, and more than that, what she had said was astounding.

"Defend Venice! What an idea!"

"It's not impossible," said Gracie. "We defeated the Barbary pirates."

"Oh, that. That was ages ago."

"But doesn't it show what Venetians can still accomplish?"

"Against the French army?"

"They won't need an army," laughed someone. "He could conquer Venice with a company of privates."

Chuckling assent ran around the group, and Gracie felt her fury rising. Beneath her mask, her cheeks grew hot.

"There are plenty of men who would fight for Venice!" she cried. She was quite a patriot, though she hardly realized it. Partly it came from growing up in the household of Mario da Riva, but partly it was her inheritance from Isabel, whom she did not even believe had existed.

"The common people are willing and even the Barnabotti would fight if the Constitution were reformed as it ought to be," she went on. She had heard Francesco and Mario talk about this. Mario had supported Francesco in some of his petitions to Council, and it had cost him the approval of the moneyed nobles.

"We'd have a democracy, if the Constitution were reformed as the Barnabottis would like it to be. That's what Napoleon wants. The Barnabottis are all in league with him."

"You're wrong!" Gracie cried. "The Barnabottis are not all in league with the French. And we won't have democracy if we're conquered. We'll have tyranny!"

Gracie's escort was embarrassed. She was making a spectacle of herself. People at other tables were looking. But she was beginning to make an impression, too. Her grasp of issues was novel in her sex, and the men liked her spirit.

"But where would we get the money for weapons?" one asked, certain she had no answer. The coffers of Venice were notoriously empty.

"Why, we'll raise it."

"How?"

"Oh, I don't know. With gambling lotteries or benefit balls," said Gracie uncertainly.

"Ha! You've no idea how much money it takes to fight a war. Those things would never bring enough."

"We might auction virgins," guffawed another. "That would bring a price!"

That brought a storm of laughter. "What virgins?" someone said. "Venice has no virgins!"

They were all taking the matter much too lightly, Gracie thought. They were making fun of Venice, and trying to make *her* look foolish as well. Gracie's pride rose and overwhelmed whatever little youthful wisdom she possessed. She rose to the challenge as thoughtlessly as a boy volunteering for war.

"Venice does have virgins, gentlemen. I am a virgin, for one. And I would be proud to have *my* virtue auctioned to save the Republic!"

A stunned silence fell over the gathering. Then everyone talked at once, the discussion centering at first on whether Gracie could possibly be telling the truth.

"She'd be in a convent if she were!"

"But maybe she's only a fisherman's daughter."

"No. You can tell by her bearing and her speech. She's a *zentildonna.*"

"There's only one way we can be sure," one said at last. "We'll have to take her up on her offer!"

Gracie gasped. She hadn't foreseen this turn of events. Wildly she turned to the man who was her companion, expecting him to squelch this insane idea. But he was looking at her as speculatively as the rest. For a moment Gracie was in a panic, but then she began to feel better. Her companion obviously intended to bid for her, and hadn't she thought of giving herself to him anyway? Why not raise some money to defend the city as well? What woman had ever lost her virtue so grandly? It would be a great adventure to remember and perhaps even to brag about someday when she was old and needn't worry about Mario and Amity.

"The winner must give me a draft made out to the arsenal," she said. Her breath came quickly as she squeezed her escort's hand to let him know that she wanted him to win. He'd stick until his last sequin, she thought, with that encouragement.

The men burst into applause. Gracie felt her feet go out from under her as someone lifted her and stood her on the table. The bidding began higher than she'd expected, but that only pleased her. She wouldn't want to barter her virtue for a pittance. Men from other tables began to cluster about, some merely to view the proceeding, others to bid. The price was a hundred ducats. Then, before she realized it, it was a thousand. Gracie was dizzy with self-importance. She imagined that other women would follow her example, and a great army would be raised to save the Republic. Most of the bidders began dropping out, but her companion hung on.

Two others continued to bid: one a student, the other a portly, middle-aged merchant from another table. Then the student dropped out. Gracie smiled and blew him a kiss. It was between her companion and the merchant now, and soon the merchant would realize that he could not have her at any price. Foolish man! She was a *zentildonna*, after all! But the bidding went on. The price had reached eighteen hundred ducats when her companion suddenly shook his head and bolted from the cafe.

Gracie was dazed. "Wait!" she cried. It couldn't be happening. But it was. The merchant claimed her, lifting her down to cheers and crude remarks. Outside she looked for her companion, hoping he'd rescue her. He'd step from the shadows and explain that a mistake had been made. But after all, there wasn't any mistake. The merchant wrote out a draft and handed it to her. Automatically, Gracie put it in her bag.

"Have you a gondola?"

She nodded and pointed the way to where Carlo was waiting.

Tenda-drawn, they headed for the lagoon. The merchant took off his gloves and cupped Gracie's breasts. "Ah," he murmured appreciatively, and drew her against him for a kiss. Gracie felt reassured. This was just like the tutor. It would be easy to satisfy this man. It might even be pleasant. He was helplessly in her power, she thought scornfully. She allowed him to undo her bodice. Chill air rushed in and made her nipples harden. The man's lips were warm and moist kissing them.

His hands went beneath her skirts, and suddenly Gracie felt pain as his fingers probed her intimate regions. He laughed and began to stroke her more gently. "Perhaps it's true you're a virgin," he said. "You're skittish enough. But I get my money back if you're not."

Gracie found his new advances disgusting. "I confess. I'm not a virgin," she said. "I'll give you the money back now."

"Not a chance. I get to find out for myself," he said, and thrust something else against her lower region.

Gracie stifled a squeal of pain. The man grunted and pushed harder. The gondola rocked dangerously. The man tried again, shoving her thighs apart roughly in the confines of the boat.

Gracie screamed.

The *tenda* came open, and she was exposed to the night air. She grabbed at her gown and tried to conceal her nakedness from Carlo. But Carlo wasn't looking at Gracie. His face filled with rage as he seized the merchant and with his powerful gondolier's arms flung him out of the gondola. The merchant hit the icy water with a splash and a ghastly yell. Carlo rowed on, while Gracie sobbed and tried to dress herself. She was still disheveled when they reached the palace landing, but a cloak drawn over her rendered her appearance decent.

"Oh, Carlo, thank you!" she whispered as he handed her out.

"There's no need to thank me, *signorina*. It's my job to take care of you."

"But Carlo—"

"Go in quickly and don't be so stupid again," he advised her.

Gracie gained the sanctuary of her room and crawled between the covers where she shivered for hours, clutching a favorite stuffed dog, given to her by the Czarina when she had been a tot. She wondered if the merchant had drowned and didn't know whether to hope he had.

She hadn't long to wait to know, for the next morning Amity summoned her into the sitting room, and there stood the merchant. Gracie paled and tripped over the edge of the carpet.

"Gracie, have you a cheque belonging to this gentleman?" said Amity. "He says it's a large one."

"Yes," said the merchant. "I've explained that I was quite drunk last night, and that when you called upon Venetians to defend the city, I gave you a donation for the arsenal, which I could not afford."

The merchant seemed nervous as Gracie handed over the cheque. Gracie was nervous, too. At least he'd made up some sort of story, but Amity was bound to be suspicious. When he had gone, Gracie tried to excuse herself.

"Just a moment, young lady. That was very odd. You had better explain hourself."

"I'm sorry, Aunt Amity. I slipped out and went to the piazza. There were some people talking about Napoleon, and I said we should defend Venice."

But Amity wasn't satisfied. Gracie had been too willing to admit guilt. There must be more that she wasn't confessing. "You must have been very persuasive, Gracie. How did you get to the piazza? Did Carlo take you?"

"Y-yes."

"Well, then, I'll ask Carlo."

Gracie listened trembling at the door while Amity interrogated the gondolier. Would he tell on her? He never had. But she had never done anything so rash. And Gracie knew she wasn't really a *zentildonna* yet.

"Please, *signora*, I cannot tell you," Carlo said. "It would cost me my life if other gondoliers found out that I had. And I would deserve to die. What you ask is against a gondolier's honor."

"Oh, I know about the gondolier's creed, Carlo. But Gracie is a child. You have a responsibility to tell me!"

Carlo couldn't be swayed, and Gracie wept with relief. But Amity decided that Mario would have to deal with the matter. She didn't like the idea because he'd be hard on Gracie, but no doubt she needed punishment. Amity spent the morning getting up her gumption to tell him about it, but when Mario arrived, the expression on his face made her forget all her intentions.

"Mario—what—"

"The doge is dead," he said.

The next few days were a turmoil. There was no time to deal with Gracie, if anyone even remembered that she needed dealing with. Amity could think of nothing but Mario. At last the moment had arrived. The palace received an endless stream of senators and government officials, who sat in the parlor, having loud debates and consuming immense quantities of food and drink. Amity hustled about greeting callers, and giving orders to servants in a state of exhaustion.

Then came the vote. Amity knew from the set of Mario's jaw that it had not gone well.

"They've elected a weakling, Am," he said dazedly. "Venice wants nothing but isolationism and appeasement. Ludovico Manin is not even a true aristocrat. His family bought its way into the Golden Book. And he is not happier about the vote than I am. It frightened him so much that he wept. His wife has run away to Murano and refuses to go to live in the Ducal Palace."

The da Riva household went into a state of shock. The thing for which they had all striven for so long was not to be. None of them knew how to rebuild their lives. Henri, relatively untouched, handled the necessary affairs of the family, while Donna da Riva shut herself up in her room to grieve over the parties she would never have in the Ducal Palace. Senator da Riva suffered a seizure, and the doctors thought he would never fully recover. As for Gracie, she lay prudently low, glad that at least the furor had drawn attention away from her.

Amity hardly knew what Mario did with his time. He would leave the palace for long periods, presumably to wander the streets or to go to the cafes. At first she offered to go with him, but he always said that he wanted to be alone. It was not so much that he had lost the election that caused him grief.

"Venice has chosen her way, Am," he told her. "The Republic cannot survive without a strong leader. Venetians have become cowardly. It will be over soon."

"Mario," she ventured, "remember when you offered to take me to America? I am ready to go. You've said yourself that America will be a great country someday. You can help make it so. Caleb Beale says a man of your experience would be a boon to the new navy."

"No, Am, no. I can't go now. There may be ways I can help Venice yet. And there's my father to think of."

So they remained in Venice. Or rather Amity did. Mario found reasons to go to sea. When he did come home, the atmosphere of the palace depressed him, and he went to the cafes. Her struggle to make his dreams for Venice reality had separated them, and though she longed to comfort him, closeness had not returned. Amity was unhappier than ever then, knowing that Velda kept him company.

32

Gracie did not misbehave for a long while, but eventually she began to grow bold again. Soon she would not have been eligible to auction her virtue to save the Republic. Chiaretta turned twelve, and Gracie kept her promise to take her along. But Chiaretta was no fun. She was constantly shocked and forever wanting to back out of what Gracie wanted to do.

"We mustn't, Gracie," she would say when a gentleman invited them to his casino.

"Why not? Don't you think that Aunt Amity does such things?"

"No, of course she doesn't!"

But Gracie persisted in believing that Amity was her real mother and that she was having an affair with Silas Springer.

"I'll prove it to you," said Gracie, annoyed at the callow Chiaretta.

"How?"

"Oh, I don't know. I'll think of a way."

Amity was aware of most of Gracie's comings and goings. But what was she to do about it? If she had kept Gracie in the convent, as Mario had wanted, things would never have come to such a pass. Should she put Gracie in a convent now? Or was Gracie too worldly to be contained there? Certainly Gracie was more Quaker than Catholic and not likely to be frightened by threats of eternal damnation. Why, the convent had not even contained demure little Giovanna, when she had been so in love with Mario!

What, then, was the solution?

Amity was overcome by loneliness. Mario was away so much, and Francesco did not satisfy her craving for romance. She had depended on Silas, half in love with him, allowing herself to dwell on their distant past together. She had not had an affair with him, and she wondered if she would. He was returning to America in a few days, and she was torn over the parting. She'd be left alone and lose her chance forever. It was a mistake to love him on the basis of their old relationship, because they had both been different then, but Amity did not consider that. She tried not to think of Silas, but to deal with the problem of Gracie instead.

Perhaps Giovanna was the one to help her decide what to do about Gracie. She and Gracie had been close during the short time Gracie had spent in the convent. And Giovanna had sent Amity a letter asking her to come to the cove off the leper island, where the quarantined could meet friends and speak to them between the boats. But why did Giovanna want to see her now? She had not had contact with the nun since she had gone to the island almost ten years ago.

She went alone as the nun requested, taking only Carlo as her oarsman. It was Carnival again, but Amity was surprised that Giovanna wore the beaked mask with her habit as their gondolas drifted several yards apart in the cove, rimmed with olive trees.

"Thank you for coming, Amity," the nun said.

"We've missed you in Venice, especially Gracie," said Amity.

"I miss Venice, but I'm happy here. Truly happy."

It was more than Amity could understand, but she was awed at the nun's dedication. "Surely you'll come back to Venice soon, Giovanna. You've served here long enough to atone for any sin!"

"Oh, Am, you don't understand. A true penitence isn't a punishment, but a privilege. I've found what few in Venice ever do, a way to make my life meaningful. There is only one thing that is difficult left to do."

"What, Giovanna?"

"I must tell you the sin for which I was given the penitence."

Amity thought she knew what the transgression had been. "You don't have to tell me about you and Mario. I already know."

"That makes it easier. But that isn't the thing that I have to tell you. After I had become a novice, I discovered that I was with child, Mario's child, Amity. The abbess sent me away until I gave birth."

Amity's voice stuck in her throat, and she was unable to ask the question that screamed in her heart. Giovanna answered it for her.

"It was a boy, Amity. I gave birth to Mario's son." There was a hint of exultation in Giovanna's tone as she remembered that indicated she had not yet managed to completely renounce the glory of her illicit accomplishment. "Oh, Amity, don't blame me. God must have meant Mario to have a son, and I was his instrument. There is a plan to all things."

"Then why wasn't he mine?" said Amity bitterly.

"I don't know, Am. I'm only human," pleaded the nun.

Amity felt an irrational surge of jealousy. What right did Giovanna have to be so complacent, when Amity's life was in turmoil? How was it that she could be so satisfied with her calling, so devoid of the passions tormenting Amity? It was unfair that she should bear Mario's son besides!

"He is called Stefano. He is twelve years old and he lives with a fisherman and his wife on Burano. I know it's painful for you, Amity, but I wanted someone to know that Mario has a son. You love him, and I will trust you to know when to tell him and how to do it."

Unexpectedly the nun removed her mask, and Amity gasped at the marks of the disease marring her once-beautiful face. Giovanna smiled wanly, and her appearance became grotesque. "You see now why I'll never go back to Venice,

Amity. I'll die here, not soon, but in a few years. It's all right. I'm useful among the lepers."

"I'll come and see you often," Amity cried, forgetting her resentment of the nun.

Giovanna shook her head and put her mask back in place, perhaps as much to hide tears as to hide her affliction. "Don't come again, Amity. It will only be worse each time."

Giovanna's gondola drifted away, back toward the island, while Amity gazed after it. Finally Carlo's voice aroused her. "Do you want me to take you to Burano, *signora*?"

She nodded. He had heard everything, naturally. But what matter? He was her gondolier. She was glad to have a confidant, for certainly she could tell no one else.

"Oh, Carlo, Mario has a son!" she said. She wasn't telling him anything, but now he could admit that he knew.

"It's a good thing," Carlo said.

"Good!" she cried. But she knew he was right. "Should he know?" she asked.

"Yes, why not?" Carlo said. "He will be grateful to you if you are the one who gives him the news. And you are lucky. It will be impossible for your husband to seek out his son's mother."

She shuddered at his assessment of the situation. Lucky that because of her Mario was not wed to the woman who had borne his son? Lucky that Giovanna had had to take on the terrible penitence?

Carlo seemed to read her mind. "You are not to blame, *signora*. Life is not so simple as that."

She tried to tell herself that he was right about this, too. She wasn't to blame—not alone, anyway. Mario was to blame. Giovanna herself was to blame. Zabetta and her witchcraft. The senator, the whole system of Venetian society had caused it.

The houses of Burano were painted bright colors, terra cotta, sienna, and blue, with red-tiled roofs and doorways that opened onto sunny, barren *callis*. Beside the dark waters of the canals women sat in the spring sunshine working the lace for which the island was known. The steeple of a church rose into the cloudless sky, and wash fluttered on lines strung between buildings.

Carlo seemed to know where to go; and when they found Stefano mending nets on his adopted father's boat, Amity knew that it really didn't matter who was to blame. He had his father's amber eyes, and his hair was the soft brown that his mother's had been as a girl. He had the nose of a Venetian patrician, even as young as he was. No one could look at this child and doubt that he was Mario's.

She bought some fish from him, purchasing, more than the fish, time to look at him. The boy returned her glance quizzically, as if noticing her emotions, and she had to turn away as her eyes filled with tears. Oh, if only he had been hers!

As Carlo rowed her back to Venice, she gave way to her feelings and wept. And she refused to stir from her room that evening even by a worried knock from Francesco, asking her to come down to dinner. She might have married him and had a fine husband, she thought. Then none of this would have happened. But she wasn't really sorry, any more than Giovanna was sorry for her affair with Mario.

Nature had not intended her to marry Mario at all. But neither had she been supposed to wed Francesco. She had been intended for Silas Springer. How far away all that seemed! How long ago her gentle ardor for Silas had bloomed like daisies in the Bucks County fields! For years she had been circumspect about her relationship with Silas. But she had been lonely so much, and life had been complicated for too long.

She was consumed with the need to return to that simple love, and going to her writing table began a note, tore it up, and then wrote it again.

In the hall she found Gracie. "Will you run an errand for me, Gracie?"

"All right."

"Take this letter to Carlo and ask him to deliver it at once to Colonel Springer, please."

Colonel Springer! Gracie drew in her breath. Here was her chance. Her opportunity to find out the truth about Amity, and perhaps about herself.

As soon as Amity had gone, Gracie opened the envelope and lifted out the note. Her eyes gleamed as she read it. Amity was planning a tryst, no less! The tone of the letter made it obvious that the assignation would be no innocent meeting.

"What are you reading, Gracie? Something you shouldn't, by the look on your face. Let me see." A hand snatched the letter away.

"Henri! Give that back!" Gracie cried in alarm.

"Would you like Amity to know you opened this?" he teased.

"No!" said Gracie.

"This letter is very interesting, Gracie. You'll keep quiet, and I'll keep quiet. And we'll have our little secret. Run on, there's a love," he said, and kissed her cheek.

Amity dressed carefully in a simple gown of green silk with a small hoop and a falling Vandyke collar. The modesty of her attire was offset by the material, a thin tiffany silk that suggested, rather than flaunted, what was beneath. She added Chinese slippers of black Spanish kid, turned up at the toe; and slipping on her Carnival mask and her pelisse, went down to the gondola landing.

"Did you deliver my message?" she asked Carlo.

"*Si, signora.*"

She drew a deep breath, and stepping into the gondola, asked him to take her to Campo San Luca. She drew the *tenda* closed and wondered if he would be waiting. She was going to have an affair. She was going to make love with the one man who could clear away the past and make life fresh and new again. Or perhaps that would not happen. She would only succeed in making his memory of her less pure. Whichever, it was too late now. The gondola drew in along a *calle*, and a man who had been waiting stepped into the craft.

She was not surprised that he was masked. She had told him to come so to avoid talk. "Take us to the lagoon, Carlo," she said. The gondolier did as he was told, aware of the reason for her command.

The man beside her took her in his arms, and quickly his hand found its way beneath the flounces of her collar. The mere touch of his fingers on her nipples made her writhe. Dear heaven, it had been so long! Her body tensed and arched, inviting him to further conquest; and she felt the welcome hardness of his eager loins as he held her, his hands busy now unfastening her gown.

She lay half-naked, her taut breasts exposed to view, while he caressed her thighs, moving inevitably upward toward pleasure's realm.

"Amity," he said, "take off your mask, so I can kiss you."

She did and felt his lips on hers beneath the dark *tenda*. His tongue flicked against her teeth, and she moaned and opened her mouth; then suddenly she began to struggle. She had realized that he was not Silas Springer at all. Without his mask, his identity was plain even in the shadows.

"Henri!" she said furiously.

"You see, Am, I always told you you would enjoy it with

me. It didn't work when I pretended to be a ghost and chased you at the villa. Disguising myself as your dear Silas was a better idea. You couldn't tell even the slightest difference!"

The fact that she hadn't disgusted her, and she slapped him. The gondola swayed.

"Take care, Am," he said. "You wouldn't want Carlo to discover your situation."

"How did you know?" she demanded.

"Gracie opened your letter and I found her reading it. I decided to save you from yourself, Am. If you're going to have an affair at last, it would be simpler for it to be with me. I exchanged your letter for one inviting Silas to have luncheon with you tomorrow. But that will be too late. The moment is now, Am; and you know it!" His skillful hands moved over her again, and her aroused body betrayed her. He was right that tomorrow was too late, and he proved to her that the moment was now.

She was in a foul temper when the bells awakened her the next morning. She had cried herself to sleep, and her head ached. Henri had made her depravity clear to her, just as the outlaw had done. It had happened just as it had that first time. But, oh, if only she had not thought he was Silas! How could she have thought he was? She rolled over and tried to go back to sleep. Maybe she could forget for a little while. But the memory of the night in the gondola intruded into her dream.

Gracie! Gracie had caused this! Gracie must be punished! She'd send Gracie to the convent this very day.

Relieved to have someone on whom to blame her distress, she burst into Gracie's room. "You're going to the convent, Gracie. Get up and pack!"

Gracie blinked at her in horror. "But why?"

"Because of what you did yesterday! You opened the note I gave you!"

"You'd send me away for opening a letter?" Gracie was trembling, but her chin rose. "It's because you don't love me. It's because of what was in that letter that you're punishing me. You're the guilty one! You're the one who should be punished! You're worse than I am with your Colonel Springer. Why don't you just admit that he's my father and that you are my mother?"

Amity stared at her. "Your mother! Colonel Springer your father! Is *that* what you think, Gracie?" It was so ridiculous it was funny. But suddenly it wasn't so ridiculous. And it wasn't funny at all. Amity reached under the bed and pulled out a trunk.

"I won't go to the convent!" Gracie cried.

Amity's spirits lifted. She knew at last what to do about Gracie. What to do about herself! Across the years the inner light she had all but forgotten shone out and told her.

"I am not your mother, Gracie, but both of us are Americans and that is where we are going. We are going home, Gracie! I am sick of Venice. I am sick of what Venice is doing to you and me. Venice is dying. It cannot be saved, and the disease is contagious. Venice is fatal to decency."

She had waited too long already, she thought, as she set the servants to packing for her. Amity worked furiously, still in her nightgown and wrapper, her uncoiffed curls askew.

"What's going on?" said a voice behind her. "Have I come too early?"

She whirled. "Silas! What are you doing here?"

He looked confused. "Why, you invited me for luncheon, Am."

His arrival was so unexpected that Amity began to laugh hysterically. The note that Henri had exchanged for the one Amity had written! But Silas' eyes held hers and she sobered.

"I'm going home, Si," she said, and saw his face light.

"Then we'll go together, Am," he said.

She was only too happy to have his company for the trip, but she did not go with him in the way that might have pleased him most. She knew the truth about herself at last, and in a way she was grateful to Henri for showing it to her. He had at least prevented her from lessening Silas with her lust.

Mario refused to see her journey in the same light, though she tried to explain it to him.

"I must go, Mario, only for a time, for Gracie's sake," she told him.

"You are welcome to go forever with Silas Springer," he returned in cold fury.

"Mario, there's nothing—"

"Don't lie to me, Amity; I have not been blind," he said.

She longed for him to take out his anger in bed and make things right as he had done on other occasions, but perhaps there was nothing to be made right.

When they left Venice a day or so later, she looked back and saw the winged lion of St. Mark's and wept for Mario and for all her dead hopes.

Epilogue

33

"Go to him, Amity," said Zenobia.

"Oh, Aunt, I have told you a thousand times that Mario must come to me."

"It seems more than a thousand times you have said it," observed her aunt dryly.

"Yes." Amity sighed. It did seem she had said it a hundred thousand times in the four years that had passed since she had left Venice. Mario had written to her at first, asking her to return, promising to lead a quiet life at the country villa if she would. But Amity knew him too well. He couldn't keep such a promise; and if he could, it wouldn't be good for their relationship. She supposed Velda was taking advantage of the situation. There was no reason now for him not to attend her salon. Gradually his letters became more infrequent and more impersonal, reduced to notes accompanying Christmas and birthday presents for Chiaretta and Gracie.

She would answer with anecdotes about the children. Gracie was a grown-up young woman and spirited for her Quaker Meeting. But lately there had been a young man who had made her blush and seem uncertain. "I think they will pass Meeting and be married in another year," she wrote.

And she wrote, too, that Silas Springer had taken Gracie to hear President Washington's farewell address. People had cried and cheered until they were hoarse. Silas had taken his charge to meet the great man, and when Washington heard that she was a babe of his camp, born on the eve of his victory at Trenton, he had invited them to dine and had spoken to her of the courage and sacrifice of women like her mother. After that Gracie had seemed more surely rooted in the soil of their Bucks County farm, in spite of her years in courts and palaces. "She is as level-headed as she is spirited," Amity wrote. "You would be proud of her."

He would be proud of Chiaretta, too, Amity thought, though she had turned out differently from Gracie. A taste for splendor must have run in her blood, for she had loved Philadelphia from the first. When she had turned sixteen Amity had allowed her to go there to live with Zenobia and Caleb, who were home from their travels. Two daughters of that happy couple made a frolicsome trio in the drawing rooms of Society Hill, and Caleb was given to saying with only half a chuckle that Chiaretta would influence national policy one day, or perhaps be the hostess at the new presidential mansion planned for the soon-to-be capital of Washington.

Amity was older, but still beautiful, and Zenobia often told her it was a crime for her to wear simple gowns of Quaker gray instead of the fashionable clothes in which she would yet be devastating. But Amity did not want to be devastating. If any man had interested her after Mario, it would have been Silas, and ardor burned in his eyes every time he came from Philadelphia to see her. Dear Silas! If only things had been different! She had been tempted many times to let him love her, but she knew that there was only one man to whom she could give love as it ought to be given.

She gazed around her at the violets that were growing in the dooryard of the farmhouse that had been restored to her, and thought of Venice. *Go to him.* Was this the time? Should there ever be a time? She sighed, remembering the songs of gondoliers and the first flowers blooming bravely in urns and boxes.

"Donna da Riva always said that the swallows come back to Venice in May," mused Amity.

"If it is good enough for swallows, Am . . ." suggested her aunt. "You might arrive with them, if you left soon."

"I am not sure that he wants me," said Amity.

"Will you leave him to the mercy of that Gypsy forever? He needs you. War will come to Venice this spring. And *you* need *him!*"

It was true that she needed him. Her heart had longed for him ever since that first day he had turned her across his lap in Zenobia's parlor. Returning to Venice would not be easy. She had left too many ghosts that she did not want to face. There was Henri, but more important there was the secret that Giovanna had told her in the cove of the leper island. Amity had penned a dozen letters to Mario to tell him of the existence of his son. But she had never mailed a one. She told herself that it was better for the boy that he be left with his humble parents instead of elevated to a palace to be trained in the ideals of a doomed way of life. But she was afraid that the real reason was her bitterness that Stefano was not her son, too. No, she would not give him such a reward for his affair with Giovanna!

But could she live with Mario again without telling him, and if she did, would he hate her for having kept quiet so long?

She began to pack her trunk almost absently, putting in all the newest gowns that Zenobia had urged her to buy for the trip. There was an elegant jacket of dark blue sarcenet trimmed with gold lace, to be worn over a high-waisted gown of white muslin; a vest of crimson velvet and a Calypso chemise of lilac. There were sandal shoes with crisscross ribbons over the instep; and her soft, stringless bonnets had holes in the crowns for her hair, worn now in ringlets that had become the style.

She thought perhaps the curls were too girlish for her, but Zenobia pronounced her traveling clothes perfect. "You might have left Venice yesterday, Am, except that the new, softer fashions suit you better."

When she had packed, she began to unpack in a panic. What would she find in Venice besides revolution? Would she find Velda in Mario's bed?

"You'll never know unless you go, Am," Zenobia said.

"Oh, do quit hounding me! I'll make up my own mind!"

The greening hills and the smell of earth being turned for planting argued she should stay where she was, safe amid the countryside she loved. But the call of palaces and canals and winding *calli* was stronger. A carriage bore her away to Philadelphia, and then the ocean swells behind her made a change of heart impossible.

The city seemed different. Even while still at sea, almost as soon as the campanile came into view over the Piazza San Marco, she sensed it. The arsenal bristled with guns pointing out over the harbor, and ships stood at the ready; but there was an air of defeat. She had a hard time finding a gondolier, and as he rowed her down the Grand Canal toward the da Riva palace, she saw that there were crowds of angry people along the streets. The stores of the Rialto were shuttered, and the vegetable markets had not opened. Her knock at the front door of the palace was answered by a weary patrician. Not Mario, but Francesco, though for an instant the glare of the canal deceived her.

"Amity!" His tired eyes lighted. She was a miraculous sun

on a landscape of bleakness. "I can't believe that you're here! By heaven, it's wonderful to see you, especially since I thought I never would again. But you've picked an unhappy time to come back, I must say!"

"What is happening, Francesco?" she said, recovering from the start he had given her.

He took her inside and made coffee for them himself, since no servants were about. "Venetians are rioting among themselves, Am," he said. "Ordinary people want to defend Venice against the French, but the Barnabotti numbers many who want to surrender. They will get their way, since the Council is all for appeasement. Thousands came from the provinces to fight for Venice, but the government sent them all away with the excuse that there were not enough weapons."

"But what started it?"

"A French ship, the *Liberator of Italy*, come to the lagoon and there was a battle. The French commander was killed. It was the excuse Napoleon had been looking for. The Council met every one of Napoleon's demands without a murmur—voted for a new democratic government, impeached the Inquisitors, and even dissolved themselves. But the French will be here by morning."

"Where is Mario?"

"At the arsenal. There is a young man with him—no, only a boy of sixteen, but he fights like a man. He came to Mario to ask him to help organize the fishermen to defend the city. They've been together for weeks now. Mario knows the city is lost, but the boy won't give up. It's a good thing, because I don't know how Mario would cope with these moments without Stefano."

"Stefano . . ." she murmured.

"He is only the child of a fishing family of Burano, but one would think he had noble blood."

Dazed, Amity did not reply to the news that Mario and his son had found each other. Did either of them know? "What of you, Francesco?" she said. "You were always for democracy. Are you glad the French will take Venice?"

Francesco made a sound of disgust. "There will be no democracy here, Am. They will cede Venice to Austria. There is a secret treaty. I would be with Mario if it were not for the senator."

"The senator? I should think he'd want you there."

"He would. But I promised Mario I'd stay here. The senator is upstairs dying. That's as it should be. I pray he dies before he hears the sound of French boots on the *callis*."

"Where is Henri? This should be his duty."

"Dead. He was determined to flee Venice, like many of the nobility; but he wanted to take Zabetta, too. But the authorities didn't want to release her, so he freed her by climbing the wall and sawing away the bars. But he alarmed some of the poor mad devils, who thought he was the vanguard of the French. They killed him, and Zabetta along with him."

Amity shuddered, Henri's obsession with Zabetta had undone him at last. He had not died a hero's death fighting for Venice, but she decided that his death had not been ignominious. "I'll stay with the senator," she said quietly.

"Thank you, Am," Francesco said. Buckling on a sword, he kissed her before he went out the door. His eyes told her he had never quite forgotten how he had once loved her.

She took a lamp and went up to the senator's bedroom. The place was eerily quiet without the gay parties of Donna da Riva, the card games, the musicales, the endless flirtation. Nothing was to be heard except the voices outside, screaming their awful accusation at the great palaces of the nobles, "*Assassini di San Marco*! Murderers of St. Mark!"

"Are they here? Have they come?" the senator said from the big bed surrounded by heavy velvet curtains on its platform.

"Not yet," she said, wondering if she should lie to him and tell him the invader would be repulsed.

"It has been eight centuries since an enemy dared enter the lagoon," he said in a strong voice. "The Genoese. Most of our fleet was away, but we sank block-ships across the channels, took away all the navigation markers. The enemy became trapped, like insects on flypaper. They had to eat rats. And then our fleet returned . . ." He peered at her. "Chiaretta," he breathed. "Come here, Chiaretta."

"I am not Chiaretta," she began, thinking of her daughter. But he could not mean that Chiaretta. He had not seen his granddaughter since she was a little girl. He meant the other Chiaretta, his wife.

Hesitantly she did as he asked, and let him take her hand in his ancient one. "Who would have thought we'd see this day, Chiaretta?" he said, his voice far away now.

She wondered if he remembered that his wife was dead. Did he think he was speaking to someone from beyond the grave? Perhaps he was, she thought with a shudder. The palace seemed full of presences tonight, a thousand years of ghosts, all mournful and shameful.

"I am Amity," she said, trying to shake off the mood.

"Amity." He sighed. "I remember you. I wish you had stayed. What was it you said when you left? Ah, that Venice was a fatal disease. You were right, Amity. I am dying of it."

She looked into the fading eyes. "It wasn't you who had me arrested, was it?" she asked suddenly.

"No." He seemed to drift away. In a little while he awakened and called for Chiaretta again. The hours of the vigil passed slowly. She heard scattered gunshots and worried about Mario. Would Venice be fatal to him, too? And if he came, would she tell him that the boy who fought with him was his own son?

It was dawn, but the bells of St. Mark's did not ring. Instead a pounding on the front door roused her from her uneasy sleep. She went to answer it, but before she reached it, it burst open, and a dozen jubliant, drunken French soldiers spilled into the hall, greeting her with catchwords of liberation. "We will quarter here," they told her.

"You can't!" she cried in horror. "A man is dying upstairs!"

"That's all right. He'll give us no competition for the wine," said one.

Another grabbed her and kissed her. She drew her hand across her mouth to wipe off the kiss and dealt him a kick to the shin. "Come on, let's eat; there'll be time for women later," a comrade advised. The soldier tipped his cockaded hat to her as they headed for the kitchen, singing and laughing.

Outside, artillery rattled in the street, but there was no sound of cannonade from the harbor. Venice had fallen with only a whimper.

The sounds of the defeat of Venice were not guns and weeping but the revelry of soldiers as they helped themselves to polenta and hard rolls, wine and cheese, and everything else they could find.

"Please! You'll disturb the senator!" she cried after them, but they were already too engrossed to listen. She hurried into his room and found him sitting up in bed with a rapt expression on his face.

"What is all the commotion?" he demanded in his old commanding tone.

Amity felt her heart quake. She was too frightened to tell

him the truth, but he was not a man it was easy to lie to. He solved her dilemma by sinking back, muttering, "Oh, I suppose it's another of my wife's parties. You would think she would stop, with the French at our gates! Venice will not fall, Amity!"

His breath was coming hard. She thought he couldn't last long. If only he did not recognize the French being spoken in the far-off kitchen. If only the soldiers would not shout so! If only the soldier who had kissed her did not eat his fill and decide to look for her! But it scarcely occurred to Amity to worry about her own safety. The important thing was that the senator not learn that the French were in his very palace. The senator clung to her hand and gasped, *"Viva San Marco!"* His eyes fixed in the distance and then went blank and flat. She knew he was dead.

"Hello, Amity," said someone behind her. "Have you come to claim Mario now that Venice is done with him?"

She turned and saw Velda, resplendent in a Turkish robe-style gown and a cloak of green net. Her flaming hair, all curls to the front, was wrapped with an emerald-colored bandeau. "I've sent the soldiers away, Amity. You might as well go, too. I've won, finally. The French have won; it's the same thing. I saw it coming, and I spied for Napoleon at the doge's very dinner table. I have influence. Enough to order the soldiers out of this palace. Enough influence to ensure that the palace remains in Mario's hands, even though Napoleon is going to call in all the mortgages and wipe out the nobility. I can even assure Mario a high position in the new government. I'll have to redecorate, of course. French furniture is the fashion, and Mario will have to entertain a great deal. I'll be his hostess, of course—among other things. Is the old man dead? It's just as well. He would have only been a nuisance. What a bore, with those old-fashioned ideas!"

"You cannot buy Mario with your favors, Velda" said Amity angrily.

"Can't I? Why not? He'll be a broken man now that Venice has fallen. I'll offer him his self-respect. It's either that or see his palace looted and sacked."

"Looted and sacked!"

"Of course. What do you think an army does when it captures a city with riches like this one? They are already tearing down molding and grillwork and making off with the paintings of Vivarini and Titian. They are talking of moving the horses of St. Mark to Paris."

"But they cannot! They must not!" Amity was surprised that she felt it so strongly. She had come to love the city in spite of herself.

Velda laughed. "I suppose you think you can stop them, Amity! How will you do it? With your little Quaker bonnet?"

Her words gave Amity an idea. "Perhaps I will," she said.

Why not? she thought, and the light seemed to shine brightly within her. Why should she not go as a public Quaker like Caleb Beale? Why couldn't a woman be an instrument for peace as well as a man? If the light sent her . . .

Her trunk was still in the hall. Hastily she unlocked it and dug down deep, where, amid the lace and satin of her gowns, there was one of dove gray with its bonnet to match. Zenobia had teased her for packing it. She herself had not known why she had, only that it seemed wrong to be without it. When she had put it on, she paused in front of a gilded mirror and arranged her ringlets carefully about its brim. It was not a Quakerish gesture, but Amity was far from the simple Quaker she might be taken for, dressed as she was. It was never amiss to look well when trying to accomplish something in the world of men.

A gondola took her to the piazza. The French were everywhere, drinking at the cafés and sprawled about the pavements. At the top of the Staircase of the Giants, where the doge had always been crowned, a group of conquerors was gathered about the statues of Mars and Neptune, seeming to discuss the feasibility of having them hauled away. A more mobile piece of sculpture in Byzantine marble was being carried away from the basilica.

A guard stopped her as she hurried up the staircase.

"Put that back. You mustn't take it!" she cried.

"Why not? The city is defeated."

"Venice may be defeated now, but in another way her victory can never be diminished. The victory of spirit that built this city! It ought to be left untouched to inspire generations to come."

The soldier looked at her in astonishment. "Who are you?"

"I'm a public Quaker," she proclaimed.

"A public Quaker! A woman?"

"Why not? In the Quaker faith a woman is the equal of a man, since the light dwells within her as much as him. Put the statues back. You don't deserve Venice, if you cannot respect her."

The soldier grinned. "Respect is it? Well, we've orders to respect the women. You're lucky that there's to be no raping, or I'd make away with you instead of this cold piece of marble! Go on with you before I forget my orders."

It was no use. Why did she have such a strong urge to do what was impossible? Why didn't she give up like the rest of Venice? Then she remembered the secret entrance to the palace and dashed into the shadows toward the canal side of the building, where the cool, wet smell of water mixed in the spring air beneath the Bridge of Sighs.

The heavy door of worn wood opened beneath its covering of vines, and she slipped through, shivering. Behind her she heard a shout. They were following!

Soon she was deep in the palace. Her sandals echoed over the floor of the Senate Room, its ceiling rich with precious gilding and on one wall the painting by Tintoretto called "The Triumph of Venice." She sighed as she looked at it and rushed on, stumbling into the Room of the Bussola, named after a carved door, shaped like half a hexagon. Here the accused and condemned had waited to hear their crimes against the Republic. Again memories assailed her, and she ran on without pausing, discovering at last the vaulted golden staircase of gilded stucco that led the way to the apartments of the doge. Here she guessed that she would find the French commander ensconsed.

The soldier caught up with her as she slipped past the unguarded door. The commander was being shaved, and brought his light jack boots down with a thump from a brocaded footstool at the sight of her.

"Who the devil is this?" he demanded of the soldier.

"A patriot. She knew a secret way in."

"I'm not a patriot. I'm not even Venetian. I'm a public Quaker come to beg you to stop the sacking, sir!"

"You are not even Venetian, and you dare to disobey my soldiers? I could have you thrown into the Leads!"

"I'm not afraid. I've been there before," said Amity, caught up in the moment. She had thought she was done with Venice and was astounded that she was not, that she was endangering herself for it. So his dream was still her dream after all! How could it be otherwise when she loved him so?

"What shall I do with her, sir?" the soldier wanted know.

The commander wiped lather off his chin. "She sounds like a patriot, even though she denies it," he said. "Bring out the other one. The one who wrecked several boatloads of my troops with his wild manuevers in the lagoon. I'll jail them together."

Amity's heart sank. She was going to the Leads again, and for no good reason. She should have stayed in America, for Venice always brought out everything in her that was reckless and irresponsible.

And then she was not sorry at all she'd come. She wasn't even sorry she was going to the Leads in the company of the patriot who'd been brought out to stand beside her.

"Mario!"

She forgot everything as she gazed at him. He gazed back, stunned. "Amity, oh, Amity!"

The French commander, the soldier, the barber, did not exist for either of them. He was dazed by defeat, his voice halting, as she had never heard it before. She felt her heart breaking as she laid her finger against his lips to quiet him.

"Amity," he whispered, "you've come back. I always prayed you would. I could not leave Venice—"

"You're wounded, my love," she murmured.

"It's only a flesh wound where a ball grazed my head. But I've lost everything. Venice is gone, even my palace. If only my father hadn't lived to see this day!"

"The senator is dead, Mario. He didn't know." She hesitated, then went on as they were led away to a cell together. She told him what she had to, at incredible cost to herself.

"You haven't lost everything, Mario. You still can have the palace and even a position in the government. Velda says so. She has influence with the French."

"Velda! I don't want my palace given to me by a woman who has warmed the beds of traitors to get it for me!"

"But she has warmed your bed, too," Amity flashed bitterly.

"My bed! No, Am. Not since Russia, before I met you. I found out long ago what sort of woman Velda is. I found out years ago that she arranged your arrest for witchcraft."

"It was Velda?"

"She was in Venice, even then, with the gypsies. Only when she had wealth did she make her presence known."

"She did always say she'd stop at nothing to have you," Amity said. "I thought—I thought—"

"I know, Am. I know, my darling. It was my fault. The fault of my terrible ambition. I was assigned by the Inquisitors to keep track of Velda's nefarious activities, and I couldn't tell you. And I was so eager to be doge that I pushed you and Silas Springer together. Afterward I neglected you. Whatever happened between you, I was not blameless. You are all I want, only you, not power, not Venice. Only you, Am!"

"None of it matters, Mario. We're together."

"God knows what will become of us, Am!"

"It doesn't matter. We'll look to the light to show us the way."

"I have missed you so," he said with a wan smile. "You and your 'light'!"

He let her cradle his head in her lap and fell asleep, exhausted. She sat there for hours, joyous to have him so near her. And then the key turned in the lock. She started with terror, instinctively thinking of Jacques, who had raped her.

But the French lieutenant who stood there only said in a bored tone, "You're being released."

She blinked. "Both of us?"

"Yes. Napoleon likes to reward bravery. Your friend will keep his life and his palace as well. Wake him up."

Amity's spirits were high when they were on the street again, but Mario remained dejected. Somehow she must restore him, return to him his courage and his will. Suddenly she intuited what she must do, the thing that might make the difference.

"Mario," she said, "is Giovanna still alive on the leper island?"

"Yes, but Francesco says she will not live much longer."

"You must go and see her. There is something important she has to tell you. Say that I sent you."

"Not now, Am," he said.

"Now," she insisted.

He sighed and acquiesced, allowed her to help him into his frock coat.

Amity waited. He would find his son, and when he had, perhaps that would be enough for him. Surely he could not need her now, after so many years. Surely he would blame her for not having told him in the first place.

It was the next day before he came home. She waited nervously, wondering if he would hate her for having kept the secret for so long. How could he possibly understand? All the sweetness of their reconciliation would be forgotten. She would lose him again.

She gazed at him fearfully as he came in, but he had about

him a newness and serenity that gladdened her heart. "I have my son at last, Amity," he said.

"Yes. If only I could have been the one—" she burst out.

"Oh, but you were, Am, as much as Giovanna! You suffered pain to give me my son, even though it wasn't the agony of childbirth. You gave me what I needed, Am. You have always known how to do that."

He swept her into his arms, and kissing her passionately, made her aware of his present need, of her own; and thrilling to his hands unfastening her clothing, she forgot the fall of Venice in her husband's devastating embrace.

By the next day the looting had stopped, and Mario thought that the French commander had reconsidered after his visit from a "public Quaker." "You are compelling when you put your mind to it, love," he told her proudly.

They remained in Venice awhile longer. Francesco came to say that Giovanna had died. Mario wept. "Franceso, I have never told you the wrongs I did her," he said.

"I forgive you, Mario. *She* forgave you. I know about Stefano. It was like seeing you twice to see you with him. I knew he must be your son, even if you did not. And I could see my sister in him, too."

They embraced before Francesco left, on his way to the Russian frontier he had always loved. Since Mario would keep the palace, Amity wondered if they would live in it.

"The palace will go to Stefano, Am," he told her. "I will see that he has the finest education, and perhaps someday he or his sons will make Venice great again."

She smiled. He was not really finished with Venice. He never would be. But now his dream for Venice was different.

The destruction was not completely over. They watched the horses removed from their place overlooking the piazza, to be loaded onto a ship to take them to Paris. The words *"Pax tibi Marco"* were scratched off the city's lions and "Rights and duties of man and citizen" inscribed instead. A tree of liberty was raised in the middle of the piazza, and the Golden Book burned beside it.

They stood close together as the smoke rose, and when it was done, he seemed satisfied that he had seen it through.

"Are we going to Russia like Francesco?" she asked.

"No. There is a country where the women are very spirited and beautiful. Once I met a woman there, and afterward I never wanted another. There are two more there I want to meet again."

She knew he meant Gracie and Chiaretta, and her heart warmed with delight.

"I would like to be a part of America, Am," he told her. "It has always intrigued me, ever since I went there for the Czarina. America will need a strong navy, and Caleb Beale has always said that a man of my experience would be valuable."

She would show him the farm. Summer was the finest time to see it, when everything was growing, ripening and beginning anew. Their lives would grow and ripen, too, like the corn and the blackberries in the hedgerows. They would lie together on the hummocks of soft grass and see the future stretching out before them as magnificently as the forested peak of Buckingham Mountain.

But first, before that future began, he kissed her, and, as always, the touch of his lips lifted her to ecstasy. Of all the empires they had known—the new of America, the grand of Russia, the ancient of the Republic—this was the most profound. She gazed into his eyes and he into hers, and both knew that this realm of love would endure beyond all others. Amity sighed with joy as he led her once more up the great stairway of the palace to love her in the splendor that would always be Venice.

ABOUT THE AUTHOR

GIMONE HALL was raised in Texas and lives in Bucks County, Pa., where she is working on a new novel. Married to a writer, she has two young children. She is the author of two other historical romances, *Rapture's Mistress* and *Fury's Sun, Passion's Moon,* also available in Signet editions.